BROTHERHOOD PROTECTORS BOXED SET 3

BOOKS 7, 8, 9

BROTHERHOOD PROTECTORS BOXED SETS
BOOK THREE

ELLE JAMES

TWISTED PAGE, INC

BROTHERHOOD PROTECTORS BOXED SET 3

BOOKS 7-9

New York Times & *USA Today*
Bestselling Author

ELLE JAMES

Montana SEAL Daddy Copyright © 2017 by Elle James

Montana Ranger's Wedding Vow Copyright © 2018 by Elle James

Montana SEAL Undercover Daddy Copyright © 2018 by Elle James

All rights reserved.

No part of this book may be reproduced in any form or by any electronic or mechanical means, including information storage and retrieval systems, without written permission from the author, except for the use of brief quotations in a book review.

AUTHOR'S NOTE

Brotherhood Protectors Series
Montana SEAL (#1)
Bride Protector SEAL (#2)
Montana D-Force (#3)
Cowboy D-Force (#4)
Montana Ranger (#5)
Montana Dog Soldier (#6)
Montana SEAL Daddy (#7)
Montana Ranger's Wedding Vow (#8)
Montana SEAL Undercover Daddy (#9)
Cape Cod SEAL Rescue (#10)
Montana SEAL Friendly Fire (#11)
Montana SEAL's Mail-Order Bride (#12)
SEAL Justice (#13)
Ranger Creed (#14)
Delta Force Rescue (#15)
Dog Days of Christmas (#16)
Montana Rescue (#17)
Montana Ranger Returns (#18)

Visit ellejames.com for more titles and release dates
and join Elle James's Newsletter at
https://ellejames.com/contact/

MONTANA SEAL DADDY

BROTHERHOOD PROTECTORS BOOK #7

New York Times & *USA Today*
Bestselling Author

ELLE JAMES

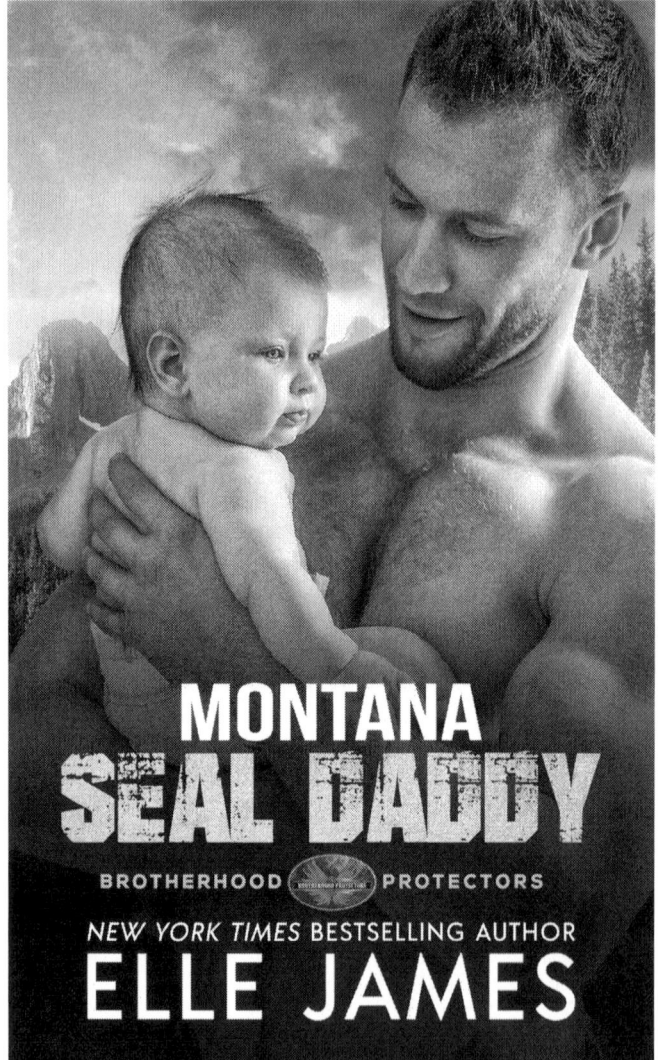

CHAPTER 1

"I don't think I'll ever get used to this heat." Daphne Miller sat on the front porch of the small clapboard house out in the middle of the hills in practically nowhere Utah. She fanned herself with a five-month old copy of a celebrity magazine, wishing she were anywhere else in the world. "Do you think they're any closer to getting the evidence they need to nail the bastard who killed Sylvia Jansen? I'd think my testimony alone would be sufficient to put him away for a very long time. Otherwise, why go to all the trouble of witness protection?"

Her forty-seven-year-old bodyguard with the gray streaks at his temples and weathered skin sat in a wooden rocking chair, his feet resting on the porch railing, a piece of straw sticking out of his mouth. Chuck Johnson rolled the straw between his teeth before answering. "You'd think after a year, the feds would have what they need."

Daphne pushed to her feet, restlessness fueling her

irritation. "All I know is that I've sat in this cabin in this godforsaken heat for longer than I can stand. I need to move on with my life. I can't stay here forever. For all we know, they've forgotten I saw anything. Harrison Cooper probably thinks I'm dead or fell off the face of the earth. He might have moved on to his next victim by now. And I'm sitting here doing nothing." She paced to the end of the porch and back, skirting Chuck and his feet propped against the porch railing.

A tiny cry sounded inside the house.

"I'll get her." Chuck dropped his booted feet to the porch and hurried inside to check on Maya, Daphne's three-month old baby girl.

Daphne held up her hands and snorted. "He's even better at parenting than her own mother." She loved Maya, but sometimes she wondered if Maya loved Chuck more than her.

Chuck returned to the porch carrying Maya on one arm, cradling the back of her head with his opposite hand. He handed the child to Daphne. "I changed her, but it's not a dirty diaper that's making her fussy. She's hungry."

Daphne took the baby in her arms, sank into the rocking chair and lifted the hem of her tank top.

Too hot for a bra, she'd left it off that morning, giving Maya free access to her milk supply.

The baby rooted around until she found Daphne's nipple and sucked hungrily, making slurping noises that made Daphne laugh.

Chuck cleared his throat and turned away. "I'll make some iced tea."

"Thank you." Daphne smiled at the man's reluctance to watch the baby nursing. Hell, he'd been there when Maya was born and helped Daphne when she'd had trouble getting the baby to latch on. Why he would feel the need to give her privacy now was a mystery. But Daphne liked to push his buttons. Anything for a reaction in the incredible boredom of her current situation.

Short of feeding Maya, Chuck did everything else with the baby, including getting down on the floor to play with her when Daphne was too tired to entertain her sweet baby girl.

How she wished things had turned out differently. But then she'd wished that for the past year. Not the part about being pregnant or having a baby. Maya was the light of her life. What Daphne despised was being stuck in this godforsaken corner of the Utah desert hill country with nothing to do but count the minutes of every day. If something didn't happen soon, she'd explode.

She switched Maya to the other breast and let the baby drink her fill. The day was much like every other day. Wake up to feed Maya, change her diaper, cook breakfast for herself and Chuck and, sometimes, one of the other guards. The sun rose, the sun set and on and on and on... Only the occasional rare, violent storm ever broke their routine. God, how she wished for one now.

Daphne leaned Maya up on her shoulder and patted the bubbles out of her tummy. She cradled the baby in the curve of her arm and then sat in the growing heat, wondering where she'd gone wrong in her life to deserve so much drama and yet so much boredom.

Chuck emerged through the back screen door and took up his position in the rocking chair. For all intents and purposes, he appeared to be relaxed and enjoying the suffocating heat of the late fall day.

Daphne sighed and rocked Maya in her arms. "I'll be glad when winter finally gets here."

"You and me both," Chuck said, his gaze on the horizon and his voice even.

"Tell me again about what you did for the Navy SEALs," Daphne coaxed.

In profile, he arched an eyebrow. "I already told you a dozen times. Aren't you tired of my stories?"

She shrugged. "Beats boredom. And it gives me an idea of what Maya's father might be doing right now, as we speak."

Chuck sighed. "There's nothing sexy about tromping through the desert, carrying all of your equipment on your back, steel plates in your vest and facing an enemy that uses women and children as shields to block the bullets meant for them."

Daphne stared down at Maya, her heart contracting. She couldn't imagine someone putting a bullet through her baby girl's chest. "Then tell me about your training to become a SEAL." She liked hearing about the rigors of BUD/S training, and how only the best of the best made it through to the end.

Chuck had survived BUD/S training. Since Brandon had made it through as well, he was another man who'd proved he was one of the best.

Again, Chuck sighed and started at the beginning of

his training and told her of the different weeks and what each entailed.

Daphne half-listened...and half-daydreamed about meeting Maya's father in Cozumel.

She'd been there on what should have been her honeymoon, but had turned out to be a solitary vacation. She'd gone with a heavy heart, having lost her fiancé six months earlier to a brain tumor. Because they'd had non-refundable tickets, Jonah had insisted she go, even though it would be without him.

During his treatment and decline, Daphne had been at his side. He'd insisted she go as part of her promise to move on, find love, get married and have children.

At the time of Jonah's death, Daphne was convinced she'd never find another man to love as much as she'd loved Jonah. He'd been her everything, from the moment they'd met in high school, through college and during his final hours on earth.

He'd loved her unconditionally and had wanted half-a-dozen children with her, the little house with the white picket fence and everything normal couples dreamed of when making plans for their futures.

Two months after he'd proposed to her, he'd fallen ill. After many tests, X-rays, scans and MRIs, the diagnosis had been grim. He had terminal brain cancer and less than five months to live.

All of their plans were pushed to the side as they fought to change that diagnosis to something that involved growing old together.

Alas, nearly five months sped by, and no amount of

medication slowed the growth of the tumor. At four months, three weeks and two days following his diagnosis, Jonah slipped into a coma and died in Daphne's arms.

Before he passed, he'd made her promise to go on their honeymoon and find a man who made her heart beat faster. A man who would love her always and provide her with the family she and Jonah had always wanted. And he'd asked her to name a little girl after their honeymoon resort in remembrance of the love Daphne and Jonah had shared in his short time on earth.

Daphne stared down at the baby girl in her arms.

Maya with her black curls, so unlike Daphne's straight blond hair. Jonah had had light brown hair and blue eyes. Nothing about Maya reminded Daphne of Jonah, except her name.

Even then, she reminded Daphne more of the man she'd met in Cozumel, her baby's father, a tall, dark, handsome Navy SEAL who'd found her sitting on the beach one night, alone and crying.

Brandon Rayne, or Boomer, as his teammates had nicknamed him, could have walked away, leaving the weepy woman on the sand in the moonlight, but he hadn't. He'd dropped down beside her, taken her hand, pulled her into his arms and held her until her tears stopped falling.

He'd listened to her sad story, patted her back and held her. When she'd wiped away the tears and collected herself, he'd stood, held out a hand and pulled her up into his arms and kissed her forehead. "Everything is going to be all right," he'd assured her.

She stared up into his moonlit dark eyes. "How do you know?"

He chuckled. "I don't. But being on a sandy beach with a beautiful woman makes me wholly optimistic." Then he'd walked her back to her room at the resort and given her his cell phone number in case she ever wanted to walk on the beach at night. He didn't like the idea of her walking alone.

And that's how their brief and fiery romance spun up into a raging flame. If Daphne believed in ghosts, she'd bet Jonah had sent the SEAL to remind her that her fiancé had died, not her. She had a life to live, and oh, by the way, this handsome SEAL seemed interested in her and wanted to spend time with her.

Once she got over the guilt, Daphne enjoyed the quiet walks at night on the beach. And what was moonlight without a kiss?

One kiss with Boomer wasn't nearly enough. By the second night, he'd invited her to dance and then to his bungalow for a drink. The remaining five days were spent together in paradise. Swimming, dancing, parasailing and learning how to love as if for the first time.

When the last night came, Daphne slipped out of his room, after he fell asleep to return to hers to pack for the trip home. She hadn't wanted to wake him, hating tearful goodbyes. She wanted to remember him as he was, big, gorgeous and naked against the sheets.

On her way from his bungalow to her room in the tower, she'd run across a young man, arguing with a woman.

The woman slapped the young man.

Daphne had been too far away to hear what she said, but clearly, she wasn't happy with the man. When the woman turned to walk away, the blond man clasped her wrist and spun her toward him.

She told him to let go.

When he didn't, she tugged hard, trying to free herself.

Daphne had sped up, trying to get closer to help the woman.

By the time she reached them, the blond man had wrapped his hands around the woman's neck so tightly, he was choking her.

The woman beat at his chest with her fists, but he wouldn't release his grip.

Daphne grabbed a stick from the ground and hit the man over and over, but he wouldn't let go of the woman until her body sagged and fell to the ground.

Then he turned his attention to Daphne.

The man blocked the path, preventing her from running back to the bungalow where Boomer lay sleeping peacefully.

With no other choice, Daphne spun and ran toward the resort, the sound of footsteps pounding on the path behind her. She'd almost reached the entrance when an arm reached out of the darkness, grabbed her, yanked her into the shadow of the bushes, and pushed her toward the ground. A hand clamped over her mouth, muffling her attempt to scream.

"Be still, or he'll find you and kill you," a voice whispered into her ear.

Steps crunched on the gravel path, heading her direction.

Daphne lay still, more afraid of the man who'd choked a woman to death than the stranger holding her in the darkness.

The killer stalked past her, his eyes narrow, his gaze darting into the shadows. In his left hand, he held a small handgun.

Freezing in place, Daphne held her breath, praying he didn't see her lying there. Vulnerable to the man holding her and to the killer brandishing a gun, she prayed she'd chosen the lesser of two evils.

The assailant tucked the weapon into waistband of his trousers and closed his suit jacket over the bulge, before entering the resort tower.

Not until the door closed behind him, did Daphne let go of the breath she'd held.

The man holding her removed his hand from her mouth and loosened the arm around her middle.

She scrambled to her feet and stared at the stranger as he pushed to his feet and stood. He towered over her, his muscular body even more proof he could have had his way with her and she'd have had little chance of fighting free.

That's how she remembered meeting Chuck.

He'd been the one responsible for saving her life and that of her unborn baby by whisking her away from Cozumel and back to the States.

"I'm Agent Johnson. Chuck Johnson." He'd shown her his credentials as a DEA agent in pursuit of a man who smuggled drugs and murdered beautiful women.

"That man chasing you happens to be the son of a high-powered senator. He's suspected of drug and human trafficking, as well as several counts of murder."

"Then why aren't you stopping him?" Daphne demanded.

"He's a slippery bastard. The witnesses or drug dealers have a habit of turning up dead before charges can be brought against him." The stranger frowned. "Why was he chasing you?"

Daphne's heart plummeted into her belly as she recalled how hard the woman had fought and how many times Daphne had hit the man with the stick to no avail. "He killed a woman."

"Show me." Chuck edged up to the path, glancing both ways before motioning for her to go ahead of him.

Before they reached the point at which the woman had been strangled, two men appeared from the direction of the beach, dressed in black. The glow of the Tiki lamps lighting the path glinted off the smooth metal of the pistols they carried in their hands.

Chuck pulled her back into the shadows and blocked her body with his.

But he didn't block her entire vision.

The two men in black moved the woman's body, carrying it toward the ocean.

"See what I mean?" her muscular rescuer said. "He has a cleanup detail following him around."

Shocked at what she'd just seen, Daphne tried to push him aside. "You can't let him get away with killing someone."

"And what do you suggest? If I kill those men, it will

appear as if I killed the woman. You and I will be split up, and more cleanup crews will be called in to deal with you and me. Our best bet is to get you out of here before they come looking for you."

At that exact moment, two more men appeared, coming from the direction of the resort, also dressed in black and carrying weapons.

Daphne sank back into the bushes, shaking. "I know the man staying in the fourth bungalow from the end of the path. We can hide there," she suggested.

Chuck shook his head. "No good. If you were there before, they'll track you down to that location again. The staff knows the comings and goings of all the guests. And they can be bribed."

But Daphne wanted to go back to where she'd left Boomer sleeping. If she'd stayed with him the entire night, she wouldn't be in this predicament. The woman would still be dead, but Daphne wouldn't now be targeted for elimination.

Again, she stayed still, waiting for the two men in black to pass by their position. She had no other choice in the matter. She had to get away from the scene of the crime. Perhaps then, they could circle back and report the crime to the local authorities.

That had been a year ago.

As far as Daphne knew, Harrison Cooper was still free, while she and Maya had been stuck in a cabin in Utah, waiting for something to happen that would put Cooper behind bars.

When Chuck paused in his description of Hell Week at BUD/S, Daphne pushed to her feet. "I'm going to go put Maya to bed. Hold that thought. I want to hear more." She smiled at the only human contact she'd had besides the doctors and nurses who'd delivered her baby in the Salt Lake City hospital and her two-man protection crew who guarded the entrance to this lonely house.

Chuck had admitted he wasn't with the DEA. He was with a super-secret government entity, assigned to clean up corruption amongst politicians. He'd come up with false identification and insurance cards to cover her and the baby. As soon as she was able, he'd packed up her and Maya and orchestrated their disappearance from the hospital into the foothills of Utah's Wasatch Mountain Range, near the Wyoming border.

Daphne had grown to love Chuck like a surrogate father or a favorite big brother. On more than one occasion, she found herself referring to him as Maya's godfather. And he was her only link to the outside world.

He had connections with the SEAL community, having retired from the Navy before taking on a role with the DEA.

Daphne knew, if she asked, he'd tell her where Boomer was, and whether he was dead or alive. When she'd been at her lowest, suffering from postpartum depression shortly after Maya was born, he'd told her Boomer was back in the States, preparing to deploy to Iraq.

She'd been tempted to reach out to Boomer and let him know he had a beautiful baby girl. But how fair would that have been, knowing he was about to deploy.

And by letting him know about his baby, she might give up her location, something she couldn't afford to do. Her life wasn't nearly as important to her as keeping Maya safe.

Now that she had a baby, she had to do everything in her power to protect Maya from Harrison Cooper's cleanup team. As effective as they'd been in Cozumel, they would show no remorse over using an infant as a bargaining chip to lure Daphne out into the open. Once they located her, she'd disappear, and then they'd have no use for Maya.

Daphne's heart squeezed hard in her chest as she laid her baby in the crib.

Maya's sweet lips puckered as if she were still suckling at Daphne's breast. She squirmed, stretched and laid still, her belly full, her comfort secured.

Daphne smiled and straightened, her attention drawn to the window overlooking the dirt road leading up to the cabin. A plume of dust rose from a vehicle moving swiftly up the mile-long track.

A second of concern rippled through Daphne, but she refused to be alarmed. Not yet.

Their dayshift gate guard, Rodney Smith, was one of two men who'd been assigned to provide backup and support. Rodney was on day shift, while Paul Caney preferred nights and slept in town during the day. They stood guard at the entrance gate to the mountain cabin a mile away, keeping in contact with Chuck via handheld, two-way radios.

"Chuck? Has Rodney checked in?" she called out.

Chuck entered the house, passed the door to Maya's

nursery and exited through the front door onto the porch. With the two-way radio held to his ear, his gaze fixed on the cloud of dust racing toward them. "Smith, report," he said over and over.

When nothing but static came across the radio, Chuck spun and raced back into the house, his face stern, his fists clenched. "Take Maya to the shed. Now! This isn't a drill."

Daphne's heart tripped and raced. They'd practiced this drill numerous times. If Chuck said take Maya to the shed, they were in trouble.

Daphne reached for her "go pack", the backpack carrying the essentials necessary for the baby, slung it over her shoulders, then she gathered Maya into her arms and ran out the back of the house to the shed.

In the shed, she pulled a baby sling over her shoulder, settled Maya into the sling and tightened it so that she fit snugly against Daphne's chest. She settled a helmet over her head and buckled the strap.

Chuck arrived a few seconds later and flung open the back doors he'd installed on the shed.

"Everything set?" Daphne asked as she swung her leg over the seat of a four-wheeler.

He nodded. "Do you want me to take Maya?"

Daphne shook her head. "I've got her."

"You can take the lead until we reach the pass. I've got your six. The paths are narrow. The vehicles coming up the road won't be able to follow for long—if they make it past the surprise I left for them."

"Where will we go?" Daphne asked.

"I have a friend in Montana. He'll know what to do. He'll help protect you and Maya."

Daphne nodded, pressed the throttle lever on the four-wheeler and sent the vehicle lurching forward and up the trail into the mountains.

Chuck followed, bringing up the rear, armed to the teeth with rifles, handguns, knives and hand grenades.

All they had to do was get far enough away from rifle fire, and they'd make good their escape from those attacking the cabin. But the race up the side of the mountain left them exposed for several minutes. What they needed was a distraction.

Daphne didn't look back, she held tightly to the handlebars of the ATV, moving as quickly as she could up the rough mountain trail, praying the men heading for the cabin didn't stop and take aim at the riders on the escaping four-wheelers.

An explosion echoed off the hillsides, followed by another, even bigger, that ripped through the air, shaking the earth beneath the four, knobby tires. Daphne nearly lost her grip on the four-wheeler handlebars. She risked a quick glance over her shoulder at the cabin. Nothing remained of her temporary home. Nothing but debris, fire and smoke.

Chuck slowed, frowning. "I planned on the first explosion, but not the second."

"Did you detonate the house?" Daphne asked.

Her protector shook his head. "No. I had some trip wires set up in front of the house. Looks like it just made them mad enough to destroy the house."

Daphne swallowed the sob rising up her throat,

threatening to choke off her air. That cabin had been her baby's first home. The crib, the extra clothing and toys had been all Maya had known. Where they'd go from here was a huge unknown.

All Daphne knew was she had to get Maya to safety. Everything that had been in the cabin was just *stuff*. She could replace stuff. She couldn't replace the life of her baby girl.

Chuck had a friend in Montana.

After a year, waiting for something to happen and thinking it never would, Daphne was now a believer. Her heart weighed heavily for the guard on the gate. More than likely, Rodney was dead.

She prayed Chuck's friend in Montana had the power and resources to protect her and Maya.

CHAPTER 2

BRANDON RAYNE LAY WITH HIS CHEEK CLOSE TO THE DIRT, wind whipping sand into his face like someone intent on sandblasting the skin from his body. Thankfully, he wore protective glasses that kept the sand from reaching his eyes. They also kept the heat and humidity contained inside the rubber seals. Sweat dripped from his forehead and down his nose.

He waited, his gaze intent on the scope, lined up with the door to a building believed to be the current location of a high-ranking Islamic State leader in Iraq.

"Holding steady, Boomer?" Irish said into his headset. Declan O'Shea, one of the more experienced members of his team, was positioned closer to the small mountain village north of Mosul.

"Holding," Boomer whispered.

"If the shit hits the fan, no worries, man," Fish said. "We've got your six. We're in position and ready to roll." Jack Fischer, the team lead for this mission, had the others ready to enter the village on command.

The main purpose of their current mission was to decapitate the head of the snake. In other words, to take out this particular leader of the Islamic State wreaking havoc on grounds once controlled by the American and Iraqi military.

With the sun setting behind him, shadows lengthened, making it more and more difficult to make out shapes and specific faces.

Taped to the inside of his gloved palm was the image of the man. His target. He couldn't miss. So many lives depended on his taking out this murdering Islamic State militant who'd orchestrated the sacking of many cities and towns, raped women, slaughtered children and destroyed centuries of historical structures and relics. He had to be stopped.

Black SUVs pulled up to the structure. Thankfully, at the angle from which Boomer was positioned, he still had a direct shot at anyone emerging from the entrance.

A moment later, the door opened. Two men in solid black uniforms, their heads and faces swathed in black, carrying semi-automatic rifles, stepped out. Behind them was a more portly man dressed in white, his face exposed, his long dark beard, thick mustache and even thicker dark brows making him easy to recognize.

Instead of the fitted black uniform, he wore the long white robe and turban of an imam. Abu Ahmed had a fierce reputation. Those who dared disagree with him were beheaded as a lesson to others.

Through the lens of his high-powered sniper rifle, Boomer locked in on his target and squeezed the trigger.

As the bullet released from Boomer's weapon, the man dressed as an imam looked up as if to stare into Boomer's scope. In that same moment, a woman carrying a baby stepped out from behind him.

A second later, a bright red dot appeared in Abu Ahmed's forehead, and he crumpled, falling at the feet of his guards. The baby in the woman's arms jerked and went limp.

The woman screamed and looked down at her baby, her eyes wide and terrified.

The black-garbed guards crouched, bringing their guns to the ready.

Fish, Irish, Nacho, Gator and the rest of the team moved into action. From their positions closer to the structure, they picked off the guards. More militants poured from the building, overrunning the woman holding the limp child.

Boomer focused on the other militants, pushing to the back of his mind the woman, now crouched on the ground, rocking back and forth, her wails echoing off the hills, her baby pressed to her breast.

He locked on another militant, squeezed off a round and watched as the man in white fell to his knees then flat on his chest.

Soon, the SEAL team converged on the structure and entered.

Boomer's job was to cover their six in case more ISIS soldiers arrived.

Soon, the team emerged, carrying backpacks filled with documents and artifacts of their operation. Fish and Gator led a man at gunpoint. He wore the black uniform of the Islamic State militants, an angry glare pushing his thick black brows together.

Women emerged from the building, clutching the hands of small children.

One woman, who didn't have a child clutching her robes, pulled something small from beneath her abaya, grabbed the top of the item and jerked her hand.

It all happened too fast for Boomer to react.

The woman tossed the grenade into the group of SEALs.

Fish scooped up the grenade, cocked his arm and threw it as far as he could before dropping to the ground. The other SEALs followed suit and dropped where they stood.

The grenade exploded in mid-air, spewing shrapnel in a three-hundred-sixty-degree radius.

The women threw their hands up to cover their faces. But the damage was done. Anyone within twenty feet of the explosion took a hit of tiny, deadly fragments of sharp metal.

From where Boomer lay, all he could do was watch and pray his team hadn't suffered any deadly injuries.

Women and children dropped to the ground, blood running like little rivers from the many wounds inflicted.

The man the SEALs had escorted out of the building clutched his throat, sank to his knees and keeled over on top of Boomer's original target.

Women and children cried. Many lay unmoving.

Boomer whispered into his mic, "Fish, Gator, Irish?" He swallowed hard and held his breath. Someone say something.

"Fish here. I'm okay. Flesh wound to the right shoulder, and maybe my right thigh. Can't tell where all the blood's coming from."

"Irish here," Declan's voice came across the radio. "Took a hit to the calf. Flesh wound. I can walk out."

"Bit in the ass." Gator laughed, the sound strained. "Won't be sitting down on that cheek for a while."

One by one, the team reported in with their statuses and

injuries. Gator called in support from the 160th Night Stalker Black Hawk helicopter team. Within minutes, three choppers landed near the small village. Medics rushed to triage and help the injured SEALs, women and children.

From the top of the hill overlooking the small Iraqi village, Boomer continued to provide cover, the image of the woman holding her dead baby replaying in his mind, over and over. He'd been tasked to take out an Islamic State militant at all costs. The man had been responsible for the deaths of thousands of innocent people.

Boomer closed his eyes for a moment and pinched the bridge of his nose. Yes, there was bound to be collateral damage in just about any operation they conducted. But that didn't make him feel any better. The bullet, meant for Abu Ahmed, had taken out the ISIS leader and the baby behind him.

A BABY'S cry pierced Boomer's consciousness. He opened his eyes and stared up at a ceiling he didn't immediately recognize.

He cursed softly.

The cry sounded somewhere outside the walls of the room in which he lay in a soft, comfortable bed. Sunlight wedged through the window, nudging aside what remained of the night's darkness and the cobwebs of memories lingering in Boomer's mind. He wasn't in Iraq anymore, and the baby's death had been well over seven months ago.

A lot had happened since then.

A light knock sounded on the door.

"Boomer? Are you going to get your lazy ass out of bed?" Hank Patterson's deep voice sounded through the door's wood paneling.

"Tell me you've got work for me, and I'll think about it." Boomer scrubbed a hand over his face.

"Oh, I have work. Get dressed and come meet your new assignment."

Boomer pushed to a sitting position, the weight of his dreams still pressing hard against his chest. "I'm up." He swung his legs over the side of the bed and stood naked in the bright light of dawn. As the sun crept above the horizon, light filled the room through the window shades he'd left open the night before.

Boomer jammed his legs into a pair of jeans. He scrounged in his duffel bag for a T-shirt, sniffed, approved and pulled it on. When he stared at himself in the mirror, he shook his head. The T-shirt's logo read FUN IN THE SUN IN COZUMEL.

Boomer snorted. The last time he'd been truly happy had been his vacation in Cozumel. Before his last assignment. Before the death of that baby. Before he'd left the military.

One reason the vacation had been so special was the woman who'd set his world on fire. He'd spent the entire week with her, laughing, playing and making love into the wee hours of every morning. On her last night, she'd slipped out of his bungalow and out of his life, disappearing so completely, he'd often wondered if she'd only been a figment of his imagination.

Boomer had spent the next two days of his vacation desperately searching the island for her, but it was as if she'd never existed. The airport showed no woman with her name having booked a flight off the island. Her hotel room had been completely cleaned of all of her belongings, and no one could tell him where she'd gone.

He reached for the hem of the shirt, ripped it over his head and pulled on a solid black T-shirt with no logos and no associated memories. Montana and this gig with Hank Patterson and the Brotherhood Protectors was a new start at a life, post-military. Granted, he'd still be utilizing the skills he'd honed as a SEAL. Hank had insisted he wanted an expert sniper on the team he'd assembled.

Why Hank needed a sniper in the wilds of Montana's Crazy Mountains, Boomer didn't know. He still wasn't sure what his role and responsibilities would be. But considering Hank's was the only job offer since he'd left the military, he couldn't be too choosy. From what he'd been told so far, he'd be something like a bodyguard or a member of a special ops team, should the need arise to deploy more than one man at a time.

Other members of the Brotherhood Protectors team had filled him in on some of their assignments since coming on board as members of the Brotherhood Protectors, letting Boomer know the mountains of Montana weren't all that peaceful, and there were some crackpot zealots in the area from time to time. Terrorist activities weren't limited to the sands of the Middle East.

Boomer ran a hand through his hair, slipped his feet into socks and his worn black combat boots and left the sanctuary of the room Hank had let him camp out in since arriving two days ago.

Voices filtered down the hallway from the main living area with the killer view of the mountains. Two deep, male voices and two female voices from the sounds of it.

Then a baby's cry brought Boomer to a complete halt.

His heart raced, his hands clenched and he broke out in a cold sweat.

How, after all this time could he still be having these insane reactions to the sound of a baby's cry? Hank and his wife Sadie had a baby girl. He'd been around little Emma for two days, and he hadn't reacted like this when she'd cried. Perhaps the lingering effects of his dream had him jittery.

The baby cried again, the sound somehow different from what he'd grown used to coming from baby Emma.

Boomer drew in a deep breath, willing the tension away. He flexed his fingers, rolled his shoulders and stepped out of the hallway into the spacious living area, the Crazy Mountains the main artwork on display through the floor-to-ceiling windows. The sun had risen, bathing the room in a bright golden light.

After emerging from the darkness of the hallway, Boomer blinked, giving his eyes time to adjust to the brighter lighting.

Hank and Sadie stood together. Hank had baby Emma in the curve of one arm. His other arm was wrapped around Sadie's waist. He smiled as Boomer entered the room. "Good. Good. Brandon Rayne, I'd like you to meet Chuck Johnson, Navy SEAL retired."

A big man with broad shoulders and salt-and-pepper gray hair stepped forward, his hand held out. The sun backlit him, making Boomer squint to see the man clearly. He gripped the guy's hand. "Always good to meet a fellow SEAL."

Chuck's grin accompanied his firm handshake. "Once a SEAL, always a SEAL?"

"Damn right." Boomer glanced toward Hank. "Are you telling me I have a partner for this assignment?"

Hank shrugged. "Actually, yes. However, Chuck isn't a member of the Brotherhood Protectors."

Boomer released Chuck's hand. "I don't understand."

"Chuck needs help protecting a woman."

Boomer returned his attention to Chuck. "What's the situation?"

"My charge has been relatively safe under witness protection for the past year. Until two days ago, when her cover was blown. We lost a man on the job and had to make a run through the mountains. I'm afraid she's in a whole lot more danger than I can handle alone. Since whoever has her number found her once, I'm betting he'll find her again. I need help when that happens."

"What did she witness?" Boomer asked.

"A murder."

"And the murderer?"

"Has gotten away with several killings. He's the son of a powerful politician with an expert cleanup team. Whenever the son commits a crime, his father cleans up the mess. His mop-up team is so thorough, they've left no evidence that can help us prosecute either the father or the son."

"This witness doesn't support a case?" Hank said, his jaw tightening.

"The body of the murdered woman never turned up. If my witness testified, it would be her against the son of a politically powerful man. They'd never get a conviction against the son. Which would also leave the father off the hook after all the laws he's broken protecting his scumbag son." Chuck shook his head. "She's a loose thread they can't afford to let live in case evidence of that murder ever does come to light."

Boomer frowned. "So what is your role in all this? Are you a U.S. Marshall?"

Chuck shook his head. "I was working with the DEA when I ran across the witness and got her out before she became another speck of dust swept under the cleanup crew's rug."

"DEA? Since when does DEA do witness protection duty?"

Chuck's lips twisted. "Well, that's where all of this is a little tricky. I wasn't really with the DEA. I was working on special assignment, following Harrison Cooper to get the goods that would nail the bastard and his father. When shit hit the fan in Cozumel where Cooper murdered a woman, I knew my witness had to get out alive. My assignment changed to protecting the witness."

"Who do you take orders from?" Boomer asked.

Chuck shook his head. "I can't say."

Hank's eyes narrowed. "If you told us, you'd have to kill us?"

"Something like that." Chuck raised his hands. "But don't worry. I'm one of the good guys. I'm still the same person who made it through SEAL training. I bleed red, white and blue."

Hank nodded. "I believe you. You had my back on more occasions than I can count when I was fresh out of BUD/S training and working my first few missions as a member of SEAL Team Six."

"Once a SEAL, always a SEAL," Chuck repeated. "That's why I came to you. I've been following what you've done with the Brotherhood Protectors. I knew that if we got into any trouble, you could help us out."

Hank shot a glance toward Boomer. "You're in luck. Rayne just hired on with the Brotherhood. He's a highly skilled sniper, and has all the training you and I had. He'll be an asset to your cause."

"Good, because I'm not sure how long it'll take for the people who breached our safe house to catch up with us. I need to get my girl to another safe location where we can see what's coming and be ahead of the next attack."

Footsteps sounded from behind Chuck.

The older SEAL turned with a gentle smile and held out his arms.

A woman with long blond hair and green eyes stepped into the room, an infant in her arms. She handed the child to Chuck and lifted her head to study the others in the room, her gaze moving from Sadie and her baby to Hank, and finally to Boomer.

She stepped closer, out of the glow of early morning sunshine, and her image solidified.

Her gaze met his at the same moment. The woman's eyes widened, and her mouth dropped open in a rounded O.

Boomer's breath caught, lodged in his lungs, and his heart pounded a wild tattoo against his chest.

Holy hell! This woman couldn't be the one he'd met and fallen so hard for on vacation in Cozumel a year ago. The woman who'd disappeared out of his life forever. She had the same long blond hair and vivid green eyes. Surely, there couldn't be two women in the world who looked so much alike.

Boomer blinked, hoping to clear his vision of the mirage standing before him. Then she whispered, the sound carrying across the room, piercing his heart.

"You," she said, her voice barely a whisper.

Boomer's knees wobbled. He took a step forward. And another.

The baby in Chuck's arms squirmed, reached for the woman and cried out when she didn't immediately take her into her arms.

The tiny cry froze Boomer's feet to the floor, and his chest tightened until he felt as though he was having a heart attack. His fists clenched so hard, his fingernails dug into his palms.

Chuck handed the baby to the woman and stood beside her, facing Boomer. "This is Daphne Miller, aka the witness, and her baby daughter Maya." His gaze met Boomer's, and his eyes narrowed slightly. "This job would require protecting both Miss Miller and her baby."

"I know it's your first assignment," Hank said, "but it's an important one. You'd be more of a backup to Chuck in his effort to protect these two ladies."

Boomer heard Hank's words but couldn't move from where he stood. His gaze remained riveted on Daphne, the baby and Chuck, standing together like a family unit.

His heart sank to somewhere in the vicinity of his gut. A year ago, he and Daphne had made such a good connection, had spent every hour of every day they had in Cozumel together, getting to know each other and making love like there would never be another tomorrow.

Then she'd disappeared out of his life, only to turn up with this older SEAL and a baby.

A thousand questions crowded his head, but he couldn't voice one.

"Boomer, are you up for the challenge?" Hank asked. "I know you're new to the Brotherhood, but I don't have anyone else available at this time."

Boomer thought of all the reasons he couldn't do the job, but none of them left his lips. Perhaps what he'd felt in Cozumel with Daphne had been blown completely out of proportion. She might not have been as attracted to him as he had been to her. Obviously, she'd moved on with her life, found someone else to love and had a baby. By the way Chuck handled the tiny infant, it appeared the someone else was the retired Navy SEAL.

As the anxiety of the baby's cry dissipated from his consciousness, determination kept his fists tightened into knots. If Daphne could forget what they'd had so easily, so could he. Or at least he could give the appearance of having forgotten, even though a sharp pain seemed to have wedged itself into his chest near his heart.

Though he'd known every inch of her body, Boomer pretended like he'd never met Daphne, never made love to her, never thought he'd fallen for the pretty blond tourist on the small Mexican island.

"I can do this," he said aloud, fearing it was more to convince himself than to convince his new boss, Hank.

Hank clapped his hands together. "Good. Then all we need to do is position you somewhere private where you can see the enemy coming from all directions. Others from the Brotherhood can be backup in a matter of minutes, but for the most part, it'll be you and Chuck protecting Daphne and Maya. I'll have my computer guru work on tracking data about the politician and his son. Harrison Cooper, you said?"

Chuck nodded.

Hank shook his head. "Senator John Cooper's son. It's hard to believe the senator would go to such lengths to keep his son out of jail."

"Yeah," Chuck's lips thinned. "But again, we can't pin the cleanups to him. We haven't been able to capture one of the men. Whoever hired them got some pretty slick mercenaries to do their dirty work. They make it their business to disappear, only appearing when they have a job to do."

"And their current job seems to be to eliminate their

one live witness," Boomer said, his gaze meeting Daphne's. She was the job. Nothing more. What they had in the past was just that—in the past.

She had a new life, a child and Chuck.

Where did that leave Boomer?

The awkward, odd man out.

CHAPTER 3

Daphne tried to breathe past the knot forming in her throat. She felt as if she'd been sucker punched. When she'd arrived in the wee morning hours at Hank Patterson's ranch, she'd hoped and prayed for help in her fight to stay alive.

She hadn't expected to run into the father of her child. Worse yet, he'd barely acknowledged her, as if he didn't recognize her. Or didn't care.

All these months, she'd fantasized about meeting Boomer again and telling him the happy news that he had a baby girl. She'd dreamed he'd be ecstatic and ready to take on the loving responsibility of raising a daughter.

But the stony, cold look on his face made her bite down hard on her tongue. Either he didn't recognize her, or he did and didn't want anyone else to know he and she had once been more than acquaintances.

Her heart skipped several beats and sank to her belly. For the past year, she'd dreamed of him, holding out his arms, taking her into his embrace and speaking of how much he'd missed her and how happy he was that he'd found her again.

Based on his response to her introduction, a real conversation would have to wait until they were alone.

"While you three decide what's next, Daphne and I will feed the babies." Hank's wife, Sadie McClain, with baby Emma on her hip, hooked Daphne's arm.

Though Daphne held Maya, she hadn't realized the baby was rooting around her blouse, searching for a breast to suckle. Her cheeks burning, Daphne ducked her head and followed Sadie out of the great room and into a small sitting room filled with morning sunlight.

Sadie settled into a wooden rocking chair, lifted her blouse and guided Emma to a nipple.

Unused to breastfeeding with another adult in the room, other than Chuck, Daphne fumbled with the buttons on her blouse and finally settled Maya on her left breast.

The baby latched on and pulled hard. The sudden tug made her milk come rushing in the expected letdown effect. Maya happily drank her fill while Daphne tried to think of what to say to the woman who'd opened her home to them in the middle of the night.

"I think breastfeeding is one of the most natural things in the world. I don't understand why people are so uptight about it." Sadie smiled across at Daphne.

Daphne stared down at her daughter, all her love bubbling up to the surface. Her joy temporarily crowded out the sense of rejection she'd experienced upon seeing Boomer for the first time since they'd created this beautiful baby girl. She swept aside the baby's soft black hair.

"I don't know what I would have done if I couldn't have breastfed her," Daphne said softly. "For the past year, we lived in the Utah foothills in a cabin with generator power. A refrigerator was a luxury that only worked some of the time."

Sadie shook her head. "You're lucky. Not all women are able to breastfeed. I like it because I don't have to carry around formula or extra water to mix with it. Whenever Emma's hungry, I can feed her." Sadie chuckled. "The only problem is I'm on call all the time. I have frozen breast milk for later use when I'm on the set and unable to be there for a quick feeding."

Daphne stared down at her daughter, still amazed at how much she'd gained in the past three months. From a tiny five-pound six-ounces to nearly twelve pounds, she'd taken well to nursing, keeping life on the lam less complicated than it could have been with a baby.

"I can't get over your wild ride through the mountains. Hank said you and Chuck rode four-wheelers into the mountains to escape the people after you. How did you do that carrying a baby?"

Daphne snorted. "Trust me, it wasn't easy. Chuck had purchased a special baby sling we kept with the four-wheelers specifically for such an occasion." Her lips twisted. "I never thought we'd actually have to use it, but it came in handy. It kept Maya close to my body when we got up in the mountains where it was much cooler, especially at night."

"The weatherman predicts our first snow will come sometime in the next few days."

Daphne shook her head. "After the heat of the Utah safe house, it's hard to believe it'll soon be cold enough to snow."

"We have had weird, unseasonably warm fall weather, but that's all about to change. Thankfully, you arrived when you did. I wouldn't be surprised to see a light dusting tonight. The temperature has dropped since you got here."

Daphne looked out at the beautiful mountains. "You have a lovely home." She wished to have a real home someday. A place she could raise Maya in safety.

"Thank you. It's fairly new. The original ranch house burned to the ground when I had a stalker causing problems."

"What?" Daphne stared at Sadie. "I can't imagine anyone wanting to hurt you."

"There are some crazy people in this world. Hank has done an excellent job hiring former military men to help protect those who need help protecting themselves." Sadie smiled. "You should be really happy with Boomer. Navy SEALs are highly skilled with every kind of weapon and hand to hand combat."

She dropped her gaze at the mention of Boomer's name, afraid her expression might give away the fact she was still in shock. "I hope it doesn't come down to a battle."

"Me, too." Sadie captured her gaze. "I could swear when you first saw Boomer, you recognized him. Do you two know each other?"

Daphne shrugged and shifted her gaze back to Maya. "He reminds me of someone I used to know."

"Boomer's fresh off active duty. He's been deployed several times to Iraq to fight against the Islamic State."

"Was he injured? Is that why he left active duty?" Daphne asked, trying not to sound too concerned or curious, but wanting to know as much as possible about the man she'd held tightly to in her dreams.

Sadie frowned. "He wasn't injured, but when his reenlistment came due, he decided he'd had enough. He hasn't said much while he's been here the past few days, but he has a faraway look in his eyes. Like he's seen too much."

Daphne frowned. "Are you sure he's stable?"

"Hank wouldn't assign anyone he didn't trust." Sadie glanced down at Emma. "Are you full?"

Emma stared up at her mother's face and grinned, with a milk bubble sliding across her lips.

Daphne realized Maya had fallen asleep while nursing. She pressed her finger next to the baby's mouth to disengage, laid her across her lap and buttoned her shirt.

When she was done, she tipped Maya up onto her shoulder and patted her back until the baby burped.

"Ready to rejoin the menfolk?" Sadie shifted her shirt, hiked Emma up onto her shoulder and stood. "I'd love to have you stay here with us, but I'm heading back to LA tomorrow. Maybe we can get our baby girls together for future play dates, if you remain in the area."

"I'd like that," Daphne said, wishing her life could be

that simple. "I have no idea how much longer I'll be in hiding."

"Hopefully, not long. Something's got to give. You can't be expected to put your life on hold forever. Hank and his team will help." She led the way out of the sitting room and back into the great room where the men had taken seats in the bomber-jacket-brown leather couches.

As soon as the women appeared, the men all stood.

Daphne stared from Hank to Chuck, and finally let her gaze travel to Boomer.

Sadie stopped in front of Hank. "Have you all decided on the next move?"

Boomer stared at Daphne, his gaze less than happy, his brows pulling downward into a frown. So, he wasn't happy to see her. What did she expect?

"We're working on it," Hank said.

"In the meantime, how about some breakfast?" Sadie handed Hank their daughter and turned to Daphne. "Would you like to help?"

Daphne nodded. Glad to escape the room again. Maybe she was imagining it, but she felt a distinct tension stretching tightly between herself and Boomer. Staying in the same room without saying anything would be pure agony. She stared after Sadie, but Chuck stepped into her way.

"Want me to take Maya?" he asked, holding out his hands.

Daphne smiled gratefully. "Yes. Thank you."

"My pleasure." Chuck took the baby and cradled her in one arm.

Maya didn't wake; her mouth still made sucking motions.

Daphne hurried from the room, her heart full of her love for her baby girl and breaking at the lack of interest from the baby's father. She was so tired from their wild ride through the night and her heart was so heavy, she feared she'd break down and cry in front of Boomer.

That would be awful. No matter what his thoughts about the child they'd created together, she'd be damned if she let his indifference hurt her. She didn't need him to help her care for Maya. Lots of mothers raised children alone. Besides, she had Chuck.

At least until the troubles with Harrison Cooper were resolved.

Chuck had been there when the baby was born. He'd helped her through the first weeks of caring for a newborn infant, while recovering from the effects of having given birth. Chuck changed diapers and rocked Maya after the baby had proven to be colicky. The only thing he couldn't do was feed her.

If Daphne were smart, she'd have given up mooning over Boomer long ago and fallen in love with the man who'd kept her safe all this time. The man who'd been there for her and Maya from the start.

No matter how much she'd tried to imagine him assuming a more intimate role, she'd fallen short. She loved him like a big brother or a kind uncle. Never had she wanted to make love to him like she still wanted to make love to Boomer.

She stopped short of entering the kitchen, sucked in

a deep breath and told herself to get a grip. Boomer wasn't interested in her. Why torture herself with memories of their last night together?

BOOMER STRUGGLED to focus on what Hank was saying. His thoughts had followed Daphne into the kitchen. If anything, she was more beautiful now than when they'd met in Cozumel. Her breasts and hips were fuller, and when she smiled at her baby, the entire room seemed to light up.

Her baby.

Anger bubbled up inside. He glared across the room at Chuck. He had to be the baby's father. Though he had salt-and-pepper gray hair, those dark strands were the same shade as the baby's, lying in the curve of his arm.

How old was the baby, anyway?

Boomer studied the infant. She couldn't sit up on her own, so she had to be between two and six months, right? Hell, when did babies learn to sit up? He knew nothing about infants.

Chuck seemed to know his way around baby Maya. Had he moved right in and stolen Daphne's heart?

How quickly had she switched her affections from Boomer to the older SEAL? If he did the math, it hadn't taken long. Then again, if Chuck had been her handler since she'd witnessed the murder, falling for the big Navy SEAL could have been the natural thing. They'd been holed up together all that time, alone.

"Are you okay with the plan, Boomer?" Hank asked.

Boomer pulled his head out of the funk he'd fallen

into and glanced across the room at his new boss. He scrambled for something to say that didn't make him sound like he hadn't been listening the entire time. "Could you go over it one more time? I want to make sure I have it right."

Hank grinned. "You and Chuck will take Daphne and the baby up to the mountain chalet near the Crazy Mountain Ski Resort. I recommend getting up there soon. The weatherman predicted snow as early as tonight. You don't want to get caught in the middle of a blizzard on your way out. Load up on provisions before you go, and stock up on weapons from the Brotherhood armory."

Chuck snorted. "You have an armory?"

Hank nodded. "When we rebuilt this house, we had an armory installed in the basement. It's a vault with every type of weapon we might need to carry out our duties. As we've expanded our operations, we've added to our collection."

"Are they legal?" Boomer asked.

Hank smiled. "I wouldn't have it any other way. I wouldn't be much of a husband if I went to jail for something stupid. I have a wife and baby to consider."

Boomer's glance shifted in the direction Daphne had gone and then back to the baby in Chuck's arms.

"I knew we could count on you, Hank," Chuck said. "I've heard nothing but good things about the Brotherhood Protectors. Word of mouth gets around the SEAL network."

Hank nodded. "The brotherhood has made an impression, not only in the SEAL network, but throughout the United States. Some of our wealthier clients have shared their experiences with their friends. I can't keep up with the requests to provide protection."

"Are you sure you have the capacity to protect Miss Miller and Maya?" Chuck asked. "I don't know if my sources can afford to pay you."

Hank held up his hands. "I wouldn't take your money, even if you offered. Not all of our work is for pay. I have an ulterior motive here," he said, with a half-smile. "I'm hoping your experience with us will convince you to come to work for the brotherhood when you get tired of all the cloak and dagger B.S. with *whatever* organization you're working for now."

Boomer's fists clenched. He wasn't sure how he felt about Chuck. He knew for damned sure working with him on a daily basis, knowing he was with Daphne now, would rub him wrong on so many levels. He'd work this one assignment with the man, nail the bastard causing Daphne trouble and move on and away from the happy little family.

"Be careful what you wish for, Hank." Chuck shifted Maya into the crook of his other arm.

"If I didn't mean it, I wouldn't have said it." Hank nodded toward Boomer. "I'm bringing on new men every day. All of them have prior spec ops experience. They're ready to go to work the moment their boots hit the ground."

Chuck shifted his gaze toward Boomer, his eyes narrowing. "I hope you're ready. The people we're up against wouldn't hesitate to kill Miss Miller, her baby and or anyone who dares stand in their way." He paused. "We lost a good man in Utah. I don't plan on losing Miss Miller or Miss Maya." He stared down at the baby in his arms. "I won't lie. They've grown on me. I'd kill anyone who harmed a single hair on either one of their heads." His gaze locked with Boomer's.

Boomer agreed with everything Chuck said, but he didn't understand why he was staring across at Boomer as if warning him not to hurt the ladies. He raised his hand as if swearing an oath in court. "I'll do everything in my power to keep them safe." He turned to Hank. "You want to show us what we have to work with?"

Hank tipped his head. "Follow me."

Boomer stood and followed Hank out of the living area and down a hallway to a doorway with a fancy lock securing it.

Chuck, carrying baby Maya, brought up the rear.

Hank entered a code on the keypad and pressed his thumb to a fingerprint reader. The locking mechanism clicked, and Hank turned the knob, opening the door wide to allow the men to pass him and descend the staircase into the basement below.

Boomer reached the bottom of the staircase first. A motion sensor triggered the lights, illuminating the room in a bright LED glow. Racks of weapons lined the walls, and boxes of ammo were stacked on shelves.

"What could you use at the chalet?" Hank asked, passing Boomer to open a large cabinet. "Not only do we have weapons, we have surveillance equipment, GPS trackers, early warning devices and two-way radios in various shapes and sizes.

"I have my own rifle and handgun," Chuck

responded. "We could use some of the electronics and radios."

Hank pulled out radios, small headsets and hand-held walkie-talkies, laying them out on a table. He dug in a large drawer and brought out a tracking device and GPS tracking chips. "I recommend you place one of these chips on whatever you want to track."

"Or whomever we want to track."

Hank nodded. "You can get lost really easily in the Crazy Mountains. But these are some of the best tracking devices that can be purchased. Be sure whoever has it won't leave it somewhere. They're only useful if they're worn or carried by whomever you want tracked."

Chuck and Boomer met gazes.

"Yes, we need to put one on Daphne," Boomer said.

"And the baby," Chuck added.

At least they were operating under the same assumptions.

No matter how jealous, disappointed or downright angry Boomer was over Daphne's decision to move on after she'd left him in Cozumel, he couldn't direct his anger toward the man who'd captured her heart. Chuck was a member of the Navy SEAL brotherhood. When shit got real, SEALs had your six.

Boomer selected a 9-milimeter handgun and looked around at the rifles.

"I've got what you need in here," Hank said.

He led the way to another cabinet, threw open the door, selected a rifle and handed it to Boomer. Hank crossed his arms over his chest. "It's a .300 Winchester—"

"Magnum with a Nightforce XS 32x56 scope and foldable stock." Boomer ran his hand over the stock and fit his finger through the trigger. "I had one in Iraq." It had been a part of his body—an extension of his arms and eyes. "It's a sweet machine with 100-700 meter accuracy."

Hank nodded. "More, if the operator knows what he's doing."

Boomer knew. He'd hit his mark on longer shots, including the one that had been taken out Abu Ahmed. The image of the baby behind Ahmed flashed in Boomer's mind. He closed his eyes to shut out the image, but the image had been indelibly seared into his memory.

For that split second, he had the urge to shove the rifle at Hank and escape the basement to the sunlight and fresh air outside Patterson's picture perfect ranch house.

Instead, he counted to five, inhaled deeply and opened his eyes. The sniper rifle was good for close range and long-range targets. He'd be a fool to reject it. Boomer tightened his grip on the weapon. "If it's all right with you, I'd like to carry this one."

Hank grinned. "I thought you would. I had you in mind when I purchased it."

Boomer's brows descended. "I've only been on your payroll for two days. You had to have ordered this rifle months ago. How did you know I'd come to work for you?"

With a shrug, Hank turned away. "I've been following you for a while."

"Really? How?" Boomer demanded.

Hank grinned. "Let's just say, I have connections."

Which meant he also knew Boomer's skills had taken a nosedive the last few months of his deployment. Since the Abu Ahmed job, Boomer had found himself hesitating over every shot. He'd missed more than one opportunity due to his hesitation. Did Hank know all this?

Boomer eyed Hank, his eyes narrowing. While Chuck checked out the electronics, Boomer moved closer to Hank. "If you've been following me for so long, why did you hire me?"

Hank's gaze met his. "We all have our issues, but we also have the same, structured training. I wouldn't have hired you if I didn't think you could do the job. You're an excellent sniper. For this mission and others, I need a skilled sniper to take out the bad guys before they hurt others. Your reputation is stellar. I figured if you got off active duty, I'd be a fool if I didn't offer you a job in the Brotherhood Protectors."

For a long moment, Boomer held Hank's gaze. The older SEAL never flinched.

Well, hell. Boomer hefted the rifle in his hands. "I hope I don't disappoint you or your clients."

"All I ask is that you do your best." Hank's lips twisted. "That's all anyone can ask. And the best effort from a SEAL can be a whole lot more effective than that of a civilian."

"Damn right," Chuck agreed. "You got a bag we can

put all this inside? I'd like to get up to the chalet as soon as possible and install some of this surveillance equipment."

Hank pulled a camouflage bag from a closet and set it on the table beside Chuck. "Take whatever you need, but please sign for the weapons. We have to keep strict accountability for them." He slipped a chart in front of Boomer and then held out his arms for Maya. "Let me have the baby, while you two get what you need."

Chuck handed over Maya.

The baby smiled and patted Hank's face.

Hank captured her little hand in his big one. "You are a charmer, aren't you?"

Boomer admired how smooth and easy Hank was with the baby, and wished he could be so open and relaxed with Maya. He heaved a sigh and signed the document in the space beside the .300 Winchester Magnum rifle and the handgun, and helped load the bag with the equipment Chuck had selected. He broke down the rifle into a couple pieces and stuffed it into the bag along with the rest of the equipment.

Once they had what they needed, Chuck handed the bag to Boomer and took Maya from Hank. He led the way out of the basement and up the stairs to the main level of the house.

"There you are." Sadie stood with Emma balanced on one hip. "Brunch is ready."

"We really need to be going." Chuck stared down at Maya. "Isn't that right, darlin'?"

"After you eat," Sadie insisted. "We have sandwiches and homemade soup. And I've packed several grocery bags full of pantry staples, as well as an insulated bag of meat, cheese and other more perishable items. You'll need to use them up soon so that they don't go bad."

"I've got a couple five-gallon jugs of gasoline you need to take for the generator," Hank said.

"After you eat," Sadie reminded her husband.

The men filed into the dining area where the ladies had set out platters of sandwiches and a tureen of piping hot soup.

The men tucked into the victuals.

Boomer ate two sandwiches and a bowl of soup, focusing on his food, while trying not to let his attention turn to Daphne, sitting across the table from him.

Soon the platters were empty. Hank and Boomer helped Sadie clear the table and stack the dirty dishes into the dishwasher.

Daphne disappeared with baby Maya, muttering something about diapers and nursing.

Boomer took the opportunity to step outside with Chuck and Hank. The wind had picked up, coming from the north, chilling the air. Clouds collected around the mountain peaks, crowding out the bright morning sun.

The rumble of an engine made Boomer turn toward the long, paved drive leading up to the ranch house. A truck rumbled up the drive and pulled to a stop beside the house. A tall, blond man climbed down and rounded the hood.

Chuck tensed and reached for the handgun beneath his jacket.

Hank touched Chuck's shoulder. "That's Swede. He's one of the good guys."

Chuck dropped his hand to his side, but continued to study the newcomer until the big guy stepped up onto the porch and held out his hand to Hank. "I got here as quickly as I could. I need to get back tonight."

"Understood." Hank turned to Chuck and Boomer. "This is Axel Svenson, better known as Swede. Prior military, Navy SEAL. Swede, meet Chuck Johnson, Navy SEAL retired, current super-secret witness protection assignment. And Brandon Rayne, who recently left active duty. Navy SEAL."

Swede shook hands with Chuck. "East or West coast?"

Chuck grinned. "West coast."

"We won't hold that against you." Swede winked and held out his hand to Boomer. "I've heard about you."

Boomer's lips twisted. "I hope you don't believe everything you hear."

Swede snorted. "Only the good stuff. DEVGRU, right? The best of the best in Navy SEALs." He gripped Boomer's hand, practically crushing his fingers in a tight squeeze.

Boomer shook the man's hand, and then pulled his free, careful not to damage his trigger finger. "Yes, DEVGRU. Call me Boomer."

"Boomer." Swede turned to Hank. "What is it you need from me?"

Hank pointed toward the Crazy Mountains. "I need you to make a run up to the resort chalet to show these two where they'll be for the next week or so."

Swede frowned. "I was up there last month. There's no electricity unless you've had the power company turn it on."

Hank shook his head. "I'll get on that as soon as possible, but that could take a day or two. They need to get the client up there ASAP. She's got some heat following her. The sooner they get her there, the better off they'll be."

Swede stared at the mountains. "The chalet is perched in a readily defensible position. You can see people coming from a distance. Why are people after her?"

"She witnessed a murder." Hank dropped down the porch steps and hurried toward the barn. "I'll fill you in later. For now, we need to help them gear up to hunker down in the cabin, off the grid."

Swede's lips thinned. "You couldn't be farther off the grid in that place." He shrugged and followed Hank down the steps and toward the barn.

Boomer moved to follow as well. When Chuck didn't, he turned back, a frown pulling his brows together.

Chuck jerked his head toward Hank. "I'll stay here and make sure no one bothers the ladies."

Despite the gathering of clouds over the mountaintops, the morning sun still had a firm hold on the valley.

Boomer had a hard time reconciling the threat to Daphne and the beauty of the landscape surrounding him. But then, he'd been equally amazed by the glorious sunsets of Iraq and Afghanistan, where the dust lingering in the air turned the sky a bright, flaming orange.

Too often, US combatants were captivated by the beauty and forgot how deadly the country could be.

With Chuck guarding the house, Boomer followed Hank and Swede to the barn behind the house, where they proceeded to load a truck with every kind of supply they might need, including firewood.

The temperatures dropped steadily. The wind added a chill factor that made Boomer wish he had his winter coat. If he wasn't mistaken, he could smell the snow in the air.

"If we get the snow the weatherman is predicting, you might have difficulties getting down from the mountain in the truck," Hank was saying. He glanced at Swede and the two men nodded. "They should take the snowmobiles."

Boomer glanced at the brown mountains and the green grass in the valley. "Snowmobiles?"

Hank and Swede laughed. "You'd be surprised how quickly snow can cover the ground," Swede said. "My first winter here, I got caught out in my shorts. Nearly froze my kneecaps off. Now, I carry a sleeping bag, a jacket and candles in whatever vehicle I'm in, winter or summer."

"I've seen it snow in July in the Crazy Mountains," Hank said. "I went on a fishing trip with some of my high school buddies and got caught in a blizzard. Thankfully, we had tents and sleeping bags or we wouldn't have made it back down alive."

Boomer shrugged. "I'll take your word for it."

"It's better to have too many supplies than not enough," Hank said.

"True," Boomer agreed.

Swede slipped into the driver's seat of the pickup and started the engine. He pulled to the back of the barn.

"We can go through here." Hank led the way through the structure to the back where two snowmobiles were parked in a horse stall. He started the engine on one and drove it to the back door of the huge barn. He flung open the barn doors.

Swede backed the trailer up to the opening, shifted into park and climbed down.

"Know how to drive a snowmobile?" Hank asked Boomer.

Boomer nodded. "We trained in Alaska for two months during the dead of winter. I learned how to dress for the occasion and I have a healthy respect for the power of snowmobiles for getting around when there are no roads and nothing but snow and ice all around."

"Good." Hank nodded. "How are you on snow skis or a snow board?"

"I prefer skis," Boomer replied.

Hank turned to Swede. "Got that?"

Swede passed Boomer and Hank. "Yeah." He disappeared into what appeared to be a tack room and emerged with two sets of snow skis.

Boomer shook his head, staring out at the green grass in the pasture.

"Seriously, you can't base your predictions on what

it looks like in the valley." Hank pounded Boomer on the back and climbed onto the snowmobile. "I've got this machine, you can get the other." After revving the engine a couple of times, he drove the tracked vehicle onto the trailer.

Boomer entered the stall, sat on the snowmobile and turned the key in the ignition. The engine roared to life and then settled into a steady hum. Moments later, he drove the vehicle up onto the trailer.

Like Hank said, it was better to over pack than go without.

Once they had all of the outdoor equipment stored and the skis tucked into the bed of the truck, Hank turned back to the house. "I'll go check on Chuck and Miss Miller. You'll take one of the company vehicles up into the mountains, while Swede drives the truck with the trailer."

Swede hefted a five-gallon jug of fuel from a row of jugs and set it in the truck bed.

Boomer loaded another, his gaze on Hank as he walked toward the house.

Before Hank reached the porch, Chuck stepped out, followed by Daphne carrying Maya. Daphne wore a ski jacket and held the baby in a sling beneath the jacket.

Chuck carried two large ski jackets. He tossed them into the backseat of a shiny black, four-wheel-drive, crew cab pickup. Then he held the door for Daphne and waited while she untangled herself from the sling and placed the baby in a car seat in back and buckled her in. Daphne slipped in next to the baby.

Chuck stared across the bed of the truck at Boomer.

"I'll drive," Boomer said, aiming his comment at Chuck, before turning his attention to Swede.

"Good," Swede said. "Stay close while following me up to the cabin. The roads can be tricky and the drop-offs are wicked." The big blond SEAL stared at the sky. "We better get going. I have no doubt we'll get up there in time to beat the storm, but I'd like to get back down before the rain or snow makes it impossible."

Chuck climbed into the front passenger seat.

Boomer slipped into the driver's seat.

Hank leaned into the driver's side window and glanced back at Daphne. "These two men will make sure you're okay."

Boomer glanced in the rearview mirror at Daphne. A tiny dent formed between her brows, and her eyes darkened to a deep forest green. Until that moment, he hadn't noticed the shadows beneath her eyes or the way she pulled her bottom lip between her teeth. The woman had worry written in every line of her face.

Her gaze met his for a moment and then returned to Hank. "Thank you, Mr. Patterson. Chuck's been great, but he can't be expected to do it alone."

"Hey, I got you out of the safe house alive," Chuck said from the front seat.

Daphne touched a hand to the older SEAL's shoulder and smiled gently. "You did get us out of the safe house. But you can't be awake twenty-four-seven. Even you have to sleep some of the time."

Chuck's jaw clenched. "I doubt Rodney knew what hit him. I sent Paul back to his family. We can't let Cooper's goons get that close ever again."

Boomer frowned. "What exactly happened at the safe house?"

"Our security was breached at the gate to the property. One of our guards was murdered in the process."

Daphne's gaze dropped and a tear rolled down her cheek. "Rodney was so young. He didn't deserve to die."

"Nor did the woman Cooper murdered," Chuck said.

"I'll send up reinforcements as my men free up," Hank said, clapping the bottom of the window frame. "I'd leave Swede with you, but he's on another assignment. I could only pull him for a day. I'd go with you, but I have a plane waiting at the airport to take me to Helena to meet with another client."

"We'll handle it," Chuck assured Hank.

Boomer frowned. He didn't like having another man answer for him. When they were settled in the cabin, he'd be sure to discuss ground rules and specific responsibilities.

And when he got Daphne alone, they'd discuss what had happened in Cozumel.

CHAPTER 4

The drive into the mountains did little to make Daphne feel any better about her entire situation.

How was isolating her and Maya in a mountain cabin supposed to make them safer?

So, they could see a vehicle coming before it reached them. They'd be stuck in the mountains, away from civilization. Just like before—and that hadn't been much of a solution. Granted, they'd had time to escape on the four-wheelers.

Daphne nodded toward the two snowmobiles loaded onto the trailer in front of them. "Why do we need snowmobiles? Don't we have to have snow in order to use them?"

Boomer shot her a glance. "Hank assured us the weather's going to get ugly. He predicts we'll have snow tonight."

"I would think, until the snow materializes, we'd have been better off with a couple of four-wheelers," she said, directing her comment to Chuck, the man who'd orchestrated their daring mountain escape out of Utah.

Chuck shrugged. "Hank knows Montana. If he says it'll snow, it probably will. If there's snow on the ground, I'd rather have snowmobiles up there than four-wheelers."

In the truck ahead, Swede took the turns slowly enough not to lose their vehicles or put the trailer at risk of falling down the steepening slopes beside the narrow gravel road. By the time they reached the remote chalet, Daphne's hands ached from the white-knuckled grip she'd kept on the armrest.

She could imagine the toll the drive had taken on Boomer. He had a lot riding on him. Not only did he have a trailer load of snowmobiles to maneuver through the mountains, he had a mother and child in the back seat. Losing control was not an option.

The chalet, as Hank had called it, was a beautiful, woodsy structure that complemented the mountain terrain and would have been a peaceful retreat for anyone else.

Boomer turned the truck around and backed it up to the side of the shed. Once he switched off the truck engine, he released a long, slow breath and uncurled his fingers from around the steering wheel.

The baby squeaked from the back seat.

Daphne turned to her baby girl and smiled. She'd slept through the worst of the bumpy roads and harrowing turns. "Hey, sweetie," she cooed, unbuckling the restraints. She lifted Maya into her arms and caught

Boomer staring at them in the reflection from the rearview mirror.

Was he as indifferent as he appeared?

Maya gurgled and cooed, grabbing a fistful of Daphne's hair. "Hey, baby girl," she said softly, prying the baby's fingers loose from the strand. "We're going to be okay up here." She spoke the words of assurance as much for herself as for the baby. Being in the crosshairs of a murderer had never been her idea of how her life would go.

Now, she had to shore up her courage and find a way to break it to Boomer that Maya was his baby. Thus far, he didn't seem to have a clue.

Chuck had been good enough to keep the information to himself. He knew exactly who Boomer was to Daphne and Maya, yet he'd held his counsel and refused to spill the beans until Daphne was good and ready.

Boomer slid out of the driver's seat and dropped to the ground.

Swede was already out of his truck, removing the tie-downs from the snowmobiles on the trailer. Once he had them loose, he climbed aboard one, started the engine and backed it down the ramp and into the shed.

Boomer followed suit with the other machine, climbing onboard and attempting to start the engine. He hit the ignition button and nothing happened. Again. Nothing happened.

"Let's just get it off the trailer," Chuck said. "I can look at it later and see if I can get it going. Might be as simple as a loose wire."

Between Chuck and Boomer, they put the vehicle in

neutral and pushed it down the ramp, parking it beside the first snowmobile inside the shed. Both faced the door for quick and easy deployment. Assuming they both would start.

Daphne made a mental note of where the machines were. Chuck had skills with mechanics. He'd have the cantankerous one fixed in no time. And, after having to make a quick escape from the safe house in Utah, she knew the value of prepositioning. If they had to use the snowmobiles in a hurry, they could. Hopefully, it wouldn't come to that. Then again, their daring escape through the Wasatch Range had seemed like a farfetched plan, until they'd had to execute it.

As Daphne pushed open her door, a frigid gust of wind ruffled her hair, sending a chill rippling down the back of her neck. She stepped down from the truck, balancing Maya in her arms. She reached back into the cab, grabbed the blanket and wrapped it snugly around the baby.

Swede glanced up at the sky as the first snowflakes descended. "I'll take the trailer back down the mountain. But I need to get going." He tilted his head toward the northwest. "Those storm clouds are about to open up."

Daphne paused beside Swede. "Thank you for helping us."

He nodded and gave her half a smile. "My pleasure."

Daphne didn't stay out in the elements for long. She entered the chalet and closed the door, grateful the building blocked the wickedly cold wind. Though the interior of the structure wasn't much warmer than outside, just moving out of the wind helped.

She lifted the blanket and checked on Maya.

The baby looked up at her with big blue eyes and a smile on her soft pink lips.

Daphne's heart swelled with love for her child. "You're such a happy baby." She glanced around the room, locating a fireplace. The sooner they had a roaring fire burning in the grate, the sooner the room would warm. She hoped the men would unload the firewood first.

Daphne stood by the floor-to-ceiling windows and watched the three men working in the bitter cold. Once Swede left and they settled into the chalet, Daphne had to pull Boomer aside and break the news to him that Maya was his daughter.

Her chest tightened, and her palms grew clammy despite the chill air in the chalet.

Would he be shocked, happy or angry? No matter what, he had to know he was a father. For the past year, she'd wanted more than anything to contact him and let him know. Now that the time was near, Daphne's courage faltered and her heartbeat skittered inside her chest.

BOOMER HELPED Chuck move the trailer to Swede's hitch. When they'd finished, Swede held out his hand. "As soon as I have a break in my current assignment, I'll head up here to help out. In the meantime, good luck."

"Thanks." Boomer shook hands with Swede.

Chuck emerged from carrying supplies into the cabin and shook hands with the big blond SEAL. "Thanks for the help."

"Anytime." Swede frowned. "If I had more time, I'd set up the surveillance monitoring equipment."

"That'll have to wait until the electricity is turned on, anyway," Chuck pointed out.

"Hopefully, that will only be a day or two." A giant snowflake landed on Swede's cheek. "That's my cue. I'm out of here."

Boomer and Chuck stood side by side as Swede maneuvered the trailer around the cabin and down the narrow road.

Once Swede was out of sight, Boomer grabbed supplies from the truck bed and hurried inside. By the time he returned to the truck, the snow was coming down in earnest, the flakes big and thick. Visibility had gone from miles to a few short feet.

Wind whipped the flakes against his cheeks, the tiny ice crystals stinging.

"Put this on." Chuck shoved a ski jacket into Boomer's arms and shrugged into the other one.

By the time they'd finished unloading the food, baby apparatus, gas, weapons, generator, firewood and skis, the ground was covered in a dusting of white. The road coming up the side of the mountain was completely covered.

Boomer hoped Swede made it down the mountain before the storm worsened.

Inside the chalet, Boomer had to admit it was more

than just a mountain hunting cabin. Whoever had built it, had done so with a vacation destination in mind.

The structure was two stories, with a bedroom on each floor. The kitchen and living room were on the first floor with a walkout deck that overlooked the mountain and the valley below. Before the clouds and snow blanketed the sky, Boomer could see down the road into the valley below.

The chalet was in an easily defensible position, with clear fields of fire. With the .300 Winchester Magnum rifle, he could take out any threat before they could get anywhere close to the cabin and its occupants.

In the living area, Daphne had stoked the fireplace with the firewood they'd brought with them from Hank's. Using tinder and old newspapers, she was able to get a fire going, but the logs had yet to catch and fill the room with much-needed warmth.

She'd set up a portable playpen in the center of the room where Maya lay wrapped in thick blankets, only her face peeking out. Her bright eyes were open and curious. She squirmed, but couldn't work her way out of the blankets.

Boomer set a box of blankets and towels on the floor beside the playpen and stared down at the baby with the soft blue eyes and dark hair. She didn't look much like Daphne, but she was Daphne's baby, no doubt.

"She's a good baby. She sleeps through most nights now, and she only fusses when she's hungry or wet." Daphne stepped up beside Boomer.

He nodded. "She's beautiful," he said, and meant it.

He straightened. "I'm going to see about setting up the generator."

"I'll help." Daphne offered.

"I'll keep an eye on Maya and see what I can scrounge up for dinner," Chuck said. "You two go ahead."

"I can manage on my own." Boomer left the room and stepped out onto the deck where they'd left the heavy generator. He checked the oil and gas levels then pulled the cord. The engine turned over, but didn't fully engage.

The door opened, and Daphne stepped out, wrapped in a black puffy ski jacket. She pulled the collar up around her neck and blew steam with every breath she took. "I can't get over how much the temperature has dropped. When we left Utah, we were still in the high nineties."

Boomer didn't respond, hoping he could get the generator going. With the loud noise of the engine, he wouldn't have to engage in small talk with Daphne. He pulled the cord. Again the engine turned over but didn't engage. It putted to a stop.

"Boomer," Daphne touched his shoulder. "We need to talk."

He shrugged off her hand and straightened. "We have nothing to talk about." He stared into her gaze, briefly, and then bent to grab the cord's pull handle.

He pulled so hard he broke the handle off the cord, and still the engine wouldn't start.

Daphne crossed her arms over her chest and raised her eyebrows. "I get the feeling you're angry with me."

"I'm not angry," he denied, though his response sounded terse, even to his own ears.

Her eyes narrowed. "What I don't understand is why you're mad at me."

He threw the handle on deck. "I know why you left Cozumel. I know you didn't have a choice. I know what happened. You don't have to give me the detailed explanation. I get it. Just don't expect me to be happy about it."

Her brows rose higher. "You know?"

"I know." He bent to retrieve the handle, tied it back to the cord and yanked with a little less force. The engine turned over, chugged a couple of times and then roared to life.

Over the roar of the motor, Boomer heard Daphne's words, "Then you don't want anything to do with your baby girl?"

Boomer's pulse raced, his stomach clenched and the snow swirling around his head made him strangely dizzy to the point he thought he was hearing things that couldn't be possible. "What did you say?"

She shook her head, her brows furrowing. "It's okay. I don't expect anything from you. What we had in Cozumel was a fling. Neither one of us had any expectations. We didn't discuss life after the island. We certainly didn't discuss children. Maya and I can make it on our own once this murder thing is cleared up." Daphne spun toward the door, her eyes glistening. "I've done my part. At least, now you know."

Boomer grabbed her arm and yanked her back around. "Woman, what are you talking about?" He bent and switched the generator off. The engine rumbled to a stop, leaving nothing but the wind howling through the trees for noise.

"You heard me," Daphne said. A tear rolled down her cheek. She reached up to swipe it away. "You had the right to know. Now that you do, I don't expect anything from you. Maya is my responsibility. She and I will be fine."

Boomer shook his head, his eyes narrowing. "Back it up about four paragraphs."

Her brows dipped. "Why?"

"I want to be sure I'm hearing this right. You said *your baby girl.*"

She nodded. "I did. Again, you don't have to do a thing. I'm perfectly capable of raising our daughter on my own. I don't need your help."

"Our daughter?" Boomer felt as if he'd been punched in the gut. "As in yours and mine." He touched a finger to her chest and then to his. "Not yours and Chuck's?"

She looked at him as if he'd grown a set of horns. "What are you talking about? Maya is your daughter, not Chuck's."

Boomer's head spun. Maya was his child? The baby in the chalet was his flesh and blood?

Daphne's brows dipped lower and then raised into her hairline. "You thought Chuck and I...that Maya is Chuck's daughter?" She laughed, the sound strained and tight.

Boomer stood straight, unable to move, not a single word coming to his lips. The truth swirled around him like a tornado, sucking the air from his lungs.

"Do you think I would hop from your bed into Chuck's so quickly?" Daphne pushed away from him. "You bastard." She yanked her arm free of his grip and stepped back. "I thought we had something going on in Cozumel. That we had a special connection." She snorted. "I guess it was only on my side. I was just another girl in a sailor's port." Another tear slipped from the corner of her eye. She swiped it away and squared her shoulders. "Well, to hell with you. You had the right to know you have a child, but now that you do, you can stay the hell away from both of us. That suits you, doesn't it? Maya and I would hate to cramp your lifestyle." She marched toward the door.

Before she could reach for the handle, Boomer jerked her around and slammed her against his chest. "You were not just another woman in a port. When I woke up the next morning and you weren't there, I didn't know what to think. I looked for you, but you were gone, everything about you seemed to be wiped clean. I didn't know how to contact you, and the airport didn't have any evidence of your departure. You were gone, as if you never existed." That empty feeling of despair washed over Boomer like it had been yesterday when he'd woken up to find his bed empty, the woman he'd fallen for so completely missing.

"I had to disappear," Daphne whispered. "Otherwise, I would have been gone for real."

"I get that." Boomer brushed the next tear away with the pad of his thumb. "But you had a baby." He shook his head to clear the cobwebs and confusion. "Why didn't you let me know sooner? I could have been there for you."

She shook her head. "You were deployed. I had to stay in hiding. I couldn't contact you. They were watching, waiting for me to make a move. Hell, I didn't even have to make a move. They found us anyway."

Boomer shoved a hand through his hair as the enormity of her words sank in. "Maya isn't Chuck's baby."

Daphne snorted. "If you knew anything about me and if you'd have quit thinking the worst of me, you'd have known." She wrapped her arms around her middle, tucking her hands into the fabric of her jacket. "I love Chuck…like a father or big brother. In fact, I don't know what I would have done without him over the past year. But the father of Maya is the rat-bastard standing in front of me, thinking I could be fickle enough to hop from one bed to another." She turned to walk back into the house. "I don't need this aggravation. I have a life, and it began with Maya."

When Boomer tried to stop her by placing a hand on her arm, she glared down at his fingers curled into her jacket. "I need you to protect me and my daughter. Other than that, leave me alone."

Boomer's chest tightened and words rose up from his throat. Before he could utter them and put his other foot squarely in his mouth, he swallowed hard. The angry, determined look on Daphne's face stopped him cold.

The door opened from the inside, and Chuck poked out his head. "Daphne, Maya's hungry. I can change diapers and rock her, but I can't feed her." He stared from Daphne to Boomer and back. "I take it you told him?"

Daphne nodded. "I did." She pushed past Chuck and entered the chalet without another word to either man.

Chuck shrugged into his jacket and stepped out onto the porch. He nodded toward the generator. "Need help?"

Boomer nodded. Boy did he. The woman he'd fantasized over for the past year had figuratively slammed the door in his face. She wanted nothing to do with him. But she'd have to get over it. Baby Maya was his little girl. He bent over and braced his hands on his knees, his stomach swirling, his head spinning. "Holy hell, I'm a father."

Chuck placed a hand on his back. "Breathe, buddy," he said, his tone wry. "It's not that hard. At this age, all they do is eat, sleep and poop. Save your panic attacks for when Maya starts dating."

CHAPTER 5

Daphne held onto her anger for the next hour, careful not to let Maya feel her wrath. She spoke to her child as she nursed, warmed by the glowing logs in the fireplace.

All the while, her thoughts churned in her head. No wonder Boomer had been so distant. He'd thought she had gone from one man to another without a break between. He really didn't know her. Or he held her to the same standard as himself or the other women he'd been with.

How many women had he slept with in the past year? Two, four, a dozen? Their week in Cozumel probably meant nothing to him.

He said he'd looked for you.

Yeah, but how hard?

Granted, Chuck had done a good job of getting her away from the little island off the coast of Mexico. When they'd arrived in the States, he'd arranged for fake identification. As far as Utah was concerned, Maya was Maya Jones, not Maya Miller or Maya Rayne as she should have been. And the Utah driver's license Chuck had given her had her name as Donna Jones.

As far as the US was concerned, Daphne Miller had disappeared. She hadn't filed a tax return in over a year, and she never had a baby.

She shifted Maya to the other breast, adjusted the baby blanket over her shoulder and Maya's head, and leaned back her head in the wooden rocking chair.

How much longer could it take to nail Harrison Cooper and his corrupt father? They had to make a huge mistake soon. One that would land them in jail and take the pressure off her and Maya. Once those two men were incarcerated, surely she and her daughter could settle into a nice little cottage overlooking the ocean and create a peaceful existence free of assassins and sexy SEAL bodyguards.

Maya fell asleep nursing on the second breast. By the time Daphne laid her in her playpen, the guys had the generator roaring outside.

Daphne carried bags full of groceries into the kitchen and unloaded them into the pantry. With the generator running, the refrigerator worked. She placed the cold items inside and hurriedly closed the door. Until the electric company switched on the electricity, they had to conserve energy. The couple five-gallon jugs full of fuel wouldn't last forever. Thankfully, they'd brought firewood, and she'd seen more stacked in the shed. At least they'd stay warm in the chalet.

Daphne found a pan in a cabinet, opened a large can of beans, flavored with tomato sauce and spices. She cooked the venison hamburger Sadie had packed with the refrigerated items and mixed it with the beans and tomatoes for chili.

Chuck entered the house, and with him, came a gust of frigid air.

"The temperature has dropped below freezing, and the storm doesn't appear to want to let up anytime soon. I'd say it's safe to say we're not going anywhere tonight."

Daphne smiled. "On the flip side of that, I hope that means we won't have to worry about Cooper's team descending on us during the middle of a blizzard."

"That would be my educated guess. You can't see much farther than the hand in front of your face out there." He shook the snow off his coat and hung it on a peg on the wall near the door.

Daphne leaned to the side, peering around Chuck.

Chuck's lips quirked upward on the corners. "If you're looking for Rayne, he went for a walk."

Daphne frowned. "In that storm where you can only see the hand in front of your face?" She stepped toward the door. "And you let him?"

Chuck caught her arm. "He only went as far as the shed. He'll be all right."

She bit her lip, wanting to go after Boomer.

"Give him time to digest the news. He looked pretty pale."

"Well, he'll just have to get over it. It's not like he has to do anything. I can take care of the baby. I don't need a man in my life."

Chuck's brows rose. "And what am I? Chopped liver?"

Daphne drew in a deep breath and relaxed the frown tugging at her forehead. "Sorry. You've been wonderful through everything. I don't know what I would have done without you through childbirth and the first three months of all-nighters." She hugged Chuck. "I know it was above and beyond the call of duty."

"Hey, you know I'd do anything for you and the kid. You two have grown on me. I like to think if I'd actually had a kid of my own, she would have been a lot like you. Flexible, good-natured and tough."

With a smile, she hugged him again. "You're not old enough to be my father. But you'd make a great big brother."

"It's a good thing we're not physically attracted to each other. Someone might get the wrong impression."

At that moment, the door to the chalet opened and a blast of cold air split Daphne and Chuck apart.

Boomer entered. When he spotted them in a hugging clinch, his brows drew together. "If I'm interrupting something, I can leave and come back later."

"Don't be silly. Supper's ready, and you look like you could stand to warm up a little." Daphne checked on Maya and returned to the kitchen to stir the pot of chili. She gathered bowls from the cupboard and spoons from a drawer and set them out on the small dining table near the fireplace. Among the supplies Sadie and Hank had provided was a box of saltine crackers. Daphne set a sleeve of the crackers on the table. When she started to lift the pot of chili, Boomer entered the kitchen.

"I'll get that." He carried the pot to the table where Daphne laid a hot pad on the wood, and Boomer positioned the pot on the pad.

Chuck held Daphne's chair for her. When she'd been seated, the men sat and filled their bowls full of the rich, steaming chili. Several minutes of silence passed while they ate.

The silence stretched.

Tension built until Daphne finally set down her spoon. Any conversation was better than none. She took a deep breath and threw out a conversation starter. "So, what's the plan?"

Chuck grinned. "My plan is to finish this chili. You make the best chili. But don't tell my grandmother, God rest her soul."

Boomer ate the last bite of his chili and nodded. "Thank you. The chili hit the spot." He took his bowl to the kitchen.

So much for conversation.

Daphne finished what was in her bowl and carried her dinnerware to the kitchen.

Boomer had filled the sink with soap and water and set a teakettle on the stove to heat water. "You cooked. I can pull KP."

"KP?" she asked.

"Kitchen patrol." He took her bowl. For a brief second, their fingers collided.

A shock of electricity raced from that point of contact up Daphne's arm and into her chest. Warmth spread throughout her body at that simple touch. When she glanced up to see if it had the same affect on Boomer, she was gratified to see his eyes flare before he turned with her bowl to immerse it in the water.

"If you wash, I'll dry," she offered.

"No, you've done enough." Chuck entered the kitchen behind her. "You're not the chief cook and bottle washer."

"But you two are protecting us. I need to do something useful."

"Taking care of Maya is useful," Chuck said. "We can handle doing dishes."

Behind Boomer's back, Daphne glared at Chuck.

He tipped his head toward the living area. "I think Maya is stirring. I'd much rather dry dishes than change a diaper."

Foiled at her attempt to be close to Boomer, Daphne left the kitchen and lifted Maya out of the playpen. As suspected, her diaper was wet. Though the baby had been a trooper for their great escape, traveling via four-wheelers through the mountains without a complaint, she didn't like being wet, and she wasn't afraid to voice her opinion.

Moments later, Maya settled into Daphne's arms, content in her dry diaper.

The men finished up the dishes and put the leftover food in the refrigerator.

The hum of the generator nearly drowned out the sound of the wind wailing through the trees and mountain passes. But there was no denying the storm had settled over the area and Daphne didn't think it would let up for a while. For now, at least, they'd be safe.

"Is there any hot water in the water heater, yet?" Daphne called out.

"We used hot water from the teakettle for the dishes," Chuck said. "You can see if the generator has been running long enough for a warm shower."

Daphne rose from the rocking chair and leaned over to lay Maya in the playpen. As soon as she attempted to let go, Maya fussed. "You poor thing. All this running around is making you nuts, isn't it?" She settled the baby on her shoulder and glanced around the room. She couldn't shower holding Maya.

Both men walked out of the kitchen.

Daphne grinned. "Who wants to hold Maya while I shower?"

Chuck held up his hands. "I want to work on that snowmobile before we lose what's left of the light outside." He slipped his arms into his ski jacket and hurried out the door.

Daphne faced Boomer for the first time since she'd told him Maya was his baby girl. She cocked her brows. "Well?"

Boomer's gaze darted around the room as if he was searching for an escape.

"She won't bite," Daphne said, with a slight narrowing of her eyes. "She hasn't even gotten her first tooth yet. She won't be hungry for another hour, and her diaper is clean and dry. All she wants is someone to hold her."

His gaze rose to meet Daphne's, and he sighed. "What do I do?"

Daphne hid a grin and settled Maya in Boomer's arms. "You can walk with her or sit in the rocking chair. If she gets fussy, sometimes lightly bouncing her seems to calm her."

"And if that doesn't work?"

"I'll be out shortly. I'm only a room away." She shook her head at the terrified look on his face. The man had to learn soon enough what it was like to care for his own child.

Daphne grabbed the bag of clothing Sadie had given her and hurried toward the master bedroom with the attached bathroom. Once inside, she leaned her ear against the door and listened for sounds of Maya's distress.

When she didn't hear any cries, she relaxed and smiled. Poor Boomer was way out of his element. Spending time with Maya would be good for him.

Perhaps it would make him realize how much he would want to be with her. And that, maybe, he'd want to be with Daphne again. And if wishes were horses...

She stripped out of the clothing she'd borrowed from Sadie Patterson when she'd first arrived at the White Oak Ranch, and pulled her hair up into a messy bun on top of her head. Then she stepped into the bathtub and pulled the shower curtain closed. When she turned on the water faucet, icy cold water poured out. She twisted the hot water knob wide open and waited, praying the generator had managed to turn the cold water warm. After a minute, she turned the cold water all the way off. At best the water was barely lukewarm. It would have to do.

She flipped the switch for the shower and gasped as chilly liquid ran over her shoulders. She quickly scrubbed her body. By the time she turned off the faucet, she shivered uncontrollably. The big, fluffy towel Sadie had sent along was heaven. She dried quickly and wrapped the terrycloth around her, tucking the corner in across her left breast.

Daphne recalled the large walk-in shower in Boomer's bungalow in Cozumel. They'd made love in that shower several times. She wouldn't be surprised if that was where they'd conceived Maya.

A sharp tug in the lower region of her belly reminded her of how perfectly they'd fit together and how attuned Boomer had been to her body and her desires.

She stripped out of the towel and stared down at her body. It wasn't the same as when she'd been on the Mexican island. Her hips and breasts were larger, and she had a little belly pooch she hadn't been able to work off after giving birth to her five-pound, six-ounce baby girl.

If Boomer saw her nude, would he still be attracted to her? Or would he be turned off by the changes in her body?

A baby's cry sounded through the door of the bedroom.

Daphne's breasts tightened, and she could feel the letdown effect of her milk rushing out to satisfy her baby's needs. If she didn't hurry and feed Maya, she'd drench herself with breast milk.

After tossing the towel over a rail, she hurried into a sweater and the thick, warm leggings Sadie had provided, forgoing the bra that would be more in the way than a help.

As she stepped out of the bedroom, she could see into the living room.

Boomer stood frozen to the floor, holding baby Maya out in front of him, staring into her screwed up face as she cried.

He didn't move, he didn't talk to her, he just stood like a statue.

Before Daphne could take a step, the front door opened, frigid air and snow blasting into the room.

"What are you doing?" Chuck's voice sounded from deep in the hood he'd pulled up over his head and ears.

Boomer didn't budge, didn't respond, just held out Maya, his eyes wide and his breathing coming in short, disturbed gasps.

Chuck reached Boomer before Daphne, took Maya from Boomer's hands and handed her to her mother.

Daphne hugged the baby to her chest and smoothed a hand over her head. "It's okay. You're all right," she said in a singsong voice.

Maya immediately calmed and started rooting around for her dinner. Daphne carried her into the bedroom and lifted her sweater.

Maya latched on and settled in for supper.

Normally content to let her daughter feed, Daphne found herself counting the minutes until Maya was full.

Then she could lay her in her playpen and find out what the hell had happened to make Boomer act so strangely toward his daughter.

As soon as Chuck took Maya and handed her off to Daphne, Boomer bent double and rested his hands on his knees, dragging in deep ragged breaths.

After Daphne left the room, Chuck demanded in a barely controlled whisper, "What the hell happened?"

For a long moment, Boomer couldn't have answered if he tried. The image of the woman in the black robes, holding her dead baby to her chest, haunted him.

For the first five minutes Daphne was in the shower, Boomer had walked around the room, staring down at the beautiful baby girl in his arms.

Maya seemed content to snuggle close, pressing her face against his shirt.

He'd tucked her blanket around her to ward off a chill and paced back and forth across the room, praying the baby didn't wake before Daphne returned to relieve him.

Then something outside made a loud banging noise, like a limb hitting the metal roof.

Maya's eyes blinked open, and she stared up at him.

Boomer had never seen eyes so blue, or such a precious, beautiful face. And she smelled like baby powder and sweetness. He'd marveled at the tiny human who was his daughter. A part of him, sharing the same DNA. Already she looked more like him than Daphne. Would she have her mother's kind heart and good sense? Or would she be like he had been when he was young—wild, hard to control and headstrong?

His arms tightened around her. Or would the people after Daphne snuff out her little life before the baby had a chance to grow, play, learn and one day marry and have her own babies?

Maya must have sensed his distress. Her face screwed into a frown, and she opened her mouth and cried.

The sound had rooted Boomer's feet to the floor, sending him into what was like a video rerun of his last kill and the death of the Iraqi baby. The wails of its mother blended with Maya's cries, and Boomer's head spun between memories and reality. He didn't know how to make the woman stop wailing, and the baby in his arms wouldn't stop crying. He held her out at arm's length, but the memories wouldn't detach from what he was seeing in front of him.

Until the door opened, and Chuck entered.

Once the other man had taken Maya from his grip, Boomer felt as if someone had removed the bones from his body. He was hard pressed to remain standing.

"What the hell happened?" Chuck asked.

Boomer recognized it as the second time the man had asked him the question. He swallowed hard and closed his eyes to block out the image of the woman crying over her dead baby. "I don't know," he said. He couldn't tell the older SEAL he was seeing things.

Chuck shoved a chair behind Boomer's knees. "Sit. Pull yourself together and tell me what just happened. No bullshit."

Boomer sat for a long moment before he looked up into Chuck's face.

The SEAL didn't look at him with an accusing stare. A frown pulled at his brows, but it wasn't an angry one, but more of concern. "PTSD?" Chuck asked.

Boomer shoved a hand through his hair and glanced away. "Probably," he said.

"What are your triggers?"

When Boomer didn't respond, Chuck added, "I have flashbacks when I hear the sound of gunfire or the backfire of a muffler. Fireworks set me off as well."

Boomer's gaze shot back to the big SEAL. "You have flashbacks?"

"A lot of guys I know have a hard time assimilating back into the real world." Chuck dropped another log onto fire, grabbed a wooden chair and straddled it backward. "We've seen too much, been shot at, and sometimes can't separate our pasts from our present. Some people take years before the sharp edges blur. Others never get over it."

Boomer snorted. "God, I hope that's not my case."

"What was your trigger?" Chuck persisted.

Boomer buried his face in his hands and whispered, "A baby's cry."

"A what?" Chuck leaned closer. "A baby's cry?" The older SEAL muttered a curse. "Wow. That's going to be tough to overcome."

Boomer nodded. "I'm a father, and I can't even take care of my own child."

"You just found out you're a father. You can't expect to fall right into being a good parent."

"I can't do it. That baby needs someone who isn't going to come apart at the seams every time he hears her cry. She needs someone who has his shit together. Someone like you."

Chuck snorted. "I didn't always have my shit together. Believe me. It took me two years after I left the SEALs to find my way. For one and half of those years, I sank so deeply into a bottle of booze, I didn't think I'd ever find my way back out."

Boomer stared across the floor at his brother-in-arms, feeling more connected to the man than he had since they'd met.

Chuck had been through the same brutal training, conducted similar missions and probably had killed his share of civilians in the course of his duties. He understood.

"Don't beat yourself up over this incident. Work through it. I don't know what kind of coping techniques you can use, but do what it takes." Chuck tipped his head toward the bedroom. "That baby girl is worth it. She needs a father who can be there for her."

And Daphne needed a man who could take care of her and Maya.

Boomer shook his head. In his current state, he was more of a liability than an asset to them. They'd be better off without him.

Chuck leaned across and punched him in the arm. "Don't talk yourself out of being in that child's life. Or Daphne's, for that matter."

"If I can't keep it together when Maya cries, what good am I to them?"

Chuck pinned him with a direct stare. "How do you think we knew where to find you?"

"You came to Hank. I just happened to be there."

Chuck shook his head. "That woman in there had you on her mind from the moment we left Cozumel to the moment you appeared in Patterson's living room."

Boomer's eyes narrowed. "We only knew each other for a week."

"Some things don't take long to gel. She couldn't stop thinking about you. Through my SEAL contacts, I followed your career. I knew when you got out of the Navy. How do you think Hank Patterson found out about you?"

Boomer's frown dipped lower. "You got me the job?"

Chuck shrugged. "No, your reputation as a sniper and a kickass SEAL got you the job. I just put the bug in Hank's ear. He made the decision to hire you. Hank's a nice guy, but he wouldn't employ just anyone. You have to be right for his vision of the Brotherhood Protectors."

Boomer wasn't sure he liked the idea that Chuck had been the one to get him on with Hank's organization. Nor did he like the idea that Chuck had been spying on him for the past year.

What did make his insides warm and his heart beat a little faster was the fact Daphne had wanted to know about him—where he was, how he was doing, when he was deployed and when he came home.

The woman had been through a lot over the past year. Probably as much trauma as he'd suffered. Hell, she'd had a baby. That in itself was life threatening. And he hadn't been there for her.

The least he could do was make sure she wasn't harmed by the bastards trying to kill her. He'd sort out his own issues after he got her past the threat on her life.

Looking over Boomer's shoulder, Chuck pushed to his feet. "How's Maya?"

Boomer turned toward Daphne. With her hair piled high in a messy bun on top of her head, a thick wool sweater and leggings hugging her long sexy legs, she couldn't have been more beautiful.

"Maya's asleep on the bed. We'll need to keep the fire going through the night to keep the house warm enough."

"I'll take the couch and feed the fire through the night," Boomer insisted. He couldn't screw that up.

Daphne nodded, her brows twisting. "Are you all right?"

Heat burned its way up his neck into his cheeks. He pressed his lips together in a tight line. "Yes."

"I'll take the bedroom upstairs," Chuck offered.

"Won't it be too cold up there?" Daphne asked.

"Heat rises," Chuck reassured her. "If Boomer stokes the fire all night, I'll stay plenty warm. Besides, I need to be up above the noise of the generator. I want to know when the storm clears. If it stops in the middle of the night, we need to be ready."

Daphne shivered. "Do you think anyone would be out on a night like this?"

Chuck shook his head. "No way. But if it clears off suddenly, the night skies can be as bright as day."

"Could they already know where we are?" Daphne wrapped her arms around her middle.

"They found us in Utah," Chuck said. "It might only be a matter of time.

Boomer glanced at the rifle he'd hung on the hooks over the door. "If they show up, we'll be ready."

"I hope so. I don't want the same thing to happen to either one of you that happened to Rodney."

"It won't," Boomer said. Not on his watch. He'd be damned if Cooper's henchmen got anywhere close to Daphne and Maya. They'd have to go through him to get to the two women in his life.

CHAPTER 6

Maya cried out, drawing Daphne's attention back to the bedroom.

She hurried in to check on the baby, torn between wanting to be with her daughter and wanting to know what the men were saying.

Daphne lifted Maya to her breast again, straining to hear the rumble of voices in the living room of the chalet. She wished she could be in both places at once. Perhaps Boomer was explaining his strange behavior toward Maya.

The baby settled against her and suckled, falling asleep every few minutes as she filled her belly.

Every time Daphne tried to break Maya's seal on her nipple, the baby woke up enough to drink more.

Finally, baby Maya fell into a deep sleep.

Again, Daphne laid her in the middle of the freshly made bed, swaddled in blankets and surrounded by pillows.

Anxious to get to the bottom of the trouble with

Boomer, she left the bedroom and returned to the living room.

Chuck and Boomer sat close together, talking softly.

When Chuck noticed her, he addressed her.

They worked out the sleeping arrangements and Chuck grabbed his duffel bag and headed up the stairs to the spare bedroom, leaving Daphne and Boomer alone.

Boomer poked at the fire, rearranging the logs to burn brighter and hotter.

He was avoiding her.

Which confused her. She was sure he'd swept her with a glance when she first entered the room. At that moment, she'd read longing in his gaze.

When he straightened and turned, he sighed. "Sorry about...before. Is Maya all right?"

Daphne nodded. "She's fine. With a full tummy, she'll sleep for the rest of the night." She took a step toward Boomer. "I'm more worried about you."

His lips thinned. "Don't worry about me. I'm here to protect you and Maya. I won't fail."

Daphne believed him, but she wanted to know more. "What happened earlier?"

He turned away. "I'd rather not talk about it."

She touched his shoulder. "Yeah, well, if it involves our daughter, we need open communication lines."

Boomer shrugged off her hand and moved away. "It won't happen again."

"How do you know?"

He glanced away, a frown denting his brow. "Because I won't hold her again."

Daphne flinched as if she'd been slapped across her face. Her heart dropped into her stomach, and she placed a protective hand over her belly. "You won't hold your own daughter?"

"I'll protect you two," he said, his voice rasping, "but I can't hold her. I'm not fit to care for her."

"What do you mean, you're not fit? All she needs is love. Isn't that all anyone needs?" Daphne stood before him, her eyes burning, her heart worn on her sleeve. This was the man she'd dreamed about for the past year. But somehow he'd changed.

He stared at the door to the cabin as if he wanted to make his escape. "Maybe I'm not capable of love," he whispered.

Though hurt by his rejection of her and the baby, Daphne recognized a man in pain. Not physical pain, but something that hurt him on a much deeper level. Pushing him to confess what had caused the injury wouldn't help. Not at that moment.

Daphne hoped one day he'd be able to tell her what had caused him so much pain he believed he wasn't fit to be her baby's father.

Although disappointed in the meantime, she'd give him the space he needed.

She crossed to stand in front of him. "Okay," she said softly. "We'll accept your protection. I won't make you hold Maya, and I won't ask anything of you that makes you uncomfortable. But I want you to know..." She reached up and cupped his hard jaw in the palm of her hand. "I'm glad you're here." She leaned up on her toes and pressed her lips to his.

When she dropped down and turned away, she was determined to run back to the bedroom before the tears started to fall. She hadn't gone two steps, when a hand grasped her arm.

The next thing she knew she was crushed to Boomer's broad chest, the air forced from her lungs by the iron band of his arms wrapped around her.

Boomer held her close, staring down into her gaze, his eyes dark with whatever emotion he was feeling. "You've haunted me since the day you left," he said.

"I never stopped thinking about you," she confessed.

He shook his head. "I can't do this." His hands tightened on her arms.

Daphne leaned into him, her unfettered breasts pressed against the hard planes of his chest. "Do what?"

"This." His mouth descended on hers, and he stole her very soul in that one kiss.

Daphne didn't care that she couldn't breathe, she felt as though she'd died and floated to Heaven. This was where she'd longed to be since she'd last been with him in Cozumel.

Boomer threaded his fingers into her hair, dislodging the messy bun.

The long strands fell down around her shoulders.

He fisted his hand in the tresses and tugged, tilting back her head to expose the length of her neck.

His mouth left hers and traveled down the sensitive skin of her throat to the pulse pounding at the base. His tongue tapped against it, and he sucked her skin gently before pushing aside the neck of her sweater.

Boomer nipped at her collarbone, tongued the flesh

there and tried to push the sweater farther over her shoulder. When it wouldn't stretch more, he reached for the hem and dragged it up her torso.

The cool air hit her back, while heat from his body and the fireplace warmed her front. Her nipples pebbled, and desire coiled low in her belly.

Daphne tugged the shirt from his waistband, dragged it over his head and tossed it to the floor. She ran her hands over the solid muscles of his biceps and across the coarse hairs covering his broad chest.

Boomer kissed her forehead, captured her lips in a hard, brief kiss and then worked his way downward, bending to take one of her nipples between his teeth. He rolled the tip around then flicked it again and again.

Her body ached with the need to take what they were doing to the next level. She wanted to be naked, lying in his arms, filled with his lovemaking. Daphne slipped her hands into the waistband of his jeans and then lower to cup his firm buttocks. He was so damned sexy, her mouth watered, her blood raced through her veins and she couldn't get close enough.

A log shifted in the fireplace, shooting sparks and making the light flicker in the dark living area.

Boomer lifted his head. "We can't do this."

She shook her head. "Yes, we can." Daphne slid her hand around to the button on his jeans and pushed it through the hole. She stared up into his eyes as she eased the zipper downward. "You know you want to, and I want it as much as you."

"We're not alone in this house," he reminded her.

"We're alone in this room." She reached into the

denim and circled his hard length, easing it free of the constraint.

Boomer tipped back his head and sucked air between his teeth. "You're making this hard."

She chuckled and ran her hand across his velvety cock. "That's obvious."

He caught her wrist and stopped what she was doing. "I can make no promises to you or Maya."

She froze, her heartbeat stuttering for a moment before it settled into a rapid tattoo. "I'm okay with that. We're here, in the moment. That's all I want." *For now.* She'd work on more, later.

Boomer cupped her cheeks and raised her face to his. "Sweetheart, you deserve so much better."

"I'll be the judge of that," she whispered and leaned up on her toes, sealing his mouth with hers.

Boomer fell into her, his tongue slicing through her lips to capture hers in a dance of desire, thrusting, twisting and caressing until Daphne's knees wobbled, and she clung to him for support.

He bent, scooped her off her feet and laid her on the couch in front of the fire.

Daphne stretched her arms above her head, her body on fire, her core aching and empty, ready for Boomer to fill. The fire's warmth and the intimate glow it created set the mood.

Boomer kissed a path across her chin and down her throat to settle on one of her breasts. He teased, tongued and nipped at the areola until Daphne arched her back off the cushions and cupped the back of his neck, urging him to take more of her breast into his mouth.

He complied, sucking hard, flicking the tip several more times before moving to perform the same magic on the other.

Daphne moaned softly, ready for him to take it lower.

With excruciating slowness, he licked and kissed his way lower, tapping the tip of his tongue on every rib, dipping into her bellybutton and, finally, coming to a halt at the waistband of her leggings.

Daphne reached for the elastic band, desperate to shed the layers standing between her and Boomer.

He pushed her hand away and caught the fabric in his hand, along with the elastic of her panties, and pulled them down over her hips and lower, exposing the triangle of hair atop her sex.

A pulse thrummed inside her core, her channel slicked with her juices and she almost cried out for him to take her before she spontaneously combusted.

Boomer slid his fingers through the curls over her sex and dipped between the folds to tap that nubbin of sensitized flesh.

Daphne dug her heels into the cushions, lifting her hips. "Oh, please," she moaned.

"Please what?" he asked, pressing a kiss to the mound of hair.

"Please, don't stop," she begged, letting her knees fall to the sides, leaving her open to him.

"I couldn't if I wanted to," he said and parted her folds.

The first touch of his tongue sent her to the edge of reason. The second catapulted her into the stratosphere. She dug her fingers into his shoulders and held on as her body rocked with her orgasm.

He lapped, twisted and flicked that very special place until she could stand it no more. She had to have him inside her, filling that hot, wet, desperate void that had gone too long without him.

Daphne dug her nails into his skin and dragged him up her body.

He still wore his jeans, but she didn't care. What mattered was getting him inside her so she could wrap herself around him.

He slipped between her legs, pressing his fingers to her entrance. One finger slid in. Her juices coated him as he swirled that digit and then pulled out. When he dipped in again, he did so with two, then three fingers, stretching her channel's opening.

"Please," she moaned. "I can't wait any longer." The tension had rebuilt, taking her to the edge yet again.

Boomer settled his big body between her legs. He leaned over, captured her lips with his and touched his cock to her entrance. When he pushed his tongue past her teeth, he thrust into her channel, claiming her in one powerful stroke.

Daphne raised her knees, cupped the back of her thighs and lifted her hips to meet him.

He pressed all the way into her, sliding easily into her dampness. For a long moment, he remained deep and still.

Then he eased out. His next thrust was hard and

swift, followed by more. Soon he was pounding in and out, faster and faster.

Daphne dropped her heels to the cushions and pressed down, lifting her hips, meeting his every thrust.

Her core tightened. A tingling sensation rippled out from her center to the very tips of her fingers and toes.

For a year, she'd dreamed of this. That long year of not knowing what was going to happen to her life and that of her baby. This was where she'd longed to be, what she'd prayed for countless times.

BOOMER THRUST one last time and buried himself deeply inside her. He drew in a deep breath and then pulled out and rested his cock on her belly as he came.

He dropped down on the couch and pulled her into his arms, balancing precariously on the edge.

"Sadly, we can't stay this way." Daphne pressed her cheek to his chest, making no effort to move any further.

"I know." Boomer pressed a kiss to her forehead, squeezed her body against his and disengaged, rolling to his feet. He held out a hand and pulled her to her feet, gathered their clothing and led her into the bedroom and closed the door behind them.

Surrounded by pillows and tucked into her baby blankets, Maya slept peacefully.

Boomer dropped the clothing on the end of the bed and kept walking, leading Daphne to the adjoining bathroom.

"I have to warn you, the water is cold."

He chuckled. "We'll warm it up between the two of us."

Daphne purposely left the bathroom door open. "To listen for the baby," she explained.

He had lots to learn about babies and Maya's needs. But for now, she was asleep and her mother was hotter than ever and naked.

Boomer's groin tightened. The shower wasn't nearly as open and airy as the one they'd shared in his bungalow in Cozumel, but it didn't dampen his desire in the least.

Once the water temperature increased to just about lukewarm, he helped her over the edge of the tub.

She shivered, her nipples tightening into tight little beads.

"We'll make this quick." Boomer grabbed the bar of soap and worked up a lather.

She touched his arm. "Don't hurry on my account. My body will adjust to the temperature."

He spread the suds over her shoulders and across her chest, moving his hands in slow, rhythmic circles around the swells of her breasts, pausing to tweak her peaked nipples.

"Mmm," she moaned. "Already getting warmer."

He spent some time tweaking, swirling and squeezing each globe until she arched her back, thrusting herself into his open palms.

"You're making me crazy," she said, her voice low, gravelly and sexy as hell.

Boomer's cock sprang to attention. "We can't keep doing this without protection."

Daphne's lips tipped upward on the corners. "True. But then Maya is proof not all protection is one hundred percent fool-proof."

"We did use protection then, didn't we?"

She nodded. "Every time." Daphne grabbed the soap, worked up a generous lather, started at his shoulders and worked her way downward until her fingers circled his cock. "But we don't have to go all the way to get satisfaction." With slow, steady strokes, she ran her hands the length of his staff all the way from the tip to the base. She rolled his balls in one palm and circled behind him with the other to cup his ass.

A groan rose up Boomer's throat, and he thrust into the circle of her hand. He wanted to take her, to bury himself inside her again, but he couldn't move out of the tightness of her grip.

Lukewarm water sluiced over his shoulder, washing away the suds.

Daphne looked up at him with a sexy smile and then dropped to her knees in front of him.

"You don't have to do this," he started.

"But I want to." Then she touched the tip of his cock with her tongue.

Boomer sank his hands into her damp hair and grabbed a handful, urging her closer.

Daphne opened her mouth and wrapped her lips around him, flicking the tip of his shaft with her tongue.

His cock jerked, and his fingers tightened in her hair.

Then she cupped his balls, pulling him toward her, taking more of him into her mouth.

He moved inside slowly, responding to the pressure of her fingers. Hell, he was on fire. Desire rushed like flames through tinder in his veins.

She clasped his buttocks and set the rhythm, moving him in and out until he was pumping like an engine's piston, in and out. Tension built rapidly, sending him up toward the edge. Before he spiraled over the precipice, he pulled free.

Her hand took the place of her lips, gliding over him until the rush of his seed had been spent.

Not until he regained his senses did he notice the water had chilled considerably. He rinsed the remaining soap from their bodies, turned off the water and wrapped Daphne in a dry towel.

With another towel, he squeezed the water from her hair then patted her face, neck and legs dry.

Daphne took over and dried his skin from the top of his head to the tips of his toes. When she was done, she handed him the towel.

Boomer wrapped the terry cloth around his waist, swept Daphne up into his arms and carried her into the bedroom. Beside the bed, he stood for a moment, staring down at their daughter, stirring in her blanket.

Maya whimpered and shoved a fist into her mouth.

"She's hungry," Daphne said. "If you'll put me down, I'll feed her."

Reluctantly, Boomer lowered Daphne to the ground. He wanted to lie in the bed with her and hold her close throughout the night.

With a towel wrapped around her middle, Daphne

sat on the edge of the bed and swung her legs onto the mattress.

Boomer lifted Maya and laid her in Daphne's arms.

Daphne let the corner of the towel drop to expose her right breast and positioned Maya's mouth over the nipple.

Maya nuzzled greedily, her head moving back and forth, her mouth open like a baby bird's. Finally, his daughter found the nipple, sucked it between her lips and pulled hard.

Daphne stroked Maya's dark hair and settled with her back against the headboard. "She has your hair."

"She does," he agreed. "But blue eyes?"

With a chuckle, Daphne glanced up at him. "Most babies have blue eyes for the first few months. I think they're turning green."

"Like her mother's." Boomer stood for a long moment, watching Daphne feed Maya, one of the most beautiful things he'd ever witnessed. His heart swelled behind his ribs with a feeling he had never experienced. Sure, he'd thought himself in love with Daphne back in Cozumel, but this feeling was a much stronger mixture of love, pride and wonder. They'd created a child. A combination of the two of them.

For a long moment, his chest tightened, and he couldn't move from where he stood.

"Do you want to lie down?" Daphne asked, scooting to the edge of the bed. She raised Maya from the right breast and switched her to the left.

Maya's little hand fisted as she suckled at Daphne's breast.

"No." Boomer grabbed his clothes and backed toward the door.

Daphne frowned. "Are you leaving?"

"I think it would better if I slept in the living room. For now." He turned to leave.

"Boomer?" Her voice stopped him, but he didn't turn back.

"Why did you freeze with Maya earlier?" she asked softly.

He didn't want to answer. But if he did, perhaps she'd better understand why he couldn't stay. Why he couldn't be a good father to Maya. "When I was on my last deployment as a sniper, my target was an ISIS militant." He drew in a deep breath and let it out. "He came out of the building dressed as an imam in white robes. The man was responsible for numerous murders, rapes and beheadings. I had him in my sights, and I pulled the trigger."

"Did you get him?" Daphne asked.

Boomer bowed his head. "I did."

"What happened?" Daphne's voice brought him back from his memories.

"At the same time I pulled the trigger, a woman stepped out of the building with a baby in her arms. The bullet travelled straight through the ISIS leader's head and hit the baby." He turned back to take in the sight of Daphne nursing their baby. "The baby died in that woman's arms." He didn't wait for her response. He left the room, pulling the door closed behind him.

Yes, he was a coward. The sudden panic attack he'd experienced reminded him he wasn't fit to be a father.

The image of Daphne cradling the baby was much like the Iraqi woman holding her dead baby. Chills rippled down Boomer's spine, along with an overwhelming feeling of hopelessness.

He was there to protect them.

What if he failed Daphne?

Holy hell. What if he failed Maya?

CHAPTER 7

Daphne woke the next morning to the wail of the wind blowing against the windows. Maya lay nestled against her side, having scooted closer to keep warm during the night.

A dull gray light filtered through the window. The morning sun was completely consumed by the cloak of the storm raging outside.

Maya stirred and whimpered.

Daphne changed the baby's diaper and then settled her against her breast.

Maya drank her fill and lay staring up at Daphne, blowing bubbles in the breast milk still on her lips.

"Hey, sweetheart," she cooed, smoothing her hand across Maya's dark, silky hair.

Maya looked so much like her father, it made Daphne's heart hurt.

Why, after making love to her twice, had he left the room to sleep in the living area? Was it the presence of the baby that made him run?

Daphne smiled down at her daughter. "You aren't so scary, are you?"

Maya's lips curled in an adorable smile.

"How could anyone not love you?" Daphne asked her daughter. She leaned the baby over her shoulder and patted her back until Maya burped.

The scent of bacon drifted beneath the door. Daphne's tummy rumbled. She wrapped Maya in her baby blankets and slipped out of the bed. When her bare feet hit the wooden floor, she winced at how cold it was. She'd have to leave the door open to the living room to keep it warm in the bedroom. Hopefully, the electricity would be turned on soon.

Daphne hurried to brush her hair and teeth. She dressed in the thick sweater and leggings from the day before. Then she gathered Maya in her arms and opened the bedroom door.

The air in the other part of the house was much warmer. The fire burned brightly in the fireplace, drawing Daphne to its heat.

"About time you two woke up," Chuck said from the kitchen. "Boomer and I have already eaten, but we saved you some bacon and scrambled eggs. I hope you're hungry."

"Starving." She settled Maya in the playpen near the fireplace but not so near that a spark could catch it on fire. Then she turned to survey the room.

A blanket lay neatly folded on the couch, but other than that, there was no sign of Boomer.

"If you're looking for Maya's daddy, he braved the

blizzard to work on the snowmobile that was acting up yesterday."

Daphne frowned and cast a dubious glance toward the window. Snow scoured the glass like sand. "He went out in that? You can't see two feet in front of you."

"What can I say? The man was determined." Chuck scraped scrambled eggs from the fry pan onto a plate and added two thick slices of crispy bacon.

Suddenly less hungry, Daphne took the plate anyway. She had to eat to produce the milk Maya needed. Taking the plate to the table, she sat in one of the wooden chairs and stared down at the fluffy yellow eggs, her appetite gone.

Chuck grabbed a chair, turned it around and straddled it, sitting across from her. "Hey, why the glum look? Would you rather have had an omelet?"

"No. This looks great." She lifted the fork and jabbed at the eggs several times before laying the utensil on the table and pushing the plate away. "What's wrong with me, Chuck?"

He shook his head. "Nothing's wrong with you, Daph." He slid her plate toward her. "But if you don't eat, my girl Maya will go hungry."

Daphne sighed and lifted the fork again. "I wish I'd never witnessed that murder."

"For your sake, I wish you hadn't either. But then Cooper would be getting away with yet another murder."

"If his daddy's cleanup crew succeeds in finding me, it'll be a moot point."

Chuck's lips thinned. "Boomer and I won't let that happen."

She reached across the table and touched Chuck's hand. "I know you'll do your best." For a moment, she sat in silence, her hand still on Chuck's. "If, for some reason, I don't make it, promise me you'll take care of Maya."

"You're going to make it, damn it." A fierce scowl marred Chuck's face. "And, by damn, you'll dance at Maya's wedding."

Daphne smiled and squeezed Chuck's hand. "That's the plan. But if something were to happen to me, I need to know someone will look after Maya."

Chuck stared at Daphne long and hard. "Don't you think Maya's father will want to have a say in who takes care of her?"

Daphne glanced toward the door, willing Boomer to come through. "Just promise me, please," she whispered.

Chuck touched her arm. "Maya has come to mean as much to me as you have."

Daphne turned and smiled at Chuck. "And you mean a lot to us. You're like the brother I never had and the doting uncle Maya needs."

With a sigh, Chuck took her hand, a brief flash of sadness making him appear older than his forty-seven years. "I only hope that one day I find a woman as smart and courageous as you."

A glance down at the way Chuck held her hand made Daphne's heart beat faster. Did Chuck have feelings stronger than that of a brother? She looked up into his eyes.

Chuck met her gaze, a crooked smile on his lips. "Boomer is a lucky man."

"Oh, Chuck. Please tell me you aren't..." she fumbled for the word, "you haven't..." Daphne rose from her chair and flung her arms around his neck. "You know I love you, Chuck."

He pulled her into his lap and held her tightly.

At that moment, the door flung open, and a swirl of snow blew in on frigid air.

Boomer stepped through the entrance.

Daphne leaped off Chuck's lap and straightened her sweater.

Boomer pushed the goggles he wore over his eyes up onto his forehead. The frown he exposed shot straight through Daphne's heart. Boomer didn't say a word. He glared at Chuck and back at Daphne, drew in a deep breath and let it out. "Just came in for a wrench. I don't guess I'll find what I'm looking for in here." He pushed the goggles back down and walked back into the blizzard.

"I should go after him." Daphne started toward the door.

Chuck caught her arm. "Don't. Maybe if he thinks he has a little competition it'll help screw his head on straight."

Daphne hesitated. Boomer had the wrong idea, and she felt compelled to tell him so. "What if he leaves me to the competition?" she said, her voice low, almost a whisper.

"Then he didn't deserve you anyway. Any man worth his salt would fight for the woman he loves." He didn't say it, but the words *I would* were loud and clear.

Daphne was heartsick for Chuck who'd taken good care of her and Maya, and who had been there when Maya had come into the world. She'd never suspected he might have more than brotherly feelings for her. The man had been nothing if not professional in his protection.

Perhaps the competition he'd mentioned had sparked in Chuck the need to fight for the woman he loved.

Maya let out a cry, as if she could sense her mother's confusion and sadness.

Daphne gathered the baby and took her back to the bedroom to nurse. Going to the bedroom was a way to escape this latest development between her and Chuck. But the quiet time while nursing Maya gave Daphne too much opportunity to ruminate about Boomer, and now Chuck.

Add a killer determined to take her out, and she had quite a mess on her hands.

HEAT FLOODED Boomer's veins though the temperature outside had sunk well below freezing with a wind chill factor of twenty degrees lower.

He stood on the porch, letting the frigid air cool his anger. The snow-laden wind blasted against his cheeks. If he didn't get out of the direct force, frostbite would be the result.

He bent against the wind and trudged through the

whiteout conditions to the shed where they'd stored the snowmobiles. At least inside the shed he wouldn't be plagued by the bite of the wind.

Once inside, he shoved the door closed and removed the goggles. With nothing but the wail of the wind pummeling the metal roof and thin wooden walls of the shed, Boomer was alone with his thoughts and, like the snow outside, they swirled around his head.

Seeing Daphne on Chuck's lap had sent a flash of rage ripping through Boomer's veins.

He closed his eyes in an attempt to unsee what he'd witnessed, to no avail.

Well hell, what did he expect? Daphne and Chuck had been together the entire year she and Boomer had been apart.

Chuck had been the one to protect her from attack. He'd been there when Maya was born. He took better care of Maya and Daphne, for that matter.

Of course Daphne would have feelings for the man.

Then why did she make love with Boomer the night before?

The rage surged again. If he counted the actual number of days he'd spent with Daphne compared to the number of days Chuck had spent with her, he didn't have a snowball's chance in hell.

If he counted the number of days Daphne had been on his mind throughout the year...

What did it matter? He'd frozen when he'd been left in charge of Maya. Though he'd made love with Daphne twice the night before, when it came right down to it, he'd run out on her and left her to sleep the night alone when clearly, she'd wanted him to stay.

Boomer had no right to be jealous. Chuck was the better man. He didn't have near the number of hang-ups Boomer had, and he obviously loved Daphne and Maya. He'd do anything to keep them safe.

But so would he. His chest tightening, Boomer realized he'd lay down his life for Daphne and Maya. No one would get past him and do them harm.

He picked up the tools he'd been using to repair the snowmobile's engine and went to work. If they had to make a quick escape, both machines needed to be up and running.

For the next hour, he tightened hoses and electrical connections and did everything he knew how to do. When he finally tried the ignition, the engine roared to life. He let it run for a few minutes to make sure it wasn't going to cut out again. Switching it off, he paused and tried the starter again.

The snowmobile sprang to life without hesitation.

Satisfied his work was complete, he shut down the engine and stored the tools in a compartment on the body of the machine.

When he straightened, he cocked his head to the side and listened.

Silence.

Boomer slung his rifle over his shoulder, pushed open the door to the shed and stepped out.

The wind had completely died down, and the swirling snow had settled. An eerie quiet hovered over the mountain, now covered in a foot-deep, white blanket. Clouds clung to the peaks, the sun blocked by their thickness.

The quiet set Boomer's nerves on edge. He glanced toward the house. The generator had kicked off.

At that moment, the front door opened and Chuck stepped out, zipping his jacket. His gaze swept the hillside, the buried road and finally the shed where Boomer stood. He gave him a brief nod before crossing the deck to the generator.

Boomer closed the shed and trudged through the snow to the steps leading onto the porch.

Chuck was reaching for one of the five-gallon jugs of fuel.

"Out of gas?" Boomer asked.

"Yup." Chuck filled the generator's tank and set the jug back on the deck. "Although, I think we should conserve what gas we have. We don't know how long we'll be up here, or when we'll have the opportunity to get out for more supplies."

As much as Boomer wanted to hate Chuck, he couldn't. The man had been there for Daphne and Maya throughout the yearlong ordeal.

The faint sound of an engine drifted up the side of the hill to where Boomer stood. He frowned and tipped his ear toward the hum. "Are we expecting anyone?"

Chuck's eyes narrowed. "No." He hurried into the house.

Boomer took a position at the corner of the porch with the best view of the road they'd driven up the day before.

A moment later, Chuck came back out, carrying a rifle with a scope.

"I told Daphne to take Maya to the back bedroom and lie down on the floor with her."

"Thanks," Boomer said.

Chuck left the porch and walked through the snow to a stand of trees. There he knelt and raised his rifle, resting his elbow on his knee.

Boomer had a good angle and field of fire. When the vehicle appeared, he'd have the best chance of hitting the target.

Now, all they could do was wait for the vehicle to emerge from the trees.

Boomer breathed in and out, taking slow, steadying breaths as he stared through the scope, getting a magnified view of the road two hundred yards downrange.

A solid black truck emerged, moving slowly over the snow-covered road.

Boomer sighted in on the driver's side of the pickup, hoping to see a face. His finger caressed the trigger, without applying force. If the driver and the passengers of the truck decided to attack, Boomer would take out the driver first. The narrow road coming up to the house had a steep drop-off. One wrong move and the truck and its occupants would careen over the edge with nothing to stop them but the ground two-hundred-fifty-feet below.

Peering through the scope, Boomer counted off the seconds it would take for the truck to get close enough to the house to cause concern. In five seconds, the truck would be close enough the driver could ram the house.

Five…

The truck slowed to a crawl.

Four…

The driver brought the vehicle to a complete halt.

Three…

Boomer inhaled and held his breath, his focus on the driver's windshield.

Two…

His finger rested on the trigger.

One…

The driver's door opened, and a man stood up on the running board and yelled, "Boomer, Chuck. Don't shoot!"

Boomer pulled his finger away from the trigger and released the breath he'd been holding in a rush. Holy shit! He'd almost shot his new boss.

Hank Patterson waved from his perch on the running board, balancing himself between the body of the truck and the door. "Don't shoot!" he yelled again.

Boomer rose from his crouched position on the porch, the rifle still in his arms, ready if for some reason Hank was being held hostage.

Chuck stepped away from the stand of trees and motioned for Hank to pull forward.

Boomer's eyes narrowed. From what he could see, Patterson was alone, but that was only based on what he could see. A full-grown man could be hunkered down in the seat, holding a gun on Hank.

The owner of the Brotherhood Protectors slipped back into his seat, closed the door and shifted his truck into drive. He eased his way up the narrow road, careful not to misjudge the edges and drop-offs.

When he finally brought the truck to a halt twenty yards from the house, Hank got out.

Chuck retained his hold on his rifle, as did Boomer, ready should a hidden threat emerge at the last second.

Hank lifted his hand as if in surrender. "You can put down your rifles. I'm alone."

Boomer nodded toward Chuck.

"If you don't mind, we'd like to make absolutely sure you aren't being held at gunpoint," Chuck said.

Hank's lips twisted. "I don't blame you. If Sadie and Emma were in danger, I'd do the same."

Hank stepped away from the truck and waited while Chuck examined the interior and the truck bed. When he was done, he lowered his weapon and announced, "All clear."

Boomer lowered his rifle and stepped off the porch. "We didn't expect anyone to come this way for a while."

"I wouldn't have come if I didn't have to." Hank tipped his head toward the door. "I'm here to add to the ranks of protectors."

Boomer frowned. "You have news." His words were a statement, not a question.

Hank's lips firmed into a straight line. "Where's Daphne?"

"She and Maya are in the back bedroom, staying low," Chuck replied.

"Good. I'd rather tell you two what we've learned before we break it to Daphne."

Boomer's gut knotted. Whatever Hank had to say wasn't going to be good.

The door opened, and Daphne stared out at Hank, her arms wrapped around her middle, her body trembling. "I heard you talking. Whatever you have to say, I want to hear."

Boomer moved to stand near her. "I don't like the fact you're standing outside. Anyone with a rifle and scope could pick you off."

"Nice thought." Daphne ducked back inside the shadows of the doorway. "Then let's bring it inside."

The men followed her into the house.

Boomer glanced around the living area noting the absence of the playpen. "Where's Maya?"

Daphne gave him a hint of a smile. "Asleep in the bedroom."

He nodded and turned to Hank as his new boss closed the door behind him.

Hank drew in a deep breath and concentrated his attention on Chuck. "Apparently, the bad guys got hold of your man Rodney's cell phone and traced his calls to you."

Chuck's jaw tightened. "I didn't call you on my cell phone."

"No, but you brought your cell phone with you, didn't you?"

Chuck nodded and pulled the device out of his pocket.

Hank's lips twisted. "This area is notorious for bad cell phone reception, but apparently, they managed to track your cell phone to my place."

Daphne stepped forward. "Sadie and Emma?"

"Are safely on their way to California. Sadie had a meeting scheduled with her agent." Hank inhaled and let out the breath slowly.

"How do you know all this?" Boomer asked. "Tracking a cell phone isn't something that sets off alarms. I mean Chuck didn't know he was being traced."

"No. But once they located my place, they hacked into our databases." Hank stood taller. "They're using some pretty sophisticated tools to get past our firewall. I have my computer guru working on shoring up our tech defenses. But in the meantime," he paused and glanced from Chuck to Daphne. "They know you're in the area. I figure it's only a matter of time before they find you."

Daphne's face paled, and she sank onto the couch. "What should we do?"

"I came up to provide support. I put a call out to others on the Brotherhood Protectors team. We should have three or four more men up here by morning. Your safe house here won't be safe for long. We need to bring you down from the mountain."

"Why not now?" Boomer asked.

"I want as many people between the bad guys and Daphne and Maya as possible, before we bring them down from the mountains," Hank said.

Boomer shifted his stance. "Wouldn't it be better to stay here and defend in place?"

Hank's eyes narrowed. "I thought about that. But I think it'd be better to bring them back to the ranch. It's not as remote."

"Then why didn't we stay there in the first place?" Boomer asked.

"I didn't think they'd find you so quickly. I thought this cabin in the mountains would be the perfect hideaway, until we could get more information on Cooper and his cohorts." Hank shook his head. "Now, I'm not so sure. They have a lot more assets to find missing persons than I'd suspected. For all I know, they could have followed me from the ranch here, despite my best efforts to keep that from happening.

Boomer shot a glance at Daphne.

Her gaze met his. "How soon can we get off this mountain?"

"I want to wait until I have more of my men here before we try to bring you and Maya down," Hank said. "We're better off taking a stand here with as few protectors as we have, than inching our way down the mountain without adequate reinforcement."

"How is the road?" Chuck asked.

Hank shook his head. "Treacherous, at best. The snow hides the worst road conditions, including the places where the shoulders are soft and ready to crumble. The best bet would be to wait until the snow melts before attempting to descend with Daphne and the baby."

"In the meantime, I'd like to get out on the snowmobiles and see if we have any visitors to the surrounding area," Boomer said.

"That's a good idea," Hank agreed. "We could look for weaknesses in our defenses and locate high ground that could be used by a sniper."

Daphne crossed her arms over her chest. "For that matter, I'd like to see what's out there."

Before she finished speaking, Boomer was shaking his head. "You have to remain inside, in hiding. You're the only witness they haven't killed. That makes you a huge threat to Cooper. Getting out on a snowmobile would set you up as a target. And then who would take care of Maya?"

Chuck raised a finger. "I'll take care of Maya. We need to recon the area. If Daphne wants to get out with you, I see no problem. As long as she puts her hair up in a cap, and she wears a baggy snowsuit."

Daphne grinned. "Looks like I'm going for a ride on snowmobile."

Boomer swallowed a groan. "If you come with us, you have to follow our orders, no questions asked."

Daphne nodded. "Follow orders, check."

"You'll ride with me," Boomer said. He glared at Chuck. "I'll deal with you later."

Chuck raised his hands. "I don't know what you're talking about. I'm here to protect Maya. What you and Daphne do is up to you. Just keep the noise down in the middle of the night."

Boomer's brow lowered. He hooked Daphne's arm and marched her to the door, and shoved her jacket into her arms.

"*Now* you're eager to get me outside," she grumbled. "Damn right I'm going."

"Damn right, you are."

She pushed her arms into the jacket and shrugged it

over her shoulders. She arched an eyebrow. "Aren't you afraid I'll be shot at?"

"I might strangle you before someone has the chance," he said, opening the door and waving her through it.

"Some bodyguard," she muttered and stepped out onto the porch.

"Stay in the shadows," Boomer commanded.

"Staying," she shot back.

Once he closed the chalet door, he gripped her arm and spun her to face him. "What the hell are you trying to prove?"

"I'm not trying to prove anything." She lifted her chin and braced her feet slightly apart, as if she were preparing for a fight.

"If Cooper's cleanup team is out here, you're barely safe inside the house. Outside, you're a damned target."

She spun away from him and paced a few steps across the deck. "I'm tired of playing it safe. I've been holed up for a year." She turned to face him. "*A year.*" Her lips thinned into a straight line. "Maybe it's time to lure these bastards out of hiding so we know what we're dealing with."

"And if something happens to you, what will become of the baby?"

CHAPTER 8

Daphne's eyes narrowed. "If something happens to me, Maya's father will have to raise her." A frown tugged her brow downward, and a sick feeling settled in her belly. "Is that what you're afraid of? Afraid you'll be stuck with a baby to raise? A little girl who'll need you to brush her hair and get her ready for school every day? Someone who will be forced to rely on you to provide for, care for and love her for as long as you live?"

Boomer didn't move. He stared at her, a muscle twitching in his jaw.

"That's it, isn't it?" Daphne snorted. "You're the highly trained SEAL with the ability to gun down a man at four hundred meters without blinking an eye. You can kill a man with your bare hands, and you can race into an enemy-infested building without fear." She shook her head. "But when it comes to that little baby in there—your little girl—you can't handle the thought of being responsible for her life."

"You don't understand," he said, his voice choked, and turned away.

"Maybe I don't, but you're not doing anything to help clarify." She touched his arm. "Tell me."

He spun and gripped her arm so hard, it hurt. "I've seen things." His Adam's apple rose and fell as he swallowed hard. "I've done things I'm not proud of. Things I can't undo or take back."

The anguish in Boomer's eyes cut through Daphne's heart. "That's the past." She pointed toward the house. "You have a possible future in there. One where you're a part of your daughter's life." Daphne held up her hands. "But if you can't or don't want to be included in her upbringing, I can't force you, nor will I try." She dropped her arms to her sides, her chest aching with longing for this man to take part in his daughter's life. "I don't expect you to be a part of my life if you can't find it in your heart to love me. But Maya is your daughter. A piece of you lives inside of her. For so long, I hoped you could love her, and that she would know her father."

Daphne drew in a deep breath and turned to look over the mountains. She should be filled with joy at the beauty of her surroundings, but her heart hurt too much for her to see it.

"Daphne, I need time," Boomer said. He touched her arm.

She flinched.

His hand fell away from her. "I don't know if I'll be a fit parent to Maya." He paused. "Chuck loves you and Maya. He'd make a much better father for her."

Daphne spun, anger replacing sadness. "But he's not her father." She poked her finger into his chest. "You are."

Boomer grabbed her finger and held it, his eyes widening, his gaze shooting past her. "Shh."

"I will not be shushed," Daphne said, her voice rising. "That little girl needs a father. She needs you."

Boomer touched a finger to her lips and then spun her around, pushing her behind him. "Be quiet." He leaned on the porch railing and stared up at the sky.

For a moment, Daphne's anger burned until she realized Boomer was staring up at the sky, his head tilted as if he were listening to something.

Then Daphne picked up on the soft humming sound. Her anger disappeared, and she leaned toward Boomer. "What is it?"

"An engine. It's too quiet to be an airplane or helicopter. But it sounds like it's in the sky."

"Are you sure it's not echoing off the hillsides? Could it be a vehicle coming up the road?"

Boomer shook his head. "I've heard this sound before. "Get back in the shadows," he commanded. "Damn. There it is." He pointed toward the cloud-laden sky.

Daphne stared hard but couldn't see what he was seeing.

"I don't see anything."

"It's a drone." He backed away from the railing, flung open the front door and ushered Daphne into the chalet.

Hank and Chuck looked up from where they sat at

the table. "Did you two get everything ironed out between you," Chuck asked.

Boomer shook his head. "I think they've found us."

Daphne's heart slipped into her belly. Her gaze went to Maya in Chuck's arms. "I thought we'd have more time."

"Apparently not," Boomer said. "There's a drone hovering nearby."

Hank pushed to his feet and strode toward the door. "Could you tell if it was equipped with anything more than a camera?"

"It appeared to be something that could be purchased by anyone. Not like the weaponized UAVs we flew over Iraq and Afghanistan." Boomer held the door for his boss, balancing the sniper rifle in his other hand. He glanced at Daphne. "Will you please stay inside for now?"

She nodded.

Hank and Boomer stepped out on the porch, closing the door to keep the warm air in and the cool air out.

Daphne paced the living room floor. "I can't keep dragging Maya all over the countryside. The weather's too cold, and the roads are too dangerous.

"Then we'll have to come up with another plan," Chuck said. He cradled Maya in one of his big arms.

"They want me, and they're ruthless enough to kill anyone in the way." Her heart flipped over. "I need to get Maya away from me. I could never live with myself if she becomes collateral damage." Daphne choked on the last word and stared at Chuck through blurred eyes. A single tear slipped down her cheek. "If I have to send her away from me, so be it. Until we stop these attacks, I need to take the danger away from her."

Chuck nodded. "You have a good point."

A loud bang sounded from the porch.

Daphne jumped. "What the hell?"

Chuck dropped to his knees on the floor, clutching Maya to his chest.

Boomer and Hank entered the chalet, their faces set in tight lines.

"What was the gunfire all about?" Chuck asked.

"I shot at the drone, but it was already dropping below the horizon," Boomer said. "It got away."

"It doesn't matter," Hank said. "The damage is already done. They know we're here."

Daphne held out her hands toward Chuck.

The older SEAL handed Maya over to her.

She held her baby against her breast, her heart racing, the fear threatening to overwhelm her. "What's to keep them from targeting this entire chalet? They killed a guard last time and blew up the safe house. We were lucky to get out in time."

"We don't know how they will attack next," Hank said.

"Exactly. And we can't keep running. Maya made one mountain escape, but she's a baby. We can't keep jerking her around."

Hank nodded. "My men should be here by morning."

"That might be too late," Boomer pointed out, his gaze on the baby in Daphne's arms.

"We need to get Cooper's killers away from this cabin. Away from Maya," Daphne said. "The only way to do that is to get me away from Maya." She stared down at her child. Maya had only been with her for three months, but she couldn't conceive of life without her. She loved her little girl more than she ever could have imagined.

"What can we do to draw them away from Maya?" Hank asked.

"Use me as bait," Daphne answered without hesitation. "We have the two snowmobiles. If I'm on the back of one of them, I can leave my hair free. It'll let them know for certain it's me."

Boomer was already shaking his head. "If you're on the back, you aren't protected."

She looked from Boomer to Chuck to Hank. "Then give me a bullet-proof vest. The hair has to be out, or they won't fall for it."

Boomer gripped her arms. "I was okay with you being on the snowmobile when you would be bundled up like one of the men. But you're painting a target on your back for them to aim at."

She stared up into his face, her jaw tightening. "I'd die rather than put my daughter at risk of being caught in the middle. She deserves to live a full and happy life."

"Yes, she does. But we can get her down the mountain and to safety without you sacrificing yourself." Boomer smoothed a hand along her cheek. "Your life is just as important."

"What if they bring in men on a helicopter?" Daphne asked.

Boomer snorted. "Then we're all in trouble."

"Exactly." Daphne gripped his hands. "And all the

more reason for me to get as far away from Maya as possible, draw them away, until we know she's in a safe place."

"The possibility of Cooper's men getting their hands on a helicopter gunship is slim to none," Boomer said.

"But he had a drone," Hank said. "They know where we are. Maybe they won't have a helicopter, but who says they won't have some kind of rocket-propelled grenade? They could lob a rocket into the chalet and kill us all."

Chuck shook his head. "You're getting ahead of the situation."

"Well, it beats being in reaction mode." She stared around the room at the three men. "I know it might seem farfetched, but these men mean business. They've proven effective at squelching others. I have to take them away from Maya. If we can distract them long enough, Chuck could drive Maya to Hank's ranch where the other Brotherhood Protectors could provide support."

"That leaves Maya with only one protector," Hank reminded her.

Daphne patted her chest. "But it's me they're after."

Boomer and Hank exchanged glances.

"We could wait it out here until morning. We don't even know if Cooper's cleanup crew is close. The drone could have been a probe. They might not be close enough to cause trouble yet."

Daphne held Maya closer. "Or they might be over the next hill, ready to hit this place hard with whatever they have. At the very least, they could have automatic rifles or machine guns that could cut this building into pieces, like we see in the documentaries on the wars in the Middle East. I'm not willing to sit around and wait to find out."

Hank walked to the window. "Daphne has a point. But if we do this and use her as bait, we have to be sure they know she's on the snowmobile, or they'll attack the house anyway."

"So we wait and watch for them to arrive," Daphne leaned forward. "But we have to be ready to go and keep them on our trail, but far enough ahead, so they won't be able to shoot us."

"I don't like it," Boomer said. "Just because you wear a vest doesn't protect all of you. If these guys are worth their salt, they could go for the head."

"She can wear a helmet," Hank said.

Boomer glared at his boss. "I thought we were here to protect her, not put her out there for the crazies to take pot shots at."

Daphne planted a fist on her hip. "Would you rather they shoot at me, or blow up this house with Maya in it?"

Boomer frowned. "I'd rather not have either scenario happen."

"And I'd do anything to protect my child." Daphne threw the words at him, knowing it was a challenge. She wanted him to care about Maya.

Maya, sensing her mother's distress, whimpered.

Instead of holding her close, Daphne held the baby out to Boomer. "You choose who will die. Me or Maya, or both."

Boomer took the child shoved into his hands and held her out in front of him.

Maya squirmed and then stared at Boomer, her eyes wide. At first she appeared frightened and ready to let out a wail, but she continued to stare until a smile curled the corners of her lips, and she batted at Boomer with a chubby fist.

Daphne's heart squeezed hard in her chest. She willed the man to hold the baby close and love her like a regular father. After a couple minutes, she'd almost given up hope, when he pulled the baby in, wrapped his arms around her and smiled down at Maya.

Boomer couldn't get over how much Maya looked like him. It thrilled and scared him all in the same breath.

Maya swung her arm and caught him on his chin.

Boomer grabbed her fist with his free hand and laid it against his cheek.

Maya giggled and bunched her fingers, then tried to grab a handful of Boomer's face.

His lips twitched as if he fought a smile. "Are all babies this soft?" he asked in wonder.

Daphne's eyes glazed, and she nodded.

"Don't let that soft skin and sweet baby scent deceive you," Chuck said with a smile. "Maya's got quite a swing." He rubbed the corner of his eye. "She almost gave me a black eye the other day. She'll give the boys a run for their money when she's old enough to date."

Boomer frowned.

Daphne touched his arm. "Please. I want her to live to date. Even if it's hard to let her out of the house with a teenage boy. She deserves a life."

Boomer looked across the baby's soft dark hair to her mother and then to Chuck. "Do you think you could get her down the mountain without any trouble?"

Chuck nodded. "If you keep the cleanup team busy, I'll get her down and take her to Hank's ranch."

"The arms room is a reinforced bunker," Hank said. "If you can get Maya there, you two will be all right until the other Brotherhood Protectors arrive." Hank gave him the access code and the workaround for the fingerprint.

Chuck glanced toward the window. "Days are getting shorter. We have what's left of the afternoon to make this happen. And that's assuming the cleanup team isn't right behind the drone."

"We should get the snowmobiles ready," Hank said. "We can pull them up to the house so we can make our move if we hear anything."

"Or we can go out and see what we can find," Daphne suggested.

Boomer arched a brow, impressed with her courage, even as her confidence rankled. He wanted her safe, not daring some spec ops bastard to take a bead on her. "We don't want to stumble on the attack team."

"No, but we don't want to wait until they get in position to blow up the chalet," Daphne reminded the men. "The sooner they think we're out of here, the better."

"You'll need snow pants, the protective vest and

warm gloves." Boomer studied her. "Have you ever driven a snowmobile?"

She shook her head. "I'm good with the four-wheeler, but I don't have any experience on a snowmobile. Besides, I need to be on the back with my hair flying out for them to take the bait."

Boomer clenched his teeth. He didn't say anything for a moment or two. Using Daphne as bait to pull Cooper's cleanup team way from the chalet went against everything in his heart. But Daphne was adamant about getting them away from the house. With a sigh, he repeated his earlier order, "You'll ride with me."

"I'll be on the other vehicle to ride interference, should they get too close," Hank said.

Chuck held out his hands to Boomer. "And I'll be ready to take this little girl down the mountain when you get the bad guys away from here."

Boomer was reluctant to release Maya, but he did, a frown pulling his brow low. "I don't like leaving you alone with the baby."

Daphne slipped a hand into Boomer's. "Chuck will take care of Maya. He's her godfather."

"Damn right, I'll take care of her. She has a way of growing on you." Chuck smiled down at her and tickled her cheek.

Maya giggled and grabbed for Chuck's finger.

"I'll gather her things." Daphne hurried toward the bedroom.

"Put them in my truck," Hank said. "The one you came up in still has the trailer hitched to the bumper."

Daphne stuffed a bag full of diapers, warm clothing and the emergency can of formula powder. She draped baby blankets over the bag and hurried out into the living room. "We'll have to move the car seat into Hank's truck."

"I'll help with it," Boomer offered.

Daphne blinked, then gave a little smile of pleasure. "Thanks."

"We'll be back in a minute." Boomer held the door open.

Hank stepped through. "I'll stand watch while you take care of things." He carried the rifle he'd brought with him and took a position on the corner of the porch, staring out over the hillside sloping away from the house.

Boomer hooked Daphne's arm and hurried her out to the shed where they'd unloaded the two snowmobiles. The truck they'd brought them up on stood beside the shed, covered in twelve inches of snow.

"Stand between me and the shed."

She did as he said.

Still, Boomer shook his head. "I don't know why I let you talk me into this craziness."

"Because you know it's what we have to do if they come after us." She stared up at him. "We have to protect our baby."

Her bright green eyes captured his gaze for a moment, before his focus shifted to the soft rose of her lips. God, she was beautiful.

"I never stopped thinking of you after you disappeared." He pulled her into his arms. "Even in the desert, so far away from Cozumel. I remembered how your lips felt against mine."

She cupped his cheek. "I wanted to tell you where we'd gone, but it was too dangerous."

"We haven't seen each other in a year, but last night felt like we picked up where we left off. As if twelve months hadn't slipped away."

"Then why did you leave me?" she asked.

He pulled her close, crushing the bags between them, and lowered his head until his lips were a breath away from hers. "Because I'm an idiot. I don't want to fail you."

"The only way you'll fail me is if you push me away."

"I'm not the same man you met in Cozumel. There are things you don't know."

"You're right," Daphne said. "You aren't the same man. You're better. More mature, and even more handsome than before. So, shut up and kiss me. We don't have much time." She leaned up on her toes and pressed her lips to his.

Boomer clutched a handful of her hair and tugged, pulling her head back just a little. He crushed her lips with his, pushing his tongue past her teeth to slide along hers in a long, sensuous caress.

For a long moment, he held her like he should have the night before. When he came up for air, the whisper of a distant engine teased his ear.

His heart thudded. He lifted his head. "Do you hear that?"

She blinked open her eyes and tilted her head. "I do."

"We need to move. If they're on their way here, we have to be ready."

She nodded and hiked the diaper bag up on her arm. "It's time to get this show on the road."

Boomer knocked the snow off the roof and opened the back door. He unbuckled the car seat and backed out. As quickly as he could, he placed the baby's car seat in the back seat of Hank's truck and secured it. As he did, he prayed this insane plan would work, and Chuck would safely get Maya to that bunker in Hank's house. With Chuck watching out for Maya, Boomer would do his best to keep Daphne from becoming a sniper's target practice.

CHAPTER 9

As the engine sound grew louder, Daphne's pulse quickened. She tossed the diaper bag into the backseat and ran back to the house.

Boomer was right behind her, holding his rifle in his hands, not slung over his shoulder.

When Daphne burst through the door, Chuck and Hank stood.

"What's wrong?" Hank asked.

"We can hear the sound of engines," Daphne said.

"Engine or engines," Chuck asked.

"Engines," Boomer confirmed as he stepped up beside Daphne.

"Time to rock and roll." Hank tossed his truck keys to Chuck. "Hunker down until we get them to follow us, and then get Maya down the mountain."

Chuck held Maya in the crook of his arm. "Will do. For now, I'll take her into the back room in case there's any shooting."

Hank nodded and shrugged into his jacket. "Let's do

this." He led the way out the door and to his truck where he pulled protective vests from the toolbox in the back. He handed one to Daphne and one to Boomer.

She shed her coat and slipped on the vest.

Then Hank reached in and pulled out a small case, popped the latch on it and lifted a small handgun out of the foam padding. "Chuck assured me you know how to use one of these."

She nodded and took the weapon.

He handed her a belt with a black leather holster.

Daphne didn't ask questions. She wrapped the belt around her waist and hooked the buckle.

Then she donned her jacket, making sure the holster wasn't covered.

The engine sounds were getting closer. If they planned on getting out of there, they had to do it soon.

Boomer threw open the overhead door to the shed and straddled one of the snowmobiles. In seconds, he had the engine humming and pulled out onto the snow. He handed her a helmet.

Daphne pulled on the helmet, letting her long blond hair tumble down her back, in sharp contrast to the black jacket she wore. There would be no denying a blond female was on the back of the vehicle.

She climbed on the back and wrapped her arms around his waist. With a gun on her hip and a SEAL to hold onto, she felt unstoppable.

Hank climbed onto the other snowmobile and revved the engine. In the next moment, four snowmobiles appeared over the hilltop.

"There they are!' Daphne shouted over the roar of the motors.

"Hold on tight!" Boomer hit the throttle and sent the snowmobile skidding around in a one-hundred-eighty-degree turn, heading past the house and up to the top of the ridge.

Daphne clung to Boomer's middle as her bottom slid sideways on the sharp turn. She tightened her arms around his middle. The only way she'd come off the seat of the snowmobile was if Boomer came off with her. She refused to slow them down.

The rear end of the snowmobile skidded to one side and then straightened, the tracks digging into the snow and gravel beneath, shooting them forward.

Hank took the rear position, covering them from behind. The plan was to split up and lead the cleanup team on a wild goose chase through the mountains. When they reached a decent position, Boomer and Hank would attempt to take them out before the bad guys had a chance to hurt them.

Daphne glanced over her shoulder, and her heartbeat rocketed.

The four snowmobiles raced toward them, flying up over bumps and across the rugged terrain.

Her grip tightened again as they topped the ridge on the other side of the chalet.

Boomer slowed long enough to make sure all four snowmobiles were following them.

Hank pulled up beside them and looked back.

The group of riders flew past the house and followed their tracks up the side of the hill.

"Go!" Hank said.

Boomer gunned the accelerator, sending the snowmobile over the ridge and down a steep slope to the valley below.

Hank followed, paralleling them, but not so close that if he lost control he'd come crashing into them.

The four snowmobiles shot over the top of the ridge and plummeted toward the valley floor.

Daphne gasped.

The bad guys were traveling so fast that if they didn't slow, they'd either wreck at the bottom or overtake the two men and one woman before they had time to escape. Boomer's snowmobile was slower with two people on it. At the rate everyone was moving, it was only a matter of time before the gang following them caught up.

On the verge of second guessing her decision to use herself as bait, Daphne was surprised when Boomer topped a hill, rounded a bend in the terrain and climbed a steep incline, placing them on top of an overhang.

Hank spent a few precious minutes swishing a tree branch to cover their trail, and then took off on his snowmobile, laying down a fresh trail for their pursuers to follow.

Boomer shut down their engine, leaped off the seat and pulled out his rifle. "Stay down." He lay in the snow on the edge of the little cliff. Using the barrel of his rifle, he cleared a V-shaped wedge in the snow.

Daphne slipped off the snowmobile and dropped into the snow, low-crawling up to Boomer's left side.

They didn't speak, just waited.

Moments later, the four snowmobiles appeared.

Boomer's body tensed. He gripped his rifle in his hand, inhaled deeply and let the air out slowly, his eye trained on the scope.

"Do we know for sure these are the men who are after me?" Daphne asked.

"You want to walk down there and ask?"

She shook her head. "What if they're just recreational snowmobilers?"

Boomer's finger froze on the trigger.

As Daphne watched, the lead snowmobile came to a halt on the path below. The rider pulled off his goggles and motioned for the next man to move forward on his machine.

"You tell me. Is that Cooper or one of his hired guns?" Boomer leaned his head to the side "Look for yourself."

Daphne laid her cheek against his and stared down the scope. For a moment everything was blurred. Then she moved a little to the right and the images cleared.

The man who'd removed his goggles had dark hair and heavily tanned skin. He pulled a rifle from the scabbard on the side of the snowmobile and turned toward their position.

Daphne sucked in a sharp breath.

"Recognize him?" Boomer whispered.

Her heart pounded against her ribs. The man below her was one of the guys who'd swept in to carry off Cooper's kill in Cozumel.

Daphne leaned away from Boomer and pinched the bridge of her nose to keep from shouting out loud.

"He's a member of the cleanup crew I saw in Cozumel."

The mercenary lifted the rifle to his shoulder. He stared into the scope and spun in a circle, searching his surroundings. The man slowed as he raised his rifle to the top of the hill where Boomer and Daphne perched on the edge of the cliff.

His eyes narrowed, and a loud bang echoed off the hillside.

The snow beside Daphne puffed upward, dusting her face.

Boomer laid a hand on her head and pushed her down.

Daphne gladly lay with her cheek in the cold, white snow, afraid to raise her head for fear of getting it blown off. She watched Boomer as he resumed his position, stared down the scope and squeezed the trigger.

Daphne gasped and shoved a fist into her mouth to keep from crying out, then couldn't resist taking a peek.

Below, the gunman staggered backward, clutching his chest.

One of the other men slid off his snowmobile and dropped behind it. The tip of a rifle appeared above the seat.

"Daphne, stay down," Boomer urged.

The crack of a rifle being fired split the snow-covered silence of the mountains.

Daphne hugged the earth, making a crater in the snow.

Engines revved and moved out.

Boomer trained his weapon on the movement below and fired off another round.

Daphne looked up long enough to see two snowmobiles race off. The man who'd been shooting at them lay on his back, a bright red stain in the snow surrounding his head.

Daphne's stomach roiled and she looked around. "Where did the other two riders go?"

"I don't know."

Her heartbeat quickened, and she came halfway up on her knees. "You don't think they went back to the chalet, do you?"

Boomer leaned dangerously close to the edge of the cliff.

Daphne grabbed a handful of his jacket to keep him from sliding off and crashing to the bottom a hundred feet down.

"Their tracks lead away from the house, but I'm hearing engine noise echoing off the hills. I can't tell where they're going." He scooted back from the drop-off and stood with his head tilted, a frown denting his brow. "Do you hear that?"

Daphne listened, her heart pounding against her ribs. The thumping sound of rotor blades whipping the air came to her over the hills.

"Helicopter," Boomer said.

"Good guys or bad guys?" Daphne asked.

He shook his head. "I don't know."

A shiver shook her from head to toe. "Do you think Chuck and Maya got away?"

"Only one way to know." He pulled her to her feet and into his arms. "We need to get back to the chalet."

She nodded, her gaze dropping to his lips. "Whatever happens between the two of us, I want you to know, what we shared in Cozumel was the happiest time of my life."

His gaze darkened. "And mine." He lowered his head and captured her lips in a swift kiss that left her breathless and wanting so much more.

When Boomer raised his head, he touched a finger to her lips. "Hang onto that thought. I don't want to lose you again." He climbed onto the snowmobile.

Her heart surged with a rush of happiness. Boomer held out his arm to help her balance as she slipped on behind him, wrapped her arms around his waist and pressed her cheek to his back. Hope surged.

Just as Boomer started the engine, a single snowmobile appeared on the road below, followed by the two that had disappeared minutes before.

"Hank's in trouble," Boomer said.

Her heart banging against her ribs, Daphne leaned close to Boomer's ear to be heard over the sound of the engine. "We have to help."

Boomer's chest swelled.

The woman he'd fallen in love with on the resort island of Cozumel was brave and selfless. She'd sacrifice her own life for her daughter's, and she'd chase the enemy to save a friend.

She deserved a better man than him, but he wanted

her and couldn't think of a future without her in it. And he wanted to get to know his baby girl. Maya looked like him. If her personality was anything like his, she'd be a handful. She needed someone who would understand her and help channel her energy and curiosity into something productive. Daphne would be patient and loving, the kind of mother any little girl could need.

Boomer shook his head to clear his thoughts. Right at the moment, he needed his wits about him, needed sharp focus to help Hank and keep Daphne from being hurt.

He raced down the side of the hill and followed the two snowmobiles gaining on Hank.

Hank veered his vehicle off the trail and climbed a hill. When he reached the top, he stopped suddenly. Then he raced his snowmobile across the ridgeline.

Why wasn't he going down the other side?

The two bad guys powered up the hill after him. Thankfully, the terrain demanded both hands on the handlebars to keep the snowmobile moving steadily forward. The riders couldn't pull out weapons to fire on Hank.

But as they climbed the hill after Hank, they were exposed and vulnerable.

Boomer brought the snowmobile to a halt.

"What are you doing?" Daphne shouted over the roar of the engine. "We have to help Hank."

Nodding, he shut off the engine, pulled his rifle from the sleeve he'd strapped to the snowmobile and rested the barrel across the handlebars.

Daphne slipped off the back of the snowmobile into

a foot-and-a-half-deep snowdrift, giving Boomer more room to take aim.

He held steady, his sight trained on the snowmobile in the lead. When he was sure, he pulled the trigger.

The man on the vehicle in the lead jerked, and his hand flew into the air. The snowmobile turned, teetered and rolled sideways down the hill, throwing its rider in the process.

The second snowmobile spun and raced back down the hill, zigzagging, making the driver a more difficult target.

Boomer aimed, anticipating the next move and squeezed the trigger.

The driver jerked the handlebars. The snowmobile rocked up on one skid and dropped back to the earth, careening to the bottom of the hill where it crashed into a tree.

Hank turned his snowmobile and eased down the hillside.

Boomer trained his sights on the figure lying beside the crashed vehicle. The man moved, dragging himself through the snow toward what appeared to be a rifle that had been thrown ten feet from the crash site.

Fortunately, Hank reached the man before the man reached the rifle.

He kicked the rifle out of range of the man on the ground and pulled the man's arms behind him, securing them with a zip-tie.

"Hank has the last man secured." Boomer sat up on the snowmobile, sheathed the rifle in its scabbard and scooted forward making room for Daphne.

"Wow," she said, her voice soft and shaky. "You're really good with that rifle."

He turned to her, his brow descending as he studied her expression. "It was either them or us."

She nodded.

He waited, looking for her reaction and wondering if she could stomach this part of him.

"I know," she said softly. "I'm just glad you're with us." Daphne slid onto the seat behind him and wrapped her arms around him.

He liked the way it felt with her arms and legs pressed close. When they got back to Hank's house, he had to come to grips with his feelings for her and Maya and somehow convince himself and Daphne that he could be a part of their lives.

Boomer drove the snowmobile to where Hank had the man secured.

His boss had tended to a wound on the man's shoulder, packing it with fabric torn from the aggressor's T-shirt. Once he'd stemmed the flow of blood, he helped the man onto the back of his snowmobile, securing his wrists to the leather strap across the seat. "Let's see who we have here." He pulled off the man's helmet and glanced at Daphne. "Anyone you know?"

The injured man had dark hair and dark eyes. His face was pale from blood loss, and his head lolled a little, his eyes rolling as he tried to remain upright.

She shook her head. "Never saw him before now."

Hank snorted. "Another mercenary." He shoved the helmet back on his head and secured the strap. "We'll have to take it slow to get back to the chalet."

Boomer nodded. "You take the lead. If he falls off, I'll help you get him back on."

Hank eased the snowmobile up onto the trail, heading back the way they'd come. From the top of the ridge overlooking the chalet, Hank slowed and waited for Boomer to catch up. He removed his goggles and shot a glance at Boomer. "My truck is still there."

Boomer's gut clenched.

"What do you mean?" Daphne slid off the back of the snowmobile and stood looking down at the chalet. "Chuck and Maya should be halfway to your ranch." She grabbed the rifle from the scabbard.

Boomer reached out to take it, but she stepped out of reach.

"Hey, what are you doing?"

She squinted, staring through the scope. "Both trucks are still there."

Boomer laid his palm over the top of the rifle. Sighing she let him take it.

Hank dismounted from the snowmobile and walked several yards across the ridge to view the chalet from a different angle. He stopped suddenly and cursed.

"What?" Boomer asked.

"There's a helicopter parked in the clearing on the far side of the chalet." He shook his head. "What do you want to bet they've captured Chuck and Maya?"

Daphne gasped. "Maya." She took off running toward the trail leading down to the chalet.

Boomer caught up to her and then, holding the rifle away, he grabbed her arm and yanked her into his embrace. "What do you think you're going to do?"

She struggled against his hold. "Whatever it takes to free my baby."

"She's my baby, too. And running down there will only get you both killed."

"I can't let them hurt Maya." Daphne shook her head, tears streaming down her cheeks. "She's my life. She's all I have. I love her so much it hurts."

With his free arm, he pulled her more tightly against his chest, trapping her arms against his body. "Sweetheart, she's mine, too. I promise you we'll get her back."

"Alive?" Daphne lifted her head and bit her lip. Tears dripped from her chin.

Her pain-filled glance tore at him. "Alive," he promised, though he wasn't sure how he'd accomplish that feat. "Right now, you're the only thing keeping them from hurting her. Maya's their leverage."

Hank returned to stand beside them. "He's right. They want you. To get you, they'll use whatever they can to lure you out into the open."

Daphne tried again to shake off Boomer's embrace. "Then let me go."

He shook his head. "If you go down there now, they'll shoot you. Once you're dead, they have no reason to keep Maya alive."

"But they want me, not Maya."

"They won't leave any of us alive," Hank said. "We'd be more witnesses to be disposed of."

"But we can't stand here and do nothing," she wailed, pushing at his chest. "There's no telling what they're doing to Maya, and to Chuck, for that matter."

Boomer's jaw tightened. "When I let go of you, can

you promise me you won't run down there and get yourself shot?"

She bit her lip and stared into his eyes.

He squeezed her gently. "I promise I'll do everything in my power to save our daughter. Promise me you won't run."

Slowly, she nodded her head. "Please save my baby."

"Our baby," he said, resting his forehead against hers. "I might not know how to take care of her like you and Chuck do, but I know I'll love her as much as you do. If you'll give me the chance to be with her and you."

"Yes!" Daphne said, her voice shaking. "Just save her. Please."

Boomer released Daphne, and with the rifle in his hands started across the ridge to where Hank stood. "We have to get in a position where we can see into the chalet. We need a headcount of the number of people holding them hostage."

Daphne followed. "How will that help?"

Boomer came to a halt when he faced the chalet's front porch and dropped to his belly in the snow. "We have to know how many people we're dealing with in order to make our move and not get Chuck or Maya kil—harmed."

Daphne stumbled, righted herself and dropped down beside Boomer.

Hank passed them, carrying another rifle with a scope. "I'll go a little farther along the ridge and let you know what I see."

Boomer nodded without saying a word. He concentrated all his focus on the door and windows to the chalet.

"What do you see?" Daphne asked.

"Not much. The shadow of the porch overhang keeps the doors and windows in the dark, and without the generator running, there are no lights on inside."

Daphne grabbed his arm. "Is the door opening?"

Boomer grimaced. "Sweetheart, don't touch, bump or nudge me while I have a rifle in my hands."

"I'm sorry, but look." She pointed. "Is that Chuck?"

Boomer had already ascertained the man who stepped out of the chalet was indeed Chuck. And he carried what appeared to be a bundle of baby blankets.

Daphne drew in a sharp breath. "Oh, my God. He has Maya, doesn't he?"

What Boomer could see through his scope that Daphne could not from this distance was the handgun pressed to the back of Chuck's head. If the gun went off and the bullet ricocheted inside the man's skull, there was no telling where it would exit, and whether it would hit Maya on the other side.

Boomer's palms sweated in the cold air.

"Daphne Miller!" a voice shouted from inside the chalet, the noise echoing off the hillsides. "If you want your daughter to live, come down now. You have exactly one minute before she dies."

CHAPTER 10

"Oh, sweet Jesus." Daphne struggled to her feet and started over the edge of the ridge. "I have to go."

Boomer dropped his rifle, snagged Daphne's hand and jerked her down beside him. His expression was taut with fury. "Don't you understand? If you go, they'll kill you."

Her heart thundered against her ribs. Her baby was down there with a psychopath. What did Boomer expect her to do? Stand by and let them kill an innocent child? "Better me than Maya," she said and struggled to free her wrist.

"You can't go." Still holding her wrist with one hand, he grabbed his rifle and fumbled with the clips holding the strap to the rifle's length.

Daphne braced her feet against the snow-covered, rocky terrain and pulled with all her might.

Boomer's grip was like an iron band. He refused to release her. When he'd freed the strap, he turned to her. "You're going to hate me for this, but I can't let you go down there. I risk losing you as well as Maya. I'm not willing to lose you both now that I've found you."

She stared down at the hand holding the strap. "What are you doing?"

He wrapped the strap around her wrists and dragged her backward, away from the edge of the ridge. "You have to stay put and let me do my job."

He looped the strap over a low-hanging tree branch and pulled it tight, knotting it snuggly.

"You can't leave me here." Daphne yanked and tugged, but his handiwork held. She wasn't going anywhere. "Damn it, Boomer, that's my baby down there. You can't keep me from her."

"I'm keeping you from getting yourself killed. Now, be quiet while Hank and I figure out how to handle this situation."

"One minute, Boomer," she whispered harshly. "A quarter of that is almost gone. You have to let me go down there." She pulled so hard, the strap rubbed her wrists raw. "Please, don't let my baby die." Tears ran down her cheeks.

Boomer resumed his position and stared through the scope. He lay for so long, without moving, Daphne thought he'd fallen asleep.

Please, don't shoot my baby. Please. She repeated the mantra beneath her breath, praying for a miracle.

Maya was not just the result of fling with a handsome SEAL on a resort island. She was the hope for the future Daphne had needed after losing her fiancé. She was the result of falling in love with a real hero. A man who'd suffered while defending their country and way of life. Maya was the glue that kept Daphne together and, hopefully, would bring and keep Boomer in their lives.

If Maya died...

More tears slipped down Daphne's cheeks. If Maya died, every happiness Daphne had dreamed of would be gone. She wasn't even sure she could be with Boomer knowing their baby was dead. Her baby looked like him. Seeing him every day would be a steady, painful reminder.

Anger replaced sadness. Anyone who could hold a baby hostage had to be the lowest form of life. He didn't deserve to live. Hell, she already knew that based on how he'd choked the life out of that woman in Cozumel. Harrison Cooper deserved to die.

"If you're going to shoot someone," Daphne shouted to Boomer, "make sure it's the bastards holding my baby hostage."

BOOMER COUNTED two people inside the chalet, besides Chuck and Maya.

After the man pointing the gun at Chuck's head had issued the ultimatum, he'd pulled Chuck and Maya back inside the building and closed the door.

"Ten seconds remaining," Hank called out. "I counted two men besides Chuck and Maya.

"I got the same," Boomer acknowledged.

"From where I am, I can take out the one further inside if you can take out the one who came to the door with Chuck."

"If they come out that way again, I can do it."

"Five seconds," Daphne said. "Please don't hit Maya or Chuck. Anyone else if fair game."

Boomer's lips twitched. The woman had fight, and she would defend her child like a mother bear.

"Four…three…two…one…" Daphne whispered.

The door opened. Chuck stepped out onto the porch, holding Maya.

"Time's up!" the voice shouted.

Boomer could make out a blond-haired younger man holding a handgun to the back of Chuck's neck.

Chuck seemed to be saying something, but no sound was coming out of his mouth. He held Maya with two fingers pointing up.

Boomer concluded the man was confirming only two men were in the chalet.

Chuck leaned to one side slightly, giving Boomer a better line of sight at the man holding the gun.

He drew in a deep breath and held it, the crosshairs of his scope on the blond man's head. One slip-up, and he could kill Chuck or Maya.

Moisture gathered on his upper lip, and his finger curled around the trigger. Images of the Islamic State militant dressed in the white imam's robe rose up in Boomer's mind.

He blinked to clear the image and focused on the blond man, a far cry from the militant with the black hair and the black beard. He couldn't loose his concentration now. Not with his baby's life depending on him.

"You just sentenced your baby to death!" the man shouted.

"That man down there is not an ISIS militant. He's a murderer, and he's threatening our baby," Daphne whispered. "Shoot the bastard."

Boomer pulled himself out of the past and focused on his future. With the gentlest of pressure, he pulled the trigger.

The bullet blasted out of the rifle and a moment later hit the target.

Not even a second later, Hank fired a round, piercing the window of the chalet.

The blond man Boomer's bullet had struck jerked backward, and his gun went off. Chuck flinched and dropped to his knees, still holding the baby in his arms.

Boomer was on his feet and scrambling to release Daphne from the tree. He ran to the snowmobile and leaped onto the seat.

Daphne flung herself onto the back as Boomer revved the engine. Then they slipped and slid down the trail toward the chalet at breakneck speed.

When they came to a halt in front of the chalet, Boomer and Daphne flew off the snowmobile and ran toward the porch where Chuck sat, cradling Maya in his arms. Blood oozed from a wound on the side of his head, just above his ear.

Daphne dove for Maya and gathered the baby in her arms, peeling back the blankets to check for injuries.

"Maya's all right," Chuck said. "I made sure of it."

"Which is better than can be said for you," Boomer said quietly.

Chuck shook his head and winced. "He just nicked me."

Boomer knelt beside the blond man and felt for a pulse. There wasn't one.

"Harrison Cooper?" Boomer asked.

Chuck and Daphne nodded.

"He's dead." Boomer glanced across at Daphne. "He won't be bothering you or anyone else, ever again."

Daphne clutched Maya to her chest, her eyes narrowing. "Good. The bastard had it coming." She kissed Maya's forehead and wrapped her more tightly in the blanket.

Boomer moved into the chalet where he found a man dressed in a business suit lying on the floor, moaning, blood pooling beneath his shoulder.

Boomer stepped over the dead blond man "Who do we have here?"

"Harrison Cooper's father." Chuck had pushed to his feet and leaned against the doorframe. "Meet Senator John Cooper."

"You murdered my son," the man on the floor said through gritted teeth. "I'll have you all in the electric chair for what you've done."

"We think not," Boomer said. "Your days of killing off witnesses to your son's messes are over. The fact you're here, supported by a team of mercenaries, isn't going to look good to the authorities."

"You don't know what you're talking about," the senator said.

"The men you sent on snowmobiles to kill us didn't accomplish their mission."

"I suppose you killed them as well. The courts will see your actions as a brutal killing spree."

"The courts might have, but we saved one of your mercenaries," Boomer said. "My bet is he won't go down with you. I doubt you could pay him enough money to lie in front of judge and go to jail for you and your murdering son."

"It'll be my word against his—and yours."

"Not so fast, Senator." Chuck pulled a cell phone from his pocket. "I recorded everything—from your threats to your son's. We have multiple witnesses, including one of your own cleanup crew, who I'm sure will be eager to cut a sweet deal. You're going to jail, and your son's going to hell."

Several trucks appeared on the road leading up to the chalet. They were followed by a couple of county sheriff's vehicles.

Hank arrived on the porch, shoving the man from the snowmobile chase ahead of him. "The cavalry has arrived."

Boomer slipped an arm around Daphne. "We need to get Maya somewhere warm." With the door to the chalet wide open, and the generator turned off, the house would be as cold as the outside.

Daphne handed Maya to Boomer. "Take care of her while I help Chuck."

Boomer took Maya and tucked her, blanket and all, into his jacket.

Daphne took charge of tending to Chuck's "nick," cleaning the wound and wrapping his head in a swath of strips torn from a pillowcase.

With the bleeding stopped, Chuck smiled and hugged Daphne.

Boomer couldn't be angry with the man. He knew how it felt to be in love with Daphne, having loved her since they'd met in Cozumel.

Once law enforcement cleared them to leave after they'd promised to give their statements at the sheriff's office the following day, Boomer and Daphne took Maya and headed to the truck. They'd stay at Hank's ranch while Hank and Chuck remained behind to answer questions and make sure the senator didn't get away with his lies and treachery.

"Are you sure you don't want to wait for Chuck?" Boomer asked as he helped Daphne buckle Maya into the car seat.

She smiled over the top of Maya's head. "I love Chuck."

Boomer's heart plummeted into his belly, and he had a hard time concentrating on the multiple buckles that were part of the intricate car seat.

Daphne's grin broadened, and she reached across Maya to touch Boomer's hand. "I love Chuck like a wonderful older brother. I don't know what I would have done without him this past year, and I want him to be a part of Maya's life." She squeezed his hand. "But you were what kept him at arm's length from me. Even when you were on the other side of the world, you were always in my heart and on my mind."

Boomer released a deep breath and stared across at her, sure she could see the moisture gathering in his eyes, but not giving a damn. He gave her a half-smile. "You don't know how happy that makes me. I'd hate to have duke it out with Chuck. Especially after he took such good care of our daughter." He lifted Daphne's hand to his lips and kissed her fingertips. "I love you Daphne Miller. I never stopped thinking about you. When I was up to my eyeballs in sandstorms and ISIS militants, I thought of you and how, when I got back to the States, I'd find you."

Her smile was sweet, her eyes misty. "And then you did."

"Thanks to Chuck and Hank," Boomer said. "Remind me to thank those two for bringing us back together." He backed out of the rear seat and closed the door. Before he could get around the truck to help Daphne into the passenger seat, she was already inside.

He'd have to step up his game if he wanted to show her how much she'd come to mean to him.

CHAPTER 11

Once he was behind the wheel of Hank's truck, Boomer eased down the road. The parade of trucks and sheriff's SUVs had packed the snow and made it easier to see the drop-offs. They made good time all the way back to the ranch.

When they pulled up in front of the sprawling ranch house, Boomer shifted into park, cut the engine and climbed down, hurrying around to Daphne's side. He opened the door and reached in, capturing her around the waist.

She laughed, the sound so much lighter and happier than he could remember. "I can get down from the truck myself."

"I know that. You're a very independent woman. Still…" He lifted her out of her seat and let her slide down his front until her feet touched the ground. "I like the way you feel against me."

"Mmm…you have a good point." She leaned up on

her toes and pressed her lips to his. "And I like the way you taste."

He lowered his head and took her mouth in a crushing kiss. The sound of Maya stirring in the backseat brought him back to earth, reminding him they had responsibilities. "I'll bet she's hungry."

"Probably so." Daphne unbuckled the baby from the car seat and carried her into house. She found a chair in the living room and settled down long enough to nurse Maya.

Boomer sat across from her. "Do you mind if I watch?"

Daphne shrugged. "Not at all."

He stared at the baby, suckling at her mother's breast. "Where did you get the name Maya?"

Daphne brushed a dark strand of Maya's hair back from her forehead. "Remember when you found me on the beach in Cozumel on what was supposed to have been my honeymoon?"

He nodded. "You were sobbing buckets of tears. Seeing you like that nearly broke my heart."

Daphne smiled. "You were so good to listen to my sad story." Her smile faded. "Before Jonah died, he made me promise to go on the honeymoon and be open to love and life. Had he lived, we would have named our firstborn child after the resort where we were supposed to have shared on our honeymoon. So you see, you were not my first love." Daphne looked up into his face.

Boomer's brow twisted. "I'm not sure how I'm supposed to feel about that."

She smiled. "Good. I truly believe Jonah sent you to

be with me in Cozumel. He was the guardian angel that led me to you." She held out her hand and took his in hers. "You might not have been my first love, but you are my last love and the father of our little girl."

"I will be sure to say a prayer for Jonah, thanking him for giving you to me and for the beautiful baby girl we have." He leaned over and kissed the baby's cheek. "Maya is a beautiful name for a beautiful little girl."

Daphne cupped his cheek. "You're not afraid of her anymore?"

"I was never afraid of Maya. I was more afraid I wouldn't be good enough for her."

"You're going to be a great father," Daphne said with a certainty Boomer wished he could feel.

"I hope so. One thing is for sure…I'm going to give it my best."

"That's all any parent can do." Daphne handed Maya to him. "You can start by learning to change her diaper. Then she'll need to be burped." Daphne winked. "Don't worry. You're going to be great."

Boomer laughed. "Yes, ma'am. I'd be honored." He gathered Maya in his arms and leaned over to press a kiss to Daphne's lips. "I love you Daphne Miller. And someday soon, I hope to marry you and Maya. You both mean so much to me."

Daphne's eyes widened. "Is that a proposal?"

He grinned. "Why yes. But if you want me to do a better job of it, I can do the whole down-on-a-knee thing." He started to get down on his knee, but Daphne stopped him by wrapping her arms around his neck, sandwiching Maya between them. "You don't have to do that. My answer is yes!"

Behind Boomer, a door opened and the clump of boots on the wooden floors heralded the entry of a number of men.

"Are we interrupting something?" Hank's voice called out. "We could go to the Blue Moose Tavern and have a drink or two and return later, if you like."

Boomer and Daphne turned to face Hank, Chuck and half a dozen of the Brotherhood Protectors.

Boomer laughed. "You don't have to leave. I'm betting you have beer and champagne somewhere in this big, beautiful house."

"Are we celebrating something?" Chuck asked, appearing like a wounded soldier with his head wrapped in white strips of fabric.

Boomer hooked his arm around Daphne's waist and hugged Maya with the other. "She said yes. Daphne, Maya and I are getting married."

Chuck's lips tightened for only a moment before he grinned. "About time. We can celebrate your engagement and Daphne's freedom from hiding."

"What happened to the senator?" Daphne asked.

"The sheriff hauled him off to jail."

"Who flew the helicopter?"

"Harrison Cooper had a pilot's license," Hank said. "His father was in the state campaigning for reelection. He flew him over to the chalet to witness what his money had bought in the way of mercenaries."

"Any chance the senator will be cleared of all charges?" Daphne asked.

Chuck shook his head. "No way. The hired gun was already asking for a plea bargain, claiming he'd spill his guts for a more lenient sentence."

Daphne sighed. "Then it's true? I'm free?"

Chuck nodded. "You're free."

She leaned into Boomer's side. "Then I can go shopping and not worry about being shot at."

Boomer laughed. "Yes, you can go shopping."

"Then tomorrow, I want to go to Bozeman to pick out my wedding dress." She stared up at Boomer. "You weren't kidding when you asked me to marry you, were you?"

He shook his head. "I want you in my life. I want to be there for you and Maya. The sooner the better."

She leaned up on her toes and kissed him. "Sooner, please."

Hank emerged from the kitchen, carrying glasses and a bottle of champagne. "If you prefer beer, there's a stash in the bar refrigerator."

Swede, Taz, Bear and Duke bypassed the champagne and went straight for the beer. Swede brought a longneck bottle to Boomer.

Daphne laughed and held up her hand to Hank. "You might as well put the champagne back in the fridge. I can't drink while I'm nursing, and I'm betting you'd rather have a beer."

Hank grinned. "You got that right."

Duke handed Hank a beer and all the men raised their bottles.

"To Daphne and Boomer!"

Boomer leaned down and kissed his bride-to-be. "Your strength makes me want to be a better man."

She cupped his cheek. "I love you, my Montana SEAL daddy."

If you enjoyed this story, you will enjoy these books by Elle James:

Brotherhood Protector Series
Montana SEAL (#1)
Bride Protector SEAL (#2)
Montana D-Force (#3)
Cowboy D-Force (#4)
Montana Ranger (#5)
Montana Dog Soldier (#6)
Montana SEAL Daddy (#7)
Montana Ranger's Wedding Vow (#8)
Montana SEAL Undercover Daddy (#9)
Montana Rescue

MONTANA RANGER'S WEDDING VOW

BROTHERHOOD PROTECTORS BOOK #8

New York Times & *USA Today*
Bestselling Author

ELLE JAMES

MONTANA RANGER'S WEDDING VOW

BROTHERHOOD PROTECTORS

NEW YORK TIMES BESTSELLING AUTHOR
ELLE JAMES

CHAPTER 1

"I GET THAT BROTHERHOOD PROTECTORS ARE bodyguards, but what kind of assignments can I expect?" Vince "Viper" Van Cleave had asked earlier that morning. His first time in Montana and his first official day as a new recruit to the Brotherhood Protectors, and he'd now gotten the answer to his question.

"It varies. For instance, I'm covering a wedding at the Brighter Days Rehab Ranch today. Not only am I providing protection for the bride, I'm driving the limousine with the bride and groom to the airport in Bozeman." Chuck Johnson went through the arsenal in Hank Patterson's basement, selecting a Glock nine-millimeter handgun and a shoulder holster. "You can come along as my backup and follow me to the airport to bring me back. I'm dropping off the limo there and need a ride back."

"That's it?" Viper stared at the array of handguns, rifles and grenade launchers that would make any Delta

Force soldier envious. "All you want me to do is go to a wedding and follow you to the airport?"

"Until Hank tasks you with your first assignment, you can hang with me and see what we do...sometimes."

Viper glanced around at the arsenal. "A glorified chauffeur needs to carry a weapon?"

"And protective service," Chuck emphasized. "Even the simplest assignments have a way of getting sticky. You never know."

"Why do you need to provide protection at a wedding?"

"The bride is a Montana senator's daughter and physical therapist at the ranch. The groom is one of our own...Taz Davila, a former Army Ranger."

Viper could appreciate the show of support for a teammate. He had been close to the men in his unit and hated leaving them when he'd retired. He was glad to see the brotherhood had each other's backs. "How long have you been with the team?"

Chuck grinned. "About a month...not long. I resigned from the DEA to come to work for Hank. I wanted to stay in the area."

"Staying because of a girl?" Viper lifted a rifle and weighed it in his hands, while imagining the amazing woman Chuck gave up the DEA for. A stab of guilt hit him in the gut. If he'd left the Navy when his wife got pregnant, he might still have a little family.

Chuck grinned. "You bet. The prettiest girl you ever met."

His chest tightened. "Congratulations. You two going to be next at the altar?"

Chuck barked a laugh.

Viper looked at him over the AR15 he held. "What? Not the marrying kind?"

"I love the girl, but I'm not marrying her. She's only a baby."

Viper frowned. "What do you mean?"

"While with the DEA, I provided support to the witness protection program. Baby Maya's mother witnessed a murder. I had to keep the two of them alive for about a year before the bad guys got wind of their location. Then the shit hit the fan, and we came here. Hank helped me protect them until we could flush out the adversaries."

Protecting innocents from murderers was the kind of work Viper could see himself doing. His interest captured, he glanced toward Chuck. "How did you know about Hank's operation?"

"He and I go back to our days as Navy SEALs."

His gaze swept over Chuck. "You were a SEAL?" The man was older than him, but his shoulders were broad and he still appeared to be in good shape.

Chuck snorted. "I know, it's hard to believe. An old guy like me."

"Seriously, you're not that old."

"I'll be forty-seven next month."

"That's not old." Viper shook his head. "I never thought I'd live to retire from Delta Force. But I proved the younger men wrong, and here I am."

"Glad you made it." Chuck pounded Viper on the back. "Us old guys have to stick together. You'll like it here. Hank has a great setup. I don't know anywhere else I could get a job doing what I love and still be close to that kid." Chuck's lips twisted into a wry grin. "Maya has me wrapped around her little finger. Never considered having kids of my own, but this arrangement is the next best thing. I get to be Uncle Chuck."

"What about the mother? Not interested?" Viper asked.

"She's a beautiful, wonderful woman." Chuck's lips pressed together. "But she loves another guy."

"That sucks."

"For me, yeah." He shrugged. "But *she's* happy. That's what counts. And he's a Navy SEAL. I can't be too mad about that. She could do worse. She could have married a Delta Force puke."

Viper frowned. "Watch it."

Chuck laughed. "Just kidding. I worked a number of missions in the sandbox with Delta Force guys. Next to Navy SEALs, they're the second-best special operations men around."

"SEALs being first?" Viper harrumphed. "Not full of yourself much, are you?"

"Damn right, I am. I worked hard to earn the right to be an ass."

"And while the Delta Force soldiers are preserving your freedom by fighting the good fight on foreign soil, you're chauffeuring a bride and groom through their wedding and off on their honeymoon."

Chuck grinned. "Damn right. I did my part while on active duty and then with the DEA. Being with the Brotherhood Protectors is a damned good job. And I get to be home tonight to watch the Cowboys play ball on the big screen at the Blue Moose Tavern. You're welcome to join me, if you're up to drinking a beer."

"You're on," Viper said. "But I'll be rooting for the New Orleans Saints."

"Then forget it. I retract my invitation."

Viper chuckled. He liked the easy camaraderie he'd found with Chuck. When Viper retired from active duty and didn't know what he'd do next with his life, Hank had given him a job.

Hank and his wife, Sadie, welcomed him into their home while he looked for a place to live in Eagle Rock, Montana. The other members he'd had the pleasure of meeting had all been like brothers. "Hank has all this equipment for the Brotherhood Protectors?"

"Only the best," Chuck said. "Like I said, you'll like it here."

LATER THAT NIGHT, after the wedding of the senator's daughter to one of his new teammates, Viper followed the limousine Chuck drove. The happily married bride and groom were on their way to their rendezvous with an airplane that would whisk them away to Maui, their honeymoon destination.

Viper wasn't well-versed on weddings, having only gone through one. His own. But, as far as Hannah Kendricks and Taz Davila's nuptials went, the event had gone off without a hitch. All of Hank's team that weren't deployed to various engagements showed up in force. The wedding was casual, the bride glowing, and the groom happier than any man Viper ever knew. And the groomsmen were an array of rehabilitating veterans with missing limbs, PTSD, and nothing but good things to say about Hannah and Taz in their many toasts.

It did Viper's spirits good to see so many people laughing and enjoying the celebration of two people who were obviously in love getting hitched. The couple's joy gave Viper hope for other veterans who were having difficulty finding their way in their postwar civilian lives.

Viper had given marriage a shot, but it hadn't ended the way he'd planned. While he'd been deployed on a super-secret mission, his wife had died. He'd never quite gotten over the tragedy. He still lived with the guilt of not being there for Emily when she needed him most. From that point forward, he'd committed himself to being a bachelor. Special Forces soldiers had no business being married. They were on call all the time and gone from home more months out of the year than they were present.

Now that he was retired and not subject to long-distance and long-duration deployments, Viper might consider finding someone to share his life with. But he wasn't ready to jump into marriage with just anyone. His wife had been special. Any other woman would have to measure up, and then some.

He studied the taillights of the limousine in front of him as they traversed the mountain roads, heading southeast to Bozeman.

Viper's parents had been the model for a happily married couple. His father worshipped his mother. The woman could do no wrong. She was the kindest, most caring woman Viper could have asked for as a mother. And she loved his father completely. His father treated his mother with tremendous adoration and respect and never had a cross word to say to her.

Viper had been lucky to find Emily, a woman very much like his mother. Kind and nurturing. She'd deserved a better man than him. One who could have been there every night.

Viper wanted that perfect union and wouldn't settle for anything less.

As he considered the woman he could potentially fall in love with, he added more qualifications to the list that started with *kind*, *gentle* and *loving*.

She didn't have to be beautiful, but petite, with long, flowing blond hair would be good for a start. And well-endowed. Yes. He liked a woman with curves in all the right places.

He focused on the road ahead as the hairpin twists grew tighter, and what he could see of the shoulders of the highway dropped off into darkness. He'd driven the route the day before to arrive at White Oak Ranch, the base of operations for the Brotherhood Protectors.

The roads had been dangerous in the light of day. They were even trickier in the darkness, requiring much slower speeds to navigate them safely.

Viper maintained several car-lengths' distance from the limousine ahead. He didn't want to intrude on the newlyweds' privacy by shining his headlights into their back window.

The limousine rounded a sharp curve, disappearing out of sight for a moment.

Viper didn't worry too much but increased his speed and then slowed as he took the curve. When he could see the limo's taillights again, he wondered at the distance between the two vehicles.

They were heading down a mountain, which explained the increased speed, but he couldn't understand why Chuck wasn't using his brakes more to slow their descent.

Viper punched the accelerator on the straight stretches in an attempt to catch up to the now racing limo. What was wrong with Chuck? Didn't he realize the roads were too crooked to take at such a high rate of speed?

The limousine didn't even slow as it entered the next curve. Nor did the brake lights blink on.

By then, Viper's pulse had picked up. His gut told him something wasn't right. He wished he'd opted for some of the radio equipment Hank had stored in his basement. At the time he and Chuck had been looking through the array of devices he hadn't thought communications equipment would be necessary for a wedding.

But as he raced down the mountain behind the wedding limousine, plunging down the road at an increasingly dangerous speed, he wished he could communicate with Chuck to find out what the hell was happening.

Chuck hit the next curve going so fast the limousine's backend spun sideways. The rear wheels skidded across the pavement, heading for the guardrail.

Viper held his breath, his foot on the brake, bracing

himself for the wreck he suspected would happen in the next second.

Somehow, Chuck managed to keep the limousine on the road, the rear bumper scraping the guardrail as they swung around the curve.

But the descent continued to be steep and the curves tightened.

At the next bend in the road, the limousine wasn't as lucky.

Viper guessed the limousine was traveling at fifty or sixty miles per hour as it plowed into a curve with caution signs indicating half that speed as necessary to negotiate the turn. With no protective guardrail to keep it on the road, the rear of the limousine swung wide, the back tires sliding off onto the dirt shoulder.

When the back fell off the road, the rest of the limousine followed and the entire vehicle slipped into the darkness.

His heart in his throat, Viper slammed on his brakes in the middle of the curve, pulled onto the narrow shoulder and brought the truck to a screeching halt.

He leaped out onto the ground and ran to the edge where the limousine had disappeared. He couldn't see anything but a black abyss. Pulse pounding, he ran back to the truck, punched the hazard lights button and fished in the glove box for a flashlight. Thankfully, he found one and ran back to the roadside.

This time, when he looked over the ledge he was relieved to see the limousine about thirty feet down a steep incline. It appeared to be wedged up against a small tree, bent at a dangerous angle.

If he ran down the hill, he could slip and fall, adding to the weight of the heavy vehicle and pushing it against the tree. His weight could be the straw that broke the tree and sent the limo crashing farther down the slope and over the cliff below.

He needed a rope and some help. Back at the truck, he checked for reception on his cellphone and cursed when it displayed No Service.

With no one looking for them for the next couple hours, Viper was responsible for handling the situation to the best of his ability.

He searched the truck bed, under and behind the backseat and finally found a rope and gloves. He tied the rope to the trailer hitch at the rear of the truck then tossed it over the edge. Stuffing the flashlight into his shirt, he wrapped his gloved hand around the rope and eased his way down the steep hillside to the limo. Surprisingly, the engine was still running.

He reached the driver's door first and shined the flashlight through the window.

Chuck lay slumped over the steering wheel, the air bag having deflated beneath his cheek. A fine layer of dust covered his face and chest.

Using the hard, plastic end of the flashlight, Viper tapped the window without using too much force. He was afraid even the slightest weight on the vehicle could cause the little tree holding it precariously in place to snap, and send the limo plummeting the rest of the way down the cliff.

Chuck didn't move.

Again, he tapped the window with the flashlight.

The limo shifted, slipping farther down the hill, bending the little tree practically in half.

Then the back window lowered, and Hannah Davila's face appeared, her eyes wide, a gash on her cheek bleeding. "Help us," she pleaded.

"Taz?"

"He's coming to. But he hit the window pretty hard." She glanced toward the driver's seat. "Chuck isn't responding to the intercom and the glass is up between us. Do you know…is he okay?"

"I can't tell. He's slumped over the steering wheel. But the airbag deployed, so hopefully his injuries won't be life-threatening." As long as they got him out of the vehicle before it plunged the rest of the way down the hill.

"You all have to help me. The slope is too steep for me to carry any of you away from the wreckage."

Hannah bit her lip. "How bad is the drop-off?"

"You don't want to know," Viper said, a frown pinching his forehead. "But the sooner we get you three out of the car and up the hill, the better."

Hannah shook her head slowly, as if weighing her options. Then she pressed her lips together in a tight line. "We're getting out of here." She ducked from sight for a moment.

Viper heard the sound of ripping fabric and Hannah's voice calling, "Taz, sweetheart, you have to wake up enough to help us move you."

"What happened?" a groggy voice sounded.

"We were in an accident."

"Did we get married?"

Hannah laughed like she was choking back a sob. "Yes, darling. But we have to leave this vehicle. Now."

"You tore your dress?" he asked.

"To hell with it. I'd rather live than worry about a silly outfit."

"Is the accident that bad?" Taz said.

"Yeah," Viper answered loud enough Taz could hear him through the opening. Holding onto the rope, he walked sideways to where he could peer in through the open window. "You need to exit the vehicle and get Hannah up the hill. The sooner the better."

Because of the angle of the limo, Taz lay scrunched against the other door with Hannah leaning against him.

She fumbled with the seatbelt and unbuckled the clasp.

"Viper?" Taz frowned up at the open window. "Are you going on our honeymoon with us?"

Viper grinned, his blood humming with a surge of adrenaline. "No, but you won't be going either, if you don't wake up and get out of the limo, pronto."

Taz touched a hand to his temple. "Must have hit my head harder than I thought."

Hannah nodded. "You have to get it together because we have to climb to reach the road." She tugged on his arm, attempting to get him out of the cramped position he maintained against the door.

"I can get up on my own," he said. "You need to get out first."

"I'm not going until you're out, so get moving," she ordered.

If the situation hadn't been so dire, Viper would have laughed at the sternness of Hannah's command and that she was yelling at a man who probably had put fear in the hearts of the Taliban and ISIS.

"I'm going. I'm going," Taz muttered and pushed himself upright, bracing his feet against the door. He reached for Hannah, grabbed her around the waist and hoisted her through the open window. "You're going first."

"Damn it, Taz. You're in no condition to argue."

"I'm not arguing." He looked to Viper. "Do you have her?"

Viper slipped the flashlight into his tethered hand, extended his free hand and took Hannah's. "You'll have to help yourself. I'm holding onto a rope with the other hand."

"I've got this," she said, but she let him guide her hand to the line.

"Follow the rope to the top of the hill and wait by the truck," Viper instructed. "And whatever you do, don't lose your grip."

"Believe me, I won't." She climbed a few feet upward and glanced back, her brows wrinkled.

"Don't worry," Viper said. "I'll make sure the groom gets out okay."

"And Chuck?" she asked, nodding toward the driver's door. "Will he be all right?"

"I'll do what I can," was all Viper could promise. Until Chuck regained consciousness, he would be impossible to extricate without the help of a rescue team with mountain climbing equipment.

Taz reached upward, grabbed the edges of the window and hauled himself onto the side of the limo.

The vehicle shifted suddenly and slipped another couple of inches down the slope, bending the small tree at an even more precarious angle.

"Now would be a good time to get out of the limo," Viper said in his calmest tone, though his jaw hardened and his heart beat so fast he thought it might leap out of his chest. He reached out to Taz. "Take my hand. I'll guide you to the rope."

Taz shook his head. "You can't get Chuck out by yourself."

"I'll help," Hannah offered, backing down a step.

"No!" both Taz and Viper said as one.

"Okay, okay, you don't have to yell," she said. "Just get Chuck out and climb the hell up the hill."

"We will. But we can't be worrying about you," Taz said. "Knowing you're safe will make our jobs easier."

"I'm on my way, then." She started up the rope, pulling herself hand over hand. "Please, don't do something stupid and get yourself killed. Because I love you, dear husband. Not to mention, I'm too young to be a widow."

"Love you, too, Mrs. Davila," Taz called out after her. Then he turned his attention to the driver's door. "We need to get that door open."

"It doesn't appear to be dented." Viper lowered himself by the rope to get closer to the limo without adding his weight to the vehicle. "With the direction the limo is tilted, gravity will make opening it difficult."

"Yeah, but we're not leaving Chuck." Taz reached for

the handle and pulled. It didn't budge. "Damn. It's locked. Chuck!" Taz yelled. "Wake up, Chuck!"

The man behind the steering wheel didn't move.

"I could crawl inside and check if I can get the window to lower between the front and the back." Taz eased toward the rear window, holding onto tree roots and rocky outcroppings as he moved.

"No," Viper said. "You need to stay outside the limo in case it breaks free of the tree holding it."

"But we can't leave Chuck in there."

"We won't." Viper pulled the Glock nine-millimeter pistol from the holster beneath his jacket.

Taz's eyes rounded. "You're not shooting out the window, are you? You might hit Chuck."

"No, I'm not. But this weapon is heavier than the flashlight." He dropped the magazine out of the handle, cleared the chamber and turned the gun to hold it by the barrel. Then, with a firm hand, he hit the window hard. The butt of the pistol made a small crack in the glass.

Praying he didn't put too much force on the vehicle, Viper swung again. This time, the window shattered, but remained intact. "Three's a charm," Viper muttered and hit it again. The glass collapsed inward. Using the pistol, Viper cleared the broken shards away from the frame and reached in to feel Chuck's neck for a pulse. Several seconds later, he let go of the breath he'd been holding. "He's alive."

"Thank God." Taz made the sign of the cross on his chest. "Now, how do we get an unconscious man out of a car before it falls the rest of the way down this hill?"

"We have to wake him up. We can't do this without his help." Careful not to put too much of his weight on the limo, Viper leaned in and lightly slapped Chuck's face. "Hey, buddy, you have to wake up."

The man didn't even flutter an eyelash.

Viper tried again, this time applying more of a pop to his slap and shouting, "Chuck! Wake up! The house is on fire! You have to get Maya out!"

Chuck jerked awake, his eyes rounding. "Maya. Where's Maya?"

"She's safe, Chuck, but we have to get you out of that car and up the hill behind me."

"What happened?"

"Doesn't matter now. What matters is helping you out of the car."

He looked at the steering wheel and the deflated airbag. "I can't seem to move."

"You have to release the seatbelt," Viper said. "And be ready, because you'll fall as soon as you do."

Before Viper could finish his sentence, Chuck clicked his belt button and slid to the other side of the vehicle. The limo shuddered and teetered on the little tree.

Taz wrapped his hand around the end of the rope Viper clung to. "Chuck, grab my hand."

Chuck fumbled as if making heads or tails of where he was. When he looked up, he frowned. "You can't pull me out of this."

"No, but I can help," Taz said.

The limousine slipped, tilting toward the front end,

the back rising. If it tilted much more, the limo would slide right off the little tree and continue down the hill.

"Take our hands." Viper leaned down, extending his free arm beside Taz's. "Now!" he commanded.

Chuck reached up and clasped Viper's hand. Taz grabbed his other arm.

The limo shifted and slid several inches.

"Get him up!" Viper yelled, dragging Chuck out through the window as the vehicle slipped farther and rolled free of the little tree anchoring it to the side of the steep hill.

Chuck's feet caught on the window, dragging him backward with the force of the falling limousine.

Taz and Viper held on.

Viper's muscles strained with the weight of the big guy pulling on his left arm.

The limousine continued down the hill, crashing over rocks and small trees and finally falling over the end of a drop off.

A couple seconds later, a loud metallic crunch sounded, echoing off the hillsides.

Chuck dangled for a moment, kicking his feet to find purchase on the rocky slope. When he did, he quickly grabbed for the rope and hauled himself up beside the other two men. "What are we waiting for? Let's get out of here."

"No kidding. That was entirely too close," Taz said.

Viper dragged in a deep breath and shook out his aching arm. "Let's do it."

Taz went first, followed by Chuck. Then Viper

pulled himself up the rope to the top of the hill where the bride waited anxiously for her groom to join her.

Once all three men stood with Hannah, Chuck clapped a hand against Viper's back. "And that's what I meant by things don't always go according to plan."

Viper shook his head. "That's all jacked up."

Taz and Chuck laughed.

But Viper didn't see anything funny. His knees wobbled and his heart raced with the residuals of his adrenaline rush. "What the hell did I sign up for?"

CHAPTER 2

DALLAS HAYES ADJUSTED HER PROSTHETIC LEG, PULLED on her blue jeans and a pair of boots and headed out of the main house at the Brighter Days Rehab Ranch.

Once outside, she stretched both arms over her head and marveled at how blue the Montana skies were and how chilly the air was even in late June.

Even though everyone on the ranch had been up a good portion of the night, the animals still needed to be cared for and work had to be done to clean up after the wedding that had taken place the day before.

Gavin Blackstock, dressed in jeans and a faded blue chambray shirt, appeared in the barn door and shaded his brown-black eyes against the sunshine. "Mornin', Hayes."

Dallas nodded. "Hear any more from the Davilas?"

"After the doc cleared them to fly, they caught a later plane out of Bozeman and made their connection to Maui. I got a text around five saying they were in their bungalow, about to crash." Gavin winced. "Poor choice of words. About to go to sleep for the first time since the wedding."

"Cruddy way to start a marriage, if you ask me." She tilted her head to the side, a frown pulling her brows together. "What about the driver? How's Chuck?"

"He's pretty banged up. He's staying the night in the hospital, but the doc thinks he'll be fine."

Dallas nodded. "Glad to hear it." She glanced around the barnyard. "What's top on your list of chores that need to be done today?"

He nodded toward the stacks of chairs and tables waiting to be loaded. "We need to load the rented items onto the trailer and drive them into Eagle Rock. I'll get Franklin and Vasquez to help."

"Looking for us?" Brody Franklin, a blond-haired, green-eyed medically retired Army private, had just celebrated his twenty-first birthday a few days before the Davila wedding. He emerged from the barn, a little worse for wear after having had his share of the kegs of beer at the reception.

He was followed by Xavier Vasquez, the twenty-three-year-old former Marine.

Both young men had been on the ranch for several months and knew their way around. They'd proven they could handle any work thrown their way. As a team. Each man had lost an arm—Franklin his right, and Vasquez his left—during their last deployments. But together, they'd established a rhythm that worked for both. They performed the work of two men despite their missing limbs.

Dallas envied their easy camaraderie, something she

hadn't had since she'd declared her intention to complete Army Ranger training. Once she'd set her sights on that goal, her friends backed away and her peers steered clear. They wanted nothing to do with a female daring to step into the formerly male-dominated world of combat.

She hadn't been the first female to go through the training, nor would she be the last. She had been fortunate to follow the first three very strong and determined women who'd blazed the trail through Ranger training. She'd wanted to prove to them, as well as herself, their sacrifices hadn't been in vain.

"Hey, Ranger," Gavin said. "Hank said he was stopping by the ranch on his way back from the hospital in Bozeman. He wanted to speak with you. So, don't disappear. He should be here in the next twenty minutes."

"Hank Patterson?" She narrowed her eyes. "Taz Davila's boss? What's he want with me?"

"I don't know. I'm just passing on the information." Gavin turned back to the barn. "I'll be working with Little Joe if you need me. He's due a good hoof cleaning. When you're done with the chairs and tables, you can help Mize in the stalls. You know the drill by now."

Dallas's lips twisted. "They always need mucking. I don't know why my therapist thought this place would be a good idea. All I've done since I've been here is manual labor. How am I supposed to move on with my life if I don't get a real job?"

Gavin stopped and turned back to Dallas. "You don't

consider working with your hands and the animals a real job?"

Dallas squirmed under his direct stare. "That's not what I meant."

"What did you mean?"

She drew in a deep breath and let it go before responding. "It's not a job I'll be doing for the rest of my life. I need to get on with my career."

"And you consider your time here on the ranch as a waste?" Gavin's jaw tightened. "Well, you better get busy wasting your time, because the chores won't get done on their own. Everyone pulls his or her own weight around here. Most do it without complaining." With that parting comment, Gavin left her standing in the barnyard.

Having been thoroughly put in her place, Dallas squared her shoulders and turned toward Franklin and Vasquez.

Both men grinned.

"You've just been initiated into the wrath of Blackstock." Franklin held up his only hand for a high five.

Dallas hesitated and then slapped his hand. It was that, or he'd hold it up all day.

Vasquez held up the opposite hand, obligating Dallas to slap it as well. "Consider yourself one of us now."

"We had a few concerns ourselves when we arrived at the ranch," Franklin admitted. He glanced at his friend and his smile broadened. "We worked it out and are better for the effort. Right?"

Vasquez nodded. "Right. It taught us we could do anything we set our minds to. We just had to find a way without the use of the limb we lost and rely a lot on teamwork."

Jimmy Young emerged from the barn, covered in hay, moving his body by planting gloved hands on the ground and swinging his torso between his arms.

Dallas couldn't help but be amazed at how well the young man with no legs got around.

"Hey, Ranger," he said. "If you'll hand me the chairs, I'll stack them on the back of the trailer." He pulled himself up onto the trailer and held out both hands. "Come on. I don't have all day. I need to exercise the ponies when we're done here."

Dallas grabbed a chair and handed it to Young. He stacked the chair against the side of the trailer wall and held out his hand for the next one.

They worked, Dallas and Young, stacking chairs while Vasquez and Franklin loaded all the folding tables. By the time they were done, a big, black, four-wheel-drive truck had pulled into the barnyard, followed by a charcoal gray truck.

Hank Patterson dropped down from the driver's seat of the black truck.

Dallas had met the man the day before at the wedding. He'd been with his pretty movie-star wife, Sadie McClain, and their daughter, Emma.

Today, he was accompanied not by his wife, but by a man who climbed down from the second vehicle. He'd been introduced to the wedding party as the new guy on the Brotherhood Protectors team, Vince Van Cleave, or Viper, as he preferred to be called.

He appeared in the nice clothes he'd worn the day

before, but they were muddy and torn. Dirt smeared Viper's face, and his eyes were slightly sunken, as if he'd had less sleep the night before than she had.

"Miss Hayes." Hank approached and held out his hand.

Dallas took the proffered hand and gave it a firm shake. "Mr. Patterson."

"Call me Hank." He gave an abbreviated smile. "Blackstock told you I wanted to speak to you?"

"He did."

"Good." He nodded toward the man at his side. "You've met Viper?"

She nodded.

"We were introduced yesterday at the wedding," Viper verified.

The deep resonance of his voice sent a strange ripple of awareness across Dallas's senses, and she gave the man another look.

He was tall. A few inches taller than Hank. He wasn't as young as Hank, based on the salt gray streaks at his temples. Light blue eyes bored into her, making her wonder what he saw. Did he find her lacking in some way?

Not that she cared. When she'd signed on to be a Ranger, she knew her status would be off-putting to most men. Especially those who served or had served in the military. So many men took issue with women in combat and snubbed her without getting to know her.

Dallas lifted her chin. She didn't need a man in her life to make her complete. What she needed was a job, a home and a place where she could start over, one leg short of being a whole person.

"Can we go inside the house to talk?" Hank asked.

Dallas shrugged. "I guess. It's not my house, but Miss Kendricks—Mrs. Davila—assured me I could make myself at home." She led the way to the sprawling ranch house, climbed the steps to the porch and held the door for Hank and Viper.

Hank entered.

When Viper stepped past her, his broad shoulder brushed against her breast.

A shock of electricity shot through her body, pooling low in her belly. The guy, dirt and all, was more man than any of the soldiers she'd accompanied through Ranger school.

"Pardon me," he said in that tone that had every one of her nerves on alert.

"No problem," Dallas said, unsure of how to respond. She had zero experience with men in any other sense than that of a battle buddy. She could provide cover fire, carry a two-hundred-pound body out of harm's way and lob a grenade like a professional baseball player. But she didn't know how to flirt, bat her eyelashes or react to a man when his touch made her insides go all mushy.

What the hell?

She shook off the feeling and followed the big guy into the house, her cheeks burning. She hoped the heat would subside before she faced him again.

Hank found his way to the kitchen and the automatic coffeemaker which still had half a pot keeping warm. "Want a cup?" he asked Viper.

Viper shoved a hand through his hair and nodded. "I could use one. And a shower."

"I can offer you the coffee, but as for the shower, you can get that when we've had a chance to discuss the situation." Hank waved a hand toward the cabinets. "Now, where can I find a mug?"

Dallas reached into a cabinet and retrieved three mugs. She hadn't bothered with breakfast, after sleeping past dawn. She preferred a stiff cup of caffeine instead of the usual eggs and bacon Cookie, the ranch cook, stirred up each morning.

She handed the mugs to Hank, who waited with the coffee pot. He poured out three cups and set them on the large kitchen table that seated over a dozen people. The day before, the table had been moved outside for the meal following the wedding.

Dallas pulled out one of the chairs and sat in front of a steaming mug. She inhaled the aroma of strong coffee, letting it calm her. She had a feeling whatever Hank had to say would be a game-changer. The serious look on his face portended nothing less. Not one to beat around the bush, Dallas launched with, "What is it you wanted to talk to me about?"

Hank stared down at his coffee for a moment as if gathering his thoughts. Then he looked up, straight into Dallas's eyes. "What happened last night nearly got three people killed. One of my men is lying in a hospital pretty banged up."

"I was sorry to hear about the incident," Dallas acknowledged. "What does that have to do with me?"

"Based on what Chuck was able to tell me, the brakes didn't work. As soon as we can collect the limousine from the side of that hill, I'll have a mechanic go over the vehicle with a fine-tooth comb. But I have a feeling the brake lines were cut."

Dallas frowned. "You don't think I had anything to do with damaging the limo, do you?"

Hank waved her worry aside with a sweep of his hand. "No, of course not. But I talked with my wife, who keeps up with the local social events more than me. She tells me a number of questionable occurrences happened at several weddings in the county over the past few weeks. In one case, the bride ended up in the hospital with a concussion after the rose arbor they'd had specially built for the wedding collapsed on top of her."

Dallas didn't understand the need to spend money on special settings that would only be torn down the day after a wedding. "Sounds like faulty construction."

"The builder was very careful, knowing how strong the winds can get in these parts. The arbor had been sabotaged. Someone sawed through the brace posts holding the upper section. All it took was a person bumping against it and it came down."

Dallas sat forward. "Sawed into it? As in deliberately?"

Hank nodded. "That's exactly what I mean. And at another wedding, the wine the bride and groom drank had been poisoned. They were lucky they threw up most of what they drank and were airlifted to the hospital in time for medical help."

"That's awful. Who would do that?"

"Some sick son of a bitch who doesn't like weddings?" Viper suggested. "Excuse my language."

"I don't give a fuck if you cuss." Dallas gave Viper a wry smile. "I've heard and said worse." She turned back to Hank. "I still don't see what this situation has to do with me."

"Or me." Viper ran his hand through his hair again and sat back in his chair, his coffee untouched. "Unless you want me to attend every wedding scheduled in the near future looking for the saboteur. That solution could be like searching for a needle in a haystack. The bastard might not even attend the event after setting it up for failure."

"Actually," Hank said, drawing out the word. "You're thinking in the same direction as I am."

"Oh, yeah?" Viper sat forward. "How so?"

"Rather than have another innocent bride and groom take a hit, I thought it might be better to have two of my own Brotherhood Protectors lay a trap and lure the culprit into revealing himself."

"What did you have in mind?" Dallas asked. Though she had an idea where Hank was heading, she wanted to be perfectly clear. Her body tensed and her pulse raced.

"A wedding, between two of my most skilled operatives who are recent arrivals. They'd have to be so new to the area, no one would know their backstory."

"I meet the new criteria, having just arrived in town yesterday," Viper said. "How will this work?"

"I need you to get married," Hank said, his tone flat, his face set like stone.

"Ha!" Viper's bark of laughter met silence. "You're kidding, right?"

Hank shook his head, his gaze swinging away from Viper to Dallas.

Dallas set the mug she'd been holding on the table and wiped her suddenly sweaty palms against her jeans. Before Hank uttered his next words, she knew what he would say. She held her breath and braced herself.

"I'm not kidding. As of now, I don't have a female protector as part of my team. But I'm all for equal opportunity and for hiring the right man…or woman for the job." He leaned toward Dallas.

She shook her head and sat back as far as she could get away from Hank and his intense stare. "Not me."

"Yes, you." Hank gave her a hint of a smile. "I've read your dossier. You kicked ass in Ranger school, and you're an expert marksman on a number of different weapons. Plus, you can take on anyone in hand-to-hand combat." His tone lowered and became even more intense. "I need someone I know can handle a potentially bad situation…a trained combatant. But most of all…a female."

Married? Her? The one-legged female who gave up any possibility of getting married when she opted into Ranger training? And now…one leg short, she most definitely was out of the marriage pool. Dallas held up her hands. "Whoa, wait just a minute. I might be all of those things, but I'm nothing like the marrying kind. I don't even look like a bride."

"My wife, Sadie, can help you with everything you need to put together a wedding. Hannah's father, the senator, will fund the effort. He's promised to pay for everything you need to stage a ceremony, from a wedding dress to a three-piece band, if that's what you think we need. The bigger the event, the better chance of flushing out our guy."

"But, you don't get it." Dallas shook her head. "I'm not the right woman for the job."

"You're female. You're good with a gun. You know how to fight. You're perfect," Hank said. "And in case I didn't say it before, I want to hire you as one of the Brotherhood Protectors. We could use another competent fighter on our team."

Hire her? Hank wanted to hire her? For a moment, a flash of hope swelled in her chest, only to be crushed seconds later when she reflected on the reality of her world.

She shook her head, heat rising in her cheeks. "I'm sorry, Mr. Patterson, but I'm not the right woman for the job. I'm not the fighter I used to be. Hell, I'm not sure I *can* fight anymore." She turned in her seat and pulled up her pant leg, exposing her prosthetic where a healthy leg had been months before. "You see, I'm not the person I was in that dossier."

Hank glanced down at the prosthetic and back up to Dallas's face. "You're everything I read in that dossier. And more. And you'll be perfect to play the part of a blushing bride. You even have the blush down pat. And you'll make a convincing bride to your groom…" Hank waved his hand toward the other man sitting at the table, "Viper."

The heat increased and spread all the way up to her ears. She shot a glance toward Viper, hoping he would back up her refusal.

His eyes had widened, and he shook his head slowly from side to side. "You want us to stage a fake wedding? I don't know…I've never done anything like this. I wouldn't know where to start."

"It's all about acting. You don't even have to like each other." Hank grinned. "Although, that would make the scenario more believable."

"Weddings are for girly-girls," Dallas protested. "I'm the furthest thing from being a girly-girl. I don't think I've ever painted my fingernails, and I couldn't begin to tell you how to apply makeup. And I can't wear high heels. The prosthetic rules that out." She laid her hands on the table. "You'll have to find someone else."

Hank's smile faded and his eyes narrowed. "Again, I don't have any women in my organization who qualify. Hell, I don't have any women in my organization. You'd be the first, and you're a highly trained Ranger. I couldn't ask for better."

"But, don't you see?" Dallas fought the sting in her eyes. Rangers didn't cry, she reminded herself. She lowered her voice to a whisper, afraid it would break on a sob she refused to release. "I'm the reason all the members of my team died. I'm poison. Worse, I'm a curse."

Hank jerked back, a frown pulling his brows low. "Who told you that?"

Every man in her unit. Every Ranger she'd sworn to protect. "No one had to tell me. My history is the proof. Of the seven-member team that went into the village that night in Afghanistan, I was the only one who lived."

Hank's fierce expression softened. "And you carried one of your own men out on your back."

"He died!" she said, her voice catching. Dallas pushed to her foot, spun on her prosthetic leg and nearly fell on her face.

If Viper hadn't leaped to his feet at the same time, she would have fallen and made a complete fool of herself.

His hands grabbed her arms and steadied her until she could get her body straight and the prosthetic squarely beneath her weight. Damn the device. And damn Viper for catching her, proving she was vulnerable when all she'd wanted was to get away from the men before the tears burning her eyes slipped down her cheeks.

Too late. A fat, wet tear slipped free and made a long damp trail down her cheek. She ducked her head. "Let go."

"Can you stand alone?" Viper asked.

"Yes." Shame burned in her chest as well as her cheeks. "I just got ahead of myself."

He hesitated a moment more, and then released his hold on her arms.

Without Viper to lean on, Dallas swayed.

He cupped her elbow and steadied her. "Please. Sit."

She shook free of his hold and walked across the kitchen, careful not to display her decided limp. Yes, she lost a leg, but no, she refused to reveal just how the loss had slowed her down...any more than she had already. Finally, she turned to face Hank and opened her mouth to decline his offer.

But he held up a hand. "Look, this is a paying gig. A job. I've read your file, I'm a pretty good judge of character. I know you're the one we need in this position." Hank stood. "Think of it this way...if I chose any other female, she'd be a liability to Viper. You and Viper will be a team. Equal pay for equal performance. I expect no less. I know you can handle yourself and that you will provide cover and backup for Viper. I know he will do the same for you." Hank turned to Viper.

Viper nodded. "I'm game if you are." He shrugged. "I was never much of an actor, but for the sake of smoking out the bastard who almost killed a few of our own, I'll do it."

"Do it for all the couples in this area thinking of tying the knot," Hank urged. "You'd be saving them from heartache and possibly an end to their happiness before it has a chance to begin."

"To hell with them," Viper said, his gaze intense and staring as if right through her. "Do it for yourself. Do you want to remain in rehab, wondering what you'll do for a real job? Or do you want to take an honest-to-goodness offer to do what you do best?" He crossed both arms over his chest. "I'd rather work to get on with my life than spend the next couple months wondering where I fit in."

Damn the man. He made too much sense. When Viper put it that way, Dallas would be a fool to pass up an offer that required the use of the only skills she possessed.

She drew in a deep breath and let it out slowly. Then she faced Hank. "Sadie can help me with whatever froufrou things I'll need to know and do?"

"She will," Hank agreed. A smile crept up the corners of his lips. "You'll do it?"

Despite her reticence, Dallas nodded. "I'll do it. How do I start?"

"By getting to know your fiancé." Hank stuck out his hand.

Dallas placed hers in his. He shook it and then dragged her over to Viper. "Viper, meet your bride to be. Dallas, you'll need to become acquainted with the man you're going to marry."

As she stared up into Viper's blue eyes, Dallas was positive she'd regret her decision.

CHAPTER 3

Viper held Dallas's strong, capable hand in his as Hank wasted no time in calling Sadie.

"Sadie, I need you to draft a wedding announcement to go into tomorrow's paper." Hank held his cellphone to his ear, nodding.

Viper stared into Dallas's eyes, noticing their color for the first time. "They're green," he said. He shouldn't be surprised that they were green, because what better color could there be for a woman with a shoulder-length swath of bright, copper hair?

"What're green?" Dallas asked, a frown forming between her eyebrows.

Viper blinked and released her hands, realizing he'd been holding them for a long time. "Your eyes. They're green. We probably need to know a few things about each other, if we're to pull off this undercover operation. Mine are blue." He stepped back and eyed her from head to toe.

"I'd noticed." Dallas's cheeks reddened, and she

ducked her head. "How far do we need to go in this wedding planning?"

"Probably all the way," Viper said. "Seems our Tango likes to disrupt the ceremony itself."

"Or in Taz and Hannah's case, *after* the ceremony." Hank slipped his smart phone into his pocket. "I didn't expect to get any cellphone reception, but the stars and antennas must be aligned." He grinned. "Sadie will phone in the wedding announcement for next weekend. We'll conduct the ceremony at Bear Creek Ranch where my father and sister live. My father is out of town for the next couple of weeks, so it shouldn't be an issue. The security there isn't nearly as tight as at Brotherhood Protectors Headquarters which is White Oak Ranch where I live. My sister, Allie, will enjoy helping Sadie with the preparations. She's had a little practice with her own weddings."

"Weddings?" Dallas asked, her voice rising.

Hank's lips twisted. "Her first fiancé was trafficking diamonds. She ditched him for her bodyguard, one of my guys, Swede. You met him last night at the ceremony."

Dallas nodded. "The tall blond guy?"

"That was Swede." Nodding, Hank chuckled. "He's kind of hard to miss. He's also my computer guru."

"Aren't you afraid you'll put Sadie and your sister in harm's way?" Viper asked.

Hank drew in a deep breath and let it go. "So far, all the attacks have been primarily on the bride and groom. Chuck just happened to be driving them. I'd host the wedding at my ranch, but the attacker wouldn't make it past the security and probably knows it. We have to give him enough rope to hang himself. That's why I need my bride and groom capable of handling anything that comes their way."

"We can do this," Viper said, catching her gaze.

"I can fight my way out of most situations," Dallas said. "But I'm completely out of my comfort zone in tulle and lace. I don't have the first clue how to plan a wedding."

"You heard the boss," Viper said. "Sadie and Allie are going to help. And I've been through one myself. I remember some of the crap that goes into the process."

Dallas frowned. "You're married?" She shot a glance at Viper's left ring finger. It was free of any jewelry.

"Was." Viper's lips tightened. "I'm a widower." He turned away from Dallas's questioning look. His marriage was a story he preferred to keep to himself. The outcome wasn't one he was proud of. Not that he hadn't been proud of his wife. Emily had been everything he could have asked for in a spouse. She was okay with his deployments, waiting patiently for his return. After each mission, she even welcomed him home with banners and champagne.

Except one mission.

No, she hadn't been the problem in his marriage. *He* had. Viper hadn't been home enough during Emily's pregnancy to know she wasn't feeling well. He'd deployed far in advance of the baby's due date, planning on being back in plenty of time for the delivery.

Only fate had other plans for him, Emily and the

baby. Due to complications, Emily and their baby girl died at their home. Alone.

His heart squeezed hard in his chest. Though it had been close to six years, not a day went by that he didn't think about how he'd failed his family. If he'd been there, he might have gotten them to the hospital in time to save their lives. If he'd been home, he might have seen signs of Emily's failing health. Though the doctor said, sometimes they couldn't predict what had happened. It just did.

Still, Viper blamed himself. He should have been there for them. Or at the very least, he should have waited to have children until he could be home to care for both his wife and child.

A hand on his arm made him look down. Dallas's slender fingers brushed his sleeve, sending warmth through his arm and chest.

"I'm sorry," she said.

He shrugged off her hand. The last thing he needed was sympathy. He didn't deserve it. "No worries. It's been a few years." Yet, he still hadn't gotten over the sense of loss and guilt.

"Well, since you two are officially on board, I'll get back to the ranch and have my computer guy dig into all the backgrounds of anyone we can come up with who might have it out for one of our lucky couples."

"Start with people having anything to do with the planning and setup," Viper said.

"You might also check on anyone local who could have been jilted or stood up before the ceremony," Dallas said.

Viper gave half a smile. "Hell hath no fury like a woman scorned?"

"Or a man," Dallas added. "Men can be just as cranky about being left at the altar as women."

"You know this from experience?"

Dallas's green eyes flashed. "I read."

Viper chuckled. "I'm betting you don't indulge in bride magazines."

"Never." Grimacing, Dallas shook her head. "My tastes lean toward news and crime fiction."

"So, you know all the best places to hide the bodies," Hank said.

Viper raised his eyebrows. "Should I be worried?"

"Only if you scorn me." Dallas's lips quirked.

If Viper wasn't mistaken, Dallas almost smiled. He liked the sparkle in her green eyes, so different from Emily's blue-gray eyes. And the fiery auburn hair was a stark contrast to Emily's golden blond. And Dallas was taller, stronger and less ladylike than Emily. All of her physical traits made Viper's agreement to the charade easier.

If Dallas had looked at all like Emily, Viper would have politely declined the assignment and asked for someone else to take his place. Having a blond-haired, blue-eyed partner would have been a constant reminder of what he'd lost and that he hadn't been there for Emily to keep her from dying.

Dallas was as different from Emily as night from day. He could treat her like one of the guys. No sweat.

As long as he ignored the little spark of electricity that shot through him every time he touched her. Why that happened, he wasn't sure. From what Viper gathered, Dallas was all Army Ranger. She was one kickass soldier, and she'd rather shoot a man than kiss him.

As much as he didn't want to admit the fact, the shine of her fiery, auburn hair and the flash of her green eyes were sexy as hell. Not his type, but definitely sexy. His type had been Emily...blond and blue.

Now...he didn't know what his type was.

His gaze swept over Dallas's shiny auburn hair, her athletic figure and the way she wore her jeans. Having a prosthetic device in place of her lower leg did nothing to detract from her raw sexuality. And the kicker was, she didn't know just how sexy she was.

Viper's groin tightened. He hadn't been attracted to anyone over the past few years. Not with the weight of guilt and regret sitting on his shoulders. Perhaps it was Dallas's background, her time in the military and her dedication to her training that made him look at her twice. She was a fighter, having proven it by qualifying for Ranger Training and completing it successfully.

He argued with himself that he admired her for her gumption. But gumption wasn't what made his cock swell and his hands itch to push the strand of coppery hair back behind her ear.

One of the guys, my ass.

Perhaps he was in for more of a challenge than he'd originally anticipated. Either way, he had work to do and a boss to prove himself to. "Let's get this wedding planning going."

Dallas nodded. "Yeah. The sooner we find our wedding saboteur, the sooner we can move on to a more palatable assignment." She clapped her hands together. "So, where do we start?"

Viper turned to Hank. "Is Sadie available for consultation this afternoon?"

"Her schedule is open, and she's ready to meet with you." Hank gave Viper and Dallas a narrow-eyed glance. "As far as anyone knows, the pair of you are a couple. Only you two, me, Swede and Sadie know what we're planning. The fewer people who know, the less likely we'll let it slip that this engagement is a setup." He looked from Viper to Dallas and back. "Got it?"

Viper snapped a salute. "Yes, sir."

Dallas lifted her chin. "I'm in."

Hank held out his hand. "Welcome to the Brotherhood Protectors."

"Are you sure?" she asked, casting a quick glance down at her jean-clad prosthetic leg.

"Absolutely certain," Hank responded, his gaze never leaving Dallas's.

Viper watched as Dallas took Hank's hand, and they shook.

"Thank you," she said.

With that handshake, Viper had a partner. He hoped they could make this assignment work. It was his proving ground with Hank. Plus, he needed the work. So far, the Brotherhood Protectors gig was the only one he'd found using the skills he'd gained over his many years in the service. Where else could he carry a gun, fight for right and protect the good people of his country?

. . .

She had a job. A real job. Not the kind of job she'd envisioned for herself, but one she'd do her best to get right.

Pretending to be a blushing bride wasn't something in her comfort zone, but then she'd been outside her comfort zone on numerous occasions and survived.

Hopefully, swimming in tulle and taffeta would be a piece of cake. A shiver slipped down her spine. Even in high school, she'd opted out of going to the prom. She couldn't remember the last time she'd worn a dress.

The Army had tried to make her wear a skirt, but she'd chosen the tailored slacks to go with her Class A uniform. Besides, she'd rarely worn a pair of high heels.

"I'll let you two get acquainted." Hank strode toward the door. When he reached it, he paused and turned back. "Oh, and I suggest you go down to the courthouse in Eagle Rock and apply for a wedding license. You want to make this engagement appear as real as possible."

Dallas bit down hard on her tongue to keep from gasping. "License?"

Hank nodded. "We don't know at what point the Tango is tipped off about the wedding. We might have to take the act from the beginning, through the actual ceremony, and all the way to the airport on your way to your honeymoon, if we don't catch him sooner."

Of course, they had to put on a show for whomever was targeting brides and grooms in the area.

Viper's throat worked as he swallowed before he spoke. "Roger."

"Now, get to know each other," Hank ordered.

"You'll run into people asking you about how you met, what's her favorite flower and color, and when you knew you were in love. Come up with a good story and agree on the details. Your relationship has to appear real, or our guy might not take the bait." Hank glanced at Dallas. "Sadie will get with you this afternoon to make arrangements to shop tomorrow."

"Shop?" Dallas said weakly.

"What's the saying? Gird your loins. Sadie's really good at shopping, and she can last for hours. If shopping was an Olympic event, she'd win gold every time."

Dallas waited for Hank to leave and close the door behind him before she let loose the groan she'd been holding back.

"What's wrong?" Viper asked.

Dallas turned a sideways glance his way. "I hate shopping."

He chuckled. "You have to be the first woman I've met who hates shopping. We'll get along just fine." He patted the table in front of him. "We'd better start now. If we're learning everything about each other in the next twelve hours, we'll have to make the minutes count."

"Okay, but wouldn't this process be easier over food?" Dallas didn't wait for his response. She strode for the refrigerator, yanked it open, and spotted the leftover barbeque trays from the night before. "Feel like a sandwich? There's leftover brisket from the wedding reception."

"I'll help." Viper jumped up from the table and joined her at the counter.

Dallas found a package of hamburger buns and pulled out two, while Viper hefted the loaded tray of brisket from the refrigerator.

"Mayo or barbeque sauce?" Viper asked.

"No mayo, but mustard instead of sauce," Dallas said.

"My fiancée likes mustard."

Hearing him call her his fiancée had a strange effect. Her chest tightened and her belly fluttered at the same time. She opened the buns and laid them each on a plate and then handed them over to Viper. "What's your favorite color?"

"Green," he said, as if automatically. "Not because of the color of your eyes, though it fits for the purpose of the operation."

She handed him a knife and fished the mustard out of the refrigerator. "Then why green?"

He smiled as he pulled the foil off the tray. "I like the color green because it reminds me of spring and summer, when everything is fresh and growing. I also like green for the evergreen trees that are green even when they're buried in snow. I know they're still alive and growing beneath the cold flocking. What about you?"

"Blue," she said and laughed. "Not because of the color of your eyes. Though, again, my preference works for our operation. I like blue because it's the color of a clear sky in the daylight. If I can see the sky, I'm not imprisoned, I'm not in a cave and I'm not dead. Sunlight and blue skies make me happy."

He glanced sideways, capturing her gaze. "You don't like the dark?"

"Not so much." Hesitant to share her reason, Dallas turned away. She'd lost her team and her leg in the dark. She'd almost lost her life in the dark.

A hand on her shoulder startled her, and she looked back.

Viper stood behind her, his eyebrows lowered. "What happened? How did you lose your leg?" He gave her half a smile. "You might as well tell me and get it over with. I'll have to know in case someone asks. No groom could marry a woman without knowing her story."

Dallas drew in a deep breath and let it out. "Can we do your story first? I want to eat while I have an appetite."

"Sure." He went back to work making sandwiches. "I'm thirty-eight years old. Six-feet-four. I served for twenty years in the Army, eighteen of which was with Delta Force. I retired at the rank of Sergeant Major. I've deployed more times than I could count on one hand."

Dallas hadn't realized just how remarkable Viper's military record was. She laid two bottles of soda and a package of potato chips on the table. She drew in a deep breath and launched. "I'm twenty-eight, five-feet-six and I served ten years, the last four as a Ranger. I'm one of the first seven females to successfully complete the US Army Ranger School. I lost my leg on a mission and was medically retired at the rank of Staff Sergeant."

"I'm impressed. Not many women can do what you did." Viper brought the two plates of sandwiches, setting one in front of her and the other across the table. Then he held out her chair.

Dallas, always the tomboy, the woman who no man fucked with, stared at him and then the chair.

Viper's lips twisted. "You might as well get used to it. I treat my woman like a lady."

She frowned. "I'm not that kind of woman."

"But you are female, and my mama taught me to respect all females—big, small, short, tall, young or old." He held the chair, challenging her with a raised eyebrow. "You wouldn't want me to disappoint my mama, now would you? Besides, I would hold a chair and open doors for any bride of mine. The gesture's non-negotiable."

Dallas crossed her arms over her chest. "What if I said not holding chairs and not opening doors was non-negotiable for me?"

"I guess we'd be at an impasse. But for this operation, we need to appear in sync. We're supposed to be in love. We're about to get married. I need to show the world how much I care for you, and you need to show the world how much you love that I do." He retained the cocked eyebrow, staring straight into her eyes, unflinching.

"You're not backing down on this, are you?" Dallas asked softly, knowing his answer.

"No, ma'am. My mama scares me a lot more than you do." Then he winked and grinned.

Butterflies erupted in Dallas's belly, and warmth spread throughout her body. No man had ever winked at her like that. She wasn't quite sure how to react. For one, she had to pick the right battles. This argument was not one of them. So…she sat. "Don't think you won that one."

"But I did, didn't I?"

"Only for the sake of the mission," Dallas grumbled.

"I'll take it." He sat across the table and lifted his bottle of soda toward her. "To our upcoming wedding."

Dallas lifted hers and touched her bottle to his. "To catching a sadistic bastard." Glass clinked and they both knocked back half of their bottles before setting them on the table again.

Viper dug into the sandwich. Dallas ate hers with the quiet, quick efficiency of one who didn't get a lot of time to eat meals in the Army. When she got food, she gobbled it down and chased it with potato chips and soda. She found eating easier than telling her story.

Viper wasn't far behind her. When he finished his sandwich and soda, he gathered their plates and carried them to the sink. "I'll wash if you'll dry."

Dallas found a dry dish towel and positioned herself beside Viper at the sink he'd filled with warm soapy water. "Did your mother teach you how to wash dishes?" she asked.

He washed a plate and then rinsed it. "No. I learned that skill on my own. Contrary to popular belief, I didn't live my entire Army life in the barracks. I had an apartment for much of my active duty time, though I didn't see it much. I had to clean a dish or two out of self-preservation. And I was married, at one time. When I was home, I didn't leave all the work to my wife."

"Gallant of you." Dallas dried the plate and set it in

the cabinet. "So, you know how to wash dishes. What else do you have going for you in husband material?"

"I'm good at fixing things. I'm handy with computers and electronic devices. I can cook, when I need to, and, as you've noticed, I open doors for the ladies in my life."

Dallas nodded. "So far, so good." Getting to know a man was new to her. She'd never dated in high school or cared to get close enough to anyone she worked with. Strangely, she enjoyed learning more about Viper.

"What about you?" Viper handed her a dish to dry. "What have you got going for you in the wife department?"

She held the plate, refusing to meet his gaze. "Sadly...not much. I was raised by my father to be tough. We ran marathons when we weren't hunting or fishing."

"Sounds like the perfect woman, to me. What guy doesn't like a companion when he's out in the woods?"

Her lips pressed together and she shook her head. "Most guys. Hunting is a very individual sport. Most hunters like to get out in the woods alone and commune with nature." She shrugged. "Must be the introvert in us."

"Maybe. Or you just enjoy nature. What did you hunt?"

"Deer and elk. The occasional grouse or pheasant." She shrugged. "I took my rifle or shotgun and my camera." At the memory, she smiled. "I liked taking pictures more than bringing home a trophy."

"And fishing?"

She laughed. "I bring home all the fish I can eat. I

love baked, broiled, fried and grilled fish. And I love even more to head out with a rod and reel and spend quiet hours along the shore of a river, casting my line to see what I'll catch." She smiled. "Most times, I don't catch a thing. That's okay with me, too."

"Ever been dancing?" Viper asked.

She took a plate from him, shaking her head. "Never. I have two left feet." She rubbed the dish dry.

"Obviously, you've never had the right dance partner." Viper plucked the plate from her hand and set it on the counter. "You'll need to learn how to waltz for the wedding dance."

"Waltz?" She recoiled. "What did you not understand about I have two left feet? Or rather, I have one left foot."

"Again, you never had the right partner. You appear to get around fine on what you have. Trust me…you can learn to dance." He took her right hand in his and rested his left hand on her hip. "It's easy if you get the rhythm down. Just remember 1-2-3, 1-2-3." He tapped his toe in time to the numbers. "Now you move like this…" He stepped back a little and looked down at his feet, moving them to the beat of his, "1-2-3." Then he glanced up. "You try."

She shook her head, her feet firmly planted on the tile. "I can't. I don't have a musical bone in my body."

"Then put your feet on mine and move with me."

She frowned at him. "You're kidding, right?"

"Not at all. Go ahead, you won't kill me."

"But I'm not a little girl."

"No, but you have to learn one way or another."

"I can't feel my foot, remember?" she argued, humiliation building inside. With the one emotion came another...anger.

"Just put your feet on top of mine. I'll show you how it feels to move to the rhythm of the waltz." Viper's grip tightened on her hand and around her waist. "On my feet, Ranger," he commanded.

Dallas hesitated another moment.

"What's wrong, Dallas?" He stared into her eyes, unflinching. "Are you afraid?"

Dallas's back stiffened. "No way."

"Then show me you can do this." He pulled her closer, forcing her to move her feet. "Go on," he urged, his breath mingling with hers. "You won't hurt me."

Maybe not. But he might hurt her. The thought flitted through her mind. Her pulse raced and her breathing became ragged, as if she couldn't get enough air into her lungs.

He was so close!

Oh, she'd been close to men before. Hell, she'd had to carry a two-hundred-pound soldier over her shoulder up a hill during a training exercise and in combat when she'd had to carry one of her team to the rear, after he'd been hit by explosives.

But this situation was different.

They were both conscious, and Viper didn't smell of sweat and gunpowder. He smelled of fresh dirt and the outdoors, and he was still dirty from having rescued the bride and groom from near death.

Why was she hesitating? They had a job to do, and if

learning to waltz would make it more believable, by God, she'd do it.

Dallas placed her foot on one of his and looked down to position her prosthetic on the other. "Don't let me hurt you," she said.

"Relax. I can handle it." He smiled down at her. "Ready?"

"As ready as I'll ever be."

And he stepped out. "1-2-3, 1-2-3, 1-2-3."

At first, Dallas remained stiff in his arms, her back ramrod straight, her knees rigid.

"It's okay to bend your legs, you know," he whispered against her ear. "1-2-3, 1-2-3."

Soon, she was on her own feet matching his rhythm with similar movements, albeit awkward and clumsy. "I take it your mother taught you to dance, too?"

"No, actually, my wife taught me to waltz for our wedding." His jaw hardened, and he quit counting for a couple seconds.

"Your wife must have been a special woman."

"She was," he replied, his words clipped.

Dallas hadn't grown up with a loving mother. Sometimes she'd wished she had. Viper might as well know about her dysfunctional family. "My father raised me, after my mother ran off with the used car salesman."

"That must have been hard for you."

"Not really. I had a great relationship with my father. My mother wasn't good with children. My father taught me a lot of things, but dancing was not one of them."

"What kinds of things, besides hunting and

running?" he asked without breaking their dancing pace.

"How to cook a mean pot of chili, and how to change the oil on my truck."

"And who taught you how to kiss?" Viper brought her to a halt.

The air disappeared out of her lungs, and Dallas nearly fell over her good foot. If not for the strength of Viper's arms, she would have crashed to the floor. "Kiss?" she said, her voice barely a whisper.

CHAPTER 4

✎

Why in hell had Viper taken Dallas into his arms? Being so close to the woman brought back feelings he'd thought long forgotten.

Though Dallas was taller, bolder and less girly than Emily, she had curves in all the right places, and she was warm and smelled like sunshine and spring flowers.

He almost laughed. If he said anything like what he was thinking, Dallas would knock him on his ass and wipe the floor with him.

But to ask her who taught her to kiss? He'd taken his life into his own hands. The woman didn't suffer fools.

"Kiss?" she said, her voice like an angel's whisper, not the usual clipped words. Then she stumbled, requiring him to tighten his hold to keep her from falling.

His arm brushed against the side of one breast, the connection making him instantly hard. Viper told himself he wasn't interested in the former Ranger. If anything, he should be afraid of pissing her off.

But he found a twisted sense of satisfaction in pushing her buttons and making her think more like a girl than a soldier. "That's right. In order to convince others we're a couple, kissing will take place."

Her tongue darted out from between her teeth and swept across her lips.

Viper's groin tightened and his hands around her did, as well. "Should we practice?"

Dallas's eyes widened, and she shoved herself away. "No." She rubbed her hands down the sides of her jeans. "We…we can cross that bridge when it comes." She pushed her hair back behind her ears. "Besides, if we're tracing the paths of the brides and grooms, you might want to get a shower first. You don't want to show up at the courthouse looking like you do."

He glanced down at his clothing still caked in the mud he'd collected on his slide down the hill to the crashed limousine. "You're right. I'll head to Hank's place for my gear, and be back within an hour. I suppose since we'll be working together, we need to stay close. We can stay here, or you can come to Hank's place. I'm sure Hank and Sadie wouldn't mind finding a room for you there."

Dallas frowned. "We're not fake married yet. Why can't our living arrangements stay the way they are?"

"They could, but if we're setting up ourselves as bait, I'd rather be close. We never know when we need one another to cover the other's ass."

Dallas's eyes narrowed for a moment, and then she sighed. "You're probably right. Since Hank's place is too locked down with security, we should probably stay here." She glanced out the window. "Which begs another question. Will we put others in the line of fire by being here? Some of the guests aren't as mobile as others."

"You're right. How about we stay here the first few nights and then check with Hank's sister and see if they can put us up at her ranch until the wedding? We can get really familiar with the lay of the ranch and any potential areas of concern."

Dallas's lips pressed together, but she nodded. "Just to be clear, we're only pretending to be a couple. It's all for show. We will not go past first base as a fake couple."

Viper held up a hand like he was swearing in court. "I won't if you don't want me to."

"Trust me, I won't want you to." She lifted her chin.

"To make myself perfectly clear, you'll have to ask me if you want more than the requisite kisses a man will give his fiancée and bride in public."

"I don't know why, but I'm not all that sure I trust you."

"I was a Boy Scout," Viper said.

Dallas snorted. "I've met a lot of Boy Scouts I couldn't trust any farther than I could throw them."

Viper laughed out loud. "I bet you threw them pretty far."

"I did." Dallas's lips twitched. "And they weren't too happy about being bested by a woman."

"Again, you'd have to ask for me to make love to you, sweetheart. I don't relish picking myself up off the floor all bruised and battered."

"Good." She lifted her chin a little higher. "Just keep that in mind. I don't give second chances."

He popped a salute. "Yes, ma'am."

"And don't call me ma'am. I worked for a living."

"Yes, sir." Again, he popped a salute.

"Good grief." Dallas shook her head. "Get out of here. I have work to do before we leave for town."

"I'll be back as soon as possible. Don't go anywhere without me. Once that announcement hits the newspaper, we're officially an engaged couple planning a quickie wedding."

Dallas nodded. "I'll remember. The question is, will you?"

His brow dipped. "What do you mean?"

"No flirting with pretty waitresses or getting phone numbers from the women you meet."

He touched a hand to his chest and gave her an innocent look. "You think I flirt with random women and ask for their phone numbers?"

"A man like you can't help but attract the attention of the opposite sex."

His chest warmed. "You think I'm sexy." Viper grinned. "Well, that's a good start."

Her cheeks blossomed with pink. "I didn't say you were sexy. Merely that you would attract *some* women."

He raised his brows, enjoying her discomfort. Perhaps too much. "But not you?"

"Of course not. You're not my type," she answered far too quickly, the pink in her cheeks darkening to red.

"Oh." He tapped his chin. "You have a type, do you?"

Viper tilted his head, knowing he shouldn't poke at her, but he couldn't resist. "And what type is that?"

"I like more cerebral men."

He fought back a laugh. "Cerebral. You mean men who are more brain than brawn?"

"Exactly."

"Oh, so you like men who can't fight back, physically."

A frown pulled her brows together. "No. That's not what I meant. I like men who can hold their own in a conversation."

"And I can't because I'm sexy." He didn't proffer his words as a question, but as more of a statement, fighting back the laughter bubbling up in his chest.

"No. I didn't say that." She glared. "You're putting words in my mouth.

"Darlin', I don't have to put words in your mouth, you're doing a pretty good job of it all by yourself." He caught her arms and pulled her close. "Since I'm not smart enough to be your type, I think we need some practice to fool the cerebral men out there into thinking we're together. Come here and lay it on this non-cerebral man." He bent and captured her mouth with his in a kiss designed to blow her socks off.

Oh, he knew how to kiss. He'd dated his share of women before marrying Emily. Not one of them had complained about his kisses. In fact, they'd all come back for more.

He dragged her against his body, with one hand low on her back, and the other buried in her hair. At first, he crushed her lips with his, then he traced his tongue across the seam of her lips.

When she opened her mouth on a gasp, he thrust past her teeth and claimed her tongue with his in a long, slow caress.

Dallas pressed her hands to his chest, her body stiff. When he deepened the kiss, he could feel the change.

The starch melted out of her arms and back. The fingers pressed to his chest curled into his shirt, urging him closer instead of pushing him away.

What had started as a kind of punishment for insinuating he wasn't all that smart played back against him. Viper wanted to show her she was not immune to his charms and then leave her wanting more. Only, he couldn't seem to let go.

The more he kissed her, the more he wanted to keep doing it. Until finally, he had to let go long enough to suck air back into his lungs.

Damn. What had he just done? No woman had made him want more than a handshake since Emily.

Until one female Ranger, who'd more or less told him he was too pretty to be smart and not her type at all.

DALLAS LEANED her forehead against Viper's chest, remembering how to breathe. Not only had the man kissed her...he'd kissed her into a daze. She'd forgotten to push him away, forgotten where she was, her mission and hell, what day of the week she'd woken up in.

Despite her insistence on keeping their partnership

purely professional, she had all kinds of unprofessional thoughts and images racing through her head. Each one had something to do with getting naked with the man and making mad, passionate love. Not that she'd made mad, passionate love to any man ever in her life. Made love, yes, but it hadn't been all that memorable.

She couldn't let that happen. They had a job to do and needed all their focus on solving the mystery of who was sabotaging local weddings.

Dallas straightened her fingers against his chest and pushed back. Adopting an air of nonchalance, she smoothed a hand over her hair and said, "Well, I think those moves should convince our Tango of our fake-commitment to each other." She laid extra emphasis on the word *fake*. She could never admit to him that the kiss had rocked her world. No man should have that kind of effect on her. Ever.

But Viper had.

Holy hell.

He pushed a hand through his hair and released his hold, dropping his hands to his sides. "I'm not so sure. I think we need more practice."

With a hand held out in front of her, Dallas put the kibosh on him taking her into his arms again. Another kiss would be a very bad idea at that moment. "You need a shower. I need to do chores, and we have a trail to lay for our perpetrator. The sooner we get to it, the sooner we can find our guy and stop the wedding day terror." She pointed to the door. "Go."

Viper chuckled.

The warm, deep sound of his mirth filled every pore in Dallas's skin, spreading heat throughout her body.

How did he do that?

No man had made her quite as aware of her femininity as Viper had in just a single kiss. Hell, no man had kissed her like Viper had. Yeah, she'd been kissed once or twice. Okay, maybe once. But the guy who'd stolen that kiss had suffered a broken nose for his audacity. Not another man had dared try again.

Going through Ranger training, she'd shaved her head like the men and worked hard to become one of the guys. None of her battle buddies dared make a move on her. Deployed and in a wartime situation, she'd been shunned by her team. Even more so after each battle in which they'd engaged had ended badly. They blamed her, saying she'd jinxed them. She didn't believe in luck, good or bad, superstition or jinxing.

All her life, she'd worked hard to establish herself as one of the guys, only to discover she wasn't and never would be. But after every operation went south, she wondered if the men had been right.

"I'm going," Viper said. "But I'll be back in less than two hours. Be ready to hit the ground running."

"I'll be ready," she said.

"Oh, and wear something pretty. A bride should want to look good for her man when they go to apply for their marriage license."

Dallas frowned and swept a hand down her length. "What's wrong with what I'm wearing?"

"It's okay for mucking stalls and feeding the livestock, but not for our undercover operation." He winked. "Do you have a dress you can wear?"

"Hell, no. I've never owned a dress a day in my life."

His lips twisted into a wry grin. "Guess we'll be going shopping sooner than I thought."

"The hell we will," Dallas said. "I'm not changing who I am."

"You want this operation to be a success, don't you?" Viper's gaze captured hers. "I don't know how you approach a new job, but this assignment is my first for Brotherhood Protectors. I figure I'm here on a trial basis. If I screw up this one, Hank Patterson will have every right to fire my ass." His eyes narrowed. "How much do you want to keep this job you've just been handed?"

Dallas pressed her lips together and forced herself to meet his gaze. After a long moment, she dropped hers and nodded. "I don't know who else would hire someone like me. I'd like to keep this job, if at all possible."

"Same here."

She jerked up her head. "What do you have to be afraid of? You're an able-bodied man, fully capable of doing anything."

"Probably the same thing you're afraid of."

"You're afraid you'll be rejected or won't be able to perform because you have a prosthetic leg?"

"Not the leg part, but the fear of rejection and inability to perform are two of my concerns. I'm not quite sure what a retired spec-ops guy can do to find a wedding saboteur. But I'm giving it my all to make sure

I capture his ass to prove to myself I can do what it takes to ensure I keep this job. Where else will I get to use my Army training in the civilian world?"

"You could hire on with a police or sheriff's department," Dallas suggested. "Whereas, I couldn't. No law enforcement agency will hire a one-legged female, except to sit behind a desk. Which isn't my style."

His brow furrowed. "You don't know that."

She snorted. "Oh, yes, I do. I've applied to more than one. Turned down at all, based on physical requirements. Even though I can probably outrun and outperform any recruit they might have."

Viper's lips quirked upward. "I don't doubt that in the least. But I, for one, am glad they turned you down."

She frowned. "Why?"

A grin spread across his face. "At least, I have a pretty partner for this undercover operation."

Her back stiffened. She had to remind herself where she was. Had she been on active duty, in her spec-ops unit, she would have taken offense at his statement. She hadn't done everything in her power to be "one of the guys" for them to tell her she was pretty. But in her current assignment, being female came with a different set of requirements. "Thanks," she said, albeit grudgingly and followed him out onto the porch.

"See ya in a few." Viper climbed into the gray truck and drove out of the yard.

Dallas's gaze followed him until he rounded a bend in the long driveway, disappearing out of sight.

"What was that all about?" Gavin joined her.

Dallas laughed. "I just got engaged."

. . .

As Viper drove to Hank and Sadie's place to collect his duffel bag, his thoughts went back to the woman who would be his partner for the assignment.

Dallas was long, lean and built like a brick house—sturdy and solid, with toned lines and a badass attitude. What impressed him most was the fact she didn't have a clue how attractive she was.

Oh, not in the usual, supermodel-perfect way, but in a striking, knock-a-guy-on-his-butt kind of way.

When he arrived at the beautiful, sprawling ranch house, Hank met him on the porch. "You're back so soon?"

"I think it best if I stay at the Brighter Days Ranch with Dallas. The relocation makes more sense, since we're supposed to be an engaged couple."

Hank opened the front door. "What do you think of Hayes?"

An image of Dallas flashed in Viper's mind. "I think she will work fine for this assignment."

"Good." Hank clapped his hands together. "Now, what can I do for you?"

"Nothing. I just want to grab my go bag and get started."

Sadie stood by the door, baby Emma perched on her hip. "Vince, I'm glad you're here. Let me know when I need to organize the wedding dress shopping trip. I can be ready at a moment's notice."

"Thank you. Dallas will need all the help she can

get." He grinned. "She probably doesn't know taffeta from satin. And neither do I, for that matter."

"Is there anything else I can help with?" she asked.

"As a matter of fact, there is." Viper studied the actress. "You're shorter than Dallas, but you might have the same waist size."

Sadie laughed. "And you need to know this because?"

"Dallas doesn't even own a dress. I thought she might want to look a little fancier to apply for the marriage license."

"That's sweet of you. I bet I have something that will fit." She handed Emma to Hank. "I'll be right back."

"Hey, my little honey bunch." Hank kissed Emma with a loud smacking sound, and then he tossed the baby into the air, catching her expertly.

Emma giggled and waved her hands high, indicating she wanted him to toss her again.

Viper watched, his chest tightening. His baby girl would have been five by now. He'd never gotten the chance to hold her.

Hank's cellphone buzzed. He kissed Emma again and fumbled to answer. With a glance at Viper, he asked, "Do you mind holding her?"

Before Viper could think of a response, Hank handed over Emma and stepped away to answer.

"Hank here."

Viper held the baby at arm's length, his body stiff, his heart racing.

Emma stared at him, her bright eyes rounding. Then she batted a chubby hand at his face and giggled.

The sound melted Viper's heart, and he hugged Emma to him.

Emma tugged at the collar of his jacket and patted his cheek, gurgling and cooing. Her grin infected him, and he found himself grinning back, though his eyes stung. "You're a charmer."

He couldn't admit, even to himself, how much he wanted this exact situation. A child of his own, a woman to love and a home to go to. All of this shined up at him through Emma's eyes.

"Oh, sweetie, let me take her from you." Sadie hurried into the room, a garment bag looped over her arm. "She can be a handful."

Viper held onto Emma. "No, really. She and I are getting to know each other." He smiled down at Emma. "Aren't we?"

Emma giggled and pulled his ear with her tiny little fingers.

Sadie frowned. "If you're sure?"

"Yes." Viper nodded toward the garment hanging over Sadie's arm. "You found something for Dallas?"

"I did." Sadie beamed. "I think this one will go wonderfully with her glorious red hair." She pulled an emerald-green dress out of the garment bag and held it up. Made of a flowing material, the dress would drape Dallas's body beautifully.

"That should do it." Viper smoothed a knuckle over Emma's soft cheek, reluctant to release his charge. But he had a job to do, and he needed to get back to the rehab ranch.

Sadie zipped the dress into the garment bag and laid

it over the back of a sofa. "I'll take Emma. I'm sure you'll want to return to Dallas."

As he handed over Emma, Viper whispered, "Be sweet for your mama."

"Come here, sweetheart." Sadie lifted the baby into her arms and kissed her cheek. "Thank you for holding her." She cast a glance at Hank, who'd walked to a far corner of the living room to take his call. "Hank loves her to the moon and back."

"As he should. She's amazing." A lump lodged in Viper's throat, and he turned toward the hallway leading to the bedroom where he'd left his bag. "I'll get my things and go." He hurried to the room, stuffed his toiletries into his kit, jammed it into his duffel bag and looped it over his shoulder. The walls seemed to close in around him as he headed back down the hallway to the exit.

"Don't forget the dress," Sadie reminded him as he passed through the spacious living area.

He grabbed the garment bag and nodded toward Sadie. "Thanks. I'll see that you get it back soon."

"No worries. She can have it. I have so many clothes in my closet from the movies I've been in. Tell her to keep it. It can be my contribution to her wedding trousseau." She winked and then her face sobered. "I wish you two all the luck."

"Thanks."

Hank glanced up from his conversation and ended the call. He hurried after Viper as he left the house.

"I've had my contact in cyber security looking into the wedding disaster case. So far, he hasn't found anything that jumps out in the area. He'll keep looking."

"I can't imagine anyone going online as a wedding day saboteur," Viper said.

"You're right. However, I spoke with Sheriff Barron earlier today," Hank said. "He's had his deputies questioning all the victims. So far, he's discovered they all used the same services." He handed Viper a sheet of paper with names of businesses written in bold ink. "They all used Daisy's Wedding Planning, Mel's Catering & Fuller's Rental."

"We'll follow the same path."

Hank nodded. "Good. In the meantime, be careful. The last attack almost killed the bride and groom. I don't want you and Dallas to be victims of this lunatic."

"We'll be careful. If you need me, I'll be at the Brighter Days Ranch."

"Glad to hear it," Hank said. "You two will have each other's six. And any time you need additional support, all you have to do is call."

Viper held out his hand.

Hank shook it.

"Thanks for this opportunity to be a part of Brotherhood Protectors," Viper said. "We won't let you down."

"I have no doubt you and Dallas can handle this mission."

"We've got it," Viper assured his new boss. He hoped he was right. He'd never participated in a mission disguised as the groom for a fake wedding. He was feeling way out of his depth. But he'd do anything needed to prove himself and Dallas as competent additions to the Brotherhood Protectors. Even if it meant going through with a fake wedding to a woman he'd just met.

As he climbed into his truck, his lips twitched upward. Dallas wasn't anything like Emily, but he wouldn't find it hard to pretend he was in love with the spitfire. No, she wasn't the girly type of woman who enjoyed having her nails done and shopping for clothes. But she could hold her own in hand-to-hand combat and didn't need any man to stand up for her.

He also sensed that behind her badass façade lurked a woman with all the same needs as anyone. The need to be accepted and loved for who she was. What got to Viper was that Dallas probably didn't think she needed anything but a paying job.

Viper had learned, through his own loss, that everyone needed to be loved.

CHAPTER 5

Dallas hurried through her morning chores, mucking stalls, feeding the horses and chickens, and worrying about her ability to perform her first assignment as a member of the Brotherhood Protectors.

Percy Pearson, the white-haired ranch foreman, stepped out of the barn office into her path. He planted his hands on his narrow hips and pinned her with his piercing blue eyes. "Hey, what's this I hear about a wedding?"

Her body stiffened. Holy hell, news travelled fast around the ranch. "I don't know," she hedged. "What did you hear?"

"Got a call from Hank Patterson asking if we could use a little help around the ranch. One of his buddies from the service needed a place to stay while he planned his wedding to one of our guests." Percy's brows lifted. "Imagine my surprise when I found out that guest was you."

Heat rose in Dallas's cheeks. She'd never been a good

liar, but this act would be her first as an undercover bride. She had to lie to a man she respected in order to keep the fakeness of the pending wedding from getting to the person responsible for sabotaging other weddings. She sucked in a breath and figured the wave of warmth blooming on her cheeks could be attributed to the blushing bride syndrome, of which she had no experience. "You heard right. I…uh…I'm getting married."

Percy's brow furrowed, and he stared through slitted eyes. "You are? You don't sound convinced."

She swallowed hard and forced a smile to her face. "It's all so new and sudden." Not a lie. "I'm having a hard time believing it myself."

"We didn't know you were engaged to be married."

"Because I wasn't when I arrived a couple weeks ago," she admitted. Again, the truth. "Hank Patterson showed him how to find the ranch today, and he came to…pop the question." Again, not really a lie, but the statement still stuck in her craw.

"I take it you said yes." Percy's frown deepened. "That's kind of sudden, isn't it?"

"Not as sudden as the wedding date." Dallas cringed inwardly. Who would believe anyone would want to get married a week after the proposal?

"So, when is the wedding?"

"Next weekend." There. She'd said it.

Percy's eyebrows shot up. "A week? You're getting married in a week?" He shook his head. "Girl, what are you doing mucking stalls and feeding the animals? Shouldn't you be planning a wedding?"

Dallas gave a nervous laugh. "I suppose, only I don't have a clue where to start." Again, it didn't hurt when she was telling the truth. She really had no idea what went into a wedding.

"Do you have a dress? What about the cake? Where will it be held? Hell, if I'd known you were getting married next week, we could have left all the tables and chairs in place from Hannah and Taz's wedding."

Another nervous laugh and Dallas held up her hands. "My f-fiancé will be back in a while, and we plan on starting today. Hank's wife will help me find a dress. And the rest...I guess will fall in place. If the event were just up to me, I'd hire a Justice of the Peace and call it done."

Percy's frown slipped back over his forehead. "Are you sure about this wedding? I mean, I don't get the feeling you're keen on the idea. Do you even love the guy?"

Dallas bit down on her tongue, the pain reminding her she had to hold true to the operation, or she could be setting up herself for failure before it had even begun. "Yes. I l-love Viper, I mean, Vince." She shrugged. "I'm just not used to all the touchy-feely stuff most women experience."

"Hell," Percy said. "I'm not a woman, but I know a marriage won't last if you don't love each other."

"You're right," Dallas agreed, glancing to the side, praying for someone else to interrupt their conversation, or looking for an escape route, but finding neither. "We know we love each other and want to start our life together as soon as possible." *So we can catch a murdering son of a bitch who preys on newlyweds.*

"Have you told anyone else on the ranch?" he asked.

"Not yet. I can barely process all I have to accomplish before the big day."

"Then let me be the first to congratulate you." He held out his hand.

When Dallas took it in hers to shake, he pulled her into a hug.

"I wish you a truck-load of happiness." He set her to arm's length. "And I'll remind you that if you decide he isn't the right man, you can back out of the wedding up to the moment you stand in front of the preacher. I'll have your back and get you out of the church or wherever you plan on having it. No questions asked."

Dallas's eyes stung. "Thank you, Percy. Knowing you care means a lot."

"I just know you deserve the best. And if he's not the best…well, you know where I stand." He dropped his hands from her arms. "Now, go get cleaned up. Your fiancé is on his way, and I want an introduction."

"You've got it. I think you'll like him. He's retired Special Forces."

"I don't care if he's a retired garbageman as long as he's good to you and treats you like the princess you are."

Dallas snorted. "I'm no princess. Ranger training kicked anything resembling princess out of my system."

Percy smirked. "You like to think that, but I've been watching you. You might be all tough and hardcore, but inside, you're as feminine as they come." He held up a hand to stop her from commenting. "And that's not a bad thing. The toughest people I know happen to be female. You don't have to be able to kick everyone's ass to be strong. You have to be smart and know when to kick ass and when to ask for help. Take Hannah, our boss…she's one of those people. She takes in a lot of strays, but she has the strength of heart and mind to make their lives better. You're like her."

Dallas's chest swelled. "Thank you. That's the nicest compliment anyone has ever paid me. I think the world of Hannah and all she's done for the veterans and horses here at Brighter Days."

Percy's face softened. "Yes, she's done a lot. We all love her and wish her all the happiness her heart desires with her new husband." He grinned. "Now, we get to do the same for you." Percy hugged her again. "Congratulations."

At that moment, a truck pulled into the drive.

Percy stepped back and shaded his eyes with a hand. "This your man?"

Dallas's pulse kicked up, and her breathing became a little more ragged.

Viper stepped down from his truck and headed their way.

"Good. I want to meet the man who has stolen our girl's heart." Percy waited for Viper to close the distance between them.

Dallas's gaze connected with Viper's. She prayed she'd given a sufficient performance to the foreman who was now acting like a protective father.

Again, her heart swelled at Percy's concern. Her own

father would have done the same, if he knew she was getting married. Only he hadn't lived long enough to see her graduate from Ranger training. He also hadn't been around to help her pick up the pieces when she'd been discharged from the Army.

Percy took half a step in front of Dallas and crossed his arms over his chest. "You looking for someone?" he demanded.

The corners of Viper's lips twitched, but he didn't let loose with a smile. "As a matter of fact, I am." He tipped his head toward Dallas and winked. "I'm looking for my fiancée."

"Is that so?" Percy remained planted between Dallas and Viper.

Dallas fought the urge to giggle.

"I understand you two are planning to get hitched," Percy said.

Viper nodded, his face poker-straight now. "We are."

"Then what's the all-fired hurry that you have to do it within a week?"

Dallas couldn't resist the smile forming on her lips. It was Viper's turn to be interrogated. She was curious to see how he handled the older man's questions and prayed his answers matched hers.

"Sir," Viper started. "When you know exactly who you love, you don't want to wait another day to start living the rest of your life with her." He held out his hand to Dallas. "Isn't that right, darlin'?"

Dallas stared at his open hand for a moment before she took it and stepped around Percy, her cheeks heating and her pulse pounding so loudly against her eardrums she could barely hear herself think. "Uh-huh," she muttered.

Viper slid his arm around her waist and pulled her close against his side. He then held out his hand to the foreman. "You must be Percy Pearson."

"Maybe I am...maybe I'm not." Percy didn't take the extended hand. "I'm not sure I approve of a wedding taking place so quickly. We didn't even know Miss Dallas had a boyfriend."

"I didn't talk about him because I didn't know he felt the way he did," Dallas added quickly. "When he showed up at the ranch and proposed, I couldn't believe he came to do what he did."

Percy snorted, apparently not ready to concede. "How do you two know each other? Did you meet in the Army?"

Viper and Dallas answered as one, "Yes."

Viper went on to add, "We met while deployed."

"Ain't it against regulations to hook up when you're both deployed?"

"Yes, sir," Viper answered. "I said we *met* while deployed to..."

"Afghanistan," Dallas finished. "We were both at the same base. We met in the—" She scrambled in her head for where they could have met.

"—chow hall." He smiled down at her. "She was frowning at the mystery meat. I offered to take it off her hands."

"The meeting was love at first bite," Dallas finished, laughter bubbling up inside her. Yes, she'd been in chow halls with what the cook called meat that looked more like shoe leather.

She gazed at Viper with more interest. They shared common experiences, having been in the military and deployed to places that served reconstituted food no one knew what it was originally.

They'd both been in chaotic combat situations and knew what losing members of your squad was like. They'd both worn the uniform proudly.

Pretending to know each other shouldn't be much of a hardship.

Finally, Percy took Viper's hand and shook it. But he held on longer than necessary, his eyes narrowing. "You hurt my girl here, and you'll have me to answer to."

Viper met the older man's gaze straight on and answered, "I'm glad to know she has someone else looking out for her. Rest assured, I'll do my best to keep her safe and happy."

Dallas had always prided herself on her independence and her ability to look out for herself. But she had to admit, if only silently, that the protective tug-of-war between the two men made her feel cherished. The only other person who'd ever made her feel that way had been her father.

Her chest swelled with something she didn't want to put a label on. Not yet. Both of these men were relative strangers to her. She hoped to remedy that situation and get to know them better over the course of her mission.

"Now, if you'll excuse us," Viper said, "we have a lot of planning to do if we want to get married next weekend."

Dallas touched Percy's arm and leaned close to whisper, "Thanks for looking out for me."

Percy lifted his chin. "We watch out for each other at Brighter Days."

"I'll be back later to help with chores," Viper promised.

"You know anything about horses?" Percy asked.

"A little. I grew up on a ranch near Malta."

Dallas studied Viper more closely. Yes, she could see the cowboy in him...the quiet strength, loyalty and good manners. He knew how to wear a pair of jeans and she bet he could ride a horse. Her heart skipped several beats.

Percy nodded. "Good. I have some that need their hooves cleaned."

"You're on," Viper said.

Dallas waited until they were out of Percy's hearing before she leaned close to Viper. "Do you really know how to work with horses?"

He cast a sideways glance down at her and winked. "We have a lot to learn about each other if we're pulling off this charade."

Dallas swallowed hard at the way his glance made her insides scramble. No man had the right to look that sexy. Especially if he was her partner.

"Are we heading for the courthouse?" Dallas asked.

"We are. After we shower and change."

She frowned and planted her hands on her hips. "Are you telling me I smell?"

"If you mean by smell, that you have the lovely aroma of horse manure, then yes." He grinned. "You're in luck. I just happen to like the earthy smell of horse manure. But I do know for a fact, others might not appreciate it the way I do. Especially on the woman I'm taking to the courthouse to sign up for a marriage license." He steered her toward his truck. "But first, I have something for you."

"For me?" Dallas stumbled a little.

Viper cupped her elbow until she righted herself. "The item's not from me," he said. "It's from Sadie, Hank's wife."

The way Dallas's brow furrowed made Viper want to kiss away the lines. The sudden thought shook him to the core. He hadn't wanted to kiss any woman since the day his wife died.

"What would Sadie be sending me?" Dallas asked.

Viper opened the back door and unhooked the garment bag from the hanger. "Check it out. I've seen it, and it's going to look great on you."

"She sent me clothing?" Dallas unzipped the bag and her eyes widened. "A dress?"

"That's right. At least now we won't have to shop for one before we go to the courthouse."

"I don't know…" Dallas stared at the dress. "I told you, I've never worn a dress."

"It can't be too complicated." Viper stared at the emerald green dress inside the garment bag.

"But don't you have to wear high heels with dresses?" She looked up. "I don't even own a pair of high heels."

"How about sandals? Surely, you own a pair."

"If you recall, I only have one foot." Dallas grimaced. "The best I can do is a flip-flop." She shoved the bag back at Viper. "I can't do it. I'm not a girly-girl. And no one wants to see a woman with an artificial leg in a dress."

"Don't underestimate yourself." Viper took the bag and felt something hard at the bottom. "What's this?" He pulled a pair of low-heeled pumps from the bottom of the bag and laughed. "Sadie thought of everything."

"But she can't possible wear the same size shoe as I do." Dallas held up her hands.

"You tell me." He handed her one.

The sinking of Dallas's shoulders almost made Viper laugh. "Are they your size?"

"How did she know?" Dallas sighed. "I've haven't worn a pair of heels since this." She patted her injured leg, then gave a shrug. "I guess I can give them a try."

"Think of the outfit as an undercover disguise," Viper encouraged. "Take one for the team."

With a glare, Dallas snatched the garment bag and the other shoe from Viper. "If I look stupid in this, I don't want to hear one chuckle or rude comment."

Viper choked back his laughter and held up his hands in surrender. "I wouldn't dare."

"Damn right, you better not."

"You could whip my ass, for one." He did grin then. "And my mother taught me to be polite to the ladies."

"Your mother was a smart woman." Dallas turned toward the house. "I'll be out in less than fifteen minutes."

"Take your time. I'll just put my bags in one of the empty rooms." He gave her a head start before grabbing his duffel bag and following her into the house. Hank had cleared it with Hannah for Viper to use one of the spare bedrooms while he stayed at the ranch.

Once Hannah and Taz received clearance from the ER doctor, they'd continued on with their honeymoon. They'd be gone for a week and return just in time for the fake wedding.

He set his bag on the floor and pulled out his cellphone. So much for reception. Not a single bar. Viper left the room in search of a landline to make a call to the hospital where Chuck had been taken.

He happened to leave the bedroom at the same time as Dallas left hers—the one beside the room he'd chosen.

She stood for a moment, one foot bare, the emerald dress draped over her arm. A frown pulled her eyebrows low. "Do you want the first crack at the shower?"

He shook his head. "No, I need to make a call."

She nodded and continued across the hallway to a bathroom before hurriedly closing the door between them.

Viper got the distinct impression she wasn't happy he'd chosen a bedroom so close to hers. The thought made him smile. For some reason, he liked getting under her skin. And he was definitely succeeding. A lot had to do with the fact she was completely out of her element.

Viper knew more about being a regular female than

Dallas. His mother had seen to it that her boys respected and treated women the way she expected to be treated.

Dallas had been raised by her father. Not that he'd done a bad job. He'd raised an independent woman. But he hadn't filled her in on the more feminine intricacies of being a modern woman.

Viper found himself relishing the task of educating Dallas on those finer points. Not that he didn't like who she was. He did. Maybe a bit too much. Based on her training, she could hold her own in any situation that required shooting a gun or taking down an adversary with nothing but a knife or her bare hands.

The sound of water rushing from a showerhead came through the door of the bathroom.

His imagination got the better of him as images of Dallas, stripped naked and standing beneath the spray, came to him in a rush. His blood rushed through his veins, angling south to his groin.

She'd be slim, athletic, with finely tapered muscles.

The fact she had a prosthetic leg did nothing to dampen the heat of desire coursing through him. If anything, the strength and determination to come back from such an injury only made his new partner more attractive.

Viper drew in a long, deep breath and let it out slowly in an attempt to ease his racing pulse. Then he continued down the hallway. In the front foyer, he found a small table with a phone resting in a charger. He plucked the phone out of the base and called the number he'd saved on his cellphone from his visit to the hospital earlier that morning.

After a couple transfers, he was finally connected to Chuck Johnson's room.

"Johnson," Chuck barked into the phone.

"Hey, Chuck, Viper here."

"Hey, dude, thanks for getting me out of that car."

"No worries."

"You think you can get me out of this damned hospital?" He snorted. "You'd think I was injured in that wreck. I keep telling them I'm fine and ready to go home."

"You had a concussion. They want to make sure you don't have any bleeding on the brain."

"My head's fine but for the splitting headache. I can't stand hospitals."

Viper laughed. "I read you. I'm sure they'll let you out as soon as they're satisfied you won't keel over dead on them."

"I hear you got your first assignment." Chuck changed subjects. "Hank wouldn't give me any details, but I'm glad you're working."

"Thanks. I'll fill you in when I can," Viper promised. "In the meantime, don't give the nurses hell."

"Ha! *They're* giving it to *me*." The man was definitely more coherent than he'd been earlier that morning.

Viper rocked back on his heels, a smile curling his lips, glad Chuck was pulling through just fine. "I'm sure you deserve it."

Chuck sighed. "Can't believe I screwed up on my only task for Taz and Hannah's wedding."

"Something had to be wrong with the brakes on that limo. You can't beat yourself up."

"I should have checked it more carefully."

"They were working fine when you left the ranch."

"I should have done something. They almost died on their wedding day."

"*You* almost died," Viper reminded him. "The sheriff's department had the vehicle recovered and taken to the state crime lab. If the brakes were tampered with, they'll discover it pretty quickly."

"That's what Hank said."

"What you need to do is get back on your feet and back to work," Viper said.

"Yeah, sitting around is making me nuts. The only thing that made my day better was a visit from Daphne and Maya. That little girl has me wrapped around her little finger, and she knows it."

"I'm glad they were able to visit. I'll talk to you soon. Take care."

"You, too. These assignments aren't all about babysitting rich chicks. They can be harder than you think."

"I'll bear that in mind," Viper said, biting back another grin. "Out here."

"Out here," Chuck repeated.

He headed down the hall to the bedroom where he grabbed clean clothes and waited for the bathroom to be free.

The sound of the door across the hall opening made Viper's pulse kick up a notch. He waited a few moments before exiting his room, giving Dallas time to cross the hall into her bedroom.

Then he entered the bathroom and closed the door, glad he didn't see Dallas freshly washed and shiny clean. Already, he was too turned on by her slim body and sassy attitude. The fact the bathroom was steamy and smelled of a floral-scented shampoo and Dallas didn't help.

After turning the faucet to cool, he stripped down, stepped beneath the showerhead and let the water chill his body and his desire. By the time he showered, shaved and dressed, he was back in control and ready to face anything. Finally ready, he opened the door.

Dallas stood in her open doorway in the emerald-green dress, her auburn hair dried and curling around her chin in a soft wave. She chewed on her bottom lip, her eyes wide and worried. "Do I look stupid?"

Holy hell. She looked amazing. Viper's body immediately forgot the chill of the shower and sprang to attention. "Oh, sweetheart, you don't look stupid." Despite the fact she could kick his ass, he crossed the hall and took her hands in his.

She stiffened, her eyes growing wider. "Are you sure?"

"You're beautiful," he whispered and bent to brush his lips across hers.

Dallas pulled her hand from his and touched her fingers to her lips. "Why did you do that?"

For a moment, Viper didn't know what she was talking about. But his confusion ebbed fast when he realized what he'd done. Quick to cover his transgression, he said, "We need to act like we're in love. You'll have to get used to public displays of affection."

Her brow wrinkled. "We're not in public now."

"Count this gesture as practice." And then he swept his lips across hers again, unable to resist.

This time, she leaned into him, her free hand resting on his chest, her fingers curling into his shirt.

When she didn't draw away, Viper circled her back with his arm and drew her closer until her hips pressed against his and his cock nudged her belly.

Sweet heaven, she felt good against him, reminding him of how very long he'd gone without a woman. He traced the seam of her lips with his tongue.

She opened on a gasp.

Viper slipped past her teeth and caressed her tongue in a long, slow, glide that left him breathless, but wanting so much more.

When he finally straightened, he realized he could possibly be in way over his head with Dallas.

CHAPTER 6

Dallas pulled away and pressed the back of her hand to her mouth. "We should go," she said, her voice barely a whisper, hating that she sounded so breathless.

Some Ranger I am. I can't even control my respiration after one little kiss. One soul-defining, toe-curling, blood-boiling kiss.

"Right." Viper glanced down at the shoes Sadie had loaned Dallas. "Will you be okay walking in those?"

She nodded. Even if she wasn't, she wouldn't tell him. They made her feel more feminine than anything she had in her limited wardrobe. For the first time in her life, she wanted to feel like a woman. Though she hated to admit it, Viper was the reason.

That kiss. Sweet heaven. She'd never been kissed like that before. Sure, she'd been kissed and groped back in high school, but she'd never understood what the big deal was all about.

Now, she knew.

Every nerve in her body and all her blood in every vein and artery was on fire. All because of a kiss. She could only begin to imagine what making love to Viper would be like. Her cheeks heated, along with the center of her being.

Making love with Viper…

Dallas had to remind herself their kissing, and anything else, was for show. Nothing about their relationship was real, except their partnership as Brotherhood Protectors on a mission to catch a wedding saboteur.

The phone in the front entryway rang, saving Dallas from having to come up with anything else to say. She jumped and hurried to grab the call.

"Brighter Days Ranch," she answered as she'd heard Hannah and Cookie respond each time the ranch received a call.

"Dallas?" a female voice said.

"That's me," Dallas said Surprised the call was for her. She never received calls at the ranch.

"This is Sadie McClain Patterson."

"Oh, hello, Sadie. Thank you for the dress and shoes."

"You're welcome. Did they fit?" Sadie asked.

"Perfectly," Dallas assured her. The material lay as soft as butter against her skin and the shoe didn't pinch her foot. She'd been relieved the foot attachment of her prosthetic fit the shoe without too much coaxing. She stared down at the shiny, black pumps, admiring how pretty the shoes were. She'd never had any so nice.

"I called to let you know I set up an appointment for you and Vince with the wedding planner, Daisy Chadwick. She's actually at her waitress job at the diner in Eagle Rock today. However, she can take a few minutes to speak with you when you come by."

"Thank you." Dallas glanced toward Viper, her breath catching at how handsome he was in his white dress shirt and black slacks. "We were on our way to apply for the marriage license at the courthouse."

"Sounds good. I wish you two all the happiness in the world. That's coming from someone who has found her forever love." She laughed. "Call me a romantic, but I want everyone to be as happy as I am with Hank."

Dallas swallowed hard on the sudden lump in her throat. "Thank you, Sadie," she choked out. "We'll get with Daisy."

"Oh, and the day after tomorrow, Daisy and I want to take you to Bozeman to shop for a wedding dress. Are you up for that? We don't have much time if the gown has to be altered before the wedding."

Inwardly, Dallas groaned. Shopping wasn't something she enjoyed, but, for the sake of the operation, she'd suck it up. "Oh. Yes. I suppose I'm up for dress shopping."

"Good. Hank's taking Vince to try on tuxedoes that day, as well. We can meet for lunch afterward."

"That arrangement would be very nice." Dallas thanked Sadie and hung up. Her gaze met Viper's. "I didn't realize planning a wedding would be so intense."

Viper laughed. "Most brides take months to plan one, and some take more than a year."

"You're kidding, right?" Dallas had never been around women planning a wedding, and she didn't watch much television to pick up on the rituals associated with planning such an event.

He shook his head. "Emily took six months to plan ours. I wanted to go down to the courthouse and get it done in a day, but she wanted the flowers, the church, cake, and her entire extended family there." He shrugged. "I just had to show up in a tux."

Dallas gave him a sad smile, her heart hurting for him. "You must have loved her very much."

The smile Viper had a few minutes earlier faded. "I did."

Dallas touched his arm. "I'm sorry you lost her."

"Me, too." He squared his shoulders and offered her his arm. "Shall we go apply for a marriage license?"

With a nod, Dallas slid her hand into his bent elbow, liking the way it felt to be escorted through the door, down the steps and across the uneven ground to Viper's truck. She was glad for the support, given she wasn't familiar with walking in even a low-heeled pair of shoes. And climbing up into the truck took some finagling without getting the skirt of her dress caught in the door.

Sheesh, she had a reason for wearing only jeans and T-shirts. She didn't have to worry about all those details. Nor did she have to brace herself for the strange looks people gave her when they saw her prosthetic in place of the leg she'd lost.

Most people never considered she was a war veteran

and were surprised when she told them she'd lost it in battle.

Whatever. She was proud of her service and wished she was still on active duty, fighting for right and freedom. At least with the Brotherhood Protectors, she could continue to fight for justice and protect those who couldn't protect themselves.

Viper climbed into the driver's seat and set the truck into motion, heading into Eagle Rock. "Let's nail down our story while we can," he said. "I'm sure the wedding planner will have questions about us, and we'll want to answer without stumbling."

"Good idea."

"Let's start with backgrounds."

"I prefer to stick to as much of the truth as possible," Dallas said. "That way we don't have as many lies to remember."

"Agreed," Viper said. "I can start. I grew up in Malta, Montana. That's on the other side of the state. No mountains, but a lot of grasslands. I'm one of four brothers. My parents are alive and well and still living near Malta."

"Why didn't you go home after you left the military?" Dallas asked.

"Hank offered me the job. I took it, and here I am." He smiled. "Your turn. I know your father raised you, but where? Any siblings? Favorite ice cream? Favorite flower?"

"Texas. Siblings...zero. I was an only child. Ice cream...rocky road. Is there any other flavor? Flower...Mountain laurel because it smells so good and reminds me of home in the hill country of Texas. But if you're talking flowers from a florist, I like daisies because they're cheerful." She'd received daisies from an unknown donor while she'd recuperated from the amputation at Walter Reed. With no family to visit her, the flowers had come when she'd been at her lowest.

"What about your dad?"

Pain knifed through her heart. "Dead of a heart attack while I was in basic training."

Viper shot a frown in her direction. "I'm sorry."

"So was I."

"No other family?"

"None." She shot him a sharp glance. "I don't need your pity, Viper. I've been on my own for years. I'm doing fine."

"Fair enough," he said, his gaze on the road ahead. "If the planner asks, Hank will walk you down the aisle at the wedding."

Dallas swallowed hard on the lump forming in her throat. Not that she'd thought about getting married, but her father had been so much a part of her life, she would have wanted him to be the one to give her away.

Again, she had to remind herself this wedding was fake. She wasn't really getting married. Still, her eyes stung and her chest hurt. She stared out the side window at the mountains, the trees and the blue sky. As she passed a dark stand of lodge pole pines, her face was reflected in the window. So was Viper's. He looked at her, a frown wrinkling his brow.

She blinked back tears and forced herself to focus on

the road ahead. What else could she do? Looking back only brought pain.

Once they reached Eagle Rock, Viper glanced at each of the buildings, searching for the courthouse with the directions Hank had given him.

"I believe the courthouse is by the sheriff's station up ahead." Dallas pointed to the old stone building next to another with patrol vehicles parked out front.

"After we get the license, I'd like to get an update from the sheriff about the wedding attacks," Viper said.

"Won't visiting the sheriff's office give away our cover?" Dallas asked.

"I think we'll be okay. Since I was first on the scene of Taz and Hannah's crash, I think it's reasonable I would ask for an update."

Dallas nodded. "Right."

Viper parked between the courthouse and the sheriff's office, climbed down from the truck and hurried around to help Dallas down.

"I can do this myself," she muttered, but she caught her foot in the hem of her dress and nearly fell.

Viper was there to catch her around the waist and transition her from the truck to the ground.

She straightened and smoothed the hair out of her face. "Thank you."

He waited until she turned toward the courthouse before he grinned.

Dallas was a stubbornly independent woman.

Viper found that he liked that. Her attitude challenged him to teach her it was all right to be independent and to accept the courtesies of the gentleman his mother raised him to be.

The more Dallas resisted, the more Viper liked to show her how good he could act.

Inside the courthouse, they followed signs to a middle-aged woman with dyed black hair wearing a leopard-print cardigan and black leggings. She sat at a desk, typing on a keyboard.

When Viper stopped in front of her, she turned her attention from the monitor to Viper's belt buckle and her gaze rose up the length of his torso. The woman's lips curved upward. "Well, well, what can I do for you, honey?"

He glanced at the nameplate on her desk and gave her a smile that probably melted her panties.

Viper's smile had that effect on Dallas, as well. That he was directing it toward another woman didn't make the gesture less potent.

"Irene," he said. "I'm Vince Van Cleave." He turned to Dallas. "And this is my fiancée, Dallas Hayes."

"Let me guess," Irene said. "You're here to apply for a marriage license." She sighed. "The good-looking guys are always taken. If I was twenty years younger…" She pulled a form from a drawer and placed it on a clipboard. "Fill out this application and bring it back to me with cash for the fee listed." She laid a pen on top of the clipboard and nodded toward the chairs lined against the wall.

Viper handed the clipboard to Dallas.

Dallas took a seat and filled in the information she could and passed the form to Viper.

When they'd both completed the form and signed their names, they approached Irene. Viper pulled bills out of his wallet and handed over the form and the money.

She took the bills and the paper and keyed the information into the computer. A few short minutes later, she printed out a marriage license on cream-colored parchment paper and handed it to Viper. "After the ceremony, you both sign this document and have the wedding official who conducted the ceremony sign, as well. You'll file this document here at the courthouse."

"Thank you, Irene." Viper slipped his arm around Dallas. "Ready, darlin'?"

He could feel Dallas stiffen at his side. Then she leaned into him.

She nodded. "Ready."

As Viper turned toward the door, with Dallas pressed against his side, he could almost believe this fake wedding was real. Which was ridiculous. Everything they would do, up to and including the actual wedding itself, was fantasy. A way to lure an unpredictable suspect out of hiding.

Dallas would never marry a guy like him. Hell, she didn't need anyone else in her life. At least, that was what she'd told him.

Somehow, deep inside, Viper knew better. Dallas needed others in her life more than she'd ever admit. She missed her father terribly. He'd been the only family she had. The thought of Dallas lying in a hospital fighting to stay alive and recover from the loss of her leg made Viper sad. That she'd had to go through the recovery alone broke his heart.

"By the way," Irene said from behind them.

Dallas glanced over her shoulder.

Irene give a tip of her chin toward Dallas. "Love the dress. It's perfect with your coloring."

A blush rose in Dallas's cheeks. "Thank you."

Viper liked that she was slightly uncomfortable with the compliment. She wasn't full of herself. He liked that about her.

Outside the courthouse, Dallas paused on the steps and glanced around. "Did you suppose Irene could be the one?" she whispered. "Middle-aged, probably single —I didn't see a wedding ring on her finger."

Viper couldn't imagine Irene tampering with the brakes on a limo. "I don't know, but we'll add her name to the list for Hank's computer guys to check into."

Dallas nodded and continued down the steps, moving slowly.

Viper hooked her arm in his hand just as the shoe on her prosthetic twisted sideways, causing Dallas to stumble.

He pulled her against him and slipped an arm around her waist. "Those shoes take some getting used to?"

"I never thought I'd use this foot they gave me for wearing high heels." She snorted. "But here I am. I prefer my running foot. I suppose I could hide it beneath the wedding dress."

"You bet." Viper agreed. "Along with your running

shoes. You'll be just as gorgeous." He bent and pressed a kiss to her temple.

Her cheeks reddened, and she touched a hand to where his lips had been. "Why did you do that? No one's watching."

He smiled down at her but his words were serious. "We don't know who is watching and from which direction. Everything we do could be under scrutiny now that we've applied for the marriage license."

"Oh, good." She smiled, though it appeared tight and forced. Then she cupped her hand to his cheek and leaned up to press a kiss to his lips. "There. How was that for a show?" And she gave him a cheeky grin.

The warmth of her lips on his spread throughout his body, pooling low in his loins. "Pretty good. But I think you can do better." He swept her into his arms and crushed her lips beneath his.

She opened to him, and his tongue slid along the length of hers.

She didn't fight or resist. Instead, her hand slid up his chest to weave into the hair at the back of his neck.

Minutes later, he set her back on her feet and waited for her to stand steady. Then he took her hand, pressed a kiss to the back of her knuckles and led her to the sheriff's office.

The color in her cheeks was bright, and her eyes appeared a little dazed.

Viper fought back a huge grin.

Dallas had a few things to learn about kissing, and he enjoyed teaching her.

Once inside the building housing the sheriff's department, Viper asked for Sheriff Barron.

Before anyone could go get him, the man stepped out of an office and strode toward them. "Mr. Van Cleave," he said and stuck out a hand. "Glad to see you this morning. I just got off the phone with the state crime lab. They didn't have to look far to see the brakes on that limo had been tampered with."

Viper clenched his teeth as images of the limo skidding off the road and over the edge of the drop-off resurfaced in his mind. "They were lucky a tree was there to stop the limo."

The sheriff's lips thinned into a straight line. "Yes, they were. Viper barely got the bride, groom and driver out of the limo before the tree snapped."

"Damn," Dallas whispered. "Thank God he was able to get them out safely."

"The accident could have been a lot worse," Viper said. "Other than the limo rental company, did anyone else have access to the vehicle before or during the wedding?"

"I asked the rental company. They staged it in Eagle Rock overnight and moved it to Brighter Days Ranch the morning of the wedding." The sheriff crossed his arms over his chest. "Anyone could have tampered with it during the night." He dropped his arms to his side, and his grim face changed to a warm smile. "I hear congratulations are in order for you and Miss Hayes."

Viper's lips twisted. "Good news travels as fast as bad in these parts."

"I'll take all the good news we can get. It helps

balance the bad." The sheriff stuck out a hand to Dallas. "Congratulations on your upcoming wedding. I heard about it from the local news reporter, Trish Sweeney. Said she got a call from Sadie McClain that the two of you were gettin' hitched next weekend." The sheriff's eyes narrowed. "Sure you don't want to put off the ceremony until we have a better handle on who's ruining weddings around here?"

Viper's arm circled Dallas's waist again. He liked the way she fit against him, and she wasn't as stiff as the first time he'd held her close. "No. We're pretty set on the date. We'll take our chances."

"As long as you play it safe. Want me to schedule one of my deputies to attend the wedding, for security?"

"That's not a bad idea," Dallas said. "We could use all the help we can get to make sure the ceremony goes off without any trouble."

Viper tipped his head toward Dallas. "What the little woman said. You know, happy wife…happy life."

Dallas dug her elbow into his side and stretched a tight smile across her face. She nodded toward the lawman's left hand sporting a bright gold wedding band. "That's right. I'm sure the sheriff knows all about keeping the peace in his marriage."

Sheriff Barron chuckled. "I sure do. My sweetheart means the world to me. I'd do anything to make her happy." He winked at Viper. "But she's really good about making me happy, as well." He clapped his hands together. "Well, I wish you two the best."

"Do you mind if we stop by occasionally for an

update on the case between now and the wedding?" Viper asked.

"Not at all. If I were in your shoes, I'd want to know, as well." The sheriff touched Dallas's arm. "Take care of yourselves. I don't want anyone else hurt."

"We will," Dallas responded. "Thank you, Sheriff Barron."

Viper guided her out of the building, ready for her anger, knowing she would have taken offense at his comments.

But when she cleared the door and didn't lay into him, he thought he'd dodged that bullet. Not until he'd helped her into the truck, slid into the driver's seat and closed the door did she address him.

"Don't ever call me *the little woman*," she commanded, in a low, dangerous tone.

He grinned. "I wondered how long you'd take to say something."

"It was all I could do not to punch you in the throat."

His smile broadened. "I'm impressed. You kept your cool throughout. Well done."

She drew in a deep breath and forced a smile as a deputy walked past her window and into the sheriff's office. "Don't patronize me, *partner*. Thank God, this is only a fake marriage. You wouldn't last a day the way you're going. I thought your mother taught you better."

"At least I got a rise out of you." He held up both hands in surrender. "I'm sorry. I just couldn't resist getting your goat."

"Oh, you got it, okay." She smiled again as another deputy left the office and strode to his patrol car.

Viper reached for her hand and lifted it to his lips. When Dallas tried to pull it free, he held on tighter. "I'm sorry. I won't tease you again."

"Good. Now, let go of my hand," she said through gritted teeth.

"I will," he said, his grip tightening. "After I show you how sorry I am."

Dallas froze, her gaze on the hand he held as he lifted it to his lips.

"Dallas, darlin', I'm sorry." Then he turned over her hand and pressed his lips to the soft skin of her palm. He hadn't planned on kissing her, but he was sorry he'd made her mad. Besides, he really wanted to kiss her again. With the console in the way, he was forced to be satisfied with pressing his lips to her hand, not her mouth.

This kiss was too brief, when he wanted so much more, but it would have to sustain him until they could be closer. Viper curled her fingers into her palm and looked up into her rounded eyes. He was more shaken than he ever thought he could be. After Emily died, he was certain he never would feel anything for another woman.

And Dallas was so very different from Emily, he would never have considered her. But the kiss they'd shared earlier and the feel of her palm against his lips made him look at her in a completely altered light. The flood of blood-pulsing desire rushing through him was nothing like the warm, comfortable love he'd had for Emily.

Perhaps he was doing Dallas and Emily both a

disservice. They couldn't be compared. And he wasn't being loyal to the memory of his dead wife.

Guilt roiled in his gut, reminding him that he'd had everything. Why was he considering Dallas in any other capacity than as his partner?

Because she was badass, determined and made him feel again.

Damn it!

She'd made him feel again.

CHAPTER 7

Dallas led the way into the diner, her gaze scanning the occupants. She wondered if the wedding saboteur was one of the patrons, watching and listening to determine his or her next target.

A brown-haired waitress nodded toward them. "Take a seat where you like. I'll be with you in a moment."

"Is that Daisy?" Viper asked.

Dallas shook her head. "Sadie said Daisy has blond hair."

"Are you Dallas and Vince?" A petite young woman with bright blond hair and blue eyes stepped out of the kitchen, smiling.

"We are," Viper said.

"I'm Daisy." She nodded. "I'll be with you in just a moment." Then she turned to the brunette. "I've got these two, Lisa."

Lisa's eyes narrowed momentarily before she shrugged and turned to help other customers.

Dallas led Viper to a corner booth at one end of the diner. She sat with her back to the wall and waited for Viper to take the seat opposite her.

He smiled and chose to sit beside her, instead of across, forcing her to scoot along the bench.

"Another seat is available," she whispered.

"We're engaged and about to get married," he whispered back, smiling as if she hung the moon. "And we want Daisy to sit across from us during our planning session. Besides, I like sitting with my back to the wall, too." He winked and lifted the menu. "And I like sitting next to you."

Dallas had difficulty concentrating on the words on the laminated card. Viper's thigh pressing against hers made her warm all over and scrambled every one of her brain cells. Not only could she not put two thoughts together, she could barely catch her breath. What was wrong with her? Surely, she wasn't so attracted to the man she'd lost her friggin' mind?

"Sorry to keep you waiting." The pretty blonde stopped at their table and pulled a pad out of her crisp white apron. "What can I get you to drink?"

"I'll have coffee," Viper said.

"I'll—" Dallas squeaked, cleared her throat and started again. "I'll have ice-water. Sadie McClain sent us. She said you could help us with planning our wedding?" She gave the woman a weak smile.

A grin spread over Daisy's face as she slid into the seat across from them. "Yes. Sadie called and said you two were planning a wedding for next weekend." She blew out a quick breath. "Wow, that's a tight timeframe."

"We're sorry for the short notice," Viper said. "But Sadie was sure you could help."

"And I will. We'll have a lot to do in the next week, so gird your loins and be ready to drink from the fire hose. Sorry for the clichés, but in this case, they fit." Daisy jumped up from the seat. "Let me get you those drinks and take care of a couple of customers. Then I can go on break, and we can get started."

Daisy dashed away, smiling at customers. She poured coffee, removed empty plates, sent orders to the kitchen and then returned with coffee and ice-water.

Dallas was tired just watching the younger woman. "Where do you find all that energy?"

Daisy laughed. "I've always had more energy than I know what to do with. That's why I work this job, have a business as a wedding planner and I'm taking online classes to get my business degree. My friends and ex-boyfriend call me an overachiever." She shrugged. "I just don't like to sit around when I could be doing something productive." She leaned across the table. "So? What kind of wedding did you have planned?"

Dallas shot a glance at Viper and back to Daisy. "Type?"

"You know..." Daisy grinned. "Preacher or Justice of the Peace."

"Preacher," Dallas said.

"Justice of the Peace," Viper said at the exact same time.

Daisy chuckled. "Okay then, you don't know."

"The setting really doesn't matter," Dallas said. "I'm comfortable with either."

Daisy shot her a narrow-eyed glance. "Are you sure?"

"I'm sure," Dallas said.

"Getting married isn't something you do every day," Daisy said. "I don't want you to have any regrets."

Heat rose in Dallas's cheeks. Who could have regrets marrying Viper? He was so handsome it hurt to look at him, knowing she would never have him as a real husband.

"Since we have such a short timeframe, let's go with whatever is most expedient or available," Viper reasoned.

Daisy nodded. "Fair enough. We'll go with whoever is available next Saturday." She lifted her pen and set it to her notepad. "Besides the wedding dress, rings and tuxedo, have you thought about cakes, reception venue, dinner entrées, music, decorations and most of all, invitations to the guests?"

Dallas wished Daisy would hand her a rifle and ask her to fire expert. She was trained and capable of anything weapon or tactics related. But planning a wedding? She drew in a deep breath. "We haven't thought of anything other than I'm going wedding dress shopping and Viper—Vince is looking for a tuxedo tomorrow."

"Wow, you really are behind the curve." Daisy smiled. "Are you set on next weekend?"

Viper draped an arm around Dallas's shoulders. "When you know you have the perfect person, you want to start the rest of your life right away."

Daisy sighed. "I agree. I just wish other people understood."

"What do you mean?" Dallas leaned forward. "You've had couples plan a wedding they weren't sure of?"

"Some. Not my most recent event with Hannah and Taz." Her smile faded. "I can't believe they ran off the road on their way to the airport. I'm glad they made it out all right and continued on to their honeymoon. Have you heard anything about the driver? I heard he was hurt in the crash."

"He's banged up, but he'll survive," Viper said.

"I'm glad," Daisy said. "He seems like such a nice man."

"One of the best," Viper agreed.

The wedding planner made a few more notes on her pad. "Do you have a venue for the wedding and the reception? It might be difficult to find a place to accommodate you at this late date."

"Hank Patterson assured us we could have the wedding and reception at his father's ranch," Viper said.

"Good. I'll need the number of guests, type of food you want at the reception and if you would like live music or a DJ."

"You planned Taz and Hannah's wedding..." Dallas wondered what about Daisy would inspire someone to want to ruin a wedding the waitress had planned? "We want everything the same. It was a beautiful ceremony."

"You're in luck," Daisy smiled. "They had barbeque and a DJ. Guests?"

"The same number." Viper laughed. "Probably the same guests, too."

"You must be a close-knit group of friends."

"We all served in the military," Viper said. "Including Dallas."

Daisy's eyes widened. "I haven't met too many women who've served. I admire you for doing that. I've thought about joining the Army, but I've never been farther from home than Bozeman."

"Bozeman?" Dallas tilted her head.

Daisy's lips twisted. "That's right. I stayed here in Eagle Rock after high school because my father was sick. When he passed, I stayed for my mother until she was stable enough to be on her own. And here I am, still in Eagle Rock. But I have plans. I won't be here for much longer."

"No? Where are you going from here?" Viper asked.

Daisy drew in a deep breath and let it out on a smile. "I'll start in Helena. I want to go to school to become a nurse. After caring for my father, I discovered I liked doing that."

"Nursing is an honorable profession and there seems to be a high demand." Dallas remembered all the nurses and doctors had done for her when she'd lost her leg. "Once you have your license, then what? The military could use good nurses."

Daisy smiled. "I hadn't thought about that option. I would love to help our men and women in uniform. I'm so ready to get out of Eagle Rock and explore the world. I don't understand those who can't see past this town or Montana."

Viper's mouth twisted. "As a native of Montana, getting out of the state was great, and even better coming back."

Daisy nodded. "I get that. I just want the chance to see something besides the Crazy Mountains. I've always wanted to go to Europe. But first, I have to finish school. I'm working the diner and my wedding planning business to pay for school. But the way things have been going, I was afraid I wouldn't get any more business. I'm starting to think I'm a jinx."

"Why's that?" Dallas asked, knowing the history of Daisy's wedding planning fiascos. Having Daisy go through the details might reveal information that could lead them to the one causing the problems.

"My past four weddings have had problems. One had an arbor collapse on the bride and groom. Another had the tent stakes pull up from the ground. The entire wedding party was caught beneath. And then last night my bride and groom nearly died when their limousine went off the road." Daisy's brows wrinkled. "Are you sure you want to hire me? I'll completely understand if you don't. Hell, I wouldn't hire me with a track record like mine."

"We're not superstitious," Dallas assured her. "Sadie highly recommended you. Plus, I don't have the first clue how to plan a wedding."

"We'll take our chances," Viper concluded.

"Okay, then." Daisy grinned. "This job will put me that much closer to my financial goals before I leave for Helena in the spring."

"Have you already been accepted into the university?" Dallas asked.

The younger woman tilted her head. "I have. And

I've been taking courses online so I'll be applying for the nursing program as soon as I can."

"Congratulations." Dallas was truly happy for this bright and gregarious woman. "I wish you all the luck."

"And I wish you two all the happiness. Now, let me get back to work. I'll make some calls on my next break to set up appointments for you to choose wedding cakes. And I'll do all the arrangements for seating, tables, decorations, etc." Daisy touched a finger to her lips. "Oh, Dallas, what's your favorite flower?"

"Mountain laurel," Viper answered before she had the chance. "They remind her of home back in Texas."

Her heart warmed. He hadn't forgotten.

Daisy frowned. "I doubt we can get some here in time for the wedding. I believe the plant's pretty seasonal."

"Her second favorite is daisies," Viper said. "Because they're so cheerful."

Daisy laughed. "I hope I live up to my name."

"You do," Dallas said.

"Thanks. No matter what flowers you love, to see them in a bridal bouquet arrangement helps with the final choice. I suggest you stop by the florist shop in town and look through the books to decide what you like. You might want to do that next, since the type of flowers could determine how long ordering them and getting them in will take."

"I have to choose an arrangement?" Dallas asked then looked at Viper and shrugged. "I'm not good at this."

"I'd go with you, but I have to work." Daisy looked to Viper.

Viper smiled, picking up his cue. "I'll help her choose."

Daisy glanced toward the kitchen. "I'd better get back to work before my customers get restless." She leaned across the table and clasped Dallas's hands. "Thank you for the opportunity."

"No, really," Dallas assured her, "thank you for helping us pull together this event on such short notice."

"I can't believe we're doing this in just five days." As Daisy rose from her seat, a young man entered the restaurant. "Great," Daisy muttered. She turned back to Dallas and Viper. "Sadie gave me your cellphone numbers, I'll contact you with information, meetings and when I need you to make decisions."

"Thank you," Dallas said.

The young man spied Daisy and made a beeline toward her.

She met him halfway across the floor and pressed a hand to his chest. "Tyler, what are you doing here?"

The young man covered her hand on his chest. "I don't like where we left off last night."

Daisy's usually smiling lips firmed into a straight line. "I told you, I'm not staying in Eagle Rock. Nothing you can say or do will keep me here. Can't you leave it there?"

Tyler's face hardened, his hand curled around her fingers and held tight. "No, Daisy. I love you. I want you to be my wife."

Dallas didn't like the way Tyler was holding onto

Daisy. It appeared Daisy didn't like it, either. Trapped inside the booth by Viper, Dallas couldn't help.

"I'm not ready to settle down. I've spent the last four years taking care of others. I want to take care of me and do what I want, without anyone holding me back." She pushed past him. "Now, go away. I have work."

Tyler grabbed her arm and jerked her around.

Viper was halfway out of his seat when another young man, wearing a white apron, burst through the swinging doors of the kitchen. "Tyler, you need to leave."

Still holding Daisy's arm, Tyler faced the other man. "Back off, Billy Joe. This matter is between me and Daisy."

Daisy glared at Tyler. "It was, but it isn't anymore. I'm not marrying you. I'm going to school."

"Then I'll come with you," he insisted.

"No, Tyler. I need to do this on my own." She stared down at his hand. "I care for you Tyler, but I'm not ready to settle down. Now, please let go of my arm. I need to get back to work."

Tyler refused to drop her arm.

"You heard Daisy. Let her go," Billy Joe said, his voice low and tight.

"Sir, release the woman," Viper said in a deep, resonant tone that brooked no argument.

"I'll do whatever the hell I want. She's *my* fiancée."

Dallas slid out of the booth, ready to take on Tyler in defense of Daisy.

Daisy jerked her arm free of Tyler's grip. "You are not my fiancé. You aren't my boyfriend anymore. Last time we broke up, you didn't even wait a day before climbing in bed with another woman. I forgave that and took you back. But your temper is the last straw. We're done." She pointed her finger at his chest. "Do you understand? D.O.N.E." Then she pointed to the door. "Leave."

Tyler's eyes narrowed. "You don't dump me after we've been dating for five years."

"Seems like she did." Billy Joe leaned against the counter, his arms crossed over his chest.

Tyler took a step toward Billy Joe, raising his fisted hand. "Stay out of this, busboy."

"We haven't dated five years straight," Daisy said. "I broke up with you a couple times because you couldn't control your temper."

Tyler stiffened. "You went out with that Brandon guy. What did you expect?"

"You and I weren't together." Daisy flung out her hand. "I'd broken up with you. You had no right to tell me who I could or couldn't date when you were dating someone else."

"You're my girlfriend," Tyler insisted, his stare hard.

Daisy shook her head. "No."

"You heard her," Billy Joe said in a low, steady voice.

Tyler's lip curled back in a snarl. "Shut the hell up."

Viper stepped between the two young men. "This show is over."

Tyler's glare shifted from Billy Joe to Viper. "Stay the hell out of my business."

"You need to leave," Viper warned, his jaw tight, his brows low and menacing.

Tyler tilted his head back to look up into Viper's eyes. "Or what?"

Dallas stepped up beside Viper. "Or we'll call the sheriff." By now, they were the center of attention in the diner. Dallas wouldn't back down. If Tyler grabbed Daisy again, Dallas wouldn't wait for the sheriff. She'd take his ass down.

Tyler's eyes narrowed as he stared from Viper to Dallas, and back to Daisy. "Go ahead. Call the sheriff."

Daisy dug in her apron pocket and pulled out her cellphone. She punched the buttons for 911 and raised the device to her ear.

Tyler slapped the cellphone from her hand, sending it flying.

It bounced against Viper's chest and clattered to the floor.

Viper took another step toward Tyler.

Tyler swung at Viper's chin.

Viper caught Tyler's fist in his hand, twisted the man's arm up and behind his back. Without hesitation, he shoved him toward the exit.

Dallas hurried ahead and opened the door.

As Viper pushed him out into the parking lot, a sheriff's deputy pulled up, climbed out of his vehicle and hurried around to take charge. "What's going on?"

"This man attacked me!" Tyler shouted.

"The hell he did," Daisy said from behind them. "And we have a dozen witnesses who will verify. Tyler swung at Mr. Van Cleave."

The deputy snapped one end of a set of cuffs on

Tyler's wrist. "Sir, do you want to press charges against Mr. King?"

"No," Viper said. "But you might ask Miss Chadwick if she does."

The deputy's brows furrowed as he glanced from Tyler to Daisy. "Did he attack you, Daisy?"

"Yes, he did." Daisy rubbed her arm where bright red fingerprints stood out against her pale skin.

The deputy jerked Tyler's other arm around behind him and snapped the cuff on his wrist. "Do you want to press charges?"

"Not at this time." She narrowed her eyes at Tyler. "But if you try anything again, I'll file a restraining order against you faster than you can say *we're through*."

Tyler glared at her. "We're not over, Daisy."

Daisy crossed her arms over her chest. "Yes. We. Are."

The deputy hooked Tyler's arm and led him toward his service vehicle.

Tyler jerked his arm free and turned back to face Daisy. "You can't just toss me out like trash. We had a good thing going." When Daisy didn't respond, Tyler's lips pulled back from his teeth. "You'll regret it, bitch." He looked past her to where Billy Joe stood in the doorway beside Dallas. "And you...I'll get you."

"The hell you will," the deputy said. "Maybe you need some time in the pokey to cool your heels. Let's see what the sheriff has to say about you disturbing the peace." He opened the rear door of his vehicle, placed a hand on the back of Tyler's head and guided him inside.

When Tyler struggled, the deputy gave him a

stronger push, sending the angry young man sprawling across the back seat.

Tyler landed with a grunt and pushed himself awkwardly to an upright position.

As the vehicle pulled away, Tyler glared at the crowd standing outside the diner, witnessing his departure.

"That man has anger management issues," Dallas said softly.

"You're telling me?" Daisy snorted. "That's why I broke up with him." She turned and forced a tight smile to her lips. "I'm sorry for the drama. You two shouldn't have to deal with that when you have a wedding to think about." She clapped her hands at the crowd of folks. "Show's over. Can I get anyone a refill on their drinks?"

And just like that, she had the guests back in the diner in less than a minute.

Viper took Dallas's arm and ushered her back to their seats. Once again, he sat beside her.

Dallas scooted across the seat to the inside corner of the booth. No matter how far she slid, she couldn't go far enough to keep Viper's thigh from touching hers. Heat spread from the point of contact throughout her body.

She cleared her throat. "Do we need to stay? Or can we go on to our next stop?"

"I don't know about you, but I'm hungry." He waved Daisy back to their table.

"Thank you so much for sticking up for me. I'm afraid you've made an enemy out of Tyler."

Viper's jaw tightened. "He shouldn't manhandle any

woman. You don't have to put up with that kind of behavior."

"I know. But he was right. We were together. I can't discount that."

"But you aren't now," Dallas leaned forward and touched the waitress's hand. "No man has any right to treat a woman that roughly."

Daisy nodded. "I just don't like making a scene at work." She smiled. "Anyway, thanks. Now, what can I do for you? Are you ready to order?"

"Yes, ma'am." Viper ordered a hamburger and fries.

Dallas ordered a hamburger as well. "With extra pickles."

"Make mine the same," Viper said.

When Daisy left with their order, Viper shot her that wickedly handsome grin. "One more thing we have in common."

Dallas's insides melted into goo. What the hell was wrong with her? Badass Rangers didn't melt at a man's smile. Just because she'd left the Army didn't mean she had to go all soft. She was an agent for the Brotherhood Protectors, not a girly-girl going gaga over a man. She shook her head in disgust, even as her body burned at Viper's closeness.

Viper gathered her hand in his. "Relax. You're supposed to look like you actually like your fiancé. Not like you're scared to death of me."

She bristled. "I'm not scared of you." But if she were honest, she was scared.

Of herself.

CHAPTER 8

Viper held Dallas's hand until their meal arrived, at which time he was forced to release it.

He liked holding her hand, more than as the cover for their operation. He wanted to continue to hold her hand and feel the warmth it spread throughout his body.

They ate in silence until both had finished their burgers and were munching on fries dipped in ketchup.

"I'm surprised you ate that entire burger," he said.

Dallas frowned. "Why?"

"I don't know," Viper backtracked, realizing he might have stepped into a hornet's nest. Hadn't his mother told him never to comment on a woman's weight or eating habits? "Just that most women I know eat salads and graze like rabbits." He held up his hands. "Don't get me wrong. I think seeing a woman with a real appetite is refreshing. Never mind. I shouldn't have said anything. I'm shutting the fuck up now." He shoved a fry in his mouth, feeling stupid.

Dallas chuckled.

Viper frowned. "What?"

"I guess I enjoy making you sweat." She smiled and lifted another fry. "I work off the extra calories. If didn't, I probably would eat salads and graze like a rabbit. But my job is hard, and I burn lots of energy."

With a nod, Viper said, "Are you ready to move on to our next stop?"

She tossed her napkin on her plate. "I am. To the flower shop?"

He dropped some bills onto the table. "To the flower shop."

They exited the diner and walked the block to the flower shop across the street from a small grocery store.

Viper clasped Dallas's hand, liking the feel of her strong, capable fingers holding his. She was a woman who could hold her own. Though she walked with a limp, she could probably still outrun him. Every muscle in her body was toned and ready for action.

He understood the effort involved to stay in shape and admired she had come back from a catastrophic injury, pushing herself to regain what she could as soon as she could. Dallas Hayes was a fighter, determined to beat this setback in her life.

His hand tightened around hers as he reached out to open the door to the flower shop. A wide arrangement of flowers, positioned in the windows in giant vases, filled the air with a subtle perfume.

"I'll be with you in just a minute," a female voice called out.

Viper bit back a chuckle at the way Dallas chewed

on her lip as she stared around at the many different flowers in all shapes, sizes and colors. "Don't worry, they don't bite."

"Yeah, but how do I choose? We should probably go with the least expensive, since this wedding isn't—"

The woman behind the counter glanced up at just that moment.

Viper pulled her into his arms and pressed his lips to hers in a crushing kiss. He told himself his action was to keep Dallas from blurting out that they were engaging in a fake wedding. But he couldn't deny the fact he liked the way her lips were so soft, when the rest of her body was so hard beneath her smooth skin.

When he raised his head, she stared up into his eyes, a small wrinkle creasing her brow. "Why did you do that?"

"Because you're so irresistible." He smiled at the pretty, dark-haired young woman heading their way and turned Dallas around to greet her. "Hi, Daisy sent us to choose flowers for our wedding."

"You must be the Van Cleaves. I just got off the phone with Daisy." She held out her hand. "I'm Brianna McCall. So happy to meet you. You must be new in town."

"Relatively," Viper confirmed. "You can call me Vince. This is my fiancée, Dallas. We need to select flowers for the wedding bouquet."

Brianna shook hands with Viper and then Dallas, her smile broadening. "I understand the wedding is just days away." She drew in a deep breath and looked around the room. "It'll be tight, but we can do this." She started down an aisle. "Are there any flowers you see that you'd like included in the bouquet? Daisy said you'll also need decorations for an arbor and the bridesmaids."

"She did?" Dallas said, then shrugged. "Oh, I guess so. She's much better at all this planning than I would ever be. I don't think I've ever actually stepped into a flower shop."

Brianna laughed. "These decisions must all be pretty overwhelming for you." She took Dallas's arm and led her toward the counter. "I have some books you can look through to get an idea of the type of bouquet you'd like to carry down the aisle."

Viper followed, loving how strained Dallas was and how out of her element she seemed. He liked that the badass woman who could outshoot, outrun and could outthink most men in tactics was way out of her league among a variety of blossoms.

But rather than watch her flounder, he stepped up to the counter and perused the book Brianna opened in front of them.

After a few minutes of flipping through the pages, he pointed to a bouquet of white Calla lilies, the stems wrapped in white shiny fabric. "What do you think about that one?"

Dallas nodded. "I think it's perfect." Her voice was barely above a whisper. She cleared her throat and added in a much stronger tone, "It's simple and not too fussy."

"Yet, elegant and beautiful," Brianna concluded. "They will be lovely with your auburn hair."

"What about the decorations?"

"Since the bouquet will be white, why not decorate with white flowers?" Dallas said. "Nothing too fancy. I'm not the fancy type."

Brianna nodded. "I know exactly what to do. I'll have it all ready and delivered on Saturday." She smiled at Viper. "I'll have a small Calla lily for your lapel. And I'll get with Daisy on what will be used for decorations."

Viper nodded. "Thank you. Now, if you'll excuse us, we have more to accomplish in the short amount of time before the big day."

"Of course." Brianna started around the counter, glanced out the window and frowned. "What the hell—"

Viper turned in time to see a boat of a car flying toward the flower shop.

Dallas shoved Brianna out of the way of the oncoming car, leaving herself vulnerable and in its path.

Viper grabbed Dallas and flung her in the opposite direction, falling on top of her as a loud crashing sound was followed by glass, wood splinters and flowers flying everywhere in front of the fender of a powder blue 1970s model four-door sedan.

When the vehicle came to a complete stop, steam spewed from the radiator and flower petals drifted to the ground.

Viper pushed up on his arms and looked down at Dallas lying beneath him, her green eyes wide. "Are you all right?"

She nodded, her breathing ragged. "I'm okay."

"Miss McCall?" he yelled, without taking his gaze from Dallas.

"I'm all right," Brianna said from the other side of the car parked in her shop. "Just shaken."

Viper ran his hands over Dallas's arms. "I didn't hurt you when I pushed you to the ground, did I?"

Dallas shook her head. "No. No."

He bent down and pressed his lips to her forehead. "I just reacted." His mouth moved as if of its own accord to the tip of her nose. "If I hadn't…"

"Knocked me down?" she said, her voice breathy.

"That car would have hit you." His lips found hers, and he kissed her. "Are you sure you're okay?"

"Um…yes," she said against his mouth, her voice nothing but air. She shifted beneath him.

"What's wrong? Are you in pain?" he studied her face.

"Can't…" she wheezed.

"Can't what?" he asked.

"Breathe."

Immediately, he rolled off her and knelt amongst the broken glass and flower stems. "Better?"

Dallas dragged in a deep breath and let it out on a chuckle. "Much better." Then she pushed up on her elbows and looked at the room around her. Her cheeks were flushed a rosy pink.

Viper rose to his feet and extended a hand to Dallas.

She stared at it a moment and then placed her fingers into his palm.

He pulled her to her feet and into his arms, holding her there longer than she needed to get her balance. But he couldn't let go too soon. After she'd nearly been bulldozed by a tank of a car, he wasn't sure he could let her go. He wanted to keep her safe.

"Are you two okay?" Brianna asked from the other side of the vehicle's hood.

Viper and Dallas turned.

The dark-haired young woman brushed dust and glass from her sleeves as she surveyed the damage done to her shop. "Wow." She shook her head. "Wow."

A crowd of Eagle Rock's inhabitants gathered outside the flower shop.

One gray-haired woman pushed her way through. "Oh dear," she said in a shaky voice. She stepped up onto the sidewalk outside the ruined storefront. "Oh dear." With a cane in her hand, she shuffled up to the back of the car. "Please tell me everyone is all right in there."

"Everyone's all right, Mrs. Davis."

"Did I forget to put ol' Bessy in Park?" The woman stared at the car and the damaged building around it. "My son keeps telling me I'm too old to drive myself. If I did this, he very well could be right."

"Do you know what happened?" Brianna asked.

"I parked my car, got out and went into the grocery store. Next thing I know, someone's shouting. Then everyone ran out of the store. I followed to see what was happening. That's when I saw Bessy." The old woman shook her head, the corners of her mouth drooping. "This accident will be the end of my driving. I can see it now. I could swear I put it in Park and secured the parking brake." She looked from Viper to Dallas. "I'm just glad nobody got seriously hurt."

Viper left Dallas standing in the rubble and moved toward the driver's side of the vehicle. "Mrs. Davis, did you leave the window down?"

"Why no. I never leave the window down. It might rain and get my upholstery wet. Then the entire interior would smell like sweaty gym socks. The last car I owned had a leak in the roof. By the time I traded it in, it smelled like a boys' locker room."

Viper leaned through the driver's side window, switched off the engine and studied the gear shift, noting it was in Drive. When his glance swept the remainder of the interior, he noted a rusty-red brick lying on the floorboard. A more accurate description would be the brick laid on the accelerator, kept in place by thick strands of duct tape.

His blood running cold in his veins, Viper pulled his cellphone from his pocket and hit the numbers for 911. Someone had rigged Mrs. Davis's tank of a car, set it in Drive and sent it powering into the flower shop.

But who?

Mrs. Davis wouldn't have been the person to send her own vehicle careening across the road.

After he reported the event to dispatch, he stepped out of the ruined flower shop and around the corner then called Hank. "We've had our first attack."

DALLAS COULDN'T DECIDE which was more devastating: the car crashing through the front of the shop, or Viper's kiss. She pressed her fingers to her still-tingling lips, her gaze following the man out of the building.

"Oh dear." Mrs. Davis clutched her hands to her breasts. "My insurance probably won't cover this accident."

Brianna picked her way through the rubble to the old woman and slipped her arm around her frail shoulders. "Don't worry, Mrs. Davis. At least, no one was injured."

"But you're bleeding," the old woman exclaimed. Tears rolled down her wrinkled cheeks as she dug in her purse and pulled out a tissue. "I don't know why this is happening. I'm so sorry." She pressed it into Brianna's hand. "You need to see a doctor."

"It's just a little cut," Brianna reassured her, clutching the tissue in her palm to stem the bleeding.

Dallas shook the cobwebs of Viper's kiss from her mind, brushed the dust off her dress and hurried over. "You have more than that one cut," she said. "But first, we need to get you out of here. We don't know how stable this building is."

Dallas cleared a path around Mrs. Davis's Cadillac to the door that remained intact. She found a chair behind the counter and carried it out to the sidewalk. Hooking Brianna's arm, she led the woman past the car and pointed to the chair. "Sit," she commanded.

Brianna's lips twisted as she eased herself onto the seat. "Really, I'm fine. None of these scratches are life threatening."

Dallas reentered the building, found another chair, and brought it out to sidewalk.

By then, Mrs. Davis shook so hard she could barely stand. She leaned heavily on a couple of spectators.

Dallas took her arm and helped her to the chair, easing her into it before she released her hold. "Do you have any alcohol and bandages somewhere in the back of your shop?" Dallas asked.

Brianna gave her a weak smile. "I have a first aid kit hanging on the wall near the back door. Everything you need is inside."

Dallas ducked behind the intact counter and weaved through the tables laden with flower arrangements in the back to the first aid kit affixed to the wall in the back. She grabbed a handful of bandages, alcohol pads, gauze and medical tape and returned to Brianna.

She'd cleaned three small cuts with the alcohol pads and pressed bandages across them when sirens wailed in the distance and a sheriff's cruiser raced toward them, lights flashing. Moments later, a paramedic's truck appeared at the end of Main Street.

"Help has arrived." Dallas smiled at Brianna, focusing all of her attention on the women and away from the man who'd curled her toes with just one kiss.

Brianna clasped Dallas's hands and held them in hers. "Thank you for saving my life."

Dallas chuckled. "I didn't do anything but give you a push. You might have gotten a few more bruises because of me."

"If you hadn't shoved me when you did, I would have been crushed," she said in a tone low enough Mrs. Davis couldn't hear.

Dallas's cheeks heated, and she stared down at the bandage she applied to Brianna's arm. "No worries."

"I promise, I'll have your flowers delivered on time

for the wedding." She gave a tight laugh and glanced around at the damage to her shop. "I can pick up the pieces and make it happen."

"Seriously, I don't want you to worry about me or the wedding," Dallas said. "You'll have a lot to deal with rebuilding."

Brianna shook her head. "Supplying flowers is my livelihood. I can't stop working. I just have to find a temporary location until my shop is set to rights." She shrugged. "People need their flowers. They're like a promise that things will be okay."

Dallas winked. "You could use some of those flowers for yourself."

Mrs. Davis sniffed and touched a tissue to her cheek. "This damage is all my fault."

Ducking back into the shop, Dallas gathered a loose white rose stem and carried it out to Mrs. Davis. "Hold onto this. I promise, things will get better."

"Thank you, dear." She patted Dallas's cheek. "Thank you."

Viper slipped his cellphone into his pocket and squatted beside Mrs. Davis. "None of this is your fault, Mrs. Davis. Someone tampered with your car and sent it crashing into this building on purpose. You did everything right." He took her hands in his and held them, muttering reassurances to the old woman until the medics unloaded their kits and hurried toward the group.

While Brianna and Mrs. Davis were being seen to by the volunteer fire department, Sheriff Barron approached the crash site and whistled. "This scenario gives a whole new meaning to drive-through service." He inspected the Cadillac and took their statements. "I don't get it. Why would someone do this?"

Viper's jaw tightened. "Looks like they targeted the shop, or us in particular."

"But you're new to town. You haven't even had time to develop any animosity in others."

Dallas clutched her hands together. "Is it true that the weddings in Eagle Rock are being jinxed?"

The sheriff shook his head. "I don't believe in ghosts. But if someone is targeting weddings, we have to catch him before anyone else is hurt or killed."

"Agreed. I'd hate for something bad to happen on my wedding day," Dallas said.

"And the wedding's Saturday." The sheriff's brow wrinkled. "I will definitely have a deputy attend in uniform as a visual deterrent."

"Though having a deputy there won't be necessary, it would be nice," Viper said. "All the guests will be former military. They'll have our backs."

The sheriff nodded. "Good, because we're stretched pretty thin, covering a lot of territory with only a few men. The budget doesn't take into account the distance between potential problems." He stuck out his hand. "But my deputy will be at the wedding, nonetheless."

"Thank you, Sheriff." Viper shook the man's hand and nodded toward the shop. "If you don't need us anymore, we have a lot to do before the sun sets."

The sheriff stepped aside. "Sure. Don't let me keep you."

Viper gathered Dallas's hand in his.

She walked beside him back to where they had parked his truck at the diner.

Once inside the cab, Dallas leaned back against the seat cushion and closed her eyes to keep from having to look at Viper, even in her peripheral vision. Since he'd landed on top of her, she'd had trouble breathing and her heart raced every time she glanced his direction.

At the ranch, she changed out of the pretty green dress and into jeans, boots and a T-shirt.

By the time Dallas stepped out of the ranch house to perform her assigned chores, Viper had already changed and was outside.

He led one of the miniature horses into the barn and was scraping the buildup out of the animal's tiny hooves. He glanced up once, a smile pulling at his lips.

Dallas's knees weakened, turning to the consistency of melted butter. She tried to ignore him by getting into cleaning the stalls and feeding and watering the animals. Whenever she passed him bent over an animal's hooves, she couldn't help but admire how nicely his jeans hugged the muscles of his ass. Nor could she erase the image of his massive thighs when he squatted beside the small horse and ran a curry comb through his mane and tail.

Yup, her job got all the harder with her thinking about Viper, instead of the mystery villain they were out to discover.

As the sun set, they both finished their assigned duties and headed for the house. The scent of roast beef wafted through the air, making Dallas's tummy rumble. "Smells good."

"Sure does." Viper climbed the steps beside her and held open the door for her to enter.

As she passed him her shoulder brushed against his chest, sending a rush of molten heat throughout her body. Her breath caught in her throat, and she fought to regain control.

Viper encircled her arm and pulled her to face him in the threshold. "Dallas."

She stared up into his eyes, her tongue too knotted to make sense with words.

"About the kiss in the flower shop…"

She lifted her chin, her lips tingling all over again in anticipation of a repeat performance of that incredible kiss.

Loud laughter floated from the direction of the kitchen.

For a long moment, Viper stared down at her mouth. Another laugh made him draw in a deep breath. "Never mind." He tilted his head toward the hallway and the bathroom. "You can wash up first. I'm changing into a clean shirt." Pressing a gentle hand against her shoulder, he turned her away.

With no other choice but to move, Dallas forced her feet to carry her down the hallway at a slow, steady pace, trying not to show how much she shook inside. She would rather have run, but she was afraid her knees would buckle and she'd fall flat on her face.

What had Viper been about to say before the sound of others made him change his mind? Had he been about to say kissing her had been a huge mistake? Did he regret it?

Her heart fell to the pit of her belly. When had she become so damned female, worrying about what a man thought about the way she kissed? How well she did or didn't kiss had no bearing on the mission. She had to keep that thought at the forefront.

Quickly ducking into her bedroom, she came out armed with a fresh blouse, clean jeans and underwear. Once in the bathroom, she slipped out of her prosthetic and hopped into the tub. For a glorious few moments, she stood beneath the shower's spray, cleaning the horse manure smell out of her hair. Used to the quick showers she'd had to take when deployed, she was out in five minutes, toweling dry and slipping back into the prosthetic leg. Another couple of minutes to brush her hair straight back from her face and dress in the clean clothes, and she was done.

She didn't wear makeup, and she wasn't going on a date. A glance in the mirror confirmed she had done no more than the basics which would have to do.

Viper needed to wash up before dinner. The longer she remained in the bathroom, the longer it would be before he could eat.

Dallas flung open the door and marched out into the hall, right into a solid wall of muscles.

Strong hands reached out to catch her and pull her against a broad chest. "Hey, steady there."

Viper's deep, resonant tone wrapped around her and sent heat to her core. Once again, Dallas fought to breathe. This time, she didn't have the excuse of Viper's big body crushing the air from her lungs. Her response was all on her for her loss of lung capacity.

He laughed. "Hungry?"

Hungry aptly described the way she felt. But food wasn't what would quell the kind of hunger building inside. "Y-yes."

"Don't wait for me. I'll be out in less than five minutes." He kissed her forehead and stepped past her into the bathroom, closing the door behind him with a soft click.

With Viper out of her sight, Dallas sucked in a huge lungful of air and let it out slowly between her teeth. She had half a mind to contact Hank and ask to be assigned to a different job. Working with Viper was proving difficult, if not impossible. The man had magnetism, and then some.

She returned to her room, reluctant to face the rest of the ranch hands when heat filled her cheeks. Dallas couldn't be around the other men at the table, yet.

So, she paced beside the length of the four-poster bed draped with an old-fashioned quilt folded at the foot. Hell, she paced until the doorknob on the bathroom door twisted and Viper stepped into the hall wearing a white button-down shirt, crisp dark jeans and black cowboy boots. He'd slicked back his dark hair. His light blue eyes sparkled when he met her gaze. "You didn't have to wait. But thanks."

She shrugged without saying anything.

"Ready?" Viper asked.

"Sure," she managed to squeak out.

He offered her his arm and led her toward the kitchen where loud voices and laughter indicated high spirits and the promise of good food.

"There they are!" Brody Franklin yelled and clapped his only hand on the table.

A cheer went up, shaking the rafters with the noise.

Dallas's cheeks reddened. These disabled vets had welcomed her into the Brighter Days Ranch family, opening their hearts to another wounded warrior without question or judgment.

"We hear congratulations are in order," Jimmy Young said from his wheel chair.

"You are inviting all of us to the wedding, aren't you?" Vasquez asked.

Dallas swallowed on the wad of guilt knotting in her throat. "You bet."

Another cheer rocked the roof. Vasquez and Franklin slapped the table while everyone else clapped with both hands.

Cookie supplied the men with more bottles of ice-cold beer and joined the group at the table. As one, they all lifted their bottles and toasted the happy couple.

Or so they thought.

Viper slipped an arm around Dallas's waist, pulling her close to his side. He smiled and shook hands through the introductions and conversed with ease.

"So, how did you keep this secret from all of us?" Young asked. "We didn't even know you were dating."

Dallas shrugged. "We haven't known each other long," she admitted.

"But when you know she's the right one for you, you don't let her get away." Viper leaned close and planted a kiss on her temple.

Another cheer went up and the men drank deeply.

Dallas offered to help Cookie carry the platters laden with roast beef, potatoes and carrots onto the table.

Cookie insisted Dallas and Viper be seated and let him wait on *them*. "You two are celebrating your engagement, for Pete's sake." He plied them with cold bottles of beer and made quick work of setting out the food.

Once everyone was seated at the huge kitchen table, Percy asked for a moment of silence in honor of those who'd fallen.

Dallas swallowed hard, memories flooding into her mind of the men who'd gone into battle with her and had returned home in body bags.

Viper reached for her hand beneath the table and held it until all heads lifted and the platters of food were circulated around the table.

Lori Mize returned that day from a trip to Helena to apply to the university there. "I wasn't gone but a night, and I come back and find out one of us is engaged?" She shook her light red hair. "I'm so happy for you." She ducked her chin and twisted her napkin in her lap. "It gives me hope that one day I can find someone who'll love me, despite my disability."

"Marry me, Lori," Vasquez said.

Franklin elbowed Vasquez in the ribs. "No, she's marrying me."

Vasquez rubbed his ribs and frowned. "Remind me to sit on Franklin's other side next time."

Everyone laughed.

Dallas enjoyed the camaraderie and jokes, her heart

warming to the love and happiness emanating from the people around the table. Though she'd been angry when the therapist at Bethesda suggested she needed more time to adjust, and Brighter Days Ranch was just what the doctor ordered, Dallas realized how right she had been.

Brighter Days Ranch had saved her life. The people understood what she was going through. Caring for and helping to rehabilitate the rescued animals living on the ranch gave her meaning and courage to continue living. She reached for Viper's hand.

He held it through several more toasts and Cookie's dessert reveal.

When the meal concluded, Viper and Dallas were shooed out of the kitchen while the others cleaned up.

Viper led Dallas out onto the porch and sat on the steps. "This place, these people…" he said and shook his head.

"I know. They're all amazing."

"We're lucky this place exists," Viper said softly.

"Very." Dallas sat beside him on the step.

A chill breeze rippled across her skin, raising gooseflesh. Dallas shivered.

Viper slipped an arm around her. "Cold?"

"A little," she lied. Aroused, attracted, aware? Yes. Every nerve in her body stood at attention, awaiting Viper's next move. Though their engagement was all for show, Dallas couldn't help but wonder, if it were real, would Viper kiss her under the light of the rising moon? Would he hold her closer and tell her how much he loved her?

Would she know how to respond? Dallas shivered again.

Viper pulled her closer and captured her chin in his hand. "They're watching us through the window," he said, his mouth lowering to hers. "We can't let them down."

"No," Dallas said, her voice nothing but air. "We can't."

Then his lips touched hers.

What started as a gentle kiss changed to a hungry, desperate connection that lasted long enough to steal Dallas's breath.

When Viper finally lifted his head, Dallas could hear the sound of cheering and clapping from the kitchen window overlooking the porch.

Her cheeks burned, but not nearly as hot as her core. She wanted more of that kiss. Hell, she wanted Viper to make love to her like he really cared. Like they weren't faking an engagement. Dallas wished, for a moment, what they were experiencing was real.

For her…even if the emotion was wrong…what she was feeling felt real.

CHAPTER 9

Viper lay for a long time in his bed, staring up at the ceiling and wondering what had come over him. When he'd kissed Dallas, he'd intimated it was all part of their cover. To make others think their engagement was real, they had to show some indication that they liked each other enough to marry.

But that kiss. Holy hell. If he wasn't mistaken, he was liking Dallas far too much for a mere partner. She made him feel things he thought long buried. Lust was a given. But tenderness, longing, protectiveness and…hope.

Dallas made him feel like his life had not ended when Emily and their baby girl died. She made him feel like a future waited for him and that he could fall in love again.

And that realization scared the ever-lovin' crap out of him.

Thus, he'd spent the night staring at the ceiling until

the wee hours of the morning when he finally fell into a fitful sleep.

He was up at the crack of dawn, dressed and feeding the chickens when Dallas stepped out on the porch, dressed in slim-fitting blue jeans, a mint-green pullover shirt and boots. Even in casual clothing, she couldn't hide her shapely body, the muscles well-defined and solid. Her hair hung down to her shoulders, the auburn locks catching the sunshine and turning coppery-gold.

Viper stopped with his hand full of hard-kernel corn and stared at the woman with her face turned up to the morning sunshine, her shoulders flung back, her chin held high and proud.

She was strong, yet vulnerable. Hard-bodied, yet soft in all the right places.

Viper's blood burned, and his groin tightened. He turned away and flung the corn a little harder than he'd intended. The chickens raced after the kernels, clucking and scratching in the dirt.

He dusted off his hands and strode to the porch. They had chores to do that morning then they'd head to Hank's place for an update from Swede, his computer guru.

"Good morning," Dallas greeted him.

"Good morning." He stopped two steps below the one where she stood. "Did you sleep well?"

She nodded. "You?"

He dipped his head in brief agreement. Two could play the vague game. "Have you eaten?"

"Not yet. Cookie's making breakfast now," she said.

"Where are the others?"

"Hanging out in the living room," she responded. "You're up early."

The scent of frying bacon and pancake batter cooking on the griddle reached Viper, making his stomach rumble in response.

Dallas smiled. "He was almost done when I dared to walk into the kitchen. Needless to say, he shooed me out."

"Let's go see if we can pilfer a pancake." Viper climbed the remaining steps and held out his hand.

For a moment, Dallas hesitated. Finally, she placed her hand in his. "For the gig," she muttered and allowed him to lead her into the house.

Viper found himself wishing Dallas wasn't holding his hand because of the undercover aspect of the mission. He wanted her to hold his hand because the gesture felt right and good. His grip tightened on hers, even as he reminded himself they were on a mission, not a date.

Cookie had just laid a heaping platter of pancakes in the center of the large kitchen table. "Breakfast is ready."

"I smell bacon." Jimmy Young propelled his wheelchair from the living room into the kitchen, pulling up to his designated spot at the table.

Vasquez followed. He paused to pull out a chair for Dallas.

Viper frowned. He'd been about to grab the chair and hold it for Dallas, but the one-armed veteran beat him to it.

Franklin held a chair for Lori and then took the seat on her other side.

Viper sat at the head of the table on Dallas's left. Close, but not close enough to lean his thigh against hers. The way he was feeling, that could only add to the rise of his desire. As it was, he bumped knees with her every time he shifted in his seat. His awareness of her was at an all-time high, and he vowed to tone it down before he found himself head over heels for the badass Army Ranger.

The meal was much like the night before, with the young veterans trading good-natured insults. For a few minutes, silence reigned as everyone dug into the pancakes and bacon.

Dallas consumed two pancakes and three slices of bacon, washing down the food with a cup of black coffee.

Lori leaned across the table. "Have you chosen your wedding gown, yet?"

Dallas shook her head. "Not yet, but we're scheduled to go tomorrow. Our wedding planner said something about giving the seamstress a day or two to do the alterations." She shook her head. "I don't have any idea how difficult it is to buy a dress. Can't you just pull one off the rack in your size and wear it?"

Lori laughed. "Oh, sweetie, you really don't have a clue, do you?"

Even Viper knew not all women were the same shape and sizes. His wife had chosen a pretty wedding dress that fit her in the bust but had to be altered for her waist and hips. Like Dallas, he wasn't exactly sure of all that work entailed, but it sounded like a lot more than a safety pin holding two seams together.

Dallas smiled at Lori "Would you like to go with me when I shop for my dress?"

Lori's cheeks colored. "Oh, you'll probably have Sadie McClain helping you choose the prettiest dress in the store. You don't need an old Army sergeant adding her two cents worth."

"I'd love to have a not-so-old Army sergeant along to keep me straight and on time. Besides, what will a movie star like Sadie and I have in common? We'll likely run out of things to say on the drive to Bozeman. I mean, I doubt she's ever fired a M4A1 rifle."

"I wouldn't be surprised if she has. She married Hank Patterson. I've heard he has quite the arsenal for his Brotherhood Protectors." Lori tipped her head to the side. "I assume you know about the brotherhood?"

Dallas nodded. She concentrated on cutting into her third pancake, her gaze avoiding Lori's. "Yes, I've heard of them. Hank's the boss, right?"

Viper bit back a smile. Dallas was doing a great job of keeping her new job as an agent for the Brotherhood Protectors under wraps.

"What's on your schedule for today?" Lori asked as she looked at the end of the table. "I bet your head is spinning with the wedding preparations."

"We're making a trip to the caterer to select the kinds of food we want at the reception," Viper answered.

"Steak," Young piped in. "You can't go wrong with steak."

"And lobster," Franklin added.

"Barbeque is cheaper, and the boys love it just as well," Gavin Blackstock offered. "Throw on some ribs and a brisket and you'll have them eating out of the palms of your hands."

Vasquez sighed. "What I wouldn't give for some of my mama's tamales."

"Mexican food sounds good," Dallas agreed. "I did some training at Ft. Hood, Texas. They had the best authentic Mexican restaurant right outside the post." She sighed. "I wonder if the caterer could conjure up fajitas with sour cream and guacamole." Dallas popped a bite of syrupy pancake into her mouth and swept her tongue across her lips.

"Whatever your heart desires," Viper said, his mouth watering, but not for fajitas. The way Dallas's tongue moved across her mouth made Viper want to capture it and suck it between his teeth.

"I think Daisy said barbeque was the easiest to conjure up at short notice." Dallas smiled. "Barbeque it is."

Viper shoved back from the table. "If you're done here, I'd like to get started on what we need to accomplish. We only have a few more days left until the wedding."

"Right," Dallas rose beside him. "We don't have a minute to spare."

"Not if we want the event to be perfect." Viper pulled

her into his arms and kissed her forehead. "Right, darlin'?"

She stared up at him, her eyes wide.

He'd caught her off guard and loved it.

"You call that a kiss?" Young snorted. "I kiss my dog better than that."

"You would," Vasquez said.

Young threw a punch at Vasquez's only arm.

"Hey!" Vasquez glared at the man without legs and rubbed his shoulder. "Watch it."

"You can do better than that," Franklin taunted.

"Leave them alone," Percy said. "They don't have to prove anything to you yahoos."

"No, we want to see a real kiss."

"Like you didn't see one last night?" Lori shook her head. "A bunch of Peeping Toms staring through the front window."

"You were staring with us, Mize," Franklin pointed out.

"Only to see what you all were gawking at," Lori protested. But her lips curled upward on a smile. "And what a kiss."

"Yeah, show us the real thing," Vasquez said. "We're living vicariously through you two."

"Get your own lives," Dallas shot back. "Maybe Viper doesn't want to kiss me in front of all of you."

"Challenge accepted," Viper whispered and crushed his mouth onto hers.

Dallas gasped, opening just enough for Viper to dive in.

He swept his tongue across hers, sliding its length in

a slow sensuous caress. She tasted of the bacon and syrup. Sweet and savory all at once.

At first, she was stiff in his arms. Then she melted against him, her body aligning with his. She slid her hands up his chest to weave together at the back of his neck. Her breasts pushed against his chest, her hips rubbing against his.

His cock hardened and pressed urgently against the thick denim of his fly. A groan rose up his throat and nearly escaped. When at last he raised his head, thunderous applause deafened him.

When the clapping died down, Lori sighed. "Now, that was a kiss."

"Damn straight, it was." Vasquez grinned. "Wasn't sure the Rangers had it in them."

Viper pulled himself together, curled his arm around Dallas's waist and straightened. "If you all have had enough of the show, we have work to do. See you later."

On her way out of the house, Dallas grabbed her jacket and purse.

Viper led the way to his truck and opened her door. She climbed in and fastened her seatbelt.

Once Viper was in the truck, he pulled away from the Brighter Days Ranch and headed toward the outskirts of Eagle Rock.

"Where are we going?" Dallas asked.

"I think we need to check in with Hank and fill him in on what happened yesterday. We can see if his computer guy found anything on any of our potential suspects."

Dallas shot a glance toward Viper. "We have potential suspects?"

"I told him to look at Tyler King and anyone else connected with wedding planning, to include the florist, caterer, party furnishings and limousine rental."

"Did you have him check on Mrs. Davis, while you were at it?"

Viper chuckled. "Please tell me you're kidding."

She waved her hand. "Of course, I am. But I feel like we haven't moved any closer to identifying our attacker. I liked it better when we knew our enemies."

"Me, too. But the wedding angle is all we have to work with."

Dallas nodded. "You're right. But it doesn't make the situation any easier."

"No, it doesn't."

As they pulled up to the spacious ranch house, Hank and Sadie came out on the porch.

Viper rounded the truck, but Dallas already opened the door and dropped to the ground. "I can take care of myself," she insisted.

"I know you can, but…"

"Don't say it. Normal people are okay with accepting a little help getting in and out of large pickups."

Viper forced a chuckle, though his chest tightened. "But you're not normal?"

Dallas tilted her head to the side. "Now you're getting it."

"For the sake of—" he started.

"Our cover," Dallas finished. "Okay, I promise to let you get my door on occasion." She leaned closer and whispered, "But since Hank already knows our relationship, you have no need to be so attentive. We're partners, not lovers."

Viper dropped a kiss on the tip of her nose and whispered back, "I don't think Sadie knows. Remember, Hank said the fewer who knew, the better."

"You think Hank keeps things from Sadie?"

Viper nodded. "I'm betting on it. When she gave you that dress, she was helping another woman, not Hank's new recruit."

Dallas frowned. "I hope you're right." She smiled and turned to Hank and Sadie, who had stepped down from the porch and were walking toward them.

Hank hugged Dallas and held out his hand to Viper. "So nice to see you two. What brings you to the ranch?"

"Dallas wanted to stop by and thank Sadie for the dress."

"That's right." Dallas hugged Sadie. "Thank you for the beautiful dress."

"You're more than welcome."

"Once I have it dry-cleaned, I'll return it."

"No, please," Sadie insisted. "I want you to have it. I used it as one of the dresses on my last movie. But it goes so much better with your coloring. I'd love to have that shade of auburn hair."

"Sadie made up a pitcher of lemonade. Emma should be waking from her nap any moment, and I wanted to introduce you to one of the men who work for me." Hank glanced toward Sadie. "Will you excuse us?"

"Certainly. I need to check on Emma and get glasses down for the lemonade." Sadie smiled at Viper and

Dallas. "Take your time. I'm sure a diaper needs changing." Sadie hurried off toward the bedrooms and her baby, Emma.

Hank led Viper and Dallas to a door practically hidden from view. He uncovered a digital keypad and ran his fingers over the buttons, leaned down and added an optical scan before the lock clicked, and he pulled open the door.

Stairs led downward into a bunker.

Viper was impressed with the state-of-the-art technology and the security Hank had installed in his home.

As Hank started down, lights blinked on, triggered by his motion. "Swede, we have company," Hank called out.

A tall, blond man emerged from another room and stretched his arms to the ceiling. "Good. I could use a break." He held out a hand to Dallas and then Viper.

After stating their names, they shook and followed him into a room lined with computer screens.

Swede slipped into an office chair and rolled up to a keyboard.

"Find anything?" Hank asked.

Swede nodded. "As a matter of fact, I did." He clicked a few keys and an image of a man appeared on the monitor. "Tim Fuller."

"Fuller." Viper rolled the name on his tongue. "Isn't he the guy who provides tables and seating for events?"

"He is," Hank said. "What do you have on him?"

"He was arrested a few months ago for assault and battery."

Viper leaned closer, studying the man's bruised face. "Looks like he got a little of the same."

"What's the story?" Dallas asked.

"From what I could gather from the police report, an article in the newspaper and the man's divorce decree, he accused his wife of cheating on him and beat up the man he suspected she was cheating with."

Hank crossed his arms over his chest. "Remember, his wife is the caterer who supplied food for the weddings that have been targeted."

"Why would Fuller sabotage weddings where he's making money?" Viper shook his head. "It wouldn't make sense." The man obviously had anger issues, much like Tyler King.

"To get back at his ex-wife?" Hank offered. "They recently divorced."

"Doing so would hurt him, as well."

"He also supplies rental furniture to local events and corporate retreats. Losing out on a couple of weddings might not impact his sales."

"Then the same would go for his ex-wife," Dallas pointed out.

"The lead bears checking into," Viper said, glad for something to check on. Perhaps the information they gleaned would lead to solving the case.

"You can start with the ex-wife," Hank said. "She runs a bakery in Eagle Rock."

Viper's lips twisted. "Is it safe for us to visit a store in Eagle Rock? The last one we were in was destroyed by a runaway Cadillac."

"You have a point. You two are targets. You can

assume you aren't safe anywhere." Hank's lips thinned. "That attack only proves someone is out to ruin local weddings."

"What's the connecting factor?" Dallas asked.

"We've only just begun the planning," Viper said.

"The announcement was sent to the local paper," Hank continued.

Dallas tipped her head to the side, a frown wrinkling her brow. "If Fuller was the culprit, why would he attack when we haven't even met with him yet?"

"Daisy said she'd contact the florist, caterer, party rental and the Justice of the Peace," Viper reminded her. "The florist mentioned she'd already heard from Daisy."

Dallas nodded. "She did."

"I looked at the others on the list of people the brides and grooms used for the weddings." Swede ticked off on his finger as he recited the list. "Tim & Melissa Fuller, Tyler King, Brianna McCall and Paul Glover, who operates the limousine service out of Bozeman. No one came up on any crime database other than Tim Fuller."

Viper glanced at Dallas. "Next stop?"

Dallas's lips quirked upward. "Melissa Fuller's bakery. Maybe she can shed some light on her ex-husband's activities. If he is the one behind the sabotage."

Hank led the way back up the stairs and into the living room.

Sadie chose that moment to return, carrying a baby. She handed Emma to Hank. "Hold her while I bring in the lemonade."

Smiling, Hank took Emma and gave her a loud, smacking kiss on her cheek.

Once again, Viper found himself longing for something that had been taken away. A life including a wife, a baby and love. His glance swept to Dallas. The former Army Ranger's gaze was fixed on the baby, her eyes wide.

"Want to hold her?" Hank asked.

Dallas backed away, her hands up in surrender. "I don't know anything about babies."

"You don't have to know anything. They teach you." Hank winked. "Really. She won't bite…well, maybe a little because she's teething. But it doesn't hurt." Before Dallas could protest again, Hank deposited Emma in her arms.

Viper could have laughed out loud at the terror in the woman's eyes, but he didn't.

Within moments, the baby had twisted her fingers into Dallas's shirt, pressed her wet lips to the Ranger's cheek and then giggled.

Dallas's lips spread into a grin and she stared down at the baby's laughing eyes. Then she chuckled. "You are a charmer, aren't you?" She smiled up at Hank. "Are all babies this engaging?"

"We like to think Emma is special. Like most parents do." Hank tipped his head toward the floor. "She loves to play on the rug. We keep a few of her favorite toys in the basket beside the sofa."

Dallas sat down Emma, pulled a couple toys from the basket and laid down beside her.

Viper's pulse hammered so hard against his

eardrums he could barely hear. This situation was what he was missing and what he wanted in his life. A home, a woman to love and children. A gut-clenching yearning swept over him, threatening to rob the very air he breathed.

"Babies have a way of stealing your heart." Hank stared at the two on the floor, as well. "I never thought I could love anyone as much as I love Sadie, but then Emma came along." He glanced at Viper. "I'm sorry about your wife and baby. I can't imagine what you went through."

Viper's chest tightened. "It's been a while."

"Yeah, but you don't ever really get over a loss like that."

"No," Viper agreed. "But life goes on." And he was still alive, breathing, thinking and feeling, while Emily and their baby were buried together in a plot of ground.

"I learned a long time ago that you can't live a life filled with guilt that you survived when others died," Hank said. "It's not much of a life, and the behavior is not something those who died would have wanted for you. If I had died during some of my missions, I would have wanted the ones who survived to live their lives to the fullest. If not for themselves, then for those who hadn't been as fortunate."

Hank was right. Viper digested his words, his gaze going to Dallas and Emma. He wanted to get on with his life and to fully embrace living. But was he ready to find love all over again? Was he willing to risk his love's life with a pregnancy that could end in her death?

. . .

WHAT HAD STARTED out scaring her to death turned out to be one of the highlights of Dallas's day. Baby Emma was a happy baby, full of giggles and joy. She brought out in Dallas feelings she never thought she'd experience.

From the moment she'd joined the Army, Dallas turned off all things feminine inside, focusing on proving to others and to herself that she was as good or better than any man. That she could hold up under the pressures of battle and provide the support her team needed.

She'd given every waking, and many sleeping, dreams to her career as an Army Ranger. When she'd lost her leg, she'd lost her career and she thought she'd lost her identity. Who was she without the Army and the Rangers? She hadn't needed to think beyond her commitment to her country. Marriage, relationships and family were all things other people did. Not her.

Now, with a new life, a new leg and a new job, she was only beginning to understand the breadth of options and choices she could have.

Emma crawled over to her and sat, holding out her arms.

Dallas lifted her and held her against her chest.

Emma nestled in the crook of Dallas's arm and sighed, her eyes drifting closed.

"She might not have been quite finished with her nap." Sadie carried a tray containing a pitcher of lemonade, four glasses and a platter of cheese and crackers.

Hank took the heavy tray from her and laid it on the coffee table in the middle of the room. He lifted the pitcher and poured lemonade into a glass, handing it to Viper with a smile. "It's not beer, but Sadie makes a mean glass of lemonade."

"Thanks." Viper took it and drank. "It reminds me of my folks back in Malta. Mom makes lemonade when we have company."

Dallas's attention perked. Viper hadn't talked much about his parents other than to say they were still alive. She wanted to know everything possible about this man who was her partner and so much more.

"Do you make it home often?" Sadie asked, taking a glass from Hank.

"Not often enough," Viper replied. "I stopped in on the drive out here."

Hank poured another glass of lemonade and handed it to Dallas. "Are your folks in good health?"

Viper chuckled. His parents were the picture of health. "I think they might outlive me. Now that they're retired, they spend much of their time either traveling or fishing. No stress."

Hank grinned. "Sounds like heaven."

"I could do with some fishing." Viper stared across the living room, images from the past filling his mind. "My father took me out to Fort Peck Lake every summer and sometimes during the winter for ice fishing. We made some great memories in the time we spent together."

"I can't wait until Emma's old enough to hold a fishing pole," Hank admitted. "I'll have her out on the river before she can spell fishing."

"Only if I'm with you," Sadie said, her eyes narrowed.

"That fact's a given. I can't imagine fishing without both of my girls." He slipped an arm around Sadie and pressed a kiss to her lips.

Sadie smiled and kissed him back.

Dallas envied Sadie and Hank's natural banter and loving looks.

Then Sadie turned to Dallas. "Let me take Emma. Your arms must be getting tired by now."

"Not at all," Dallas said.

Sadie took Emma anyway and laid her in a nearby playpen. The baby slept. "She was up half of the night, teething. Poor thing." When she straightened, she gave Dallas a pointed look. "We need to get moving on finding a wedding dress."

Dallas nodded. "Do you know where I can start looking?"

"Daisy and I conferred and set up an appointment to try on dresses at one of the shops in Bozeman tomorrow. She can't make it, but I'll be there."

Dallas pushed to her feet. "I hate to take you away from your family. I can do this task on my own."

"The hell you will," Sadie exclaimed. "A bride needs her peeps around her when she's choosing a dress. Besides, we're driving there with our guys. They have to try on their tuxedoes." Sadie tipped her head to the side. "Have you decided on your bridesmaids?"

"Bridesmaids?" Dallas grimaced. "I don't know anybody."

"You don't have to have bridesmaids, but if you do, you can bring them along. My SUV will seat eight."

"I would like to bring Lori Mize. She said she would like to be involved."

"Great," Sadie said. "We'll swing by the ranch to pick up you three around nine in the morning. Plan on having dinner before we return."

Dallas swallowed a gasp. "Choosing a dress will take that long?"

Sadie laughed. "It could. There are three bridal shops in Bozeman. If we don't find what we want at one, we'll go to all three until we do."

"Wow," Dallas said. "I didn't know finding a wedding dress could be that hard. Can't I just get married in my jeans and boots?"

Frowning, Sadie shook her head. "A woman's wedding day is something she'll remember for the rest of her life. You need to make it special."

"How much do you actually remember from ours?" Hank asked.

Sadie blushed. "Well, the day was a blur. But I remember seeing you at the end of the aisle, waiting for me, and thinking I was the luckiest woman in the world."

Hank tilted his head back and stared at her down his nose for a moment before grinning. "Good answer." Then he kissed her. "As it is, I have a new recruit flying into Bozeman tomorrow. We can add him to our dinner celebration."

Sadie nodded. "Then it's a date."

"What about Emma?"

"I'll ask Chuck Johnson if he'd like to watch her for the day." Sadie smiled. "He's so good with Maya, and Emma adores him."

"You can't keep using my guys as babysitters," Hank protested. "And Chuck's only been out of the hospital for a day."

Sadie straightened her shoulders. "Chuck offered. And he really is good with babies. I think he misses being with Maya all the time now that Daphne and Boomer are together."

"Okay, but you really can't rely on them. They have real jobs."

"I know. But who better to protect our baby than a Brotherhood Protector?" Sadie smiled up at her husband.

He shook his head, though his lips quirked upward on the corners. "You have a point."

Dallas glanced at Viper. If they were really in love and getting married, would they laugh and poke at each other so easily, like Hank and Sadie?

At that moment, Viper locked gazes with Dallas.

Heat rose in her cheeks, and she looked away. "I guess we should be going. We need to meet with the caterer."

"Let me know if we can help you with anything," Hank shot a glance at Viper. "Anything."

"Thanks, but I think we've got this. With Daisy's and Sadie's help, this wedding will happen on time."

"With a beautiful dress," Sadie added, giving Dallas a pointed look. "Tomorrow. We'll find one."

Dallas smiled. "Thank you for all your help."

Sadie laughed. "Don't thank me until we bag that dress."

Dallas led the way out of the house and down the steps.

Viper reached the truck before her and opened her door. He handed her up into the cab and closed the door once she was settled. He waved at Hank and Sadie standing on the porch and climbed in beside Dallas. "Think she knows we're faking it?"

With a sigh, Dallas shook her head. "No. She thinks our relationship's all for real."

Viper glanced her direction. "Why the glum face?"

"I hate lying to her. She's so helpful and cares."

"She'd be the first to understand." Viper backed away from the house and turned onto the road leading off the property then accelerated to the highway.

For the first few miles, Dallas sat in her seat staring at the road ahead. "They're a nice family," she said at last.

"What?"

"Hank, Sadie and Emma," she clarified. "They make a nice family."

Viper nodded. "Yes, they do." He maneuvered the truck around a curve in the road. "What about you, Dallas? Do you see yourself married and with children?"

Dallas shrugged. "Up until now, no."

"And now?"

She glanced out the side window, not wanting Viper to see the longing in her face. "I don't know what I want. I never dreamed past the Army and being a Ranger."

"I never thought past Emily and the baby. But life happened." He snorted. "In my case, death happened. I guess I'm finally coming to terms with reality."

Dallas rested her hand on the knee below which was her fake leg. "Me, too. Seeing Hank and Sadie with Emma…well…their life shows me other choices exist besides being a Ranger."

Viper nodded. "Those choices can be equally important and life-shaping."

"That Emma…" Dallas chuckled. "Can wrap you around her little finger in a heartbeat."

"My daughter would have been five this year," Viper said softly.

Dallas shot a glance in his direction. "I'm sorry. I don't know how anyone gets over losing a child or a spouse."

"You don't. You just learn a new way to breathe. A new normal." He looked her way. "You've lost friends. It's not any easier."

Her chest tightened. "No."

They entered Eagle Rock and drove to the bakery where they were to meet with Melissa Fuller.

Viper pulled into the parking lot and shifted into Park.

Dallas opened her door before Viper could get out and do it for her. She was on the ground and rounding the front of the truck when the door to the bakery slammed open and a man backed out with his hands in the air.

Dallas ducked back behind the hood of the truck, her pulse racing.

"Damn it, Mel!" he said. "Put down that gun. We can talk this out."

"Like hell we can," a voice said from inside. The barrel of a shotgun emerged through the door, followed by the petite woman holding it. "I told you, I'm done. We're divorced, and I intend to stay that way."

"What's going on here?" Viper asked.

The woman with the gun nodded toward the man she targeted. "That good-for-nothing son-of-a-bitch thinks he can waltz back into my life like nothing happened." She snorted. "Well, I'm here to tell him, the divorce was final over a month ago. I don't want you back, Tim. Get it through your thick skull."

He shook his head slowly. "But you're my wife. I love you."

"*Was* your wife. I'm now your ex-wife." She waved the shotgun at him. "Now get out of my life and stay out."

"That's my gun," he muttered.

"*Was* your gun. I got it in the settlement."

He pointed at the shotgun. "That weapon belonged to my grandfather."

"I don't care if it belonged to your Great Aunt Gladys, get out of here before I use it."

"You don't even know how to load it."

"No?" She waved the gun again. "You think I didn't load this before pointing it at your lousy ass?" She aimed the barrel at Tim's feet. "Are you willing to take that chance?"

Tim backed away a few steps. "No. Of course not.

What man would be stupid enough to go up against a crazy woman with any kind of gun?"

"Apparently you are stupid enough, if you don't leave now." She pointed to a truck with lettering on the side proclaiming it as Tim's Party Rental.

"I'm going. I'm going," he said and jerked open the truck door. "But we're not over. I'm not giving up."

"Idiot," Mel called out.

"Crazy bitch," Tim shouted as his tires spun on the pavement in his exit.

Once Tim's truck disappeared down the street, Mel lowered her gun and smiled at Viper and Dallas. "Hi, you must be Vince and Dallas. Come on into the bakery. I've been expecting you."

Dallas shot a glance at Viper.

He smiled back. "Like I was saying, life has a way of moving on. Some of us just need a little push."

Dallas tried, but she couldn't hide the smile spreading across her face as she agreed. "And some need a loaded shotgun as added incentive."

CHAPTER 10

Viper held out his hand, anxious to relieve the woman of the shotgun. "Mind if I take that shotgun for now?"

Melissa Fuller sighed. "Not at all." She ejected the shells, cleared the barrel and handed over the empty weapon.

Viper glanced around the shop with the glass cases full of tarts, cookies, cakes and pie. "Do you mind if I put this somewhere safe?"

"Not at all," Melissa said. "Make yourself at home."

Viper stepped behind the counter and into the back room where he leaned the shotgun into a corner. He returned to the front and inhaled the scent of confectionary sugar and cake.

Melissa planted her hands on her hips. "Tim makes me so mad I could spit nails."

"Apparently," Dallas commented. "What did he do that made you want to shoot him?"

"The son-of-a-" Mel covered her mouth with her hand. "Sorry. The fool proposed again."

Dallas's brows shot up into the hair hanging over her forehead. "He what?"

Melissa rolled her eyes and entered the bakery. "He asked me to marry him."

"And that made you mad?" Dallas shook her head.

"Yes. The divorce has been final for over a month, and he came traipsing into the bakery, armed with flowers and my old engagement ring." She turned back to Dallas and Viper, her eyes filled with tears. "What was I supposed to do? Say yes?"

Viper could think of better ways to let down the guy than to threaten him with a shotgun, but he kept his opinion to himself and let her continue.

"He accused me of cheating, something I would never do. If he knew me at all, he'd know it was the truth."

"Why did he think you cheated?"

"Because I talked to my old high school sweetheart when he came back into town. We had dinner to catch up on old times. He was feeling down because his wife left him. I helped him through a rough patch. That dinner was it. The man isn't interested in me any more than I'm interested in him. I'm married, for heaven's sake." She swiped at the tears slipping down her cheeks. "*Was* married."

Dallas snagged a tissue from a box on the counter and handed it to Melissa. "Are you all right?"

Mel flung a hand in the air. "No, I'm not all right. The crux of the matter is that I still love the dumbass."

She sniffed loudly and blew her nose. "And to make matters worse…" Her bottom lip trembled, and more tears spilled from her eyes. "I'm pregnant."

Viper started to ask if it was Tim's baby, but he bit back the words. From what Melissa was saying, it was and asking her could possibly get him shot. "Does Tim know?"

"No. You two and my doctor are the only ones who know. I don't know why I told you." She frowned heavily. "Don't tell Tim. I don't want him coming back to insist I remarry him because of the baby."

"But you just said you loved him," Dallas pointed out.

"I do. But he hasn't learned anything. I can't take him back until he knows how important controlling his temper is. I won't have my baby growing up in a house where we're always yelling at each other."

"Or pointing weapons at people we love?" Dallas said with a gentle smile.

When she looked at Melissa like that, she made Viper wish she looked at him. Who knew the tough Ranger girl could be as gentle and caring as she was?

Viper knew. He'd seen beyond the façade she'd erected to bluff her way past her male Army counterparts. But deep down, she was empathic, kind and caring. And she'd hate it worse than anything if he pointed out the fact.

Being raised by her father and then entering the Army, going through the extreme training she'd endured, made hiding that side of her second nature.

"Hey, come have a seat." Dallas led Melissa to one of

the bistro tables in the bakery. She urged the pregnant woman to sit on the small chair and then she sat across from her. "Has Tim abused you in any way?"

Melissa jerked back her head. "No, of course not. He beat up Rob, my old high school sweetheart after we had dinner. Rob suffered a few cuts and bruises but, thankfully, he didn't press charges. Tim's never raised a hand to me or hurt me in any other way than to call me a liar and a cheat." She smiled through the tears. "If anything, I'm the one who could have hurt him." She laughed, the sound catching on a hiccup. "Besides threatening to shoot him with a shotgun, I squirted him with ketchup one time when we got into an argument. The sauce stained his favorite shirt." She looked at Dallas, her eyes rounding. "Oh, God. I'm as bad as he is. Maybe worse."

The bakery owner buried her face in her hands. "Why am I such a mess?"

Dallas slipped into the one across from Melissa.

Viper sat beside the distraught woman. "You're fine. And arguing isn't a bad thing. My folks would have shouting matches at least once a quarter. If they didn't, then we started to worry. They've been happily married for thirty-five years."

"They shout?" Melissa asked, her tears slowing. "Loudly?"

Viper nodded. "Loud enough the neighbors once called the sheriff. They all had a good laugh later, after everyone calmed down."

Shaking her head, Melissa sighed. "I didn't cheat on him. But he never apologized for accusing me."

"Will you take him back?" Dallas asked.

"Probably," Melissa said. "I miss him. And I want my baby to have a father." Her lips firmed. "But he has to apologize first." She placed her hands on the table and pushed to her feet. "But now, you two are here because you're getting married." She smiled. "Are you sure you want to, after witnessing what marriage can make you do?"

Viper grinned. "We're pretty committed to this adventure."

Melissa wiped her face with the tissue, tossed it into the trash and squared her shoulders. "Then let's plan the food for the reception. I promise I'm not a flake. I'm hormonal and weepy, but I can make a beautiful wedding cake and cook a mean brisket and barbecue ribs."

Viper laughed, amazed the woman had the time to do both. "Those sound amazing."

"Good. All I need is the number of guests you expect and what sides you'd like to go with the barbecue."

The wedding guests would include all of the Brotherhood Protectors and their women, and the veterans from the Brighter Days Ranch. Hank had given him the list of names, and Dallas had added her list to come up with a total number that would make sense to anyone on the outside observing their efforts.

In between helping customers with cakes and cookies, Melissa worked with Viper and Dallas to develop a menu for the wedding reception. Then she handed them a book with pictures of wedding cakes and asked them to decide on one.

Viper let Dallas choose the design and was surprised when she chose the same one he'd been considering. The cake was simple but elegant, with three layers, buttercream frosting and white and pale, rosy-pink accent flowers.

By the time they concluded their meeting, the afternoon had waned.

Viper stood and helped Dallas to her feet. His cellphone vibrated in his pocket. When he pulled it out, he noted Hank's name on the screen. He answered immediately.

"Need you at the Blue Moose as soon as possible," Hank said without preamble.

"On our way." Viper thanked Melissa and hooked Dallas's arm.

Once outside, Dallas frowned up at him. "What's wrong?"

Viper opened the passenger door of his truck. "Hank called. He wants us at the Blue Moose Tavern ASAP."

"Did he say why?" she asked as she slipped into the passenger seat.

"No." Viper closed the door and hurried around to the driver's side. They could have walked, but he wanted his truck close in case they needed to leave quickly. Only a minute or two passed in the time it took to drive the short distance from the bakery to the tavern. Vehicles were parked all around the building and down the side alleys. "Looks like this is the place to be for dinner."

"I've only been here a couple of times, but these are the most vehicles I've seen out front," Dallas noted.

"I wonder what's going on. Must be something important for Hank to want us here." Viper got out and met Dallas at the front of the truck. He entered the tavern first. If there was trouble inside, he didn't want Dallas hurt.

The inside of the tavern was dimly lit with lamps hanging over each table, making them more intimate.

The people gathered around the bar all had mugs of beer, but they were silent until Viper entered with Dallas close behind.

Then a loud cheer went up, and everyone in the room yelled as one, "Surprise!"

Viper shielded Dallas's body with his for a full second until he realized Hank's team had come together to celebrate his and Dallas's upcoming wedding. His heart swelled at the thoughtfulness of the group of men he was just beginning to get to know. Not only were the men there, their women had come, as well.

Swede handed him a beer and winked. "Go with it," he said. "Chuck had the idea to throw the party. Blame him."

Chuck, the oldest of Hank's men, pushed through the crowd, a dark-purple shiner marring his face and bandages covering one hand. He enveloped Viper in a bear hug. Then he swept Dallas into his arms and crushed her.

"We're glad to see you out of the hospital already," Viper said.

Chuck grinned. "Had to twist the doc's arm to make him sign my release."

Dallas laughed and pounded Chuck's back. "I'm sure

you're exhausted. You shouldn't have gone to all this trouble."

"Maybe I shouldn't have," Chuck said with a wink, "but we can always use a good excuse to get together."

She leaned back and studied his face. "Are you sure you're up to all this excitement after nearly being killed?"

He shrugged and grinned. "Just another day in my life."

One by one, the team introduced themselves to Dallas.

Boomer carried his baby girl, Maya, on his arm. "This is Maya, and you met my fiancée, Daphne, at Taz's wedding."

"I did." Dallas shook hands again with Daphne and smiled up at Maya.

Kujo, former Delta Force, introduced his fiancée, FBI special agent Molly Greenbriar. His dog, Six, nudged his way between their legs, looking for attention.

Dallas looked to Kujo. "May I pet him?"

Kujo nodded. "Go ahead."

Squatting beside the German Shephard, Dallas held out her hand for the dog to sniff before she ventured closer to scratch behind the dog's ears.

Not only was she good with babies, she appeared to love dogs. Viper was having feelings for his partner that had nothing to do with friendship and more to do with the heat building in his loins.

He gulped down the beer and held out his hand for

another. A long, cold shower was in his near future, or he wouldn't get any sleep again that night.

Hours later, Dallas leaned back her head against the seat in Viper's truck, smiling.

"What are you smiling about?" Viper asked.

"I can't believe Chuck pulled everyone together on such short notice, after just being released from the hospital."

"Knowing Chuck, he made all the arrangements from his hospital bed. Not much keeps that man down."

"To honor us with the celebration was really nice of them." Her smile slipped as guilt filled her gut. "The get-together was fun, but I feel like such a fake."

"Every one of the Brotherhood Protectors would do anything for each other. And they would absolutely understand the need for complete silence on this particular mission."

"I know." She tilted her head sideways, a nice alcohol-induced buzz making her more relaxed and talkative. "They reminded me of what being a member of a military unit felt like. Everyone looking out for everyone else."

Viper's mouth pressed into a tight line. "Is that how your unit was for you?"

Dallas sighed. "That's how my peers were before I signed up for Ranger training. And that's how the men were to each other on the Ranger team I was assigned to." She shook her head. "Not to me. Some weren't ready to accept a female amongst them. I was their Achilles heel."

"I call bullshit," Viper said. "Male or female, we're on the same team. You went through the training just like they did and earned the right to wear the patch. They shouldn't have ostracized you just because you don't have a dick."

A chuckle rose up her throat. "I'd look awfully funny with a dick."

Viper's lips curved upward. "You're drunk."

"Maybe a little. But mostly just feeling good about the organization I belong to now. Hank's got a good thing going with the best of the best. I'm honored to be a part of it, even if I don't have testicles." She giggled.

"I, for one, am glad you are female."

"Oh yeah?" she countered, her heart fluttering in her chest. "Why?"

"I'd feel silly kissing a guy dressed as a bride."

Dallas burst out laughing.

Viper frowned. "Not that I have anything against guys who like guys, but I'm not one of them. I happen to like kissing girls."

She turned toward him, emboldened by alcohol and the good feeling of having been surrounded by people who cared. "Why did you kiss me back in the flower shop when no one was looking? And why did you kiss me on the porch when you didn't know anyone was looking?"

For a moment, he didn't answer, his hands holding tightly to the steering wheel, his gaze on the road ahead.

The bravado ebbed out of Dallas as the alcoholic

haze wore off. Heat rose up her cheeks as she realized she'd just gone fishing for answers she might not like. "Never mind. Just forget I asked," she muttered and turned away.

"No. I'll answer. I just...don't know how." He drew in a breath and let it out slowly. "I hadn't really kissed someone since Emily passed. I felt like such a gesture was betraying her memory. But when you came along all tough and ready to kick my ass, I couldn't help sparring with you. And I liked it." He faced her for a moment, taking his attention from the road. "I. Like. You. After you were nearly mowed over by Mrs. Davis's Cadillac, all I could think was that you were safe and I had to kiss you. So, I did."

Dallas couldn't believe what she'd just heard. Viper liked her. Liked her enough to kiss her. "Why do you like me? I'm not even a whole person."

He frowned. "Sweetheart, you have to get over the fact you don't have part of one leg anymore. The amputation doesn't make you any less of a person than someone with two legs. You're whole where it counts." He touched his fist to his chest. "Here. You care about people, you work as hard as any man at the ranch, and I like the fact you could kick my ass, if I let you. Don't think of yourself as anything less than what you are, a beautiful, smart badass female with eyes the color of emeralds and hair that shines like copper in the sun. You're beautiful, and working with you is an honor. I consider it even more of an honor you didn't knock off my head when I kissed you."

Dallas sat back, warmth filling her chest, radiating outward.

They'd arrived at the Brighter Days Ranch and pulled up to the front of the house. She didn't know how to respond to Viper's declaration. Dating had never been something she was good at. All she knew was she wanted him to kiss her again. But how did she tell him? Should she be blunt and let him know he turned her on?

Or should she play a little hard to get? Weren't men turned off by women who came on too strong? For that matter, what was too strong?

Her head spun with a multitude of different scenarios—all of which felt awkward and out of her skillset. At this rate, she'd be old and wrinkled before she told Viper how she really felt.

The door on her side of the vehicle opened, and the man who'd been foremost in her thoughts held out his hand. "Want to go inside, or have you decided to sleep in the truck?" He smiled. "I'm sorry if I scared you with my long speech. I promise I won't kiss you again, unless you want me to." He held up two fingers on his free hand. "Scout's honor."

Dallas put her hand in his but hesitated, her heart beating so fast she had trouble breathing. She swallowed hard and stared at where their hands touched. Heat radiated all the way up her arm and into her chest. "About that promise."

He tugged on her hand, forcing her to step out onto the running board. "The promise not to kiss you unless you wanted me to?"

"Um. Yes."

"I meant every word," he said softly.

She squared her shoulders, as she did anytime she faced something that scared her so much her knees shook, and she looked into his eyes. "What if I want you to kiss me?"

His eyes flashed surprise and then his mouth curved into a gentle smile. "Sweetheart, all you have to do is ask."

Having come that far, she couldn't go back. "I'm asking," she whispered.

He cocked his head a little to the side. "A little louder?"

"Seriously?" She drew in a deep breath and would have shouted that she wanted a kiss, now, if only to prove a point, but she didn't get that far.

Viper swept her into his arms, his lips crashing down onto hers, stealing away her words, her thoughts and her breath.

He held her above the ground, crushed to his chest, his arms like vises around her middle. None of that mattered when his lips were on hers, drawing a response she'd only dreamed of giving. Dallas wrapped her arms around his neck and gave as good as she got. She opened to him and met his tongue with her own, tasting the mint he'd popped into his mouth on the drive back.

Slowly, he set her on her feet but didn't back away or end the kiss. He did allow her to draw in a breath so that she could kiss him longer.

His hands slipped up the back of her shirt, his calloused fingers smoothing across her skin, kneading her flesh. Then he shifted the direction and slipped downward into the waistband of her jeans and panties to cup her ass.

Other than how good he tasted, the only thing Dallas could think of was that she wore entirely too many clothes. She wanted them both to be naked, their bodies pressed together, her legs tangled with his.

The sound of someone clearing his throat brought them back to earth. She broke away from Viper and glanced around.

"Sorry." Percy stepped down from the porch. "I didn't realize you two were out here. I'll just be going to the bunkhouse. Don't let me interrupt."

But he had, and the moment passed.

Dallas sucked in ragged breaths, her body on fire. She started to reach for Viper's hand to drag him into the house and to her room where she could make love to him all night long. But then the reality of the situation hit her like a ton of bricks.

Getting naked with Viper meant removing her prosthetic and then lying next to him with only one good leg. Nothing was sexy about a woman with a missing leg. And she'd be damned if she let him have pity sex with her.

A bitter mixture of longing and bile burned in her mouth. The truth was, she wasn't ready to have sex with a man since losing her leg. She wasn't even sure how she'd manage. "We'd better call it a night. We have chores in the morning and need to be ready to go when Sadie and Hank arrive." Dallas turned away.

Viper grabbed her arm and pulled her back against him. "What's wrong?"

"Nothing," she lied. "I'm just tired."

He lifted her chin and stared into her eyes. "Not buying that excuse, but I'll let it go for now." He released her arm. "Go on to bed. I'll see you in the morning."

Dallas would have run for the house, but that action would only have shown Viper how scared she was. And she didn't want him to think she was scared. Instead, she took her time climbing the stairs. But the truth was, she was terrified of her feelings and too scared to admit she wanted more. Rejection was not something she was prepared to handle.

CHAPTER 11

No amount of icy cold water would chill Viper's desire. He went to bed as hard as he'd been when he'd stepped into the shower and lay there all night, wishing he could go to Dallas and find out why she'd been so hot and pliant in his arms one moment and then shut down the next.

Granted, being caught making out by the ranch foreman had to have put a damper on her libido. But the interruption had done nothing to chill his.

He'd finally fallen asleep only to wake with the first rooster's crow. He'd even beaten Cookie to the kitchen and started a pot of coffee. He'd need the infusion of caffeine to make it through the day.

Footsteps sounded in the hallway, and Dallas entered the kitchen, fully dressed and ready for chores. When she spotted Viper standing by the coffee she came to a complete stop, her eyes wide and her cheeks turning a bright red.

Viper couldn't leave it the way they'd parted the

night before. They were partners, so they needed to be able to talk. "Dallas, about last night—"

She held up a hand. "I'm sorry. I shouldn't have come on to you like that. You don't owe me anything, and I didn't want you to feel obligated to kiss me."

He closed the distance between them and gathered her into his arms. "Are you kidding? I wondered if I had come on too strong and scared you away." His arms tightened around her. "I'm sorry if I offended you."

She stiffened. "I'm not afraid of you, Vince Van Cleave. I just didn't want to continue something that couldn't go any further."

"What do you mean?"

"I mean, we need to leave our connection at a kiss. I want nothing more." She looked away, leading him to believe she wasn't sharing the whole truth.

He clasped her chin in his hand and tilted her face upward, forcing her to look him. "Tell me you didn't feel anything when I kissed you and I'll leave you alone."

She closed her eyes. "I didn't."

His chest tightened. "Look at me and say those words."

She opened her eyes, her jaw tightening beneath his fingertips. "Why kid myself? I'm not good at this kind of thing. I'm not the right woman for you."

"Tell me you didn't feel anything and I'll leave you alone," he repeated, his tone softer. Her answer meant more to him than he wanted to admit to himself.

"You're pretty arrogant, aren't you?" she countered.

He lowered his mouth to hover over hers. "Shall I remind you?"

She opened her mouth, and when she did, Viper swooped in and claimed her lips, slipping his tongue past her teeth to caress hers. God, she tasted so good, and her body fit perfectly against his.

The clump of footsteps pierced his haze of lust. He stepped away, muttering, "Too damned many people live in this house."

Cookie entered the kitchen, chuckling. "Save it for the wedding night. I have breakfast to rustle up."

"And I have chores to do." Dallas ducked and hurried for the door.

Percy blocked her exit. "Not today, you don't. I understand Sadie McClain is taking you shopping for your wedding dress. You concentrate on that. We'll cover your chores." He tilted his head toward Lori standing behind him. "And I hear Lori's going with you. She's excused, as well. Now, don't you have to go put on some makeup or something?"

"I could use some help moving feed bags from the storage area to the bins this morning." Gavin Blackstock stepped up behind Percy. "Viper, you up for that?"

"I can do that," Dallas protested.

"I know you can, but today's a big day for you. From what Lori's been telling me, wedding dress shopping is a big deal." Gavin winked. "I won't have you chipping a nail or something before you go."

"I don't give a rat's ass about my nails, and I can haul feed just like any one of your men."

Viper chuckled. "Dallas."

"What?" she answered, her voice curt.

Viper grinned. "I think they're yanking your chain."

Dallas glared at Gavin and Percy. "You are?"

Percy crossed his arms over his chest. "Would I do that?"

Gavin raised his eyebrows. "Me?"

Dallas glared a moment longer and then relaxed. "You had me going for a moment. But since you're both a couple of jerks, I'll take you up on the day off from chores. I think I'll go paint my nails." She flipped her hair over her shoulder and marched out of the kitchen.

Viper laughed, admiring the way her hips swayed as she left.

"You'll have your hands full with that one," Gavin said.

Percy nodded. "Yeah, but she'll be one to work alongside you. She won't need to be pampered and babied."

"No," Gavin agreed. "But you better treat her right."

"Uh-huh," Percy said.

"Or she'll kick my ass," Viper finished. "I know. She's one in a million, and I'm lucky she picked me."

If only.

Viper could learn to love a woman like Dallas. He enjoyed showing her what being appreciated by a man who knew her worth was like.

Gavin jerked his head toward the door. "I wasn't kidding when I said I could use some help moving sacks of feed."

"Lead the way." Viper followed Gavin and Percy out to the barn.

"I'll have breakfast ready in twenty minutes," Cookie

called out as they crossed the threshold. "Don't go too far."

Viper helped Gavin move twenty bags of grain and sweet feed from one side of the barn to the other. They finished with a couple minutes to spare before Cookie yelled out the door that breakfast was on the table.

Franklin, Vasquez and Young hurried out of the bunk house, wearing clean T-shirts and blue jeans, their faces freshly washed. Percy had mentioned something about going into Bozeman for the day to purchase fencing supplies, and the guys were game to ride along.

Breakfast was noisy as usual, consumed quickly, and the dishes were washed in record time. Dallas disappeared into her room immediately after the last plate was stacked in the cabinet.

Viper wanted to go after her and finish the kiss that had been interrupted earlier, but he needed a shower before Hank and Sadie arrived.

He was just stepping out of the bathroom, clean, shaved and dressed when Percy called out, "The Pattersons are here!"

Dallas emerged from her bedroom, wearing Sadie's green dress, her hair combed neatly, mascara enhancing her thick lashes and lipstick coloring her lips. She looked like a model stepping out on the runway.

Viper swallowed hard to free his vocal cords. "Wow. You look amazing."

"You've seen me in this dress before," she said.

"Yeah, but something's different." Yes, he'd seen the dress, but that had been before he'd kissed her and felt her skin beneath his fingertips. That act had changed everything.

Heat flooded Dallas's cheeks. "Must be the lipstick. Is it too much?"

"No, but it makes me want to kiss you."

Her pulse quickened.

"Dallas?" Lori called out from the front door. "Are you ready?"

"I guess that kiss will have to wait," Viper said.

Dallas nodded and then hurried out of the house.

Lori met her on the porch wearing cream slacks and a powder-blue top. She'd pulled back her blond hair and secured it in a loose messy-bun.

Sadie and Hank stood beside the SUV. Sadie wore a peach dress that fit her top to perfection and flared out in soft chiffon around her hips and legs. She looked like the movie star she was, her hair hanging down around her shoulders in soft, golden waves.

Dallas couldn't begin to compete with someone that stunning, and she had no intention of trying. Her only hope was not to trip in the heels.

"Since your wedding planner had to work, it's up to us to find your wedding gown," Sadie said.

"Between the three of us, we should be able to find a dress." Dallas forced a determined grin to her face. "Let's do this."

The women climbed into the back of the SUV, giving the men the front.

Sadie brought brides magazines with her and talked about styles and materials all the way into Bozeman.

By the time the men dropped them at the bridal shop, Dallas felt as if she knew a little more about wedding dresses and wouldn't be completely ignorant or overwhelmed.

Still, she'd rather have been on the M240 machinegun range, shooting holes in old refrigerators. Trying on wedding dresses seemed so foreign to a girl raised by her father who shared hunting, fishing and riding four-wheelers. The closest thing to a dress she'd owned had been the black skirt she'd been issued as part of her formal Army Service Uniform when she'd graduated Basic Combat Training.

Until Sadie had given her the green dress, she hadn't seen a need to purchase a dress, or wear one.

Walking into the bridal shop was like walking into an alternate universe. One in which Dallas Hayes was an honest-to-goodness female kind of female. Not a graduate of the all-male club of Army Rangers. She left the selection choices to the dress consultants, Sadie and Lori.

After the first ten dresses, she gave up on any kind of modesty. Not that she'd had that luxury in the Army. Showering in an open shower with twenty other women at a time had broken her of shyness during the first week of Basic. But dressing in front of the beautiful actress reemphasized all her insecurities about having lost a leg.

None of the women made mention of the prosthetic or her stump of a leg. They acted as if nothing was different or unusual about Dallas, other than her auburn hair and green eyes.

Lori had salads delivered to the shop for lunch, and the hunt for the perfect dress and accessories continued into the early afternoon when Dallas slipped into a dress that had her reconsidering her stance on all things female.

The dress was a light peachy-pink, almost white, chiffon that moved and flowed with her body like a thin, beautiful cloud. It transformed the Ranger in her into an ethereal fairy princess she didn't recognize. Her breath caught in her throat, and tears burned in her eyes.

"Oh, my," the saleswoman whispered. "The others have to see this one." She hurriedly pinned the back of the dress and opened the door.

Dallas stepped out of the dressing room and walked toward Lori and Sadie, her heart beating fast and her breaths coming in shallow gasps. The dress made her feel so incredibly feminine she wasn't exactly sure who she was, but when she glanced in the three-way mirror, she decided she liked what she saw.

Sadie's eyes widened, and she pressed a hand to her mouth. "Oh, Dallas."

Lori's mouth dropped open, and she shook her head. "Wow."

The consultant beamed. "I think we've found your dress."

"Yes," Sadie said. She caught Dallas's gaze in the mirror. "Do you like it?"

"I've never seen a more beautiful dress," Dallas said, her voice barely above a whisper.

"You have to get this one," Lori said. "It transforms you."

"I don't want to be different than who I am." Or did she?

"You're not so much different," Sadie said. "You're still the same you, only better."

Dallas's heart swelled at the feeling of acceptance she experienced with Lori and Sadie. "Do you think Viper will like it?"

"If he doesn't, he'll need his eyes examined." Sadie clapped her hands. "The style's absolutely perfect. Now, let's find the veil and shoes to match."

An hour later, they'd purchased the dress, matching shoes, veil and a pale blue garter to wear underneath the dress.

"That's the something blue," Sadie said. "I have a string of pearls you can borrow that were my great-grandmother's. That will cover the old and borrowed. And, since the dress is new, you're covered on all fronts."

"Something old, something new," Lori recited.

"Something borrowed and something blue," Sadie finished and glanced at her watch. "The men should have collected the new guy at the airport and be back by now. Lori, could you check outside and see if the SUV has arrived?"

Lori nodded and hurried out the front door.

"How much was the dress?" Dallas asked. "I need to pay for it."

Sadie shook her head. "Hannah's father is footing this bill. Hank said he was extremely thankful Viper saved Hannah, Taz and Chuck from that limousine."

Dallas frowned, guilt hanging like a pall over an otherwise fun day. The dresses in the bridal shop cost a small fortune. How could she spend so much, knowing the wedding was a fake? "I can't let him do that."

"Consider it his wedding gift to you and Viper."

Lori came back into the shop. "The guys are outside waiting, and they're hungry."

"We're ready," Sadie said.

Dallas looked around. "Where's the dress?"

"It needs a few alterations," Sadie explained. "They'll have it done by Friday and deliver it to the Bear Creek Ranch."

The women left the shop and climbed into the SUV. A stranger sat in the very back.

"Ladies," Hank said. "Meet Trevor Andersen, the newest member of the Brotherhood Protectors."

Dallas turned to shake the man's hand. "I'm Dallas Hayes."

His hand was terribly scarred, and he was missing his trigger finger, but he shook hers with a strong grip. "Nice to meet you, ma'am."

"What branch of the military were you a part of?" she asked.

"Navy."

"Trevor is a Navy SEAL. He served under my former commander on nine missions," Hank said over his shoulder as he pulled out of the parking lot and drove several blocks to a steakhouse.

The food was excellent, and the company even better. The evening went so well, Dallas was beginning to feel as though their fake engagement and upcoming wedding were real. She and Viper were a couple planning to spend the rest of their lives together in wedded bliss.

They laughed, they touched, and they shared a joke or two like people who really liked and cared for one another.

By the time they left the steakhouse, the sun was setting, coloring the sky a stunning array of mauves, purple and brilliant red-orange.

"Look, I can sit in the back." Lori crawled into the backseat before anyone could protest.

"I'm sure the happy couples would prefer to sit with each other than with me." Trevor slipped in beside her.

Viper held the front passenger door for Sadie. "You should ride up front with Hank. I want to sit with Dallas."

Nodding, Sadie smiled. "Thank you. I kind of like my forever protector."

Viper held the door for Dallas.

She brushed against him as she climbed into the SUV. Butterflies fluttered against the inside of her belly and heat coiled at her center. After trying on the most beautiful dress she'd ever seen, Dallas was feeling strange. Seeing herself in a wedding dress most girls only dreamed of had stripped away the tough-gal façade, leaving her feeling somehow vulnerable.

When Viper slipped onto the seat beside her, her heart beat faster and her breathing became labored. The control she prided herself on escaped her entirely when the former Delta Force operative took her hand.

With her tongue tied, her heartbeat erratic and her core melting, Dallas was an utter mess. Thankfully, she was saved from saying anything by the sudden chirp of her cellphone. She'd almost forgotten she had it with her. Using it as a reason to pull her hand free of Viper's, she dug into her purse, hoping to stop the annoyingly persistent ringing.

The number wasn't one she was familiar with, but she answered anyway. "Hello."

"Dallas, this is Daisy."

"Oh, hello, Daisy," she said. "Is everything all right?"

"Yes, of course. I called to see how dress shopping was."

"We found one. It'll be altered and delivered the day before the wedding."

"Great," Daisy said. "I also wanted to let you know what I've been working on." She paused long enough to take a breath and then launched into her description. "I called Tim Fuller. He's supposed to deliver the chairs and tables this evening. I scheduled the Justice of the Peace to perform the ceremony on Saturday. Wallie Strange will install a temporary wooden dance floor in the barn, the day before the wedding, and I double-checked with Melissa Fuller about the catering. I've also lined up Lisa Benton to help with the decorations on Saturday. She's really good at them and has helped me on my other weddings. So, she knows what to do."

Sadie turned in her seat. "Tell Daisy, we all can help with the decorations."

Daisy laughed. "I heard her. Good, it might take all of us to get it done on time for the wedding Saturday afternoon," Daisy said. "Oh, and I can't remember if we discussed alcohol."

"We didn't," Dallas said.

"Would you prefer an open bar, or will you want to supply the alcohol yourself?"

Viper leaned close to Dallas's hand holding the cellphone to her ear. "We'll supply the alcohol," he said into the device. He took that moment to drop a kiss on Dallas's temple.

"I'll have one of my guys pick up a keg and a couple cases of beer," Hank said.

"Not all people drink beer, sweetheart," Sadie reminded him.

Hank chuckled. "I'll have them include several bottles of wine in the order."

"And whiskey," Sadie added.

"Since when do you drink whiskey?" Hank shot his wife a glance.

"I don't," Sadie said. "But I know several of your guys do. And I'm almost certain some of the folks from Brighter Days might like something harder than beer and wine."

"Maybe we should consider the open bar," Viper said.

"I think we can cover this," Hank said.

"Isn't it a little early for the tables and chairs to be delivered?" Dallas asked. "The wedding is still a few days away."

"Oh, sweetie." Sadie chuckled. "To set up for a wedding can take days."

"And we don't have that much time," Hank reminded them. He captured Dallas's gaze in the rearview mirror.

Dallas ended the call and settled back in her seat.

Viper reached for her hand again and squeezed it gently. "It'll all work out."

"I certainly hope so. Seems like a lot of work to go through for one day," she commented.

"One very special day," Sadie agreed.

Dallas nodded. Oh, the event would be special, all right. If the wedding day saboteur struck again, the situation would be even more unsettling than it already was.

Dallas stared at the back of Hank's seat. If the wedding went as planned and nothing happened…then what? They couldn't do it again to lure out the troublemaker. They'd have to wait until one of the other Brotherhood Protectors scheduled his own wedding, or someone else in the community, and then pray they'd invite them to the wedding so they could keep an eye out for the Grinch, wreaking havoc on young newlyweds.

The drive was smooth, but for the curving roads weaving in and out of the foothills at the base of the Crazy Mountains. The steady rumble of tires against pavement made Dallas sleepy. She closed her eyes only for a moment, the day's activities and strain of pretending dragging her eyelids downward.

Just as she closed her eyes, Dallas pitched forward against the shoulder restraint. She woke instantly and leaned toward the gap between the front seats to see what was going on.

The back tires skidded, but not enough to slow the momentum of the big vehicle.

"What is that?" Sadie cried.

"I don't know, but we're going to hit it. Brace yourself!" Hank swerved, but the front tire hit whatever was in the road, flipping it up to slam into the grill and block the view of the road ahead.

Viper gripped Dallas's arm.

Her seatbelt tightened, jerking her back against the seat.

The SUV bumped over the edge of the road and down into a ditch.

Dallas jerked from side to side with each huge bump. She couldn't see much through the side windows and her brief glimpses out the front were a nightmare of bouncing headlights.

The vehicle slowed, and Hank regained control, pulling out of the ditch and back onto the road, bringing the big SUV to a halt.

For a moment, everyone sat still, breathing hard.

Then Hank, Dallas and Viper yanked open their doors and leaped out onto the pavement.

"What the hell was that?" Viper strode back down the highway to what was left of the object that could well have killed them all.

The moon shone bright enough to illuminate something long, white and rectangular.

"Looks like a folding table," Dallas said.

"It is," Hank agreed. "The question is, what the hell is it doing in the middle of the road?"

"Isn't this the kind of table they used at Taz and Hannah's wedding?" Sadie joined them, carrying a flashlight. She shined the beam on the table and focused on the writing on the underside.

FULLER PARTY RENTALS

"Seems we need to pay Mr. Fuller a visit."

"That table could have caused a major accident," Viper said.

"Do you get the feeling that weddings in this area of Montana are jinxed?" Sadie whispered.

Not only were they jinxed, but someone was making an effort to ruin the party for the happy couple and all those invited to be a part of the ceremony.

The second attempt at ending the wedding before it began had nearly succeeded.

The trouble was, they couldn't have predicted anything like running over a table in the middle of a curving mountain road.

How could the culprit set up the latest attack, knowing the table would affect them and not others? Or could the table have fallen off a truck by accident?

Dallas was afraid to ask.

What next?

CHAPTER 12

Viper's heartbeat had barely returned to normal by the time he and Hank moved the folding table out of the road. A few miles farther, they drove past the entrance to Bear Creek Ranch where all the tables were supposed to have been delivered.

Everyone agreed waiting until morning to pursue the problem of the rogue table wouldn't make much of a difference.

Hank passed the turnoff for White Oak Ranch and drove on to Brighter Days where he pulled up to the ranch house.

Viper helped Dallas out of the SUV and then moved out of the way to allow Trevor to alight and assist Lori.

After a round of female hugging, Sadie climbed back into the front of the vehicle and Trevor slipped into the middle seat.

"I'll touch bases with you in the morning," Sadie told Dallas.

Dallas nodded. "Thank you for all your help today."

"It was my pleasure. I remember shopping for my dress. I would have loved having someone with me to help me decide."

Hank hooked his arm around Sadie's waist and hugged her close. "You would have looked just as beautiful in a burlap sack."

Viper admired how open Hank and Sadie were about their love, actions that didn't make either of them weak or silly. It had the opposite effect, showing the strength they shared as a cohesive team.

As the SUV pulled away, Viper, Dallas and Lori turned toward the ranch house.

"I'm headed for my bed," Lori said with a wave. "Thank you for sharing your day with me."

"Are you kidding? I should be thanking you." Dallas hugged Lori. "You really were a big help. Three heads were definitely better than one. I owe you. When you're ready to go wedding dress shopping, I'd be happy to go along."

Lori snorted. "Like that will ever happen." She tipped her head to the side. "But then again…you and Viper give me hope." She gave a mock salute. "Don't do anything I wouldn't do." She winked and sauntered into the house.

Darkness cloaked the countryside in shadows, but the stars overhead shined down on the Crazy Mountains.

"I guess I'd better hit the sack," Dallas said. "We need to talk with Tim Fuller tomorrow."

"Dallas…" Viper reached for her arm.

She stepped away, out of his range. "I'm glad you're my partner."

Viper frowned. He could feel her pulling away, and he didn't like it. "But?"

"But, don't you see? That's all we can be."

"Why can't it be more?"

"You deserve someone who isn't a mess as I am."

He wanted to reach out to her, but she was too far away. "What if I like the kind of mess you are?"

She shook her head. "I'm not even comfortable in my own skin. How can I let someone else in on that kind of crazy?"

Viper moved toward her, determined to close the distance growing between them. "I'll take my chances."

Dallas took another step away from Viper, her ankles bumping into the bottom step leading up to the porch. "You don't want to start something with me. I promise," she whispered.

He stopped in front of her and touched a finger to her chin, lifting her face to stare up in his. "You don't realize what you've done to me, Dallas Hayes."

"I'm sorry. I didn't mean to."

"I'm not sorry." He bent to touch his lips to her forehead. "I'm glad I met you. I'm even happier you're my partner for this assignment. Because I get to spend more time with you." He touched his lips to the hollow below her earlobe.

Dallas's moan set off fireworks across Viper's nerves.

"I can't be what you need," Dallas said, her voice a breathy whisper.

"Oh, but you are." He lowered his head and claimed her lips in a sweet, gentle kiss.

When her knees buckled, he held her up with an arm around her waist and deepened the kiss.

All evening, he'd watched her, especially the expressions chasing one after the other across her face. He liked when she laughed, when she smiled and when her forehead creased in a stubborn wrinkle.

He kissed her, hoping to erase her doubts, to show her that what was happening between them was good and right.

When he raised his head, he smiled down at her. "Now, go get some sleep before I change my mind and keep you up the rest of the night." He stepped back, forcing his arms to fall to his sides. He'd rather throw her over his shoulder, march her into his bedroom and take her in a storm of passion. But he suspected she wasn't ready, and he didn't want to rush her and possibly scare the dauntless Ranger. Yes, she could hold her own in combat, but she wasn't as sure of herself in the relationships arena.

He turned her around and gave her a little push up the stairs onto the porch. "Go to bed, Dallas. We can solve the problems of the world in the morning."

He mustered all possible control to turn and walk away. But he managed. She needed time. And he needed a cold shower.

DALLAS LAY awake until the early hours of the morning, wondering if she'd done the right thing by backing away from Viper. Logic dictated she keep their relationship professional. But nothing at all was professional about Viper's kiss, or her response.

Even though she'd said she wasn't what he needed, she still wished she could be. But the thought of getting naked and climbing into bed with Viper scared her more than she would admit. What if he was turned off by her stump? How would she feel?

What did her concern matter? She wasn't getting naked with Viper. He was her partner, not her lover.

Around three a.m. Dallas finally fell into a fitful sleep. When she woke, the sun was halfway up in the sky. She glanced at the clock on the nightstand and flew out of bed. Ten-thirty? Holy hell. How had she slept so long? Why hadn't anyone roused her? She had work to do.

After dressing in jeans, boots and a T-shirt, she hurried toward the kitchen. As she passed Viper's room, she glanced in—empty and the bed was neatly made. Damn, she'd missed him.

Cookie had left a note on the counter.

Sleeping Beauty, should you wake, your breakfast is in the refrigerator. I've gone to Bozeman for supplies.

Dallas skipped the cold scrambled eggs and cut some thick slices of ham to make a sandwich. She wrapped it in a sandwich bag and headed for the barn.

Gavin and Percy were nowhere to be found.

Franklin and Vasquez worked together in one of the stalls, mucking the soiled hay into a wheelbarrow.

"Where is everyone?" Dallas asked.

"Blackstock and Pearson headed to Bear Creek Ranch to help lay the floor in the barn for dancing."

"I thought you two were going with Cookie to get supplies?" Dallas said.

Franklin pitched a forkful of hay into the wheelbarrow. "We decided to stay and work on the chores."

Vasquez winked. "They won't get done by themselves."

"And if you're looking for Viper," Young said from behind her, "he left an hour ago and said to tell you he'd be back at lunchtime."

She glanced around at the interior of the barn. "What's left of the chores?"

"Not a damned thing. We're considering going into Eagle Rock to the diner for lunch." Franklin grinned. "Wanna come?"

Dallas smiled. "Thanks, but no. I packed my lunch. I thought I'd take Little Joe out for a ride."

"Good, he could use some exercise," Vasquez said. "Young's been feeding him too many sugar cubes."

"Shut it, Vasquez. So, Little Joe has a sweet tooth. What're a few going to hurt him?"

Vasquez set aside his pitchfork. "You want one of us to go with you?"

"Thanks, but I'd like some time alone." Dallas appreciated that the men cared enough to offer to accompany her. But she needed time to think and sort through her growing feelings for Viper.

While the men flung good-natured insults, Dallas caught Little Joe, saddled him and slipped a bridle over his head. Wanting to get away on her own, Dallas hurried on the off-chance Viper returned early.

Less than fifteen minutes later, she rode out into the pasture, heading toward the Crazy Mountains. The sun beat down, making her hot. After several cooler days, she was ready to ride, sweat and soak up the rays. Summer didn't last long in the mountains.

Dallas took off at a gallop, letting the warm, late summer air blow the cobwebs out of her mind and clear her thoughts. Eventually, Little Joe settled into a smooth trot and then a steady walk as he climbed into the hills.

She didn't stop until they'd reached a stream. Dallas dismounted and walked along the banks, leading Little Joe by the reins and letting him stop to drink when he wanted.

When she reached what Hannah had called the fairy pools, she looped Little Joe's reins over a low-hanging branch and sat on a rocky ledge near the water's edge.

Hot, sweaty and alone with her thoughts, she tried to expel the ones of Viper and how being kissed by such a handsome man felt. How she wished he was there, kissing her again.

The sun found her on the rock, baking her body until the cool, clear water called. With most of the guys in Eagle Rock and nobody around, she figured, what the hell?

She yanked her top over her head, slipped out of her boots and jeans and unstrapped her prosthetic. Down to her bra and panties, she debated whether to keep them on as a kind of bikini, but she nixed that idea and slipped out of them, too. Then she scooted to the edge of the rock and slid into the stream, gloriously naked and loving how cool and refreshing the water was when it enveloped her.

While swimming, she didn't have the added weight of her fake leg. She floated in the dappled shade, finding an occasional patch of sunlight to warm her skin.

Her therapist had been right. Brighter Days Ranch had been exactly what she needed. She hadn't felt this relaxed since she'd been medically released from the Army.

Here in the pool, no was judging her, no one could see her deformity. The trees, shadows and sunshine didn't care if she had one or two legs. The water wrapped around her like she belonged.

Dallas swam until she tired and then turned onto her back, closed her eyes and floated. The only thing that could make the day better was if Viper was in the water with her.

Viper had peeked into Dallas's room earlier that morning to see if she'd risen before him and headed out to do chores early.

When he'd seen she was still sleeping, he smiled, closed the door, grabbed a cup of coffee and a piece of toast. He left the house and the ranch, heading into town to find Tim Fuller. Hank had provided the address while he'd been trying on tuxedoes in a men's store around the corner from the bridal shop.

Fuller lived in the apartment above the warehouse where he stored the tables and chairs he rented to local groups for weddings, funerals, revivals and other gatherings. The warehouse sat on the northern end of Eagle Rock next to an auto repair shop with cars and trucks crowded into a tight fenced space.

As Viper pulled up to the warehouse, a man waved from the front of the auto repair shop.

Viper parked the truck and glanced at the Fuller's Party Rental building. The door stood open but no movement was evident inside.

The man at the auto repair shop started toward him. He wore faded blue jeans and had tattoos from his wrists all the way up his arms into the sleeves of his T-shirt advertising a name brand of motorcycles. The man appeared to be in his mid-thirties, his dark, shaggy hair having a hint of gray at the temples. He stuck out an oil-stained hand. "Rusty Benton."

Viper took the man's hand and shook it. "Vince Van Cleave."

"Looking for Tim?" Rusty asked.

"Yes, sir," Viper said. "Know where I can find him?"

The man smirked. "He's in the office of the warehouse, where he's been sleeping since his wife kicked him out."

Not wanting to discuss another man's business in front of a complete stranger, Viper gave the other man half a smile and turned toward the warehouse.

"You know, I wouldn't go in there right now, if I were you," Rusty said.

"Oh yeah," Viper countered, glancing over his shoulder. "Why?"

Another grin followed. "He ain't alone."

About that time, Melissa Fuller emerged from the warehouse, adjusting her shirt inside the waistband of her slacks and calling back over her shoulder, "Don't you forget to pick up milk and orange juice. I'll be working late—"

A man Viper recognized as Tim stepped out into the sunshine, grabbed Melissa around the waist and pulled her back against his front, kissing her on the neck. "I won't forget."

She turned and wrapped her arms around his neck. "Love you, babe."

"Love you, too." Tim kissed her full on the lips.

The couple seemed completely oblivious to their audience.

"Guess they're back together," Rusty commented.

Viper smiled. "Appears so."

"I'll be by later with lunch." Tim swept a hand across Melissa's tummy. "Gotta take care of my sweetie and our baby."

"Umm. See you in a few." Melissa cupped his cheek and kissed him again before turning toward her car. At that point, she noticed the two men standing nearby. "Oh. Hello, Mr. Van Cleave." Her cheeks bloomed with color. She gave a little wave of her hand, ducked into her car and drove away.

Tim rocked back on his heels, his fingers hooked in his belt loops, a smile spreading across his face. When he turned to Rusty and Viper, his smile widened. "She took me back."

Rusty grinned and hurried over to Tim, reaching out

to shake the man's hand. "Glad to hear it. You two were meant to be together."

"I think so. And apparently, Mel does, too." He chuckled and shook his head. "And she's pregnant with our kid." He turned to his friend. "I'm going to be a daddy."

Again, Rusty shook hands with Tim and clapped him on the back. "That's great, man. So happy for you."

Tim finally noticed Viper standing nearby. "Can I help you?"

Viper closed the distance between them and held out a hand. "Vince Van Cleave. I came by to discuss the table settings you were supposed to deliver to Bear Creek Ranch yesterday evening."

Tim nodded. "You're the groom, right?" He smiled, stepped forward and shook Viper's hand. "Congratulations." His smile faded. "Did you need more tables than Daisy requested?"

Viper shook his head. "No, but we found one in the middle of the highway last night. We nearly wrecked our SUV with six people inside. Had we been in anything smaller, the crash could have been fatal."

Tim clapped a hand to the side of his face. "Holy shit." He frowned. "I don't know how that could have happened. Billy Joe and I delivered all of the tables I took with me yesterday, along with one-hundred and fifty chairs."

"You weren't short one table when you set up?" Viper asked.

Tim shook his head. "I had fifteen on my work order. I loaded fifteen and delivered fifteen. I would have noticed then if one was missing." His eyes narrowed slightly. "Are you sure the table was mine?"

Viper nodded. "Your company name and logo were printed on the underside of the table. It's still lying on the side of the road where we moved it out of the way." He gave Tim the general location.

"Let me check my inventory." Tim disappeared into the warehouse, calling out over his shoulder, "You're welcome to come inside. I have nothing to hide."

Viper entered the warehouse, followed by Rusty.

Tim walked to a stack of rectangular tables similar to the one they'd run over the night before. He counted them once. Then he counted again. "I should have a total of fifty rectangular tables. Less the fifteen I delivered yesterday, there should be thirty-five here." He looked up, frowning. "I only count thirty-four. But I know I only took fifteen with me."

Viper crossed to the stack of tables and counted them for himself. He came up with thirty-four as well. "Do you keep the warehouse locked?" He studied the interior, noting the number of doors and windows.

He nodded. "Mel thinks I'm crazy for locking it, but I do. I spent too much of my hard-earned cash on buying all of this inventory."

"Any sign of a break-in? Tampering of the locks on the doors?" Viper asked.

"You can come look for yourself," Tim offered, leading the way first to the front door and then to the rear.

The locks were intact, with no signs of forced entry. "Who has keys?" Viper asked.

"Only me and Mel," Tim said. He pulled his keys out of his pants pocket. "I keep mine in my pocket. Mel has hers locked in a safe in the bakery."

"I have one," Rusty said. "Tim gave me a copy once when he locked himself out. I keep it hanging on a hook in my office."

"Who would steal a table and leave it out on the highway?" Tim scratched his head. "The action doesn't make sense."

"Teenage pranksters?" Rusty offered.

"Yeah, but why would they drop the table on the way to Bear Creek Ranch?" Viper asked.

"To make me look like I was careless." Tim's lips formed a straight line. "That table could have gotten someone killed. I would have been responsible."

If Viper was at all superstitious, even he would think anything to do with weddings in the area was jinxed. But he wasn't superstitious. Someone was sabotaging his wedding to Dallas. The circumstance was what he'd wanted in order to lure the saboteur out of hiding, but it still pissed him off.

Tim seemed genuinely concerned and upset that one of his tables might have hurt someone. Yeah, he had anger issues related to who his wife was seeing, but it didn't mean he was out to hurt anyone else.

Viper considered himself a good judge of character. From what he'd observed of Tim, the man wouldn't have deliberately left a table in the road. What would doing so have accomplished? Other than destroying his business.

"I'll have to report the incident to the sheriff," Viper said.

Tim's jaw hardened. "I understand."

"If you come up with a name or motivation someone might have for stealing one of your tables, will you let me know?" Viper asked. "I'd like to keep an eye open for whoever did this."

"I will." Tim shook Viper's hand again. "Thanks for letting me know. I'll retrieve the table and dispose of it properly. I'll change the locks on my building."

Viper and Rusty left the warehouse.

"Nice meeting you, Vince. If you ever need any work done on your truck, I'd be happy to help. I give a discount to veterans. I served in the Army. I know what coming home is like."

As Viper climbed into his truck, his gaze followed Rusty as he strode toward his shop.

A brown-haired young woman dressed in an oil-stained coverall exited the building and stopped to talk to Rusty before slipping into a full-sized pickup and driving away.

As she passed Viper, he remembered where he'd seen her. She was one of the waitresses at the diner where Daisy worked. He almost didn't recognize her in the coverall. What was her name? Lisa?

Who was she to Rusty? Business partner? His girlfriend? She looked too young. Daughter? Too old. Sister?

Maybe.

Not that she had anything to do with the case, but she

made Viper curious. He'd have Swede run a background check on Rusty and the employees of the diner. As small as Eagle Rock was, he was bound to run into the same people over and over. Her appearance might not mean anything, but then again, some connections meant everything. But was it only coincidence that Lisa was something to Rusty, the next-door neighbor to Tim Fuller's warehouse? And Billy Joe, also from the diner, helped Tim deliver the tables and chairs. Had he loaded one extra onto the truck and conveniently knocked it off on the way?

As Viper pulled away from Fuller's warehouse, he called Swede and gave him what little information he had gleaned, asking him to check on Lisa and Billy Joe, as well as Rusty.

Viper checked his watch. At half past ten, he figured Dallas would be up and mad that he'd left without telling her. He wouldn't be surprised if she left the ranch on her own mission to solve the case without him. Much like he'd done by interviewing Tim without Dallas.

He pulled his cell phone from his pocket and punched in the numbers for Brighter Days and let it ring seven times before he ended the call.

Viper told himself that just because no one answered the phone, didn't mean anything was wrong. Everyone on the ranch worked. They could be outside tending to fences and animals.

Once he cleared Eagle Rock city limits, he pressed the accelerator to the floor and raced down the highway back to Brighter Days. More specifically, to Dallas. The closer he came to the ranch, the more worried he became.

If someone was trying to ruin his and Dallas's wedding and was willing to throw a table in the road the group would be driving down, what else might that person try to stop the wedding from happening?

Taz and Hannah had almost died in the crash on their wedding day.

Viper glanced at the clock on his dash. He'd been gone for almost two hours. Anything could have happened to Dallas in those two hours.

As he bumped across the cattle guard at the Brighter Days Ranch gate, he tried to tell himself Dallas was okay. She could take care of herself. And she had other trained military men around her if she needed help.

Despite his self-coaching, Viper couldn't help worrying. He skidded to a stop in the barnyard and leaped out of the truck.

"Hey, Viper. What's wrong?" Young called out. He'd forgone the wheelchair, preferring to propel himself across the ground using his gloved hands and the denim-encased lower half of his body. The man was fast for someone with no legs.

"Nothing." That he knew of. "Dallas around?"

Young shook his head and tipped it toward the pasture. "She took off an hour ago on horseback."

"By herself?" Viper asked, fighting the panic entering his tone.

"Yup," Young said. "Said Little Joe needed exercise."

Viper didn't wait for Young to finish speaking before he took off at a jog.

He was halfway to the barn when he heard Young

say, "Take Blondie, the buckskin mare. She's the fastest, and she's been pacing since Little Joe left. Those two are inseparable. If you hope to find Dallas, let Blondie find Little Joe. She has a way of sniffing him out."

"Thanks," Viper called over his shoulder. He caught, saddled and bridled the mare and was out of the barn in less than five minutes.

Blondie danced sideways as Viper maneuvered through the gate and out into the pasture. Once he had the gate secured, he gave the mare her head. She shot off like a rocket, galloping across the fields, up over a rise and down into a valley.

Viper hoped the mare knew where she was going, because he sure as hell didn't. He committed landmarks to memory in case he had to find his own way back. Other than that, his gaze panned the horizon, the shadows and the gullies, searching for Dallas and Little Joe.

He'd begun to think the mare was out for a joy run when he spotted Little Joe tied to a tree branch near a creek. He reined in the mare, bringing her to a begrudging walk.

Blondie strained against the bit, breathing hard, anxious to reunite with Little Joe.

When they reached the other horse, Viper dropped to the ground, wound Blondie's reins in a branch and set off on foot, following the creek upstream to locate Little Joe's missing rider.

What he found was better than he could have ever expected.

Where the banks widened and a crystal-clear pool

spread out before him, he found Dallas, floating on her back, her eyes closed. And she was completely and gloriously naked.

For a split second, his heart raced and he thought she might be dead. Then he noticed the smile on her face and the way her hands moved beneath the surface of the water.

She was far from dead. Viper's body, and parts in the deep south, sprang to life.

CHAPTER 13

Dallas floated through the cooler shadows and into a patch of sunshine, enjoying the way the water buoyed both her body and spirit. She'd done physical therapy in a pool, learning to swim with only one leg. Now, she reveled in the cool water, letting all of her worries about her new job, her new partner and her new life float away.

A rippling motion in the water made her peek one eye open. When she didn't see anything out of the ordinary, she closed it again and lifted her face to the sunshine.

Eventually, she'd have to head back to the barn. Viper would probably have returned, wondering where the hell she'd gone. She couldn't put off their wedding planning with only a day to spare.

Too bad he couldn't find her there in the pool and join her. They might bring a whole new meaning to the word *partner*.

Again, the water rippled around her body.

Dallas opened both eyes but didn't see anything in front of her. She straightened, treading water, letting her foot drift beneath the surface.

"Hey," a deep, familiar voice said from behind.

For a moment, Dallas thought she'd conjured the man of her thoughts. She spun in the water and slipped beneath the surface.

Arms went around her and brought her back up into the sweet mountain air.

She sputtered, pushed the hair out of her face and stared into Viper's clear blue eyes.

"What are you doing here?" she demanded. "And h-how did you find me?" His hands on her skin made fire burn through her veins, turning up the heat at her core.

"Apparently, you split up an equine romance by taking Little Joe out without Blondie. They're a pair. Or at least, Blondie thinks so. She brought me straight here." He nodded toward where the two horses were grazing on the long, green grass by the shore, several yards away.

Her cheeks heated, and she crossed her arms over her chest, covering her bare breasts. "But you can't be here."

"I already am." He held her at arm's length, with their legs intertwined. Her smooth thighs slid against his thick, hairy ones.

Her insides tightened, desire roaring to life. This reaction couldn't be good. "I mean, I didn't expect anyone else to be out here. In case you didn't notice... I'm naked." She lowered her voice and whispered the last word.

Viper laughed out loud, the sound echoing against the creek banks.

To Dallas, nothing was funny about being naked with Viper. She wasn't ready to expose her body and lack of a leg. What if he was repulsed? Her belly knotted.

"Dallas." He kissed her forehead. "You're frowning."

"You can't be in here with me."

"Why?" He kissed her cheek and drew her body closer. "Give me one good reason."

"Because…I'm…not…"

He nibbled on her earlobe, and their chests brushed against each other.

Dallas moaned, her hands moving to rest on his shoulders and her hips nudging his.

His erection nudged her belly, tempting her to throw her misgivings and caution to the Montana wind.

Maybe, if they remained in the water…

"Why couldn't you stay back at the barn?" she said, her mouth moving over the stubble along his jaw. She liked the way it abraded her lips. Liked it so much, she brushed across his chin again, angling toward his mouth and the promise of a kiss.

"I was worried about you. The guys said you left alone." He kissed one eyelid and then another. "You shouldn't ride by yourself."

"I wouldn't have found or made use of this pool if I'd been with anyone."

"And I wouldn't have found you naked if you hadn't gone off by yourself. Hell, anyone could have come looking and found you like this." He brushed his lips across hers, his hands slipping down to cup her buttocks.

Dallas's legs wrapped naturally around him, her sex sliding across his length. She swallowed hard to dislodge the breath caught in her throat. "I'm glad you were the one to find me, and not someone else."

"Me, too." He captured her mouth with his in a kiss both gentle and demanding.

Dallas gave back all she got, meeting his tongue with her own. She threaded her hands in his hair, deepening their kiss as his cock nudged her entrance.

"I want you, Dallas."

Tired of second-guessing herself, she threw caution to the winds. "Anything stopping you?" she said, against his mouth.

"No protection."

"I'm clean, and I'm on the pill."

"I'm clean, and I can't resist. Are you sure this is what you want?"

She quivered all over and then kissed him hard before saying, "Yes."

Viper thrust upward, impaling her with his thick, hot staff.

She eased down, taking all of him.

He held her close, letting her channel stretch and accommodate his girth. Then he slid in and out of her in excruciatingly slow movements.

She didn't want slow. Pressing her cheek to his, she whispered into his ear, "Faster."

His feet planted firmly on the bottom of the pool,

Viper increased the speed and pumped in and out of her, splashing water between them.

Dallas gripped his shoulders and rode him hard, loving the way he felt inside her, loving how he filled the void and then some.

Her body tightened with his as she flew into the atmosphere, her core bursting into flame, shooting electricity to the far extremities. She floated for a long, sweet moment in the heavens before she drifted back to earth and into the water with Viper.

He thrust one last time, his cock pulsing inside her.

She kissed his lips, his chin and his neck, hungry for him, not wanting the magic to end and real life to intrude. Alas, her skin was pruning and reality set in as her skin cooled. A shiver racked her body from head to toe.

"Oh, sweetheart, we need to get out of the water and dry off."

She shook her head, still hesitant to let him see all of her. "I'd prefer if you got out and went back to the barn. I'll be right behind you in a few minutes."

He crossed his arms over his chest. "I'm not leaving without you."

Her lips pressed together. "I'm not getting out of the water until you leave." She shivered again. "Which puts us at a stand-off."

"Only one way to settle this," he said.

Bobbing in the water, she crossed her arms over her chest. "Oh, yeah? How?"

Viper scooped her up in his arms and strode through the water and up onto the shore. He didn't stop until he'd laid her on the huge rock beside her clothes and prosthetic.

Dallas's cheeks burned, and she sat up on the smooth, stone surface, covering her stump with her other leg. "You're impossible," she said through gritted teeth.

"I'm a realist." He dropped down beside her, grabbed his own T-shirt and used it as a towel to dry her body.

"I can do that myself," she said as he worked his way over her back, her breasts and down her torso toward her leg. "Please. Don't do this," she whimpered, hating how pathetic she sounded. "I didn't want you to see me like this." She finally covered her face with her hands.

"Why?" He pried away her hands and kissed each palm before resuming his work. "You have a beautiful body. I want you to know how much I appreciate it." He dried her intact leg and worked his way over to the other.

Shame, self-loathing and fear warred for top emotion inside Dallas. "But, I'm not…"

"Not shy when it comes to sex in the water?" He glanced up and smiled. "I can live with that."

"You know what I mean." She watched in horror as he dried her thigh and then the smooth skin of what was left of the lower portion of her leg below her knee.

"Don't sell yourself short, Dallas." He leaned over and kissed the scars. "You are beautiful inside and out. And you don't scare me in the least." Then he laid her back on the rock and showed her how beautiful he thought she was by making love to every inch of her body, one kiss, one caress and one nibble at a time.

By the time they came together again, Dallas held back nothing. She gave him everything she had.

When they finally came back to earth, Viper helped Dallas reposition her prosthetic, asking questions and showing an interest that didn't make her squirm. Instead, his attitude made her love him all the more.

Love.

Was that emotion too soon? Could anyone know something that important after only a few days together?

Dallas couldn't be certain, but the way her heart swelled in her chest each time she looked at Viper had to indicate something special. Only time would tell.

The ride back to the ranch was deliciously uncomfortable after making love so many times. But she couldn't complain. In fact, she was looking forward to spending the night in bed with Viper, making love until the wee hours of the morning.

When they trotted into the barn yard, Percy met them, wearing a frown. "You have company. I'll take your horses."

Concerned by the expression on Percy's face, Dallas hurried toward the house.

Viper caught up and took her hand. They entered the ranch house together.

Sadie, Daisy, Lori and another woman waited in the living room with Franklin, Vasquez and Young.

Daisy stepped forward. "You had me worried. I thought you and Vince had decided to elope after all."

"Where were you?" Lori asked.

Dallas averted her gaze. "We went for a ride to blow off some steam."

"Or make some of your own?" Chuck Johnson stepped into the living room with Swede, Kujo and Hank.

Hank pulled the new woman forward. "Dallas, meet my little sister, Allie. Allie, these people are Dallas and her fiancé, Viper."

Allie shook hands with Viper and hugged Dallas. "Hank's told me all about you two. We're happy you decided to have the wedding at Bear Creek. I hardly recognize the barn. You'll be pleased with the decorations. We have a few more to place before we're done."

"Thank you so much for hosting our wedding there," Dallas said, more guilt rising up her throat. These people had done so much for her and Viper, who were barely more than strangers.

Daisy clapped her hands together. "Well, let's get going. We have a rehearsal to conduct."

"Followed by the bachelor party," Chuck interjected.

"Rehearsal, yes," Viper agreed. "Bachelor party?" He shook his head. "I don't know about that."

"Don't worry, the ladies are taking Dallas out for a bachelorette party. We're having them both at the Blue Moose Tavern. We have the bottom floor, and the ladies have the second-floor meeting hall."

"We have your bag packed for the night," Daisy said. "Your dress will be delivered to Bear Creek Ranch this afternoon and the cake and flowers will be there in the morning." She smiled. "We're all set."

Dallas frowned. "What do you mean, my bag is packed for the night?"

"You're staying with Allie tonight." Sadie gestured toward Hank's sister. "Besides, you're not supposed to see the groom on the wedding day until you walk down the aisle."

Dallas had no choice but to go along with the ladies planning her wedding. She cast a longing glance over her shoulder at Viper. Her heart filled with hope and optimism for the future.

Viper's gaze was on her as she left.

Hopefully, tomorrow they'd catch the wedding saboteur and then they could decide just where they fit in each other's lives, besides being partners on an assignment.

CHAPTER 14

Viper watched as Dallas was whisked away in Sadie's SUV. He didn't like that the date was so close to the wedding and they still didn't have a viable suspect.

He followed the guys out to Hank's truck. He, Kujo and Swede climbed in. The other men loaded into other trucks and promised to meet them at the tavern after the rehearsal.

Hank nodded toward Kujo, the dog handler. "I caught up Kujo on what's going on."

Viper was glad someone else was on the lookout for them. He stared at Hank's reflection in the rearview mirror. "Find out anything from the names I supplied?"

"Nothing," Hank said. "I even called the sheriff and asked if he had anything on Lisa, Rusty or Billy Joe. Sheriff Barron reported they've never been in his jail. Lisa Benton is Rusty's sister. He left the military and raised her after her parents died in a flash flood. Apparently, he gave up a lot for that girl. Sheriff Barron said she's working the repair shop and the diner to earn money to go to school."

"She works for Rusty?" Viper asked.

"That's what the sheriff said. She's a pretty good mechanic."

"What about the busboy from the diner, Billy Joe?" Kujo asked.

"Another good kid, according to the sheriff," Hank said. "He's helping his family by working at the diner. His father has a small ranch on the north side of town, but he can't do much since he hurt his back. Billy Joe does all the chores before he goes to work at the diner. What little he makes, he shares with his family."

"Not much motivation to sabotage weddings," Swede noted.

"Do Lisa, Billy Joe, Rusty, Tim or Melissa have a grudge against Daisy?" Viper glanced out the window, thinking through all they'd learned. "Or vice versa?"

Swede shook his head. "We can't say without canvassing everyone who's ever worked with her. We looked at Daisy's record. She's clean as a whistle. The sheriff said she's one of the nicest people in town."

Hank shifted into gear. "Who would want to hurt Daisy?"

"Who would *she* want to hurt?" Swede questioned.

Viper frowned. "For Daisy to be causing the trouble wouldn't make sense. She's earning money to go to college. She has no reason to sabotage her own business. What about the ex-boyfriend, Tyler Blount?"

Hank nodded. "He's a hothead. He could have done it. But I've had Kujo conducting surveillance. Tyler couldn't have been the one to leave the table in the middle of the highway. He was at the Blue Moose Tavern that entire afternoon and well into the evening. When Mrs. Davis's car crashed into the flower shop, he was still answering questions at the sheriff's office."

Viper's fists clenched. "Where was Billy Joe?"

"Still at the diner," Swede said. "The sheriff sent a deputy by to get his statement about Tyler picking a fight. The deputy talked to Daisy at the same time."

"What about Rusty?" Viper asked. "He had a key to Fuller's warehouse. He could have taken the table."

"I'll get in touch with Sheriff Barron," Hank said. "I'll see if he knows of Rusty's whereabouts during the florist attack and the evening of the table drop."

"Thanks." Viper sat back, all the pieces of the puzzle swirling in his head. "We might be grasping at straws, but you never know."

"True." Hank followed the SUV to the Bear Creek Ranch. The ladies had already climbed out of the vehicle and were headed for the barn.

"Just because Tyler and Billy Joe don't have a police record doesn't mean they're in the clear," Swede reminded them. "Someone could have a grudge against any newly married couples. Someone who might have been jilted or passed over for someone else."

"Those details are not something you read about in the newspaper," Viper said.

"This is a small town," Hank reminded Viper. "Surely, someone knows the gossip."

"We're running out of time to figure it out. As it is, we're the bait for whoever is causing the problems. If it was just me, I'd be all for luring the attacker out of hiding. But I don't like the idea of Dallas being a target."

Hank shot a glance back at Viper in the rearview mirror. "Dallas knows what she signed up for. She's a trained combatant."

"I know," Viper said. "But I don't like it. I was there and saw what happened with Taz and Hannah. No one predicted that event coming and they, along with Chuck, were almost killed."

"Already covered. One of the guys will guard the limousine scheduled to take you two to the airport," Hank said.

"Each attack has been different and increasingly more dangerous." Viper pinched the bridge of his nose. "We can't be certain from which direction it will come."

"That's why we have you and Dallas on this. You were both trained to handle any kind of enemy attack."

"In the service, we were armed and had a full team as our backup." He felt as if his hands were tied in the civilian world.

"You have all of the Brotherhood Protectors who could make the wedding. They're your backup, and they'll be armed," Swede reminded him.

"Beneath your wedding duds, you and Dallas will be armed," Hank said. "I have whatever weapons you might need."

"Good." Viper's jaw hardened. "I guarantee, *I'll* be packing."

EVERYTHING WAS HAPPENING SO fast Dallas's head spun.

Sadie and Lori knew what to expect and what the bride and groom should be doing. Thank goodness, because Dallas didn't.

Allie met them at the barn, a worried frown on her face. "I just got a call from the bridal gown shop in Bozeman."

Sadie touched Allie's arm. "What's wrong? Is it the dress? Were they unable to alter it in time?"

"Worse." Allie slumped her shoulders. "Last night the shop burned to the ground with everything inside."

Dallas's heart sank to her knees at the thought of that beautiful peach-pink dress burnt to a crisp.

Sadie pressed a hand to her chest. "Oh, dear Lord. Was anyone hurt?"

Allie shook her head. "No, but the owner was pretty shaken."

"So, we don't have a gown." Sadie bit her lip and turned to Dallas then smiled. "Don't you worry. We'll fix this. You will have a wedding gown on your wedding day if I have to call in every one of my markers in Hollywood to make a delivery happen overnight."

Dallas smiled. "Please. It was just a dress." A very beautiful gown that made her feel like a real bride. "I can wear the green one you gave me. The color doesn't matter."

"Like hell, it doesn't." Lori planted her fists on her hips. "You're getting married. You deserve to be the princess at your own ball." She laughed, her cheeks flushing with color. "Listen to the crusty old sergeant going on about princesses and balls."

Allie held up her hands. "Whoa, wait a minute. You

don't have to come up with a dress for Dallas. The seamstress had the dress at her house, making last-minute adjustments. It's all right. It was delayed, but should be here any minute. A courier is bringing it up from Bozeman, special delivery."

Sadie drew in a deep breath and let it out slowly. "Thank goodness. Although, I'll feel better when it arrives."

At that moment, a van pulled up the drive, its headlights piercing the impinging darkness. When it stopped, the driver jumped out, reached into the back of the van and brought out a long garment bag. "Is a Dallas Hayes here?" he called out to the people standing around the barn.

Dallas held up a hand. "That's me."

The delivery driver strode toward her, handed her the bag and held out the delivery confirmation document for her to sign. Without saying another word, he climbed back into the van and left.

"I'll take the dress into the house and put it somewhere safe," Allie offered.

"After we take a peek to make sure it truly is in the dress and intact, not smoke damaged," Lori said.

While Dallas held the bag, Sadie and Lori pulled free the tape and lifted the lid.

A collective sigh sounded from all four women.

"You'll be beautiful in that dress," Allie said, her voice full of awe. "Wow."

"What have you ladies got there?" Hank asked.

He and Swede reached them just as Sadie and Lori closed the bag.

"Nothing." Sadie lifted her face for her husband's peck on her cheek.

Dallas's heartbeat ratcheted up a notch when Viper stepped out from behind the other two men. Heat burned a path from her chest down to her core, making her hot all over. His gaze met hers, and all conversation faded into a soft hum.

Allie took the garment bag from her nerveless fingers. "I'll just put this in the house. You all have a rehearsal to practice."

"Dallas, did you decide if you're having bridesmaids and who you want to walk you down the aisle?" Sadie asked.

Dallas looked around at the people standing nearby. "I'd like it if you and Lori would be my bridesmaids. You don't have to dress up or anything, but having someone up there with me would be nice in case I pass out."

Sadie laughed. "You'll be just fine with or without us up there. But, thank you."

"I've never been a bridesmaid." Lori's eyes widened and then filled with tears. "I'd be honored."

"And, if Hank doesn't mind, I'd like him to walk me down the aisle." Dallas smiled at Hank. "I'd be honored if you would."

Hank gave her a semi-bow. "I'd be proud to."

Viper stepped forward. "If Swede and Kujo could stand with me, that would be great."

Swede nodded. "I'm in."

"Me, too," Kujo seconded.

With the positions assigned, the rehearsal went off

without a hitch until the time came when the Justice of the Peace's stand-in, Allie, granted permission to kiss the bride.

Dallas's cheeks were so hot she was sure her face had turned beet-red. Viper didn't spare her one inch. He drew her into his arms, swept her in a low hold and kissed her so soundly she forgot where she was. When he set her back on her feet, she could barely stand. Her knees wobbled and the barn walls spun around her.

Sadie clapped her hands. "That was perfect. Tomorrow will be in the bag before you know it."

Hank nodded. "Now, let's get to the bachelor party before the others drink the tavern dry."

"That's right." Sadie took one of Dallas's hands. Lori took the other. "We have a party of our own to attend."

The four women loaded into Sadie's SUV. The men, again, followed them down the highway and into Eagle Rock, parking outside the crowded Blue Moose Tavern.

Music blared from inside, filling the night with noise.

The men joined the ladies outside the door.

"Might as well kiss your guy goodnight." Allie grinned. "You won't see him again until you walk down the aisle."

Viper swept Dallas into his arms and kissed her again. If he was doing it for show, he was doing a good job.

The other women hooted and hollered.

Viper whispered in her ear, "Stay safe tonight, darlin'." Then he turned her toward the group of women and gave her a gentle push in their direction.

Dallas let the ladies drag her up to the second level of the tavern where they were joined by the other women associated with the Brotherhood Protectors.

Dallas met Mia Chastain, Bear's lady, Angel Carson, Duke's woman, Molly Greenbriar and Daphne Rayne, Boomer's new wife. They played drinking games, downing shots and beer. Then they turned up the music and danced until after midnight.

When Sadie proclaimed they'd had enough, they loaded Dallas into the SUV and drove back to Bear Creek Ranch where Allie had a room set aside for her wedding preparation.

Dallas didn't know how she managed to crawl into the bed, but she did and lay thinking about what her wedding day would bring.

If someone decided to burn down the house, she'd have to go up with it. She wasn't moving until the alcohol wore off or Viper arrived on a white horse to carry her off into the sunset.

Her last thought as she slipped into a numb sleep was of Viper and how he'd kissed her. The intensity of that connection couldn't all be faked, could it?

MORNING CAME with the sun glaring through the window, piercing Dallas's eyelids like a sharp knife. She squeezed them tighter, but the motion didn't help to block the light.

A door opened, and footsteps crossed the wood floor.

Dallas played dead, hoping whoever was there

would go away and come back when her head didn't hurt and she could manage actually opening her eyes.

"Good morning, beautiful," a voice called out. "Rise and shine. We have a lot to do before the Wedding March plays."

Dallas groaned and cracked open an eyelid.

Allie stood before her with a wide smile, a glass of water in her hand and something else curled in her other fist.

"I'd shoot you, if I had a gun," Dallas muttered and pulled the pillow over her head.

"I have something for a headache, if you need it," Allie sang.

Dallas shoved aside the pillow and held out her hand. "Yes."

"The time's already past ten o'clock. We have a light lunch planned for you and the other ladies of the wedding party. We'll serve it here in this room, if that's okay by you?"

"Sure." Dallas tossed the pills to the back of her throat and downed the entire glass of water. So much for being at the top of her game on D-Day. If anything was taking place to clobber this wedding that hadn't already happened, the incident would occur that day. She needed to be alert, ready for action and minus one helluva hangover.

"I'll give you time to shower and wash your hair. Thirty minutes enough?"

"Sure," Dallas repeated, not sure she was capable of any more conversation until the painkillers worked their magic.

"I'll be back then, with reinforcements. Gird your loins, today will be a busy one," she said with that incessant smile.

Once Allie left the room, Dallas pulled the pillow back over her head and gave herself permission to wallow in pain.

A few minutes passed and the pills started to work. Dallas could sit up without puking. Then she stood without falling. That's when she realized she'd gone to sleep without removing her prosthetic. Before long, she'd stripped out of her clothes and her fake leg and hopped into the shower. She let the spray wash over her head and down her body, warming her skin and rinsing away the fog of sleep.

After she'd washed every inch of herself, she used a big fluffy towel to dry off. Then she slipped on her prosthetic device and wrapped a bathrobe around her naked body. Gone was her headache. Back was her sharp sense of situational awareness. She felt almost normal. Well, as normal as a bride could feel on her wedding day.

Her heart beat faster as she thought of Viper somewhere else, either on Bear Creek Ranch or at Brighter Days Ranch, dressing in his tuxedo.

Dallas was amazed at the amount that had been spent creating the stage for this wedding trap. What a huge waste the funding would be if they didn't catch the culprit.

Not that she wanted anyone hurt, but Dallas hoped the saboteur made his move that day. They'd be ready and could take him down when the time came.

She'd slipped into the pretty panties Sadie insisted she purchase to wear beneath her dress. Dallas would never have chosen lace. Every pair of underwear in her go-bag was made of cotton, sturdy material that could handle sweat and dirt from field training and operations. None were sexy in the least possible way.

She slipped into the matching strapless bra that pushed her breasts up and out, giving her the cleavage she hadn't realized she possessed.

A soft knock on the door made her grab for the robe and hold it against body.

The door burst open and Sadie, Lori, Daisy, Lisa and Allie entered.

Sadie sailed through, smiling. "Oh, good, you're up and ready to get started."

"We just finished decorating the barn," Daisy announced.

"It's like a fairytale," Lori said.

"It's amazing," Allie agreed.

Sadie smiled. "It's perfect."

Dallas's eyes stung, and she had to blink to keep from crying. These women had awakened early to come decorate for her wedding. A stranger. Someone they hadn't known a week before. But they'd done it selflessly and happily.

When the time came to reveal the truth, Dallas would hate to see the disappointment in their eyes. She would have violated their trust.

Daisy took over and gave each of the ladies a task to perform.

While Daisy dried and styled Dallas's hair, Sadie

applied a light foundation to her face and then added contour, eyeshadow, eyeliner, blush and mascara.

Dallas's heart warmed with the care and acceptance these women showed her. For the first time in her life, she liked feeling feminine and actually beautiful.

Allie ran errands, brought refreshing drinks and delivered finger sandwiches for lunch. Lori smoothed the wrinkles out of the wedding dress and commented when solicited for advice on makeup or hair.

The ladies were upbeat, excited and happy. Dallas almost caught their excitement, but she was too focused on what happened next.

"Are you nervous?" Lori asked.

"No," Dallas lied. "Should I be?"

"You're about to promise your life to another human being. I think I'd be petrified," Lori said, her brows wrinkling.

"It's not that bad," Sadie said. "I would give my life for my husband, I love him that much. When you find the right guy, you'll feel the same way. Like Dallas, here."

Daisy sighed and pulled a strand of Dallas's hair through the curling iron. "That's exactly what I'm waiting for. The right guy."

"And Tyler wasn't the one," Dallas stated

"You saw him," Daisy said. "There's no reasoning with him. I've broken up with him before. He wore me down, and I went back to him. But the relationship is toxic. I want a guy who loves me no matter how bad his day has been."

"When you broke up with him, did you date

someone you thought might be better for you?" Dallas asked.

Daisy looped hair over the curling iron and smiled. "I dated a couple pipeline guys who were passing through and thought…maybe." She shook her head. "But no. Not yet."

"How'd Tyler take that?"

"Oh, he was mad as a wet hen," Daisy said. "Although I don't know why. I had every right to date who I pleased. As did he. In fact, I heard he was seeing someone, but he wouldn't tell me who. Once he found out I was dating, he got all mad and must have dumped her ass, because he came back after me with a vengeance."

Dallas perked up at that piece of news. "You have no idea who she was?"

Daisy sighed. "No clue. He wouldn't say."

"Aren't you afraid of Tyler?" Sadie asked.

Daisy shrugged. "I can handle him. He really does love me and would never hurt me. Someone else, maybe, but not me." Her lips pressed into a tight line. "I just hope he doesn't do anything stupid like show up at this wedding unannounced. I don't want him to cause a scene on your special day. Maybe I'll leave before the ceremony starts to keep that from happening."

Letting out a surprised gasp, Dallas captured Daisy's free hand. "No, please stay. I need you to tell me what to do."

"All you have to do is march down that aisle, say I do and stand around for all the pictures. The ceremony will go smoothly with or without me."

"Still, I'd like for you to be there," Dallas insisted. If

someone was doing these acts to get back at Daisy, that someone might not make the effort if she wasn't there. No matter what, all the trouble they'd gone to had to pay off.

Sadie glanced at the clock. "Oh, my, look at the time. The men will be gathering in the barn." She looked out the window. "Look, there's the Justice of the Peace and the woman who will play the piano."

"There's a piano?" Dallas asked.

"Of course," Daisy said. "You can't have a wedding without the wedding march. And I've chosen a lovely song she'll play and sing while you're queuing up for your big entrance."

"Wow, this process is all too much. We could have just eloped and saved a ton of money," Dallas said and looked around for someone who agreed.

Lori frowned. "And deprive us of all this fun? Not on your life."

As the hour neared, Dallas's stomach knotted. Though the wedding was all a fake event, she couldn't help but get caught up in the excitement. Deep inside, she was a little sad that the occasion wasn't for real.

Viper would make some lucky woman a wonderful husband. He'd be kind, gentle and care about her above all else. He'd understand if she wasn't a girly-girl and love her no matter what. Because he would love with all of his heart.

Dallas's chest tightened as she slipped into the beautiful wedding dress and let Sadie zip up the back. The seamstress had altered the seams perfectly, and the dress seemed to be made for her.

Daisy settled the veil over the lovely curls she'd pinned into her hair.

Dallas slid on the matching satin shoes and straightened in front of the mirror.

All the ladies in the room sighed as one.

"Wow," Lori said. "Who'd have thought you were an Army Ranger? You could be a movie star, like Sadie."

Dallas laughed. "Don't be silly." Then she caught a glimpse of her reflection and had to do a doubletake. The woman staring back didn't look like Dallas Hayes. Color was high in her cheeks and her eyes sparkled. The dress…dear, sweet Jesus… the dress flowed around her like a soft, sunset-tinged cloud.

One by one, the ladies hugged her and filed out the door, leaving Daisy.

"Hey, I have to say it, because it's true, and I feel it's my duty to the brides I help plan for."

Dallas stared at Daisy in the mirror's reflection. "Say what?"

"It's not too late to change your mind." Daisy held out her hands. "No matter how much money was spent, how much time was invested in the preparation, you don't have to go through with this wedding if marrying Vince is not what you truly want."

Dallas swallowed the lump rising in her throat. "Aren't you afraid you'll lose business if you tell your brides they can back out?"

She chuckled. "I haven't lost a bride yet. I just want them to be absolutely certain of their love." She turned Dallas to face her. "Are you in love with Vince?"

Her pulse hammered so hard through her veins a

tattoo beat against her eardrums. Did she love Viper? After knowing him for the few days they'd been assigned to the project? Was such emotion possible? Without realizing it, Dallas nodded. "Yes."

Holy hell. She was in love with Viper. Her head spun, and she nearly toppled off the satin heels.

Daisy laughed and reached out to steady her. "You'd think you only now acknowledged your feelings. But you must have known from before the day he proposed."

Since he hadn't proposed, she hadn't known until that moment. Dallas's knees shook, and she fought to regain a grip on reality.

This wedding wasn't real.

Her feelings were, but that didn't mean Viper returned them.

Fuck. What had she done to herself? She couldn't fall in love with her partner.

But she had.

And now she was marrying him.

Granted, the marriage wasn't real, and they wouldn't be husband and wife, but damn, she felt like it was really happening.

"Okay, then, let's have a wedding." Daisy stepped back and looked at her creation. "You're a beautiful bride. Vince must love you so very much."

If only.

Dallas gulped back a sob threatening to rise up her throat.

"I'll cue the pianist to play the special song and give you time to come out to the barn. Do you need help with your train?"

"No," Dallas said. "I can manage." If she could remember how to breathe.

"Then I'll be waiting by the barn door." She gave her one last look and left the bedroom.

Once more, Dallas glanced in the mirror. She didn't look like herself. Then again, she did. A much-improved version of Dallas Hayes. Would her appearance make Viper feel any differently? She knew he liked kissing her. But that circumstance didn't mean he wanted to marry her for real.

Movement in the corner of her eye caught her attention. She turned to find Lisa Benton standing near the door to the bedroom.

Where did she come from? A prickle of unease skittered across the back of Dallas's neck. "Lisa, thank you so much for helping decorate the barn."

"I like to decorate for weddings. I would have liked to decorate for mine."

"I'm sorry," Dallas prompted her. "Are you engaged?"

Lisa snorted. "No. That won't happen."

"Why not? There's someone for everyone."

"Not me," she said, her brows drawn low. "I'm not loveable."

"Oh, Lisa," Dallas said, her gut clenching, gooseflesh rising on her arms. "Of course, you are."

She shook her head, her body planted in front of the door. "No. He said I was too weird for anyone to love."

"He?" Dallas asked, stepping a little closer, knowing by then that this was the person they'd been looking for. But why?

"Tyler." She shook her head. "He would have loved me, if he hadn't loved Daisy first. He was *my* friend first."

"Lisa, surely you have other friends."

"I don't want other friends." She raised her hand, clutching something in her fingers. "I wanted Tyler, but he wants Daisy."

Dallas's muscles bunched. "Are you the one who has been ruining the weddings?"

"He should have loved *me*. I care for him, unlike Daisy." She sneered. "Everyone thinks Daisy is so nice, so perfect. But they're wrong." She raised her hand higher. "Not everything she does is good. The weddings she plans end up bad. People will figure it out and quit asking her to arrange them. Tyler will see that she's not all that great. He'll come back to me."

"Lisa, you can't blame the broken relationship all on Daisy."

"I can!" she said, her eyes flashing. "You'll see. Daisy is Tyler's weakness. When she falls from grace, he'll lose interest. And when he gets over her, he'll see how much I love him."

Whatever Lisa had in her hand, it wasn't a gun. The object didn't even appear to be a knife. Maybe a cellphone?

Dallas could take the woman. She had no doubt. All she needed was to get a little closer. She lunged for Lisa, reaching for the woman's arm.

Instead of pulling away, Lisa leaned into Dallas and pressed something against her side.

A shock of electricity bolted through Dallas. She

tried to move away from Lisa, but the woman held onto her, still pressing the device into Dallas's side.

Dallas's thoughts scrambled. She couldn't figure out why. Her knees wobbled and then gave out and she crumpled to the floor, shaking.

What was happening? Why couldn't she move?

Lisa stood above her, her lip curling into a snarl. Next, she dropped down beside Dallas, pulled her arms over her head and around a bedpost then zip-tied her wrists together.

Dallas could do nothing. Her body wouldn't cooperate, and her mind could barely take in what happened. She couldn't even form words to call out for help.

"Sorry." Lisa walked toward the door. She paused at the threshold and faced Dallas. "Daisy has to pay, and you're the price." Then she shut the door behind her.

In the next few moments, Dallas smelled the acrid scent of gasoline, followed by the pungent aroma of smoke.

CHAPTER 15

"Everyone is in place," Kujo assured Viper.

"Good." Viper adjusted the bowtie at his neck, even as he felt the reassuring weight of the pistol beneath the tuxedo jacket. "If our attacker is here, he'll be pressed to act within the next hour or so."

"And we'll be ready," Swede said.

"Damn right, we will," Kujo muttered beneath his breath.

The seats in the barn were filled with members of the Brotherhood Protectors and their women.

Sadie stood at the barn entrance, looking back over her shoulder.

Lori waited beside her, whispering into her ear.

Daisy joined the women and then motioned for the pianist to start the music.

Still, Viper saw no sign of Dallas. He hadn't seen her since the rehearsal the night before. The more time that passed without him having her at his side, the more restless he became.

"Hey, don't worry, she'll be here." Swede chuckled. "And just think, if this wedding was real, you'd probably be a lot more nervous than you are now."

"I don't see how. I'm tied in knots," Viper said. "Where is Dallas? Why hasn't she shown up yet?"

Hank joined the ladies at the barn entrance and spoke to them for a moment, then glanced toward Viper. With a nod, he disappeared.

"I have to check on her." Adrenaline coursed through Viper's veins.

"Just wait." Kujo touched his arm. "Hank looked like he was doing just that."

"I don't care. Something doesn't feel right." Viper walked down the aisle, heading for the barn's exit.

Kujo and Swede moved behind him. Soon, Boomer, Chuck, Bear and Duke were on their feet, as well.

As Viper reached the barn door, someone shouted, "Fire!"

His heart leaped into his throat, and Viper broke into a run toward the ranch house.

Hank was ahead of him, just reaching the porch as a wall of flame rose up on the house front, as if an accelerant had just been lit. Hank fell backward off the steps, landing on the ground.

Viper raced past him, leaped through the flames and slammed into the front door. The door knob didn't budge—locked from the inside.

Then Viper jabbed an elbow into the nearest widow, shattering the glass. He kicked out the remaining jagged shards with his foot and dove into the living room.

Flames licked at the curtains and furniture, smoke rising to the ceiling.

Viper covered his mouth and nose with his elbow and ran through the room into the hallway.

A woman appeared in front of him, carrying a jug, slinging liquid onto the walls and floor. Gasoline. "You can't save her."

That woman was Lisa, the waitress from the diner. "Lisa," Viper called out. "Don't do this."

"It's too late." She splashed gasoline on the walls, some of it getting on her dress. "You can't stop it. This house is going to explode and you can't stop it." She dropped the jug, its contents spilling out onto the floor. From her pocket, she pulled out a box of matches.

"Don't!" Viper yelled and lunged toward her. But he was too far away to stop her action.

She struck the match, a flame flared, and she dropped it. On its way down, it caught the edge of her dress on fire and then hit the gasoline on the floor and ignited the hallway in a wall of flame.

Lisa screamed as the fire consumed her dress and licked at her skin.

"I'll get Lisa," Hank yelled. "Find Dallas."

Viper grabbed Lisa and shoved her back into Hank's arms. Then he covered his mouth and nose with an arm and raced down the hallway, throwing open doors until he came to the last one, which wouldn't open. A knife had been jammed into the lock and smoke was filling the hallway.

His lungs burning, Viper threw his shoulder against the door. The door frame cracked but didn't give. He raised a foot and kicked as hard as he could, again and again until the door finally flung open.

Smoke billowed out, blinding him for a moment. Crouching low, he ran inside and searched the room for the one person he realized he didn't want to live without.

He found Dallas on the floor with her wrists wrapped around the leg of the bed, her body unmoving. She lay like an angel in her wedding dress, her veil fanning out beneath her head. Viper couldn't take the time to feel for a pulse. He had to get her out or smoke inhalation would kill her anyway.

Without hesitation, he lifted the heavy four-poster bed off the floor and shoved it away from Dallas. Then, he scooped her into his arms and turned back to the door. The hallway was consumed in flames. He couldn't take her out that way. Blood pounded hard through his body. He kicked shut the door and turned to one of the floor-to-ceiling windows. If he didn't get her out immediately, they wouldn't have a chance.

With Dallas in his arms, Viper ran toward the window and made a flying leap. Right before he reached the glass, he twisted around and hit it with his back. Tinkling of broken glass echoed in his ears as he fell through. Viper hit the ground hard, using his own body to cushion Dallas's landing.

Broken glass tore at his legs and cut into his backside, but he didn't care. He had Dallas out of the burning house and into the open air.

He rolled to his side and lifted her in his arms and carried her off the porch and away from the inferno that had been the ranch house. Away from the flames, he laid her on the ground.

"Dallas, sweetheart," he said, his voice rough and gravelly. He coughed, the smoke he'd inhaled making talking hard. "Dallas, talk to me." He felt for a pulse, his hand shaking. At first, he didn't feel the reassuring thump. When he did, he pulled her against him and held her close. "You're not moving. Why aren't you moving? Oh, baby, you'll be all right. You have to be all right. I love you so much."

When he held her again at arm's length, she'd opened her eyes and her mouth was working but the words were too quiet to hear.

Viper leaned closer. "What did you say?"

"I love you, too," she whispered.

That's when Viper realized he'd said it first. And he meant his statement. "I never believed I could ever fall in love again," he said, pushing the veil back from her face. "But then you came into my life, all feisty and ready to take on the world." He laughed and kissed her forehead. "I think I fell in love the moment I saw you."

"I'm glad you do...but how can you love..." she coughed and continued, "someone like me?"

He smiled down at her and cradled her in his arms. "How could I not?" Then he kissed her lightly and raised his head, missing her body pressed close. "Why aren't you moving? Did Lisa hurt you in some other way?"

"That bitch hit me with a stun gun." Dallas lifted a trembling arm and cupped his cheek. "I'm just now getting back the feeling." She craned her neck and looked around. "Did you catch her? Did you get Lisa?"

"Hank was getting her out of the house."

"That's good because she did it all. She's the one who ruined the weddings and..." Dallas sighed. "And my beautiful dress."

Viper leaned closer. "Your what?"

"My beautiful dress. You didn't even get to see me in it."

A glance down at the sooty, pink dress had Viper laughing out loud. "You're worried about a dress? Darlin', you're beautiful, even covered in soot." He kissed her again, still chuckling. "The dress is the least of your worries. I'm just glad I got you out before you died of smoke inhalation."

Dallas pushed to a sitting position.

Beyond her, the wedding guests had formed a bucket brigade to help quell the fire tearing through the ranch house.

"We need to help," she said, trying to get to her feet.

"I think you've done enough." He pressed a hand to her shoulder. "Besides, I hear fire truck sirens."

The wail of sirens pierced the air, and soon fire engines, pumper trucks and ambulances rolled into the barn yard.

Before long, the fire was extinguished, but the house was a loss.

Lisa was loaded into an ambulance and whisked away under Sheriff Barron's supervision.

When the smoke cleared, the wedding party stood

around in their soot-covered clothes, relieved no one else had been harmed.

Dallas felt stronger by the minute as the effects of the stun gun finally wore off.

Viper hooked his arm around her waist and led her over to join the others.

Hank clapped Viper on the back and hugged Dallas. "You two did it. Your work uncovered the culprit behind the wedding disasters."

"Yeah, but she got me before I could get her." Dallas couldn't hide her disappointment in herself for failing at her first assignment. "I'm sorry I let you down. If I'd taken her out first, Allie wouldn't have lost the Pattersons' family home."

Allie shook her head. "We're just lucky Viper got to you before…well…before. Houses can be rebuilt."

"Don't sell yourself short. You were brave enough to be bait for this project," Hank said. "I couldn't have asked for more."

"Wait a minute." Sadie touched her husband's chest and glanced between Viper and Dallas. "So, this whole event was just a hoax to reveal Lisa as the wedding destroyer?"

Hank drew her into his arms. "That's right. And you did a fine job getting our bride ready. Only a very few knew the event was all part of the plan. Thank you very much."

Sadie pouted. "But we picked the perfect dress. It's a

shame she didn't get to wear it down the aisle, even if the wedding was fake."

"The day's not over." Viper turned to Dallas. "We've only known each other a few days, but I feel as though I really know you." He dropped to one knee and took her dirty hand in his. "I want you to be a part of the rest of my life. Would you consider taking a huge leap of faith and marrying this old Delta Force soldier?"

"Like this?" Dallas glanced down at her sooty peachy-pink dress and torn veil.

Viper laughed out loud. "Like that. Even with a smudge of soot on your nose. I don't think I've seen you look more beautiful."

She touched her finger to her nose as her heart fluttered and her knees trembled. "You mean it?"

"The part about you being beautiful?" His brow furrowed. "Or the part where I asked you to marry me and you didn't say yes?"

Daisy stepped closer. "The barn is intact, the flowers are beautiful and the Justice of the Peace hung around hoping to have some of Melissa Fuller's heavenly barbecue, despite the fire. If you think Vince is the one…"

Dallas nodded, her heart filling with joy so complete she thought it might explode. "I do."

"Then go for it," Daisy said. "You only live once. Or in your case, twice. You got a second chance. Don't waste it."

Dallas drew in a deep breath and stared down at Viper still on his knee, looking up at her. "Yes!"

He straightened, wrapped his arms around her and swung her in a circle. When he set her down, he turned to the gathered crowd. "Did you hear that? A wedding is taking place after all."

A cheer rose from the crowd.

The guests left the firefighters to their job of tamping down the last burning embers and headed back into the barn.

The pianist, a bit sootier, cranked up the tunes and played the wedding march a little livelier than usual.

Instead of Hank marching her down the aisle, Dallas held onto Viper's arm and walked between the rows of chairs at his side.

The Justice of the Peace smiled and then performed the ceremony until the part where Viper and Dallas were to exchange rings.

Dallas laughed, and Viper joined in. They'd thought of everything during their preparations...but the rings.

"No rings?" Percy asked. "Hold on." He ran to the back of the barn where hay bales were stacked to the ceiling. He sliced off a piece of hay string from one of the bales, cut it in two and tied knots in each. He returned to Dallas and Viper and handed each a twine ring. "What the rings are made of don't make a hill of beans. It's what they stand for that determines the strength of a marriage."

With their twine rings, Dallas pledged her love to Viper and he pledged his to her. The JP pronounced them man and wife, and Viper pulled her into his arms and kissed away her breath.

When he set her back on her feet, he turned her to the audience and raised their joined hands above their heads.

The Brotherhood Protectors, their women and the residents of Brighter Days Ranch cheered as the newlywed couple led the way to the barbecue banquet arranged beneath the trees.

"I can't believe the ceremony really happened." Dallas smiled up at her new husband.

"Me, either," Viper said.

"Any regrets?" She held her breath, almost afraid to hear his answer.

"Only that I took so long to get around to asking you to marry me. I've never seen a more beautiful bride than you, standing there in that pink dress."

She glanced down at what had once been the perfect dress. "And yet, you still married me. Soot stains, one leg and all."

"Darlin', I wouldn't have had it any other way. I got you, didn't I?" He pulled her close and kissed her until her toes curled. "I couldn't have picked a better partner. You brought me back to life."

A lump formed in her throat but she swallowed it back. She cupped his face between her palms and stared into his eyes. "You saved my life in more ways than one."

Again, he kissed her. When he finally let her up for air, he leaned close and whispered, "Any idea where we're spending our wedding night?"

She laughed. "We didn't get that far in the planning. How about the Brighter Days Ranch?"

He raised an eyebrow and grinned. "Do you think anyone will notice if we leave now?"

She kissed him. "Do you care?"

"Not a damn bit."

"Our chariot awaits." She placed her hand in his, and they left the reception dinner. The retired Delta Force soldier and the Army Ranger made a dash for the waiting limousine, both eager to start the wedding night and their lives together in the Crazy Mountains of Montana.

MONTANA SEAL UNDERCOVER DADDY

BROTHERHOOD PROTECTORS BOOK #9

New York Times & USA Today
Bestselling Author

ELLE JAMES

MONTANA SEAL UNDERCOVER DADDY

BROTHERHOOD PROTECTORS

NEW YORK TIMES BESTSELLING AUTHOR
ELLE JAMES

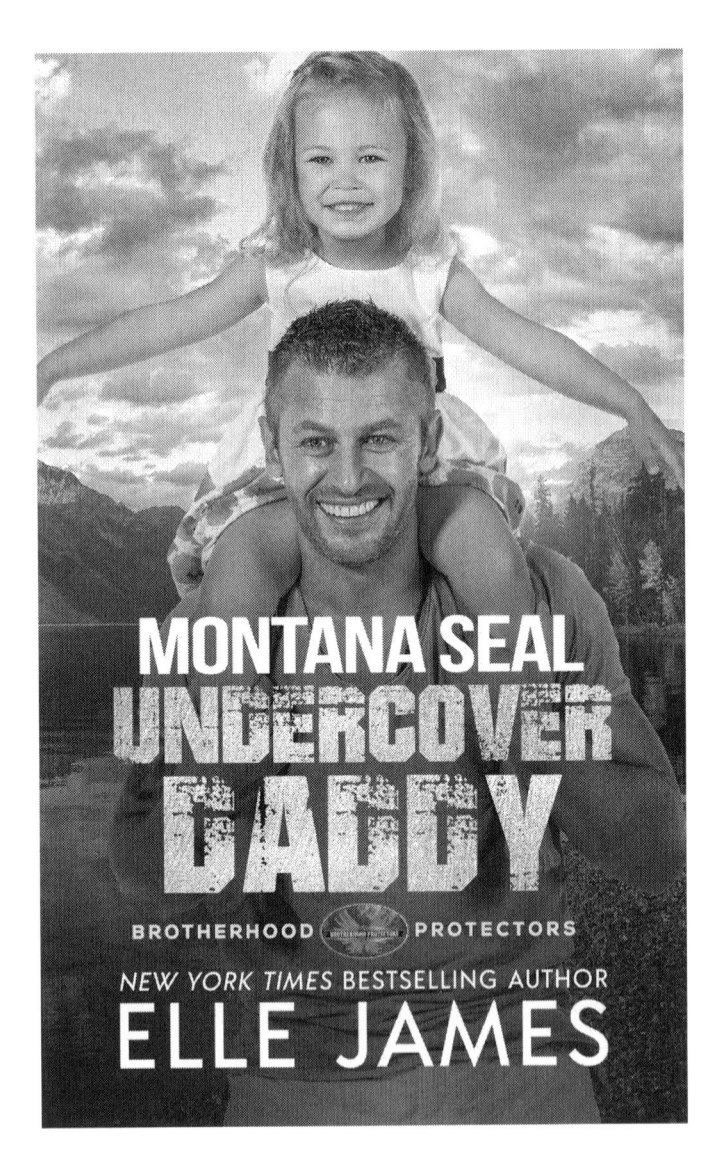

CHAPTER 1

The incessant vibration of the cellphone on her nightstand woke Kate Phillips from a melatonin-induced deep sleep. She would have ignored the urgent ringing if it hadn't been the third time in as many minutes that it had gone off.

She rolled over and blinked to clear the sleep from her eyes.

Unknown Caller.

Then a text flashed across the screen.

IT'S RACHEL. ANSWER YOUR PHONE. 911!

The phone vibrated again.

Kate frowned and hit the button to receive the call. "Rachel? What's wrong?"

"I need you to open your door." Her younger sister's voice sounded strained, almost desperate.

"Why?" Kate sat up in her bed and untangled her legs from the sheets.

"Open your door, Kate. Now!"

She dropped her feet to the ground, grabbed her

robe from the end of the bed and rushed toward her apartment door. "Okay, okay. Keep your pants on."

"Hurry. It's very important. And don't hang up yet. I have to know."

"I'm at the door," she said. "Unlocking." She fumbled with the two deadbolts and the chain, and looked through the peephole before she twisted the lock on the handle. She didn't see anyone standing outside the door. "Where are you? I don't see anyone outside."

"Just open the door!" Rachel cried.

If Kate wasn't mistaken, her twin sister's voice caught on a sob.

"What's wrong, sweetie?" she said as she pulled the door open and nearly fell over the bundle lying on the ground at her feet.

"Is she there?" Rachel asked, her voice a shaky whisper. "Kate, please. Tell me. Is she there?"

"Is who…" The bundle on the ground moved and rolled over. A sweet, pink face turned toward her, and silky, blond hair spilled from beneath the edge of a child's blanket. "Oh, sweet Jesus," Kate whispered. "Lyla?"

"Oh, thank God!" Rachel cried. "She's still there. She didn't wander off." Rachel's sobs filled Kate's ear.

She squatted next to her sister's three-year-old daughter and brushed a strand of golden hair from her face.

The child remained asleep, her cherubic face peaceful, despite being left on Kate's doorstep.

Kate looked around, fully expecting to see Rachel.

She rarely went anywhere without Lyla in tow. Her sister was nowhere to be seen. "Rachel, where are you?"

"I can't say." She sniffed. "Oh, Kate. I'm afraid. I'm doing the only thing I know to keep Lyla safe. You have to help me."

"Slow down, Rachel," Kate said, careful not to wake Lyla. "I need to put the phone down to bring Lyla into the apartment. Hold on."

"No! Kate, don't put the phone down. I only have a moment. You need you to listen."

"Okay," Kate said. "I'm listening."

"Take Lyla. Get out of your apartment. Take her to Eagle Rock, Montana, to a man named Hank Patterson. He has a protection agency. He'll help you protect Lyla. And Kate, you have to make everyone believe Lyla is your little girl. No one can know she was mine. No one."

"Rachel, what's going on? Do you need me to call the police?"

"No! You can't. Please, don't. Involving the police will only make things worse. If you love me and if you love my baby girl, you'll do this. It's the only way to keep her safe."

"What about you, Rachel?" Kate gripped the phone so tightly, her hand cramped. "Who's going to keep you safe?"

"Until I figure this out, I have to disappear. It's the only way. So, please, in your own way, you and Lyla needed to disappear. Hank will help you accomplish that."

"Rachel, you're scaring me. Where's Myles? Why isn't he helping?"

"I can't talk right now," Rachel said, her voice catching on what sounded like a sob.

"I'm your big sister." Big sister by five minutes. But still the older of the two. "You know you can tell me anything."

"I know, Kate, but there are some things better left unsaid. In this case, the less you know the better. Keep Lyla safe. Change her name. Change your name. Do whatever it takes to make her your own."

"For how long, Rachel?" Kate clutched the phone to her ear, afraid to hear her sister's answer.

"I don't know if I'll be able to come back."

"What do you mean?"

"As long as I'm anywhere near her, Lyla is in danger. In order to keep her safe, I had to leave her." Her voice hitched. "You have to be her mother. You're her only chance."

"Rachel, you're scaring me."

"Believe me," Rachel said, "I'm terrified. Not so much for me, but Lyla is caught up in this mess. They'll use her to get to me."

"Who will use her?" Kate asked.

"I don't have time to go into it. I have to run."

"Rachel, I don't know anything about little girls. I barely know Lyla."

"You look enough like me. The important thing is for you to be Lyla's mother. She has to believe you're her mom so that everyone she comes into contact with believes you're her mother."

"You don't understand," Kate stared down at the sleeping child. "I don't know how to be a mother. You were always the nurturing one."

"Just love her. Lyla makes it easy."

"Rachel, just come back. I'll protect you."

"I can't. Lyla deserves a real life. The way things are right now, I can't give that to her."

"Rachel—"

"I love you, Kate."

"I love you too, Rachel."

"Go to Montana. Find Hank. Protect my baby."

"Please, don't hang up," Kate begged.

The call ended.

Tears slipped down Kate's face as she stared down at the cellphone.

The small bundle lying at her feet moved.

Lyla blinked her eyes open. "Where's Sid Sloth?" she mumbled, her tiny voice hoarse with sleep.

"I'm sorry?" Kate didn't understand.

Lyla rooted around in the blanket and pulled from the jumble a stuffed animal that looked suspiciously like a sloth and tucked it beneath her chin. Then she yawned and closed her eyes again.

Headlights glared in the parking lot of her townhouse apartment. A dark sedan pulled into a parking space, and the lights blinked off.

Kate's heart leaped. She gathered Lyla and her blankets into her arms, and hunkering low, swung her into the apartment and closed the door. She laid the entire bundle on the floor and quickly spun around to close the door.

Footsteps sounded on the sidewalk in front of the apartment.

Kate reached out to turn the button on the door handle lock as the steps stopped. She eased the deadbolt in place as quietly as possible.

The handle moved as if someone on the other side might be trying it.

Her pulse hammered so hard it beat against her eardrums. She waited by the door, afraid to move, not knowing what to expect.

She wanted to call her sister back and ask her what the hell she'd gotten into. The last she'd heard from her sister was a phone call a couple of months before.

Rachel and her husband, Myles, had moved to a small town in Wyoming three years ago, when Rachel was pregnant with their first child. They were concerned about raising their daughter in the hustle and bustle of Los Angeles where Rachel and Kate had grown up. With drive-by shootings, horrendous traffic and pollution, it wasn't the ideal place to raise a child.

Rachel's husband had found a job as a communications specialist with a church in a small community. They'd seemed happy. But lately, Rachel's phone calls were short and not very newsy.

Kate had been so busy with her own career, she hadn't thought much about it. She'd figured Rachel was busy being a full-time mom.

When her husband of ten years divorced her, Kate gave up on the idea of marriage and children. Her husband had never wanted children. Though she'd later learned he never wanted children with her. As soon as they divorced, he married his pregnant secretary.

Kate had thrown herself into her career in freelance news reporting and left the marriage and mommy business to her little sister, who'd seemed to be doing it the right way.

Until now.

Kate stared down at the bundle on the floor.

Lyla slept on.

A knock on the door jerked Kate back to her predicament.

She lifted Lyla, blankets and all, carried her into the bedroom, shut the door and locked it. Then she grabbed her cellphone and dialed 911.

"You've reached the emergency department. Please state your emergency."

Kate had never called 911 in her life. What did she say? "There's someone at my door," she blurted.

"Are they trying to break in?"

"I don't know. But it's late, and I'm not expecting anyone."

"Ma'am, I'm sending someone over right away. Are you somewhere relatively safe?"

"I'm in my bedroom with the door locked."

"You might also go into the bathroom and lock the door. Please stay on the line until help arrives."

"I will." She laid the phone on the sleeping child, gathered her in her arms and carried her into the bathroom and locked the door.

With nowhere else to sit, she closed the toilet lid and

sat on the seat, holding Lyla and rocking her gently, more to calm herself than the sleeping child.

She strained to hear what was going on outside her bathroom and bedroom. The doors and walls muffled sounds. Was that the sound of the wood splitting on a doorjamb?

Her heart hammering against her ribs so hard she could barely breathe, Kate held Lyla tighter and prayed the police would arrive before whoever had just broken the deadbolt on her front door made it through the measly lock on the bedroom door, and then the equally pathetic lock on her bathroom door.

Kate laid Lyla in the bathtub. She had to do something to protect her sister's child. Waiting for help that might not make it in time wasn't good enough. She pulled down the curtain rod and thought about jamming it between the walls over the door. She shook her head. That little bit of flimsy metal wouldn't hold under the weight of a full-grown man. Instead, she took off one end of it and held the other in a firm grip.

If her intruder made his way through her apartment and into the bathroom before the police arrived, Kate would be ready.

She'd never hit anyone before in her life. But she'd do whatever it took to protect Lyla.

A crashing sound heralded the destruction of her bedroom lock and doorframe.

Kate stood back from the bathroom door, holding the curtain rod in both hands like a baseball bat. When the man shoved through the door, she'd hit him hard and fast. She'd have the element of surprise on her side. He wouldn't know it was coming.

Footsteps sounded in her bedroom. She was eternally grateful for the wood floors in her apartment. She knew exactly when he stopped in front of the bathroom door.

She held her breath, tightening her grip on the curtain rod as she pulled it back and stood like a baseball player ready to slam a home run.

The door handle jiggled, making Kate jump.

Then nothing.

She braced herself for what would come next.

In the distance, the sound of a siren wailed, moving closer.

Please hurry, she prayed silently and bent her knees, ready.

Then the door exploded inward.

A man charged through the door, dressed in black, with a black ski mask covering his face. He carried a gun in his hand.

Scared out of her mind, Kate didn't hesitate. She swung that curtain rod as hard as she could right for the man's head.

The metal rod connected with the intruder's face, making a crunching sound as if she'd broken his nose.

The man fell to his knees, clutching at his nose, and moaned. Blood seeped through the knitted mask onto his hands.

All Kate could think was that the man was still upright and able to continue his attack.

She swung again and again.

The masked man raised his arms to protect his head. Then he grabbed the rod.

Kate pulled hard, knowing that if she released it, he'd be able to turn it on her. She couldn't let that happen. Lyla need her to protect her.

Refusing to let go, Kate swung out her foot and put all her kickboxing training into one mighty sidekick.

She caught the man in the side of the head.

For a moment, her kick didn't seem to have done anything.

Then her attacker let go of the rod and tipped over sideways.

Kate grabbed Lyla and ran out of her apartment into the parking lot and was almost run over by a cop car.

The police officer slammed on his brakes, skidded sideways and came to a stop inches away from Kate and Lyla.

The police officer jumped out of his vehicle and pulled his gun out of the holster. "Which apartment?"

She pointed to the open door.

"Get into the squad car until my backup arrives." The officer didn't wait to see that Kate made it into his vehicle. He ran for the apartment, speaking into the radio clipped to his shoulder, and paused at the side of the door.

Kate slid into the back seat of the police car and held Lyla in her arms.

Another siren wailed nearby, and soon, another police car arrived.

With two officers now on the scene, they entered Kate's apartment.

Watching through the window, Kate held her breath, hoping they'd caught the guy. She'd never been so frightened in her entire life. And not for herself, but for the innocent little girl lying sleeping in her arms.

Kate stared down at the child's golden hair so much like hers and her sister's. Kate and Rachel were twins separated by only five minutes. Now, there was a world between them, and Kate didn't know where to look for her sister. "Oh, Rachel, what's going on?"

CHAPTER 2

"Chuck, I have a new assignment for you." Hank Patterson didn't preface the telephone call with niceties like "Hello." He got right down to business.

His boss's directness was one of the things former Navy SEAL Chuck Johnson appreciated about Hank, the founder of the Brotherhood Protectors agency and the main reason he'd jumped ship from the DEA. Not only was he direct, Hank was a Navy SEAL as well. And once a SEAL, always a SEAL. The bonds between SEALs were unbroken and forever.

Chuck had just left Daphne and Boomer's house. After spending the evening babysitting their baby, Maya, he was ready to head to the bed and breakfast where he'd taken up residence. He'd shower, drink a beer and maybe drown his sorrows for another night.

Hank's call, a welcome distraction, got his blood moving. He'd much rather work than go back to his little room by himself, especially after holding and cuddling baby Maya.

If Daphne and Boomer weren't so crazy happy in love, Chuck might have fought to win Daphne's affections. Knowing how much Daphne loved Boomer made Chuck realize he hadn't been in love with Daphne at all. If anything, he'd been more in love with Maya and pretending to be a father to the baby, than he was in love with Daphne. Daphne had been more like a daughter to him. He'd never really felt more than a fatherly or brotherly affection for Maya's mother.

Chuck's problem was that despite having sworn off family and relationships for so long, he really longed to have another child and a woman to come home to. Not to replace the loved ones he'd lost, but in addition to them.

Chuck slowed his truck, preparing to turn if he needed to. "What's the assignment?"

"I need you to come to the ranch. Your assignment is waiting here."

"On it." Chuck made a U-turn in the middle of the deserted highway and applied his foot heavily to the accelerator, speeding his way to White Oak Ranch where Hank had set up the headquarters for his brainchild, Brotherhood Protectors.

Chuck needed the work to distract him from his longing to be a father to Maya. Not that Daphne was keeping him from the baby he'd been with since her birth. But the child needed to bond with her father who had only recently come into her life. Chuck didn't need to muddy Maya's waters.

If he wanted children, he could find his own wife

and have babies. Borrowing another family's children... well, he'd just have to stay clear of those situations.

Surely, he could find a woman who wouldn't mind marrying a man past his prime and heading unflinchingly toward the mid-century mark. He wasn't old, but women of a childbearing age might consider him too old to father their children.

Why he was even thinking about a wife and children was self-defeating. He'd been a bachelor for so long, he would be terrible at a relationship.

He arrived within fifteen minutes of the call and pulled up to the sprawling rock and cedar house that had been built with a bunker beneath it, housing the armory, computer system and conference room for the brotherhood.

Chuck dropped down from his truck and climbed the steps to the front porch.

Hank met him at the door and opened it to let him into the wide-open living room with the cathedral ceilings and stone fireplace.

Sadie smiled at him from across the room. She carried her baby Emma in her arms. "Hey, Chuck. Would you care for a drink? I was just going to make tea for our guest."

Normally, Chuck would have accepted a beer, but he didn't know when his new assignment would begin, and he wanted an absolutely clear head going in. "No, thank you."

Hank waved Chuck toward a seat in the living room. "You might want to sit down for a moment. Your client will be out shortly."

Chuck shook his head. "Thanks, but I've been sitting in a rocking chair for the past three hours."

Hank grinned. "Practicing for your old age?"

Chuck laughed. "Not quite, though some would say I am. I just left Boomer and Daphne's house. I kept Maya while they went out for date night."

"Makes sense. You've been with Maya since she was born. She's comfortable with you and Daphne knows you." He glanced toward Sadie, his wife. "Sadie and I still find it difficult to leave Emma with anyone." He winked at Chuck. "I'll have to keep you in mind."

"Do," Chuck offered. "I'm pretty good with babies. I can change a diaper in five seconds flat." He wrinkled his nose. "Well, depending on the damage."

"You're hired," Sadie said. "Oh, wait. You're already hired as a Brotherhood Protector."

"And your skills with children is part of the reason I chose you for this assignment," Hank said.

Chuck frowned. "Why?"

"You will have two clients. And you're pretty much conducting the same kind of operation you led with the DEA when you were assigned to protect Daphne and her baby."

"Witness protection?" Chuck guessed.

"Not quite, but close. One of your clients is a marketing executive." Hank looked past Chuck. "Ah, here they are now." He held out his hand. "Kate, let me introduce one of the newest members of my team, Chuck Johnson."

Chuck turned toward a striking woman with sandy-blond hair and clear, blue eyes. Her skin was tanned, and she wore a white blouse, khaki slacks and leather loafers.

"Chuck, meet Kate Phillips," Hank said.

Kate held out her hand. "Thank you for coming so quickly. I didn't want to show up anywhere else around here until I had my cover firmly in place."

"What cover?" Chuck asked.

She frowned. "You, of course." The woman darted a glance toward Hank. "I did specify the man had to be of above-average intelligence, did I not?"

Hank's lips twisted. "Don't let all those muscles fool you. Chuck is one of the smartest and most mature men on my team."

Chuck leaned toward Kate. "That's code for old." He inhaled and caught the scent that could only be described as plumeria. He hadn't smelled that scent in a very long time. Anne had loved the aroma of plumeria. Whenever he was in Hawaii, Chuck picked up bottles of lotion with that scent.

She'd still had one left when she'd...

Chuck shook himself out of the past and held out a hand. "Nice to meet you, Ms. Phillips."

"Please, call me Kate," she insisted, her grip firm though her hands were small.

In keeping with his promise to himself to steer clear of relationships, he shook his head. "If you don't mind, I'd like to keep it on a professional level."

Kate shot a glance toward Hank. "Perhaps Mr. Johnson isn't so perfect for this job after all."

"I can do anything," Chuck protested.

She arched an eyebrow. "Can you do as requested?

Because I need someone who can follow orders as well as give out a few of his own."

His back stiffened. "I've done my share of following and giving orders, Kate." If he put too much emphasis on her name, so be it. She'd questioned his ability to do a job.

Her eyes narrowed on Chuck, and then she faced Hank again. "My sister recommended you. Is this the best that you have? Because I need the best. I need someone who will lay down his life for us."

Hank touched her arm. "It's all right, Kate. With Chuck, you'll be in good hands. And he has the perfect skill set for the job."

Chuck frowned. "You keep saying that. I assume any one of your men has the same skill set I do."

"They do…for the most part." Hank grinned. "You have one more skill most of the others do not."

Trying to figure it out himself, Chuck gave up. "And that is?"

Sadie said, "You have daddy skills. I knew you were the right man for the job as soon as Kate mentioned that requirement."

"Requirement?" Chuck glanced from Sadie to Hank, and then to Kate. "I don't understand."

"Mama?" a little voice called out.

Everyone in the room turned toward the sound.

A little girl with bright, blond hair emerged from the hallway leading to the bedrooms.

Kate hurried toward the child. "Lyla, you should be asleep." She patted the child's back awkwardly.

"I can't find Sid." Lyla looked up at Kate. "I can't sleep without Sid."

"Who's Sid?" Chuck asked. "Is there another child?"

Kate shook her head. "Sid is Lyla's stuffed sloth." She knelt on the floor in front of Lyla. "Did you look under the covers?"

She nodded. "I want *you* to look," she whispered.

Chuck's heart constricted. His Sarah hadn't been much younger than this little girl. Seeing Lyla standing there in a T-shirt too big for her little body reminded him so much of Sarah. His chest squeezed so hard, he could barely breathe.

Kate took Lyla's hand and faced Chuck. "This is Lyla. She's the reason I need someone with daddy skills. I need to blend into wherever I land. And that means we have to look like a family. Mama, Daddy and Lyla. Anywhere we go, we have to pretend we're a unit. No one can know she isn't mine."

Panic tightened his throat. Chuck held up his hand. "I can't do this."

"Can't, or won't?" Kate hit him with that direct stare. "I need one hundred percent commitment."

"Why do you need protection?" Chuck bit out. "What are you afraid of?"

"I'm afraid of whoever broke into my apartment and tried to take Lyla. I don't know who they are or why they were after her, but I have to keep her safe. I promised."

"Promised who?" Chuck asked.

Her lips firmed into a narrow line. "That doesn't matter. What matters is that we protect Lyla in the best way we can. I need everyone who comes into contact with her...with us...to think we're a family. The people looking for her will be looking for a lone woman and child, not a family of three."

Chuck studied Kate, his eyes narrowing. "How do we know you didn't..." he lowered his voice to a point Lyla wouldn't hear or understand, "How do we know you didn't kidnap Lyla? Is she even yours to hide?" His gaze shifted from Kate to Hank. "Do you know?"

Hank's lips quirked. "You have a good point, Chuck." He smiled at Kate. "Kate is actually Lyla's aunt. Her sister left her on her doorstep and disappeared."

Chuck crossed his arms over his chest. "And how do you know Kate didn't off her sister to steal her daughter?"

Lyla leaned her cheek against Kate's leg.

Kate's eyes filled. She blinked several times and lifted her chin. "I love my sister. I wouldn't *off* her." She patted Lyla's head, without picking up the child.

Chuck couldn't understand why the woman wasn't taking the child into her arms to reassure and comfort her. Impatience and concern for the little girl won out. Chuck bent to Lyla. "Hey, do you want me to hold you?"

The child stared up at Chuck, clutching her hands against her chest. Her big, blue eyes showed fear at first, but then she yawned and held up her arms.

Chuck lifted Lyla into his arms and held her close. He gently rubbed her back until she laid her head on his shoulder and closed her eyes. She drew in a deep breath and slept.

Kate's eyes rounded. "How did you do that?"

"Do what?" Chuck asked.

Sadie chuckled. "The man has a magic touch with small children. Emma took to him from the moment he held her in his arms."

Hank nodded. "Exactly like Lyla just did. That's why I knew he was the right man for the job."

Chuck ignored them all and carried the sleeping Lyla back down the hallway.

"Second door on the right," Sadie called out.

He found the door and entered the room with a full-sized bed in the middle of the floor decorated in light blues and grays.

A small child's blanket lay in the middle of the bed. He'd found the right room.

Careful not to wake Lyla, he laid her down, covered her with the blanket. He found Sid, the sloth, hiding under a pillow, and slipped the stuffed animal beneath her arm. Then he backed away slowly.

At the door to the bedroom, Chuck paused to look back at Lyla and wondered what his own little girl would have looked like at that age. Sarah never made it to three.

His heart contracted, squeezing hard in his chest.

Lyla lay sleeping, her silky blond hair fanning out around her on the pillow, her stuffed animal tucked beneath her arm.

He'd just convinced himself the best course of action for him was to steer clear of women with small children. They reminded him too much of what he was missing, and he got too attached.

He still missed being with Maya every day, like he

had when she and Daphne were under his care in witness protection.

But if he didn't do this job, who would? He thought through the other men on the Brotherhood Protectors team. Only a couple had been around kids. And those were on other jobs.

Chuck stared at Lyla lying there, so innocent, so vulnerable, and he struggled inwardly.

"I'm sorry I was rude," a voice said behind him.

He didn't have to turn to know it was Kate. "It's all right. You're worried about your niece and your sister."

"You were very good with her." She moved up beside him. "I'm afraid I don't know much about children. I left all of that up to my sister. While she was raising Lyla, I was concentrating on my career. I didn't know what I was missing, and I liked it that way."

Chuck understood all too well. He knew what he'd been missing after his wife and daughter died and, at times, wished he could forget. He loved children.

When Daphne had given birth to Maya during the time they were under his protection, he wasn't sure he could handle being so close. But Maya came along and wrapped herself around his little finger so fast he didn't know he was in love with her until it was too late. Now that Maya's father was back in the picture and one of the Brotherhood Protectors, Chuck had made the decision to back out and give them time to bond as a family.

She locked gazes with him. "I need someone who can help me protect her."

Chuck nodded.

"Lyla needs someone who understands what she

needs." Kate sighed. "I'm not sure I'm that person. Frankly, I need help."

"She's lost her mother, for all intents and purposes. Until your sister returns, she needs stability in her life. She needs to know she's safe and loved."

Kate stared at Lyla, her brows dipping into a concerned frown. "My sister moved away when Lyla was born. I barely know my niece. I don't know how to take care of a child."

"It's not hard," Chuck said.

"For you, maybe." She turned to face Chuck. "So, will you help me?"

"A moment ago, you didn't think I was the right man for the job."

"Then I saw you with Lyla. She took to you right away. And Hank says you're a Navy SEAL, one of the best." She touched his arm.

A shock of electricity shot through his nerves. He glanced at the hand on his arm.

She pulled back her hand. "Please," she said softly.

His gaze rose to connect with hers.

She had blue eyes, just like Lyla's. "Lyla looks like you," Chuck said.

Kate laughed. "She does. But then I look like my sister. We're twins."

Kate's blond hair was a shade darker than Lyla's, but the eyes were unmistakably sky blue and matched the child's perfectly. Her skin glowed with a healthy tan, and when she smiled, her entire face lit up.

Beautiful.

Not in the runway model way, but in a real, girl-next-door, simple loveliness.

Chuck shook his head. And there were two of them?

"I'll double whatever Hank pays you," Kate said, her eyes wide and pleading.

"No."

Kate's shoulders sagged. "I get it. I was rude. If it helps, my father was military. I have great respect for our country's men and women in uniform."

"No," Chuck said. "You don't have to pay me double. I'll do the job."

"But Lyla already likes you. It makes sense for you to be the one…wait…what?" She stared at him with her pretty brows drawing together. "You will?"

He nodded. "I will. When do you need me to start?"

"Now," she replied, without hesitation. "We need to start now. Before I show up in town in broad daylight."

"Then we start now." He tipped his head toward Lyla. "No use waking her until we figure out the logistics."

Kate threw her arms around Chuck's neck. "Thank you."

Her body felt warm and soft against his. Chuck wrapped his arms around her middle as if they belonged there. She was just the right height. Not too tall or short, and her muscles were firm. He drew in a deep breath, inhaling the subtle scent of her perfume. He liked it. And he liked the way she felt pressed against him. A little too much for having just met her.

She was now his client. Other than pretending to be

her husband and the father of her child, he had to keep their relationship professional.

He set her away from him and dropped his hands to his sides. "If we're going to pretend to be a family, we need a place to stay. The bed and breakfast I'm renting now isn't big enough for the three of us. Let's talk with Hank. He's more familiar with the area than I am."

Kate rubbed her arms, her cheeks flushing a pretty pink. "Of course. We should talk with Hank. He'll know where we can go."

"In the meantime, we need to come up with a cover story. Since I've been here a few weeks, folks might have noticed I've been alone. They'll wonder how a wife and child came from out of nowhere."

Her eyebrows drew together, and her gaze sharpened. "You could have been scouting Eagle Rock for a place to live. I could have been wrapping up my job in LA. Which I did, as soon as my sister dropped Lyla on me."

"Will Lyla have any problem calling you Mommy?"

"I don't think so. I've already started wearing my hair like Rachel's and have referred to myself as what she called my sister…Mama."

Chuck nodded. "Good. Then all we need is to get her to start calling me Daddy." He swallowed hard on that word. Sarah had called him Daddy. No child had called him that since. "And if she can't do that, we won't worry. I've known small children to get confused and call their parents by their first names."

"How will you bring us into town?" Kate asked.

Chuck thought for a moment. "You're safe in Hank's

house for tonight. I'll go back to my bed and breakfast for the night. Once I find suitable lodging for *our family*, I'll come get you and bring you in like you're coming in from Bozeman's airport."

Kate nodded. "Sounds good. Let's talk with Hank."

Chuck glanced once more at Lyla. "She should sleep the rest of the night. But she's probably missing her mother. You might consider sleeping with her for the night."

Kate nodded. "I will. Poor thing. I know how she feels. I miss her mother, too."

Chuck held the door for Kate and half-closed it before following her down the hallway back to the living area.

He wasn't sure what he was getting himself into, or how long the assignment would last, but somehow, he had to keep his distance from the woman and child or risk breaking his heart all over again.

CHAPTER 3

Kate slept that night with Lyla snuggled up against her. She couldn't believe how much a little girl could move in her sleep. At times, she lay sideways with her feet pressed into Kate's belly. At other times, she slept with her arm around Kate's neck, her face buried against Kate's cheek.

The sweet smell of baby shampoo etched itself into Kate's memory. She'd pulled Lyla up against her and draped her arm over the child's middle. Her heart swelled and warmed to her sister's baby girl.

While she'd been busy building her career, she'd been missing the beauty of caring for such a wonderful little human being.

Sleep was slow in coming and greatly interrupted, but she couldn't be upset. Lyla hadn't asked to be caught up in whatever intrigue Rachel was up against. She hadn't asked to be dumped into the inexperienced arms of her Aunt Kate. She had suffered enough. Kate accepted the responsibility of taking care of the little girl for as long as Rachel needed. That's what family did.

Lyla settled into a deep sleep in the wee hours of the morning.

Kate finally slept as well. She woke before Lyla just as the sun was rising and edging around the curtains covering the windows.

Wanting to get a head start on the day, Kate rose, dressed in the adjoining bathroom and brushed her hair.

By the time she reentered the bedroom, Lyla was sitting up in the bed, yawning.

Kate gathered her into her arms like Chuck had suggested. "Come to Mama," she said. She carried Lyla to the bathroom to relieve herself, wash her hands and brush her hair.

Once they were finished, she took Lyla's hand. "Ready to find something to eat?"

Lyla nodded. "I'm hungry."

Together, they walked into the living room. One easily trusting little girl, and one adult scrambling to figure out the ins and outs of parenting.

Sadie stood in front of a massive fireplace with Emma playing at her feet. "Oh, good. You're awake." She lifted Emma into her arms. "Hank told me to wake you by now. He was able to find you and Chuck a cottage just on the edge of our little town of Eagle Rock."

A trickle of excitement and anticipation rippled through Kate, even while the thought of seeing Chuck again disturbed her. "That's good news."

"He contacted Chuck and let him know. Chuck will

be here in thirty minutes to collect you two. I've been busy gathering items you might need for the cabin." She waved to several boxes laid out across the floor. "You'll need linens, kitchen utensils, towels and so much more. I tried to think of as much as I could. Anything else you might need, just give us a call, I probably have something. No use going out and buying all new stuff."

Bemused, Kate shook her head. "I could have purchased all of that."

Sadie smiled. "That would have defeated the purpose of looking like you're joining Chuck with things from your previous home. I have a couple of outfits I picked up in LA for when Emma gets older. They might fit Lyla now."

"I couldn't possibly take Emma's clothes."

Sadie waved her hand. "Please. Lyla needs to have something to change into. She can't show up in town in her pajamas. I'm due back in LA in a few weeks. I'll pick out more clothes for Emma. She usually goes with me."

"Are you still acting?" Kate asked.

Sadie laughed. "I am. I have gone longer between films, but I'm still showing up on the big screen."

Kate shook her head. "I don't know how you do it. Juggling a career and a baby daughter. How do working mothers manage?"

"We find good caregivers and *make* time to be with our children." Sadie grinned. "I have a fabulous nanny in LA. She's happy to work when I'm there. She keeps Emma at the studio so that I can see her on my breaks. Fortunately, I can pay her well enough that she doesn't have to work when I'm not there."

Kate didn't say it, but Sadie implied that she understood not all working moms could afford to pay a nanny.

"Let me get those outfits. If they fit, you can keep them."

"I can afford to pay you for them," Kate offered.

"I wouldn't let you. They're my gift to Lyla. Poor little thing has to be feeling the stress of all the changes in her life." Sadie held out Emma. "Do you mind holding her for a moment?"

Before Kate could beg off, Emma leaned toward her.

Kate had to take her, or the baby would have fallen.

Emma wrapped her arms around Kate's neck and gave her a wet baby kiss.

Instead of being repulsed by the baby spittle, Kate laughed. "Is she always this good with strangers?"

"Not everyone. She seems to be a good judge of character." Sadie grinned and hurried from the room.

While Kate held Emma, Lyla found a basket full of brightly colored toys. She pulled out one toy at a time until the basket was empty.

Emma batted at Kate's gold hoop earrings, determined to capture one and put it into her mouth.

Kate held onto the squirming baby, afraid she'd drop the child. She kept a close eye on Lyla to make sure she didn't get too close to the fireplace or stick her fingers into a light socket. She'd heard that little kids did things like that.

Emma grabbed both of her ears and deposited a kiss on Kate's cheek.

"Thank you, Kate." Sadie emerged from the hallway,

carrying a stack of little girls clothing. "I'll take Emma." She laid the stack of clothes on the back of the sofa and relieved Kate of her burden.

Kate glanced through the outfits on the back of the sofa and held them up to Lyla's back, one at a time.

The child played on with the toys she'd found, oblivious to her aunt.

"All three of these outfits should fit," Kate declared. "Thank you."

"You're more than welcome." Sadie glanced out the front window. "Looks like your bodyguard has arrived. We can load the boxes into the back of his truck."

Kate's heartbeat sped. A cautious look out the window made it beat even faster.

Chuck dropped down from his truck and strode toward the house. Tall, broad-shouldered and rugged, the man had swagger and probably didn't know it. Even the graying at his temples only added to his attractiveness.

Heat coiled in Kate's core. She hadn't been that aroused by a man in a very long time. And this guy wasn't a spring chicken. Perhaps that's what she liked most about him. He was mature, confident in his skin and exuded pure masculinity out of every pore of his body.

Sadie met him at the door. "Come on in, Chuck. We were just about to start breakfast. You can join us."

His gaze scanned the room, slowing as it passed Kate. "Where's Hank?"

"He's been up for hours, working on some background checks for one of the other new agents. He'll join us once I get the bacon cooking." Sadie winked. "The man likes bacon. I'm sure it'll harden his arteries, but he reminds me all the time that life's too short to skip the bacon."

"I couldn't agree with him more." He nodded toward Kate. "But I thought we'd hit the diner in town. We might as well establish our cover right away."

"Oh." Kate twisted her fingers into the hem of her shirt. She'd thought she'd have a little more time before she was alone with Chuck. Time to adjust to the thought of pretending to be his wife, acting like a loving couple with a daughter. "Okay. I can be ready in just a few minutes." She shot a glance toward Lyla.

"I'll watch her," Chuck said. He held out his hands. "How's my little girl this morning?"

Lyla lifted her arms, still holding the stuffed unicorn she'd picked out of the box.

Chuck lifted her up and settled her into the crook of his arm. He leaned in and gave her a noisy, smacking kiss on the cheek.

Lyla laughed and kissed him back with just as much bravado. Then she hugged him tightly around the neck.

Kate shook her head. She never got that kind of reaction from Lyla, and she was blood-related. The man had the child completely charmed.

And he was charming Kate in the process. "How do you do that?"

Chuck stared across at Kate, his lips still curved in a smile. "Do what?"

Charm the fool out of me, she wanted to say, but clamped her lips tight to keep from telling him exactly how confused he made her feel. "Nothing. I'll be right back." She spun on her heel, grabbed the clothes Sadie had given Lyla and ran into the bedroom, closing the door behind her.

Kate stood with her back to the door, pressing her hands to her heated cheeks. How *did* he do that? With only a smile, he turned her knees to mush. And the way he was so at ease with Lyla melted Kate's heart like nothing she'd ever experienced.

She straightened and pushed back her shoulders. Kate hadn't taken an indefinite leave of absence from her work to flirt with Lyla's bodyguard. The sooner she got that through her head, the better. Having Chuck pretend to be her husband and the father of her child was a temporary arrangement, necessary to protect Lyla. Once the threat was vanquished, Kate would head back to LA, Lyla would return to Rachel and her husband, and Chuck would move on to his next assignment.

Don't get personal with the hired help, she schooled herself.

In short order, she packed her toiletries and Lyla's new clothes into her suitcase, zipped it and set it on the floor. Then she gathered Lyla's blanket and Sid, reminded again of how little she had.

Her thoughts returned to her sister, and her heart ached. What had Rachel gotten herself into? Where was Myles? How could he let anything happen to his family? What kind of man let his wife ditch their baby and run?

Unless he hadn't known Rachel would run away

from him and take their child. In which case, was she running because Myles was abusive?

Kate wished Rachel was there. She had a hundred questions for her. The only thing she knew was that her twin was in trouble. When she was sure Lyla was safe, she'd work on finding Rachel and helping her through whatever trouble she was up against.

With the blanket under one arm, Kate wheeled the suitcase out of the bedroom and down the hallway to the living room.

Chuck sat on the floor, pulling Lyla's hair up into a ponytail.

Lyla had been changed into colorful knit pants and a shirt with polka dots and ruffles.

"I found another outfit for Lyla," Sadie said with a smile as she handed Chuck an elastic band. "And we thought Lyla might like her hair up and out of her face." Sadie motioned toward the window. "It's pretty windy outside today."

The man handled the child's baby-fine hair like a pro, appearing at ease despite how incongruous the big man looked next to the little girl.

When he finished, he rose to his feet, lifted Lyla into his arms, and nodded. "Ready?"

No, she wasn't. Not when it meant being alone with this man who ignited flames in Kate when she'd thought herself flame-resistant. "Yes." Given she'd more or less begged him to take the job, she couldn't balk now. He was the only man she knew, or felt she could trust, to take care of her and Lyla until they figured out what to do next. "Let's go."

Chuck led the way through the door, pausing long enough to scan the area before holding the door wide for Kate.

Sadie, holding Emma on her hip, exited as well and stood on the porch. "We're so glad you came to us, Kate." She smiled. "Don't worry. Chuck's an amazing man. He had to be to make it into the Navy SEALs." Sadie hugged Kate. Emma giggled and grabbed Kate's hair in her fist.

Kate laughed, unclenched the child's hand from her hair and kissed her little fist. "Thank you for helping and for all the things you've given us."

"Maybe we can set up a play date for the girls," Sadie suggested.

A play date. Sure, she'd heard of them, but she wasn't sure she was comfortable with the idea. "Uh, that would be nice. I guess."

"Let us assess the situation first," Hank said from behind Sadie.

The former SEAL curled his arm around his wife's waist and dropped a kiss on top of Emma's head. "Let us know if you need anything. The cottage is right on the edge of Eagle Rock on a less traveled road. Only people with a reason to go down that road should be going down that road."

Chuck nodded and held out his hand to Hank. "Thanks. I'll keep a close watch over these two."

"I know you will." Hank clasped his hand. "I knew you were the right man for the job. You need anything, just give me a yell."

Chuck led the way off the porch and to the passenger side of his pickup. "Do you have a car?"

Kate shook her head. "No. Hank picked me up at the airport. I didn't want to risk driving cross-country with Lyla. Not when I might have a tail following me."

"Good thinking. Though, if someone wanted to find you badly enough, they'd follow your credit card purchases."

Kate frowned. "To move fast, I had to use what I had."

Chuck settled Lyla into the back seat and adjusted the seat belt to fit as snugly as possible across her little lap. "After we meet the realtor at the cottage, we need to find a place to purchase a child's car seat."

"Definitely," Kate agreed. "And we need to stock the pantry with food. I'm not sure how long we'll be at this."

"Hank said the cottage came furnished." Chuck moved out, closed the back door and turned to hold the front passenger door for Kate. "That will be one less expense you'll have to incur."

"How big is the cottage?" Kate asked.

"I have no idea. We'll find out when we get there."

That was what Kate was afraid of. Any small cottage would be all the smaller with Chuck inside. His broad shoulders filled even the largest of rooms.

And if it had only a single bedroom? Where would they all sleep? That same trickle of excitement rippled through her center. All because of one tall, well-muscled Navy SEAL who would be Lyla's bodyguard and pretend daddy for however long it took for Rachel to return for her daughter.

And what if Rachel didn't come back?

Kate's breath lodged in her throat. Being twins, she'd always felt an awareness of her sister. Surely, she'd know if something awful happened. But then she hadn't known her sister was in distress. If she had, she would have offered to help in any way possible.

Yet, it had been Rachel who'd reached out in her time of need.

Kate hated that she'd been such a terrible sister she hadn't known Rachel was in trouble. Hell, she hadn't seen Rachel since she'd moved to Idaho over three years before. Sure, they'd talked on the phone, but Kate had always been in a hurry to end the call and get on with whatever project she'd been working. And she hadn't met Lyla, until the child had landed on her doorstep.

Her heart hurt at her failure as a sister.

What was important now was to take care of Rachel's daughter and then find Rachel.

WHEN CHUCK HELD Lyla in his arms, all the feelings he'd felt for Sarah came flooding back. No matter that it had been years since he'd held his daughter, the same emotions were still there. With Maya, he'd had the advantage of her growing on him from an infant to a healthy one-year-old. She'd sneaked into his life one day at a time. But Lyla was about the same size, if a year older, than Sarah had been when she'd been killed in a car wreck.

Sarah had had blond hair and smelled of baby shampoo, just like Lyla.

His chest constricted, making it difficult to breathe. He forced air into his lungs and marched on, like he always did, reminding himself this was a job. Once the situation resolved, he'd be on to the next assignment. Kate and Lyla would be gone from Montana.

Don't get attached.

He glanced toward Kate.

She was a pretty woman with blond hair and blue eyes, much like Lyla. He could imagine her twin looking exactly like her and how much trouble they must have caused growing up.

He thought it strange that she didn't have the slightest clue how to be a mother. What happened to good old maternal instinct? Kate seemed so awkward around her niece.

"Are you sure you're Lyla's aunt?" Chuck asked as he slid into the driver's seat.

"I'm pretty sure. All I've had from my sister was an occasional photograph of Lyla. But there's no mistaking her features. She looks just like we did at her age. But if you're concerned I might have kidnapped the child, why don't you take us straight to the sheriff's office? I probably should have started there in the first place. My sister begged me not to take the situation to the police, or I would have." She stared out the window. "Do you know where we're going?"

"Not hardly," he muttered, shaking his head. "I have the address. It can't be too hard to find. Eagle Rock isn't a large community."

They accomplished the drive into town in silence. Kate glanced all around, keeping an eye on the road ahead and behind them. After what happened at her apartment in LA, Kate wasn't sure about anything. The man who'd broken down her door had meant business. Thankfully, the cops had arrived in time to help.

Following Hank's directions, Chuck drove through the quaint little town of Eagle Rock with its one main street, several side streets, a medical clinic, sheriff's office, tavern and diner.

Kate stared out the window eagerly, wanting to know whatever she could about the little Montana town she'd be spending the next couple of days in while hiding out.

ON THE OTHER side of town, Chuck slowed and glanced down at the directions on his cellphone. He turned left onto a short road that ended in a field of green hay.

Two houses lined one side of the road. One was white with blue shutters. The other, the one they were renting, was yellow with white shutters.

The houses were separated by a dingy white picket fence in need of fresh paint, and a row of pink, climbing, tea roses that softened its appearance and made it appear quaint rather than neglected. Chuck rolled down his window and inhaled the lush, rich scent of roses and freshly cut grass. Apparently, the yard had recently been mowed and smelled like spring.

Having lived in apartments when he wasn't deployed, Chuck couldn't help but feel a connection to this little cottage on the quiet little road. Yes, it could stand a fresh paint job, and the bushes needed trimming, but the yellow and white combination reminded him of daisies and sunshine.

If he, Lyla and Kate were a real family, this was the kind of place he'd want to come home to.

Chuck pulled into the driveway and turned off the truck engine. "Let's check it out for a few minutes, make a list of what we need, and get to the diner for that breakfast I promised."

Kate nodded and pushed open her door before Chuck could jump down and hurry around to her side. He chuckled softly. Apparently, she was used to opening her own doors.

Which was just as well because, whenever he was close to Kate, he struggled for words and his libido reminded him of how long it had been since he'd been with a woman.

He had to remind himself that his reaction to Kate was purely chemical. Nothing he could stop. But he'd have to minimize its effects to avoid any complications in their relationship. Kate and Lyla were a job, nothing more.

He opened the back door to the truck, unbuckled Lyla's seat belt and set her on her feet in the grass.

She shot off like a rocket toward the house. "It's yellow. Our new house is yellow," she cried. She was up on the porch and swinging on the porch swing before Kate or Chuck could warn her to wait until they checked it out.

Kate smiled. "She likes the color. Rachel also likes yellow."

Chuck stared at Kate, amazed at the transformation

a simple smile could make to a woman's face. For a moment, the worry and heartache were gone. In that fleeting moment, Chuck could see how beautiful Kate was.

Then the shadows returned, and Kate looked at Chuck. "I hope Rachel is all right."

"I do too." He shifted his gaze to Lyla, swinging on the porch. "A child needs her mother."

"What if Rachel doesn't come back?" Kate touched his arm. "What if something awful has happened to her?"

He covered her hand with his. "My mama always told me, *Don't borrow trouble*." Chuck gave her hand a comforting squeeze. "Take one day at a time. I'm sure Hank's working on finding your sister." He nodded toward the house. "Let's get moved in and start looking like a family." Drawing her hand through the crook of his elbow, he led her to the front door. If anyone was watching through a window, they'd see a man, his wife and their small daughter.

All the way across the yard to the front door, Chuck used his SEAL skills of situational awareness, scanning the area for potential threats. No matter how good it felt to have a beautiful woman on his arm, or to hold a child in his arms, he had to maintain his focus. These two people were only his to protect, not to fall in love with.

CHAPTER 4

Kate held tight to Lyla's hand as she brushed past Chuck and stepped through the door.

The interior of the house was perhaps as quaint as the exterior. The rooms had been freshly painted and smelled like new.

Fortunately, the house came furnished, so they wouldn't have to invest in couches, beds and other items. What was there appeared to be rather dated, but lovingly cared for. A floral-print, overstuffed couch and a lounge chair in a coordinating, solid burgundy graced the original hardwood living room floor and faced what appeared to be a working fireplace. The coffee table probably dated back to the late 1960s with dainty crocheted doilies spread across the surface.

Paintings on the wall depicted snow-covered mountains and fields of wildflowers. A picture window looked out over a backyard of lush, green grass and rose bushes planted along the fence line.

"This is really cute," Kate commented. She strolled

through the living room into the kitchen where a retro table stood with a Formica top and metal legs. The chairs were covered in bright-red, shiny fabric.

"I feel like I stepped into the past on the set for one of those family shows from the fifties," Chuck said.

"I know. But I like it. It makes me think of a simpler time." Kate studied the antique gas stove and the deep, white, porcelain sink. "I bet there's a clawfoot tub in the bathroom." She hurried to the only bathroom in the three-bedroom house to find what she knew would be there. "Ha! See?" She stood back and let Chuck lean into the bathroom.

A huge old clawfoot tub stood against the wall with a shower curtain hung on a circular rod above.

Lyla ducked between their legs and ran to the tub. "Can I have a bath?"

Chuck laughed. "If we'd had a tub like that when I was a kid, I would have loved taking a bath." He patted Lyla's head. "Later, darlin', we have to unload stuff from the truck and go get some breakfast."

Kate's stomach rumbled, reminding her that she hadn't eaten since the night before.

Chuck left them in the hallway and made a quick inspection of the rooms and closets, probably looking for bogeymen hiding out there.

Kate did her own appraisal. The house had three bedrooms. Two of them were set up with beds. One had been used as an office with a large desk and office chair, no bed. The smaller bedroom had a twin bed and a matching dresser. The master bedroom wasn't very large but had a queen-sized bed in the middle of the room and a long, low dresser with a mirror. The bed was made up with a blue and white comforter. White, lacey curtains hung in the windows. Two beds, two adults and one child. If Kate and Chuck were really married, the bed situation would work.

But they weren't, and it wouldn't. Kate stared at the bed that would fit a husband and wife, and her pulse beat faster. Her imagination took flight. She could picture lying in that bed with Chuck. He'd take up most of the space with his broad shoulders and long body. It would mean sleeping up against his hard muscles, pressed close to keep from falling off the bed. What woman would complain?

"We'll need to run by the hardware store for a deadbolt lock and a few replacement locks for the windows." Chuck's voice jerked Kate back to reality.

"We can do that," Kate said. She spun away from the master bedroom and forced a smile to her face while her heart pounded against her ribs.

"I'll unload the boxes, then we can leave."

"I can help," Kate offered, following him to the door.

"Just keep an eye on Lyla." He nodded toward the toddler peering through the picture window into the backyard. "It won't take me long. There isn't much."

"Can I go outside to play?" Lyla asked.

"Not yet, sweetie," Kate said. She went to stand beside Lyla and stared out into a yard that would be the perfect size for a swing set.

Lyla reached up and slipped her little hand into Kate's. "I'm hungry."

"We'll go to the diner in just a few minutes." She

knelt on the floor. "Do you think you'll like living here with Mama and Daddy?" Kate figured she'd better start training Lyla to call her and Chuck by their pretend titles. The sooner she did, the better their cover would be.

Lyla tilted her head. "Yes. It's pretty." She ran to the couch, pulled herself up onto the cushions and patted the space beside her. "Come. Sit down. It's soft, too."

Kate sat beside the little girl and smiled. "You're right. It's very soft and comfortable."

Chuck carried in the boxes Sadie had sent and laid them on the floor in the front entryway.

"Daddy," Kate called out, making it a point to call Chuck Daddy. "Sadie said there was a doll in one of those boxes. I don't suppose you see it, do you? Lyla might like to take it with her to the diner."

Chuck stopped halfway through the front door, his eyes widening. For a moment, he remained as if frozen in time. Then he drew in a deep breath and entered, set down the box he'd been carrying, and dug into the one beside it. A moment later, he held up a soft doll with a ruffled dress and bright, blond hair. "Is this what you were looking for?"

Lyla squealed and launched herself off the couch. She ran toward Chuck with her arms reaching out for the doll.

He held it out of her reach. "What do you say?"

She stopped and stood as straight as an arrow and said, "Please, may I have it?"

Chuck dropped to one knee and handed her the doll. "Yes, you may."

"Say thank you, Daddy," Kate prompted.

Chuck remained kneeling in front of Lyla.

"Thank you, Daddy," Lyla said and clutched the doll to her chest. "She's beautiful. I'm going to call her Sarah."

Chuck's jaw tightened, and he closed his eyes as if he was in pain. Then he pushed to his feet and left the house.

If she hadn't witnessed his reaction to Lyla, she might have missed the fact Chuck was affected by the little girl's words. What had upset the former SEAL? That she'd called him Daddy? Or that she'd named the doll Sarah?

He was back a few seconds later with the last box. Once he set it on the floor, he stood straight. "Are you two ready for breakfast?"

"Yes!' Lyla ran toward the door.

Chuck scooped her up into his arms and waited for Kate to join them. Then he walked with them out to the truck and helped them inside.

Kate liked that he took the time to adjust the seat belt across Lyla's lap and worried that she didn't have a car seat. He cared about the child who wasn't even his. She imagined he'd be the same with his own children. At his age, he should have had a family of his own. Kate wondered why such a good-looking guy was still single. Not that she was in the market, but she was curious about the man who was pretending to be her husband.

Perhaps that evening, she'd ask him a few questions and get to know him better. It would help to make their pretense more believable. At least, that's how she'd pose the questions. It wouldn't hurt to get to know the man better.

On a professional level, not a personal level, of course.

She studied him out of the corner of her eye as he slid into the seat beside her. Yeah, a purely professional level. Getting personal would be dangerous.

Chuck drove the few short blocks to the only diner in town. He'd been there a couple of times, by himself and with other members of the Brotherhood Protectors. The food was good, and he didn't have to cook it.

His chest still hurt from what Lyla had said. First, she'd called him Daddy. Then she'd named her doll Sarah. Where she'd heard that name was a mystery. But it hit him square in the heart. Sarah had been her daddy's girl. She could do no wrong in his eyes and he would give his life to have her back. But that could never be. She'd died years ago, and he thought he'd gotten over it.

But he knew it was all a joke to think you ever got over losing a child. He never wanted to forget her, and why would he? The memories he had were good ones. He held onto them because he'd loved Sarah with all his heart.

He pulled up in front of Al's Diner, mentally pulling himself together. Now wasn't the time to stroll down memory lane or start feeling the heartache of loss all over again.

When he shifted into park, he opened his door and

dropped down out of the truck. By the time he rounded the hood, Kate had already climbed out and was unhooking Lyla's seat belt.

"You've got to let me open doors for you," Chuck said softly enough only Kate could hear.

"Why?" she asked and lifted Lyla out of the truck and into her arms.

"Because that's what husbands do for their wives."

She stared at him as if he'd grown a horn. "Really? In this day and age?"

Chuck ground his teeth together. "My mama taught me to treat ladies with care and respect. Opening doors is a part of that."

Kate's eyes narrowed. "Just how old are you? Ninety-three?"

A frown pulled Chuck's brows together. "I might be older than you, but I have a lot of life left in me."

"I'm sure you do." Kate's mouth curved into a smile. "Better get all that living in while you can. Your days are numbered." Then she winked. "You know I'm yanking your chain, don't you?"

He shook his head. "I believe you say exactly what you mean."

When she turned with Lyla in her arms, he smacked her ass.

"Hey," Kate spun around and glared at him.

"What?" He held up his hands. "I'm just doing what a husband would do with his wife. Good job acting like you're offended." He gripped her arm and pulled her up against his chest. "Now, kiss me and look like we're making up."

He bent his head and captured her mouth with his.

She didn't have time to protest, and he liked that he'd caught her off guard.

When he stepped away, he moved back far enough she couldn't slap the smile off his face.

She raised her hand, all right, but not to slap him. Instead, she stared at him, pressing her fingers to her kiss-swollen lips.

When Chuck was sure Kate wouldn't slap him, he leaned close to Lyla's ear. "How's my sweet little girl? Want a kiss, too?"

"Yes, please," she said and presented her cheek for him.

He bent close to land a noisy smack on Lyla's petal-soft face.

She giggled and raised her shoulders. "That tickles."

"Oh, yeah?" Chuck blew a raspberry on her neck.

Lyla squealed and giggled again.

Chuck glanced over the top of the child's head. "Now, we look like a family." He held out his elbow.

Kate hooked her arm through his and walked with him to the entrance.

As soon as they entered the diner, a man wearing an apron stepped out of the kitchen. "Have a seat, your waitress will be with you in a minute." He pushed through the swinging door into the kitchen, yelling, "Daisy! Need you out front."

"Coming!" a feminine voice called out. A blond-haired, blue-eyed waitress backed through the swinging door, carrying a huge tray laden with plates of food. "Grab a seat anywhere. I'll be right with you."

Chuck steered Kate and Lyla to a booth in the back corner of the diner. He guided them onto one of the bench seats and took the other, facing the entrance.

A few moments later, Daisy plopped laminated menus in front of them. "Good morning," she said with a big smile. "I'm Daisy. I'll be your server. What can I get you to drink?"

Chuck chose coffee, Kate chose hot tea and asked for a cup of milk for Lyla.

"Got it," Daisy said. "Be right back."

The pretty, young woman practically sprinted back to the kitchen. Moments later, she appeared with the glasses balanced on a large tray.

Once she'd set down their cups and glasses, she pulled out a pad and pen. "What melts your butter today?" she asked.

Kate ordered a yogurt and a cup of fruit.

Chuck ordered two eggs over easy and toast.

Kate leaned toward Lyla. "Would you like eggs or cereal?"

"Cereal, please," Lyla said. "The kind with the marshmallows."

"Cereal, it is—with the marshmallows," the waitress said with a smile. She pocketed her pen and reached for the large tray. When she had it perched at her shoulder, she grinned. "You're new in town, aren't you?"

Kate returned her smile. "We are."

"Are you visiting or staying?" Daisy asked.

"We're thinking about staying," Chuck responded. "We're renting a place now but will be looking around to buy."

"Looking for a house in town? Or a piece of property a little farther out?"

"In town," Chuck said.

"A little farther out," Kate said at the same time.

Chuck laughed. "We haven't decided. Since we're new around here, we'll leave the decision open until we've seen a few places."

"Out in the country gives the little ones a place to run wild, but in town they can go to the park and play with other children." Daisy shrugged. "It's whatever you prefer. People around here make it happen."

"What about you," Kate asked. "Did you grow up in Eagle Rock?"

Daisy nodded. "Yes, ma'am. But a lot of my friends lived out of town. I visited some of the ranches around here and learned to fish, hunt and ride horses. So, I guess I didn't miss much."

"Eagle Rock is pretty small," Kate remarked. "What keeps people from leaving?"

Daisy shifted the tray at her shoulder. "Many of the young people leave. Some go into the military, and then come back later. Me…I'm limited by money. Soon as I get enough, I'm off to college."

Kate nodded. "Good for you. Even if you come back to Eagle Rock, you'll come back with more than you left with."

"That's what I figure. But I plan to learn a lot and see the world before I come back."

"Admirable aspirations," Kate concurred.

"Well, I'd better get back to it. We're shorthanded today." Daisy rushed back to the kitchen with their order and emerged with another tray loaded with food. She delivered the food to a large family at a set of tables and refilled their glasses. A few minutes later, she appeared at their table again, this time with their food.

She set the plates in front of them. "Anything else I can get you?"

"No, thank you," Chuck replied. Though Daisy was nice, she was standing in the way of him studying every person in the diner.

Once the waitress left them, Chuck lifted his fork, stabbed the fried eggs and a piece of toast and brought it to his lips. He bit into the savory flavor and glanced around the diner, studying every face, committing them to memory.

The family at a table on the other side of the diner had the typical mother and father. What wasn't typical was the fact they were accompanied by a cool eight children. How their parents could afford to feed that many at a diner was beyond Chuck.

A couple of middle-aged men in jeans and jackets sat in a booth two over from the one where Chuck sat. They wore shirts with matching company logos embroidered on them. Before them on the table lay blueprints of a building.

Two gray-haired women sat at a table sipping tea, and four young men wearing reflective vests, jeans and work boots filled another booth, all drinking coffee and eating big platters of eggs and pancakes.

A young couple entered the diner with their daughter who appeared to be a couple years older than Lyla.

"Find a seat. I'll be right with you," Daisy called out.

Daisy topped off Chuck's coffee before she moved on to the newer customers.

"See anyone who looks like they could give us a headache?" Kate whispered.

"No," Chuck said, but he wasn't letting down his guard.

"Should I make a list of the groceries we need?" Kate asked. "I don't know what kind of meals you like to eat."

"I eat anything I don't have to cook."

Kate chuckled. "That narrows it down."

"I don't expect you to do all the cooking." Chuck lifted his chin. "I can cook a handful of meals. Nothing fancy. Chili, spaghetti, grilled anything and eggs."

"Good. Between the two of us, we won't starve or resort to eating out every meal." Kate twisted her lips into a wry grin. "At the grocery store, you can pick your ingredients, and I'll pick mine. I have a limited repertoire. I can make a mean lasagna, gumbo, pot roast and chicken salad."

Chuck nodded. "Point is not to get wrapped up in meal prep. Whatever is easy is fine with me. We can buy lunch meat and hot dogs, and I'll be fine."

"You're on." Kate finished her yogurt and fruit.

Lyla played with her doll, forgetting to eat her cereal.

"Lyla, sweetie, finish your cereal so we can get back to the cottage and you can play with Sarah."

Chuck winced. How could he tell a little girl she couldn't name her doll Sarah? Hell, he couldn't. Lyla had every right to name the doll anything she wanted. Just because it made a grown man want to cry every time he heard the name wasn't reason enough to force a three-year-old to change the doll's name.

He glanced up and caught Kate's gaze. His eyes narrowed. Had she seen him wince? Vowing to do a better job of hiding his emotions, Chuck shuttered his eyes and dug out his wallet. He tossed bills onto the table, enough to cover their meals, and stood. "Ready?"

Kate turned to Lyla. "Did you eat enough?"

"Yes," Lyla rubbed her tummy. "I'm full."

They left the diner and headed for the hardware store first.

There, Chuck purchased deadbolt locks for the front and rear doors. He bought replacement locks for the windows that needed them. He also picked up a couple of security devices to attach to the windows and doors that made piercing noises when set off. They weren't a real security system that connected with the sheriff's department, but they might scare off a would-be intruder.

While he hurried down the aisles of the hardware store, he made Kate and Lyla stand at the end of each aisle he was on. That way he could keep an eye on them. Others might have laughed. What could possibly happen in a hardware store?

While he found hardware, Kate found a pair of denim overalls in Lyla's size, a pink blouse and a pint-sized pair of cowboy boots to fit her as well.

Chuck insisted on paying for the purchases. He didn't want Kate's credit cards to show up in Eagle Rock and alert anyone who might be tracking her.

Chuck wasn't taking any chances. No one was looking for him, so using his cards posed no threat. He just had to keep Kate from alerting anyone to her whereabouts until her sister could be found and the situation resolved.

CHAPTER 5

Kate didn't like it, but it made sense for Chuck to pay for their purchases. When she could, she'd pay him back any money he spent on them. She had employed *him*. He shouldn't have to pay for anything. Hopefully, he'd put all his receipts on an expense report, to be paid when the situation was resolved.

Kate couldn't believe how everything seemed to be upside down in her life. From a neat, orderly existence to utter chaos. For now, all she could do was go with the flow.

She sat back in her seat and stared at the road ahead as Chuck drove them to the grocery store.

Once inside, Kate said, "Lyla's getting tired. We can cover more ground if we split up. I'll take Lyla with me. You get the juice, milk, eggs and cheese. I'll find the meats, cereal and spices."

Chuck hesitated for a moment, his gaze moving around the store's interior.

"Look, the store isn't that big. We won't be out of

yelling distance if anything should happen," Kate insisted.

He sighed. "Okay. But I'll make it fast and join you as soon as I have my items."

"Deal." Kate took one of the shopping carts and lifted Lyla to sit in it.

After a few minutes, Kate had selected the items on her list—hamburger for Chuck's chili and cereal with marshmallows for Lyla's breakfast. When she rolled down the candy aisle, Kate paused in front of the nuts and raisins.

Lyla pulled her legs out of the holes in the cart and stood up.

"Lyla, sit down," Kate admonished. She tried to get Lyla to take her seat again, but the child was having none of it.

"I want candy," Lyla said. "Please."

"No, sweetie. Candy is bad for your teeth and will make your tummy hurt."

"I want candy," she said, her voice rising. She leaned out of the cart.

If Kate hadn't grabbed her, she would have fallen to the floor. Once Kate had her in her arms, she struggled to hold onto the squirming child.

"Lyla, please. I can't hold you when you wiggle so much."

"Want down."

Kate set her on her feet. Before she could grab her hand, Lyla snatched a package of candy and darted away.

Kate lunged for her but missed.

Lyla disappeared around the end of the aisle with Kate chasing after her.

"Lyla!" Kate called out. "Chuck!" She needed help. One three-year-old couldn't be so fast she could get away that quickly, but she had.

Kate cleared the end of the aisles but didn't see Lyla anywhere.

Chuck burst from a couple aisles over. "What's wrong?"

"Lyla got away from me." Kate didn't wait for him to catch up to her. She swung right and ran past the next aisle. Lyla wasn't in that one either.

Kate kept going. When she rounded the end of the one, she spotted a flash of blond hair.

Kate ran to where Lyla stood in front of another little girl and her parents. "Lyla, sweetie, you scared me."

"I found a friend." Lyla pointed to the other little girl who was a little older and a foot taller.

"We wondered where her parents were," the mother said. "Hi, I'm Becca, this is my husband Daniel and my daughter Mary." She held out her hand. "We're new in town."

Kate let go of the breath she'd been holding since Lyla ran off. "Thank goodness she didn't get far." Kate took the hand the woman extended and shook. "Thank you for being here to stop her. I'm Kate and this is Chuck, my…husband and my…daughter, Lyla."

"You have no idea how glad I am to meet someone else with a child," Becca said. "I was afraid Mary would get lonely here. I haven't seen a whole lot of children."

"Me either," Kate admitted. "Please, don't let us keep

you. I don't know what got into Lyla to make her run off like that."

"Three can be a difficult age." Becca smiled down at Lyla. "Some children like to think they're independent. They can be stubborn or unruly. Sometimes it just takes a firm hand and structure to guide them," Becca said. "Mary's terrible twos lasted until she was almost four."

Kate's eyes narrowed. "I don't remember telling you my daughter was three."

Becca's eyebrows rose. "No? Well, I guessed based on her size and vocabulary."

The woman's explanation wasn't great, but it was plausible. Kate turned to Becca's child. "How old are you, Mary?"

At first the little girl didn't answer.

Becca gave her a nudge. "Tell Miss Kate how old you are."

The little girl had dark braids and big, brown eyes. She turned those eyes up to Kate and held up her hand with all her fingers extended. "I'm five."

"Nice to meet you, Mary," Kate said. "We hope to see you around town." She glanced back at Chuck.

He moved forward and extended his hand to Becca. "Nice to meet you." Then he held out his hand to Daniel. The two men shook hands and exchanged nods.

"If you'll excuse us, we need to get going," Chuck said. He lifted Lyla into his arms, removed the package of candy from her fingers and stared into her face. "No candy," he said firmly. "You can have a banana when we get back to the house."

Lyla puckered up as if to start crying. "But, I want—"

Chuck shook his head once. "No."

Lyla sniffed, her eyes wide, but she didn't argue. Instead, she laid her head on Chuck's shoulder and wrapped her arm around his neck.

"It was nice to meet you," Kate repeated to Becca. And she hurried off to find her cart and Chuck's. A few minutes later, they'd purchased their groceries and loaded them into the truck along with a car seat they were lucky enough to find for Lyla. When Chuck buckled her in this time, Kate felt a lot better about the child's safety.

Once they were all settled into the truck, Kate leaned back against the seat and let go of a long breath. "I never knew how hard it was to raise a child. I think I lost a year off my life with the scare she gave me."

A chuckle rumbled beside her. "You'll get used to it. Most children come as infants. That gives you the time you need to adjust as they grow."

Kate turned to Chuck. "Why are you so good with Lyla?" Then a thought occurred to her and her face heated. "Oh my God. You're married, aren't you? And you must have children of your own." Holy crud, she'd been lusting after a married man.

Chuck's jaw tightened, and he got that same look he'd had when Lyla had named her doll Sarah. He looked as if he was in pain.

Kate held up her hand. "I'm sorry. It's none of my business. Forget I said anything. This is all just a job. You don't owe me any information about you and your life outside the Brotherhood Protectors."

A minute passed, stretching into two as he navigated

the streets of Eagle Rock. He didn't say anything, and Kate had decided to forget she'd asked.

It wasn't until they'd carried all the groceries into the house and closed the door behind them that Chuck spoke. "I'm not married," he said.

A rush of relief washed over her, making her lips curl upward. She stopped short of saying *Thank God.*

"I was married many years ago. And I had a daughter."

He'd *had* a daughter. Kate shot a quick glance his way. His gray eyes seemed darker, and his lips pressed tightly together. "Had?" she asked, and then wished she hadn't.

The raw pain in his gaze nearly took her breath away.

"My wife and daughter were killed in an automobile accident when our little girl was only two."

Kate's heart dropped to the pit of her belly. "I'm so sorry," she said, a sob choking her words.

"Don't worry about it. That was a long time ago."

"Maybe so, but I can't imagine anyone really gets over something like that." She touched his arm. "Was your daughter's name Sarah?"

He nodded.

Kate closed her eyes to the man's agony. "Is that why you didn't want to work with us?" She knew the answer before he responded.

"Yes."

She tipped her head and frowned. "Wow. Then why did you agree to help?"

He nodded toward Lyla who'd curled up on the

floral couch with her doll named Sarah and had fallen asleep. "Because of her. I knew Hank didn't have anyone else experienced at working with children." He gave a twisted smile. "I couldn't walk away. She needed me to help look after her."

The man was breaking Kate's heart. "You must have loved your family so very much."

He nodded. "At the time, I had wished I could have died with them," he admitted. "But they were in Virginia. I was in Afghanistan on a mission. I didn't know until two days after they'd died. I flew back in time to attend the funeral."

Kate could imagine his heartache at seeing his wife and little girl lying in eternal repose in caskets. Her own heart ached for him.

"How long ago did it happen?" she asked so softly he could ignore the question if he wanted.

"Fourteen years, two months and…six days."

"And you haven't remarried," she stated.

"I couldn't. As a Navy SEAL, I couldn't do it again. I wasn't there for my wife and baby. I refused to subject another woman to that kind of responsibility and loneliness."

"Or yourself to more heartbreak," Kate concluded.

Chuck drew in a deep breath. "Now, if you'll excuse me, I have work to do to make this place a little more secure."

She stepped back. "Thank you." Kate didn't say more.

By the tightness of his jaw, Chuck had withdrawn, choosing to handle his grief in stoic silence.

He deserved to be left to his own personal space.

Kate fought the urge to wrap her arms around the big man and hold on tightly until all his pain went away. But that would be silly, and the gesture would be unwanted. They'd only just met. A big, tough guy like Chuck wouldn't appreciate sympathy or empathy. A former SEAL probably powered through everything life had to throw at him.

From her own experience, it could be lonely shouldering through life by yourself. Now that she had Lyla, Kate realized not only the level of responsibility, but also the capacity for love.

Her gaze shifted from Lyla's sleeping form to follow Chuck.

The man knew how to wear a pair of jeans. They hugged his hips like a second skin and pulled tightly across powerful thighs. His T-shirt stretched across impossibly broad shoulders, straining against thick biceps.

Rather than make him appear old, the gray hair at his temples made him look dangerously sexy.

Kate worked through the house, finding places for the groceries and cleaning supplies they'd purchased. Then she went to work making the two beds with the sheets and pillows and pillowcases Sadie had sent in the boxes. She placed towels in a neat stack in the bathroom and marveled about how the few things they'd added to the cozy cottage made it feel even more personal, like a home.

Her gaze wandered often to Chuck as he installed new deadbolt locks to the front and back doors. Making the beds with Chuck in the room working on the window latches was more exhilarating than Kate would have thought. Her heart beat fast, and her breathing became so erratic, she felt as if she'd run a marathon by the time he left the room.

If he wasn't the hired help, and she wasn't so worried about her sister, Kate might consider asking Chuck out for a drink. Maybe dinner and a nightcap.

She smoothed the sheets over the queen-sized bed and imagined what might come after the nightcap.

Kate shook her head and squared her shoulders. Her sister was missing, she had a niece to protect, and Chuck wasn't on the market for anyone. Kate had to get a grip or risk a little frustration and possible heartache of her own.

She carried her suitcase into the bedroom and pulled out a T-shirt. She might as well get comfortable and do some cleaning. Maybe it would help get her mind off the sexy Navy SEAL.

CHUCK HADN'T TALKED about his family with anyone for a very long time, preferring not to reopen the wound. But talking about his wife and Sarah with Kate hadn't been as bad as he would've thought. Opening up had been more cathartic than painful. Perhaps the time lapse had helped to numb his response from a sharp pain to a dull ache. Either way, it felt good to get things off his chest with someone who wouldn't judge him for hiding out the past fourteen years.

Feeling a little lighter and more optimistic, he

worked his way around the interior of the house, tightening the locks on the windows, replacing the ones that were missing, damaged or broken. The deadbolts took a little longer, but he installed them, and then went outside to look over the exterior of the house.

The day had warmed with bright sunshine, making him sweat.

The cottage appeared to be structurally sound with some areas of weathering that needed repair. Depending on how long they were there, he could knock out the repairs with a little manual labor, lumber, nails and paint.

As he passed the master bedroom, he could see Kate moving around inside, placing clothing from her suitcase into the dresser.

The woman was graceful, even when no one was watching. Every move flowed like a dance.

Chuck knew he should look away, but he was captivated by the sway of her hips and the way her hair fell over her shoulders and down her back.

She shook out a T-shirt and laid it on the bed. Then she unbuttoned her blouse and let it slide over her shoulders.

At that point, Chuck should have turned away. But he couldn't. He remained riveted to the window.

He was captivated by the smooth symmetry of Kate's back, the sleekness of her skin and the way her hair brushed across her shoulder blades and halfway down to her waistline.

Heat pulsed through his veins and coiled in his groin.

When she lifted the T-shirt over her head, she turned slightly, exposing the swell of her breast encased in a lacy, black bra.

A groan rose up Chuck's throat. He swallowed hard to keep from emitting it.

All he needed was to be caught behaving like a peeping Tom. He could lose his job. And worse…he would lose Kate's trust.

Though he desperately wanted to continue watching the woman, he turned away, walked to the covered patio and pulled out his cellphone.

Surprised to have any kind of reception in such a small town, he dialed Hank's number.

"Chuck. Tell me what's going on." Hank never bothered with greetings. He always got right down to business.

"Have you found anything on Kate's sister, Rachel?"

"I have Swede working on it now. He was able to hack into her phone records, but none of them led to Kate's phone number."

"Do you think she used a burner phone to contact her sister?" Chuck asked.

"That's exactly what she did. We traced the phone number she used when she called Kate the night she dropped off Lyla. From what we could tell, it was purchased in Idaho a couple days ago. No credit card records, so she probably used cash."

"Trying to hide her trail," Chuck mused. "What about her home? Have you hacked into her home phone or computer?"

"We haven't located a home phone or computer IP

address." Hank continued, "We looked up the town where she supposedly lived in Idaho with her husband. It appears to be a sleepy little community in the mountains."

Chuck stiffened at the tone of Hank's voice. "You don't think it was sleepy, do you?"

"Swede found some news articles about the town. Apparently, a survivalist cult set up a compound just outside the town limits. They've stirred up the residents on a number of occasions with their religious practices and suspected abuse of their children and women."

Chuck's hand tightened around his cellphone. "Great. Have you said anything to Kate?"

"No. We're still verifying sources. Kujo and Six are between assignments. I'm sending them up there to do some snooping around."

"Good." Chuck glanced through the picture window into the living room where Lyla lay on the couch, still sleeping. "If Rachel was part of this cult, they might have returned her to the fold."

"That's what we're counting on. Kujo will go in as a hiker on vacation. With his dog Six along, it'll be more believable. They will have a good reason to be out mucking around in the mountains."

"Great. As soon as you know anything—"

"You'll be the first to get the call," Hank finished. "Other than that, everything okay at the cottage?"

"It is. The girls are settling in." Chuck smiled at Lyla sleeping on the couch. Kate entered the living room wearing the T-shirt she'd put on. And she'd pulled her long, blond hair back into a ponytail, giving her the appearance of a much younger woman.

"Let me know if you need help."

"Roger."

Hank ended the call.

Chuck slipped his cellphone into his pocket before entering the house through the back door.

Kate had entered the kitchen and set a bucket on the counter. "The place appears clean, but I'm going to do a little surface cleaning." She shrugged. "It makes me feel better to have something to do."

"Stick to the inside of the house. I'm going to jump in the shower." He nodded toward Lyla. "She should sleep for a little longer."

"We'll be fine. I'll leave the doors locked."

"Good." Chuck checked the front deadbolt once more, collected his duffel bag and strode down the hallway to the bathroom. He wouldn't take any longer than was necessary. Though the town looked sleepy and the people were friendly, he didn't know anyone well enough to trust except for the men of the Brotherhood Protectors. They were cut from the same cloth—loyal, honorable, and they had his back. Anyone else was all bets off.

CHAPTER 6

Kate cleaned the kitchen counter, stove, sink and walls. Then she went to work mopping floors and dusting the furniture. Her hand in mid-swipe with a dust rag, she paused at a noise coming from the front door.

Someone knocked. Not a heavy rap but a light tap. No wonder she had barely heard it the first time.

She rose from her kneeling position by the coffee table and walked toward the front of the house, remembering Chuck's orders to leave the door locked.

Kate pulled the living room curtain to the side, hoping to see whoever it was standing at the front door.

A gray-haired little woman stood on the porch, balancing a plate stacked with sandwiches in one hand while she knocked with the other.

After a quick glance around the porch, the front walkway and the road beyond, Kate determined the woman was alone and harmless.

She hurried to answer the door.

"Oh, thank goodness," the diminutive woman sighed. "I almost dropped this plate twice, knocking." She grinned at Kate. "I'm Louise Turner. I live in the house next door. Welcome to the neighborhood." She held out the plate of sandwiches. "I would have baked a casserole, but since I just got home from a doctor's appointment, this was the quickest thing I could make in time for lunch." She shoved the plate into Kate's hands.

"Oh, thank you." Kate took the plate and smiled at the array of diagonally-cut sandwiches. "My, that's a lot of sandwiches."

"What you don't eat, you can bag and put in the refrigerator for a late-night snack. I used to make sandwiches for my husband at lunch for just that purpose. It kept me from having to get up and make them in the middle of the night when he had a hankering for a snack."

"This is a very nice treat. I was just wondering what to do for lunch." Kate noted the woman's gray hair and bright, blue eyes.

"Well, now you have it."

"Won't you join us?" Kate asked.

Mrs. Turner shook her head. "No, thank you. I know you've got a lot to do, having moved in today. I'll leave you to it. But I wanted to invite you to dinner tonight. I'm having a few people over and thought it would be nice to introduce you and your husband."

Lyla sat up on the couch and rubbed her eyes.

Mrs. Turner smiled. "Oh, and you have children as well as a dog?"

"No dog, just one child," Kate corrected. "I'm not sure what my…husband had in mind for dinner."

"Well, the offer is open. If you can make it, you're more than welcome. There won't be more than three others coming. I'd better get going. I have to water my flowers and put a roast in the crockpot." She waved at Lyla. "Hope to see you there." And Mrs. Turner was gone.

Kate was turning the lock on the front door when Chuck strode down the hallway, bare-chested and rubbing his head with a towel. And he was scowling. "Did you open the door?"

Kate held up the tray of sandwiches. "Our neighbor brought lunch and invited us to dinner."

"You shouldn't have opened the door," he said and pushed past her to check the locks and look out the window at Mrs. Turner's retreating figure.

Kate lowered her voice. "It was a little old lady, not the guy who broke into my apartment."

"You don't know if she was a setup. Did you actually *see* who broke into your apartment?"

"Well…no, but—"

"You can't be too careful. If they set her up as a decoy, they could have pushed past her as soon as you opened the door."

Kate sighed. "We don't even know if they've found us here."

"Exactly. They could have followed you here. They might know where you are and are waiting for the right time."

Lyla toddled over to where the adults were standing. "I'm hungry."

Kate stared down at the plate of sandwiches in her hand. "Do we eat them or not?"

Chuck checked out the window again.

Mrs. Turner had made it to her house and bent to pull weeds in her yard.

"She doesn't look like someone playing the part of a decoy," Kate said. But she couldn't discount the fact that Chuck was the expert bodyguard. He had experience as a witness protector.

"Let me have a bite off each one. If it doesn't kill me, you should be all right. And if I die, call Hank for a replacement bodyguard."

Kate frowned. "Are you sure?" She didn't like the idea of Chuck being the taste tester for poisoned sandwiches.

He grimaced. "You're probably right. The old lady appears to be who she says she is."

Mrs. Turner pulled a garden hose out to water the flowers in the window boxes, unaware of the people watching her.

"She invited us to dinner tonight. Should I have told her no?" Kate asked.

"If we go, we go together."

"She invited three other locals to the gathering," Kate added.

"We'll watch and see who shows up. We can decide then."

"Fair enough." Kate carried the sandwiches into the kitchen and cut a corner off all of them. She laid the corners on a plate for Chuck. "Better test these fast. Our little miss is eyeing the rest of them."

Lyla stood beside Kate, watching every move.

"Can I have little sandwiches, too?" she asked.

"After Daddy eats," Kate said.

"Are you going to eat now, Daddy?" Lyla asked. She licked her lips, staring at the plate of sandwich corners.

"Yes, ma'am." He grinned down at her. "Why don't you wash up while I see if these are as good as they look?"

"Okay," she said and ran off to the bathroom to wash her hands.

"I'll go help her. I think the sink is a little high for her to reach."

"I'll build her a step to stand on," he said and took a bite of one of the corners Kate had cut from the sandwiches.

Kate froze, her gaze on his face, watching, praying he didn't fall over dead after having been poisoned by an old woman.

"Hmmm," he tilted his head and tugged at his collar. Then he coughed and opened his eyes wide.

Kate's heart raced. "What? Are you all right? Was it poisoned?"

Chuck swallowed and laughed. "I'm sorry, I shouldn't tease you. But you looked so concerned, I couldn't help it."

"You're awful!" Kate grabbed his arm and shook it. "Don't do that. I think I lost a year off my life."

His smile faded. "I'm sorry. That was mean of me.

But the good news is, the sandwiches aren't killing me. Mrs. Turner is probably just who she said she was."

Kate drew in a shaky breath. "Still, I'm not sure I want to feed Lyla any of the sandwiches for another hour or so."

"Just to make sure it's not a slow-acting poison?" He chuckled. "Glad to know you care."

With a snort, Kate turned toward the bathroom. "It would serve you right if you dropped dead, choking on a sandwich."

His laughter followed her all the way to the bathroom, the sound warming her insides more than she cared to admit.

The man was entirely too attractive and had a wicked sense of humor. In her mind, that was a killer combination, and she wasn't sure she could resist it for long.

Chuck made fresh sandwiches for Lyla and Kate, while they were busy in the bathroom. By the time they emerged, he'd set the table with plates, glasses of ice and napkins.

"Have a seat, ladies," he said. He held the chair for Lyla and helped her into it. "Would you like water or juice?"

"Juice," Lyla said.

"Water for me." Kate took her seat, her gaze on the plate of sandwiches. "Are those different than the ones Mrs. Turner brought?"

"Yes, ma'am. I didn't want you to worry, so I made

them specially for my girls." He winked at Lyla and placed Mrs. Turner's sandwiches in front of his plate. "I'll take care of these."

Kate helped herself and Lyla to the ones Chuck had prepared while he poured juice into Lyla's cup and filled Kate's with tap water.

Then they sat at the table like a family.

Chuck took one of Mrs. Turner's sandwiches and let the image of Kate and Lyla sink in.

God, he missed having a family. Why hadn't he moved on? He felt as if he'd been in a holding pattern for so long, he didn't know how to land.

For the next twenty minutes, he pretended to be a father to Lyla and a husband to Kate.

And it felt good.

At the end of the meal, he helped Kate clean the table and wash the dishes by hand. The cozy cottage was mid-last-century-dated. No dishwasher existed in the small kitchen.

Chuck insisted on washing. Kate and Lyla dried the dishes and put them in the cabinet.

Thankfully, Sadie had included four place settings of dishes and flatware. They wouldn't have to resort to paper plates and plastic forks to eat, unless they wanted to.

That afternoon, they worked on organizing their few belongings and the toys Sadie had sent.

Kate opted for a long soak in the clawfoot tub while Chuck kept an eye on Lyla. All the while Kate was in the bathroom, Chuck couldn't help but imagine her naked body lying in a scented bath.

Chuck had to get a grip on his attraction to his client or risk jeopardizing the mission. He needed to focus on keeping Kate and Lyla safe.

The sun was setting when Kate emerged from the bedroom wearing a simple, white dress that hugged her torso and flared out around her legs. The fabric lay softly against her and swayed when she moved.

Chuck had helped Lyla into one of the pretty dresses Sadie had given her and pulled her blond hair up into a single ponytail, twisting the strands into a smooth braid.

Kate smiled and shook her head. "You are good at being a daddy."

"She's a good kid and stayed really still while I brushed her hair."

"He doesn't hurt me when I have tangles," Lyla said. She smiled up at Kate. "You're pretty, Mama."

Kate's cheeks blushed a rosy pink as she curtsied in front of her niece. "Thank you. And so are you."

"Isn't Daddy pretty?" Lyla slipped her hand into Chuck's.

"Yes, Lyla. Daddy's pretty, too."

Chuck frowned, though his lips twitched on the corners. "Handsome. Boys aren't pretty."

Lyla tipped her head to one side and looked up at Chuck. "Why?"

Kate didn't help. She raised her brows and crossed her arms over her chest. "Seriously. Why?"

Chuck tugged at the button-up shirt he'd changed into for the dinner at Mrs. Turner's. "Never mind. We'll be late for dinner if we don't leave now."

"How do you know?" Kate asked, but she dropped her arms to her sides and draped a sweater over her arm. "I don't recall Mrs. Turner setting a time."

"I saw an older couple and a woman enter her house a few minutes ago. I assume those are the guests she spoke of."

"Probably." Kate said. "I'm ready."

Together, they walked next door to Mrs. Turner's house.

She met them at the door, smiling broadly. "I'm so glad you decided to come. Please, come in and meet my friends."

When Kate stepped inside and Chuck followed, Mrs. Turner stared at him and frowned. "Oh."

Chuck's brows furrowed. "Is something wrong?"

She shook her head, the frown still firmly set. "I don't think so. It's just you aren't who I expected."

Kate tilted her head. "What do you mean?"

"You're not the man I saw walking the dog earlier. I thought that man was your husband."

"I'm sorry," Kate said. "What man?"

"There was a man walking a dog on our road earlier today. He was shorter, not as big." Mrs. Turner held her hands out demonstrating how broad the other man's shoulders were. "And he was bald." She pointed to Chuck's head. "You have a full head of hair. I know I wasn't seeing things."

"Whoever it was, wasn't my husband," Kate said. "Is it unusual for someone to walk his dog on this road?"

Mrs. Turner shrugged. "Not unusual, just unusual to

have new people move in next door and a stranger walk down the road on the same day."

One of the older women smiled. "We're a small town. Not much changes."

Her husband cupped her elbow and laughed. "But when it does…we notice." He held out his hand. "Hugh Landry."

Kate gripped his hand. "Kate—"

"Johnson," Chuck cut in. "Kate, Lyla and Chuck Johnson."

Mr. Landry shook Chuck's hand next. "This is my wife Greta and our friend, Wanda Wilcox."

The introductions over, Mrs. Turner led the way into the dining room. The aroma of roast beef and onions filled the air and made Chuck's mouth water.

"Please have a seat," Mrs. Turner said.

Chuck helped Lyla into one of the chairs, and then held another for Kate. He helped Mrs. Turner with her chair, and then sat on the other side of Lyla, figuring they could better meet her needs if they worked as a team.

Kate settled Lyla's napkin in her lap and one in her own.

"You're just in time," Mrs. Turner said. "We were about to sit down for dinner."

"Would you carve?" Mrs. Turner passed the carving knife to Chuck, and soon, they were passing plates and platters of food around until everyone had been served.

The conversation was lively, the older guests filling them in on the gossip about other members of the community.

Chuck didn't recognize any of the names, but he listened in case he heard something that might concern him, Kate or Lyla.

"Your dog-walking man might be one of the men here working the pipeline construction," Wanda said. "Rita's Bed & Breakfast has been booked solid for the past couple of weeks. I expect they'll be moving on, once they complete the section they're working north of town."

"The Blue Moose Tavern has been pretty busy lately with them and some people getting a jump on the tourist season. We already have hikers up in the Crazy Mountains. The forestry service had to rescue some just yesterday."

"Wow," Kate's fork paused halfway to her mouth. "Was someone lost?"

"No, but a hiker got crossways with a mama bear. The bear won, and the hiker had to be air-lifted out."

"Wow. I hadn't thought about bears." Kate's gaze met Chuck's over Lyla's head.

"Don't worry, we haven't had a bear in Eagle Rock in over ten years."

"Only ten years?" Kate gulped.

"We emphasize bear awareness," Mrs. Turner said. "Don't leave your trash out in bags. Use bear-proof trash cans. Don't leave your pets out at night. Not so much because of the bears but because of the wolves and coyotes."

"I lost my malti-poo, Sweetpea, because she wandered out of the yard one evening. I think a coyote got her." Wanda sniffed. "I miss that little dog."

Greta patted her friend's hand. "We all miss Sweetpea. She was a good, little dog."

"Goes the same for children," Hugh said. "Don't leave them unattended outside."

Chuck had no intention of leaving Lyla unattended. Not only because of the wild animals, but because of the threat from whoever was after Kate's sister.

"I suppose the man with the dog could be one of the pipeline workers. I won't worry about him." Mrs. Turner smiled at Kate and Chuck. "We look out for each other here. Being on the edge of town, no one would think much of us. JoJo Earles was the previous owner of the cottage you're living in. She was a lovely woman and a good friend. We miss her dearly, don't we?" Mrs. Turner's gaze swept over her older friends, who nodded their agreement.

"Did she pass away?" Kate asked.

Mrs. Turner laughed. "Oh, dear. No, she didn't. Her children moved her to Florida. They were afraid she'd slip on the ice in the wintertime and no one would find her until she'd frozen to death."

Kate's eyes rounded. "That would be awful."

Mrs. Turner nodded. "That's why we look out for each other."

"Now that JoJo's gone, will you be moving south to live with your daughter in Alabama?" Wanda asked.

"No way," Mrs. Turner shook her head. "I like my independence. I don't plan on losing that until I can't take care of myself."

"Well, I must say I feel a lot better now that you have

good neighbors living next door," Hugh said. "Someone looking out for you."

Kate cast a glance toward Chuck, her jaw tight, her eyes sad.

"We'll do what we can," Chuck said. "After all, what are neighbors for?" He nearly choked on the words he figured they would expect out of him. What he didn't add was the disclaimer of *while we're here.*

The dinner was tasty, the company warm and inviting. But by the time it was over, Chuck was ready to leave and so was Lyla.

"I'm sleepy." She yawned and stretched. "Can we go home now?"

Kate gave Mrs. Turner an apologetic smile. "I'm sorry. She's had a big day with us moving in."

"Oh, please. Don't you worry about it. I had three children of my own. You're on their schedule while they're little."

Wanda chuckled. "And well into their twenties."

"So true," Hugh agreed.

Greta sighed. "I miss my boys."

"I'll be glad when they return to the states," Hugh said. "We'll meet them in Virginia when they come home."

"Where are they?" Chuck asked.

"They're in the Navy. They're deployed now to the Horn of Africa."

Chuck perked up. "I'd love to hear more, but we need to get Lyla to bed. Perhaps next time?"

"Oh, you won't get Hugh to quit talking about David

and Michael," Greta said. "He's so proud of their accomplishments. They're Navy SEALs."

Chuck's chest swelled, but he didn't tell them that he had once been a Navy SEAL on active duty. They didn't need to know that. No one needed to know. As far as he was concerned, he was Kate's husband and Lyla's father. The less Lyla's attackers knew, the better. And the only way to keep that information from them was to keep as much to himself as possible.

He lifted Lyla into his arms and carried her toward the door.

Kate caught up and slipped her arm through his empty one. They walked away from Mrs. Turner's little white, clapboard house and into their yellow cottage, a family for all to see.

Once inside the house, Kate took Lyla and carried her into the bedroom with the twin bed and helped her change into her pajamas.

Chuck went around the house one more time, checking all the windows and doors. He regretted that there were so many windows. If someone wanted in badly enough, all he had to do was break one window.

Chuck could hear Kate's voice as she read a story from one of the books Sadie had packed in a box.

He stood outside Lyla's room, listening to the clear, sweet sound of her voice and wishing she was talking to him in the shadows as they lay in bed. He would hold her in his arms, close his eyes and just bask in the smooth silkiness of her tone.

Kate tiptoed backward out of Lyla's room, pulling the door halfway closed. When she turned toward

Chuck, she started, her hand flying to her mouth. "Oh. I didn't see you there."

"I'm sorry I scared you."

Her hand dropped to her chest. "No. I'm okay." She looked back through the door. "Poor thing was so tired, she didn't make it through the entire book."

"She's had a tough twenty-four hours. A lot of changes."

Kate nodded, her gaze rising to Chuck's. "She's holding it together much better than I am." Her eyes filled with tears. "I wish I knew my sister was safe."

Without letting himself think, Chuck pulled her into his arms and held her.

Kate laid her cheek against his chest and let the tears fall. "I should be braver," she said and sniffed. "Lyla needs me to be strong."

"You don't have to be strong all the time," he said, stroking his hand over her soft hair. "That's why you have me."

"Thank you for being here," she said, her fingers curling into his shirt. "I don't think I could do this without your help."

"It's what I do. It's my job," he said, as much to reassure her as to remind himself he could not fall for this woman. She was a client. Nothing more.

Then why was his heart beating so fast? And why was he still holding her in his arms?

CHAPTER 7

Kate would have stayed in Chuck's arms for as long as he would let her, but Lyla made a noise that brought her back to reality.

"I'd better check on her," Kate said and slipped from Chuck's arms. Back in Lyla's room, Kate called herself all kinds of a fool for taking advantage of Chuck. The man was only holding her to make her feel safer. He wasn't making any other kind of move on her, nor did she expect him to.

He was a man of honor and wouldn't take advantage of the situation to slake his own desires.

Heat coiled low in her belly. Oh, but she wished he would take advantage of her. Her desire was strong and getting stronger.

Lyla twisted in the sheets, trying to kick them off.

When Kate pulled the blankets back up over her, the little girl squirmed and moaned.

Was she having a nightmare?

In the faint glow spilling in through the half-opened door, Lyla's cheeks glowed a ruddy red.

Kate touched her forehead and felt the heat. Lyla was burning up.

"Chuck," she called out.

He was there in a heartbeat, looking over her shoulder at the small child lying against the white sheets, her face coated in a sheen of sweat.

"She's feverish," Kate said. "What do we do?"

He touched his palm to her forehead, his eyebrows drawing together. "A cool compress will help." Without another word, he hurried to the bathroom across the hall and returned a minute later with a cool, damp washcloth.

Gently, he laid the cloth across Lyla's forehead.

"Was there a thermometer in any of those boxes Sadie sent?" Chuck asked.

"I don't know," Kate said, her gaze on Lyla. "Wait. She sent a first aid kit. Maybe there's one in it." Kate rose from beside the bed and ran into the kitchen. Where had she put that little, red box? She'd been so caught up in watching Chuck fix the doors and windows earlier that day, she hadn't paid much attention to where she was putting things.

After searching three kitchen drawers, she finally found the first aid kit in a deep drawer next to the sink. Inside the kit was a thermometer. She grabbed it and ran back into Lyla's room.

"Here it is." She held it out to Chuck, who took it and rolled Lyla onto her back.

"How are you going to get her to hold it under her tongue?" Kate asked.

Chuck shook his head. "I'm not."

He pulled Lyla's pajama top up and placed the thermometer under her arm. He waited a solid minute before he removed the thermometer and pulled Lyla's shirt back in place before staring down at the number in the display.

"One hundred degrees," Chuck said. "It's not good, but it could be worse."

"What should we do?" Kate asked. "I don't recall seeing a hospital in town."

"There isn't one," Chuck confirmed.

Kate paced the length of the room, her head down, her lips pressed tight. She stopped in front of Chuck. "Do we need to take her to the ER in Bozeman?"

"I think we need to see where it goes. If she gets worse, then yes, we take her to another town where they have an emergency room." Chuck lifted the damp cloth, fanned it to cool it off, and then laid it back on Lyla's forehead. "In the meantime, I'll stay up with her. You should get some sleep. We don't know what tomorrow will bring. You need to be physically prepared for anything."

When Kate didn't move, Chuck gripped her arms. "Go to bed."

"But I can't leave Lyla while she's sick." Kate shook loose of Chuck's grip and slipped around him to enter Lyla's room.

Her niece lay like a miniature ghost, her face red and her entire body flushed with heat.

"Will she be okay?" Kate's words caught in her throat on a sob. The one job she had to do was to keep Lyla safe. How could she keep her safe if she was so sick?

"We should take her to the hospital in Bozeman," Kate insisted.

"The doctors don't start worrying until a child's temperature spikes to over one hundred and three. Lyla's not there yet."

"But should we wait that long?" Kate smoothed her hand over Lyla's angel-soft hair. "I don't want anything bad to happen to my niece. Rachel trusted me to do the right thing." Kate snorted. "She should have known I don't have a clue about what the right thing is regarding small children."

"Like I said, the doctors aren't much concerned until the fever spikes to over one hundred and three."

"Then I'm staying with her all night."

"That won't be necessary. I'll stay with her," Chuck said. "I consider it my duty and responsibility."

"As her aunt, it's my duty and responsibility," Kate insisted, lifting her chin. "I should be with her."

"Rather than argue over a sick little girl, how about we take turns?" He raised his brow. "I'll take the first shift until one in the morning."

"And you'll wake me when it's my turn?" She stared at him through narrowed eyes. "You won't try to be all tough-guy on me, will you?"

"What do you mean?"

She lifted her chin. "You won't just say you'll wake me but actually leave me to sleep all night?"

Chuck laughed and raised his hand. "Scout's honor,"

he said.

Kate's frown deepened. "Something tells me you were never a scout."

"You have my word," Chuck said. "I'll wake you."

"Okay, then." She leaned over Lyla and kissed her forehead. "I hope you feel better soon, sweetie. I love you." Then she straightened and pointed a finger at Chuck's chest. "Wake me for anything."

Chuck smiled. "Yes, ma'am."

If Lyla wasn't feverish and Kate wasn't worried, she might have melted into the floor. Chuck had charm all wrapped up in that smile.

Kate glanced once more at Lyla, reluctant to leave the child's room. Could a three-year-old die from a fever? Her heart squeezed hard in her chest. Rachel would be devastated. Hell, Kate would be devastated. Lyla was growing on her, as well as the idea of having a child in her life. Her career seemed so secondary to the responsibility of a little girl's life.

Kate hurried to the bedroom, changed into her nightgown and lay down on the bed. For the next thirty minutes, she stared at the ceiling, imagining every scenario that could happen. The more she lay there, the more worried she became. Sounds made her jump, thinking it might be Lyla calling for her or Chuck asking for help.

When she couldn't take another minute, she grabbed the comforter from the bed and padded barefooted down the hall and peeked in on Lyla.

Chuck had moved a rocking chair into the room and set it beside Lyla's bed. He sat still and held Lyla's hand with one of his and brushed the hair from her fevered brow with the other.

Not wanting to disturb them, Kate quietly laid the comforter on the floor and curled up inside it. If she was needed, she'd be there. If anything changed, she'd know immediately.

Exhausted from her mad escape from LA and her subsequent journey to Montana, Kate fell into a deep sleep.

In the middle of the night, her sleep became troubled with dreams about men in black ski masks, breaking into the little cottage to steal Lyla away.

She tried to tell them Lyla was sick. If they took her she could die. But they didn't care. They grabbed Lyla from her bed and ran.

Kate cried out, horrified and heartbroken, but unable to go after them. Her feet felt mired in quicksand. When she looked down, she couldn't see her shoes. They had sunk into the floor of her executive office, and she was being sucked into the carpet, inch by inch. "Lyla!" she called out.

Lyla couldn't help her. She was only a small child.

"Chuck!" she called out, her cries turning to sobs.

Warm arms wrapped around her and held her against a solid wall of muscles.

"Shh, darlin'," a deep, resonant voice whispered in her ear. "Everything is going to be all right."

"But Lyla…" she said without opening her eyes.

"Is asleep in her bed. The fever broke, and she's sleeping soundly."

Kate pressed her face into her rescuer's chest and let the tears flow until there were none left to fall.

Warm lips pressed against her forehead. "You're going to be okay," he promised.

"How do you know?" she whispered, unwilling to wake up from the dream. The arms around her felt so real and comforting. She wanted to stay there forever.

"I know, because I'll make it happen. Lyla's going to be fine. Just sleep."

"Mmm." She rested her hand on his chest and curled her fingers into his shirt.

Strong arms lifted her from the floor, comforter and all.

At that point, Kate realized she was no longer sleeping and Chuck was her rescuer. Still, she refused to open her eyes, preferring to bask in the reality of being in his arms.

When he laid Kate on her bed and started to straighten, she finally opened her eyes and stared up into his. "Are you sure Lyla's okay?"

He nodded and swept the hair out of her face, tucking it behind her ear. "Her temperature is back to normal. She's sleeping peacefully."

Then he did something she never expected.

He bent and brushed his lips across hers.

Kate froze, her eyes widening.

"Sorry," he said. "I just can't…" And he kissed her again.

Kate raised her hand to his chest. Not to push him away, but to clutch his shirt and bring him back to her mouth. She tipped her head and kissed him back.

He wrapped his hand around the back of her head and held her to him as his lips pressed against hers and his tongue traced the seam of her mouth.

She opened on an exhilarated gasp, allowing him to sweep in and own her tongue.

He caressed, teased and stroked her, tasting of mint and the tea he'd had at dinner.

Kate couldn't get enough of him. She clung to Chuck, holding him close, reluctant to let go.

And he seemed in no hurry to release her.

He sat on the edge of the bed and gathered her closer, pulling her across his lap, deepening the kiss. His hands slipped down her back and up her sides, his thumbs brushing below her breasts.

A moan rose up her throat and escaped. God, she wanted more from this man than just a kiss.

When he at last raised his head, she stared up at him in wonder. What had just happened seemed almost a part of a dream. Not the nightmare he'd rescued her from, but a sweet, lusty dream she wanted to go back to.

"We shouldn't have done that," he said.

"No, we shouldn't have." But she was glad they had. And she wanted to kiss him all over again. Her body physically ached for him.

Chuck straightened. "I'll sleep on the couch."

"You don't have to, you know." Kate wished he would take her up on her hint and stay with her in the bed.

He stood tall and straight, his jaw tight, his hands curled into fists as if he struggled with something difficult. "You tempt me," he said, his voice deep and sexy.

"But I can't." He shook his head and performed an about-face. "I'll check on Lyla on my way to the couch."

"Chuck?"

He turned back.

"I know we shouldn't have...but I'm glad we did."

CHUCK STARED at Kate for a moment longer, drinking in her beauty and the swell of her very-kissed lips. Then he turned and walked away.

A thousand thoughts rippled through his mind at once. Images of his wife the last time he saw her flashed through his memory. She'd stood with Sarah, seeing him off as he boarded the bus that would take his team to catch the plane to Afghanistan.

She'd smiled, though her eyes shone with unshed tears.

Sarah had waved goodbye, and then held up her arms for Anne to carry her.

As the bus pulled away, Chuck watched them as long as he could, knowing it would be months before he saw them again. He hadn't dreamed it would be the last time he saw his wife and child.

Now, after kissing Kate, he could see the potential for pain and heartache happening again. Kate and Lyla reminded him so much of Anne and Sarah, in appearances anyway.

Anne had been a stay-at-home wife and mother to their child. She'd been content to manage the household and greet him with open arms and a hearty meal when he came home.

Anne had no ambition for working outside the home. Chuck had worried she would be lonely with him gone most of the time. And she had been. Her world revolved around him. Each time he left on a mission, she would be sad and depressed. He'd tried to get her to join the military wives club, but she preferred staying home. Knowing she was unhappy made it hard for Chuck to focus on his work.

Kate, on the other hand, was a woman who had a successful career, no children, no marriages. She took charge and could stand on her own.

Chuck believed Kate could protect herself and Lyla without him. But she was smart enough to know it helped having someone else around to cover her back.

She was beautiful, confident and intelligent. And that kiss...

He was in deep trouble. As soon as he'd touched her lips, he'd known there was no going back. He had to kiss her again.

Now, he was running scared. Scared he was falling for a woman after all the years he'd sworn off love, marriage and family. He didn't believe in happily-ever-after. Not after losing Anne and Sarah.

He stopped on the way down the hall to duck into Lyla's room.

She lay with her arm wrapped around Sid Sloth, her stuffed animal.

Chuck held his breath and felt her forehead. Cool and dry.

He let go of the breath on a sigh. Thank goodness, she was okay. He left her door open and made another pass through the house, testing the door locks and the window latches. He stood by the front window, staring out at the night.

On the edge of town, the little cottage wasn't inundated with street lights. Stars shone down, providing enough light to illuminate the road and houses. But there were deep shadows he couldn't see into.

Had Lyla's pursuers traced them to Montana? Would they catch up to them soon?

Chuck's hands clenched into fists.

He wouldn't let anything happen to Lyla and Kate. Not on his watch.

A soft hand touched his shoulder.

Kate stood behind him.

He didn't have to turn to see her. He could tell it was her by the scent of spring flowers.

"Are you worried they've found us?" she whispered.

"I have to think of all the possibilities," he answered.

"Thank you for being here for us," she said. "I couldn't have done this on my own."

He shook his head. "You would have found a way."

She emitted a gentle snort. "I would have done my best, but there's so much I don't know about protecting a child and taking care of her."

"You're doing fine by letting her know you love her. That's all she needs."

Her lips curled upward. "And Sid Sloth."

Kate's smile melted Chuck's heart. He turned and gripped her arms. "I don't know what happened a moment ago, but we can't let it happen again."

She stared up at him, her eyes wide. "No," she breathed, her lips rosy from their kiss. "We can't."

His control was slipping, and he struggled to regain it. "I'm serious." He shook her gently.

She raised her hands to his waist, nodding. "I know."

"Then why can't I resist?" he said. "Oh, hell." All reason flew out the window, and he lowered his mouth to hers, crushing her lips with a kiss both desperate and beautiful.

He gathered her close in his arms, pulling her body flush against his.

She wrapped her arms around his middle and held on, giving back as much as he gave.

When he traced her lips with the tip of his tongue, she opened to him, letting him in.

Chuck thrust in, claiming her mouth, tasting her in a long, sensuous caress. Their tongues tangled and twisted around each other while their hands explored.

Kate slipped her fingers beneath his shirt and splayed them across his back. They were warm and strong, kneading into his flesh.

He dragged the hem of her nightgown over her hips and slid his hands across her lower back, loving the silkiness of her skin.

His groin tightened, and his shaft swelled, pressing against her taut belly.

Kate's hands shifted lower and into the waistband of his jeans.

Chuck moaned. "Don't go there if you don't mean it," he said against her lips.

"I mean it," she whispered into his mouth, and her

tongue thrust between his teeth and tangled again with his.

Bending, he scooped her up by the backs of her thighs and wrapped her legs around his waist. Then he backed her against a wall and deepened the kiss, like a man drinking from a bottomless well. He wanted to be closer…couldn't get enough of Kate.

She wrapped her arms around his neck and wove her hands into his hair.

"I want you," he said.

"Inside me," she agreed. "Now."

"Protection." That he could think about it was a miracle. But he refused to risk bringing another child into the world because he was careless.

She leaned back, a frown puckering her brow. "You have some?"

"Back pocket." He kissed the column of her throat and nibbled on her earlobe. "Wallet."

Kate slipped her hand into his back pocket and extracted his wallet. While he feasted on her neck, she pulled out a foil packet and slipped his wallet back into his pocket.

She tore open the packet and pressed her hands against his chest.

He held her far enough away from him that she could reach the button and zipper on his jeans. In seconds, she had flipped open the rivet and slid the tab down.

Unfettered by denim, his cock sprang free.

She laughed. "Commando?"

Chuck growled. "Damn right."

Her smile faded as she hurriedly rolled the condom over him. Then she captured his cheeks between her palms and looked him square in the eye. "Foreplay is overrated."

"Sweet Jesus, yes!" he pushed aside her panties and nudged her with the tip of his staff.

Kate was slick with her own juices, ripe and ready for him.

He eased into her and paused, the act taking all his diminishing control. "Say no, and it stops here." He could barely say the words. His chest was so tight, and his body was on fire with need.

"Don't stop now," she cried. "I've never been so... so...on fire."

He thrust into her, pushing deep until he could go no farther. Drawing in a deep breath, he waited, letting her adjust to his girth.

Kate wasn't waiting for long. She pressed down on his shoulders, lifting up his shaft, only to ease down again. "Yes, please," she said as she exhaled and dragged in another ragged breath.

After another slow glide in and out, he couldn't hold back any longer. He leaned her against the wall, grabbed her hips and thrust into her, hard and fast.

"Better," she said and held on for the ride.

Chuck powered into her like a piston on a racecar engine, pounding her as hard and as fast as he could and still balance her. A bed would have been easier, but he couldn't take the time to move her there. Not when he was so...very...close.

One more thrust, and he shot over the precipice. He

drove deep, clutching her bottom, digging his fingers into her flesh as he held on, milking the orgasm to the very last shudder.

Kate kissed his forehead, his temple and his eyelids. "Wow," she said. "That was amazing."

His desire slaked for the moment, regret set in. Part of the beauty of making love to a woman was watching her lose herself in the process. "I should have gotten you there first."

She swept a hand through his hair. "I didn't need you to. It felt good."

"We aren't done yet," he said and carried her to the floral couch, still deep inside her. Instead of laying her on the cushion, he perched her bottom on the back of the couch and pulled free. After disposing of the condom, he spread her legs and stepped between. "Now, it's your turn."

CHAPTER 8

Kate balanced on the back of the couch, her channel slick with her juices, and her core coiled and ready for whatever Chuck had in mind. "Aren't you afraid we'll wake Lyla?" she asked, her gaze going to the hallway and the open door.

"If we didn't wake her before, she'll sleep through this." He stepped back. "But I'll check on her. Don't move."

He zipped his jeans and hurried to the bedroom.

Kate took the moment to shed her panties and stuff them into the cushions of the couch. Chuck had moved them aside to make love to her, but she didn't want anything in the way of what he might have in mind next.

She waited, her breath catching in her throat, her heart pounding hard against her ribs.

The few short moments he stepped away gave her entirely too much time to think about what she was doing.

What was she thinking? This man was hired to protect her, not to make love to her. If she was smart, she'd pull on her panties and hightail it back to her bed. Alone.

But she wasn't thinking with her mind. Her body burned for more and wouldn't let her leave the couch to save her soul.

When Chuck returned, he stalked toward her like a tiger on the prowl for its prey. His eyes narrowed as he studied her face. "Having second thoughts?"

She nodded, her throat tightening to the point she couldn't push air past her vocal cords.

He parted her legs again and stepped between her knees. Then he cupped the back of her head and tipped her head up, forcing her to meet his gaze. "Want me to change your mind?"

His deep tone resonated through the room, making her nerves spontaneously combust and shoot electrical pulses throughout her system.

She wanted him to do wicked things to her.

"Please," she said.

"Please what?" He lifted the hem of her nightgown but didn't pull it up over her head.

Kate raised her arms. "Please, change my mind."

Chuck ripped the gown over her head and flung it across the room. For a long moment, his gaze swept her body, taking in every curve and swell.

Kate's nipples puckered, and her core heated. She held her breath in anticipation.

He reached out and lifted the necklace she'd worn

beneath her nightgown. "Do you always wear this?" His knuckles grazed the swells of her breasts.

Dragging a deep breath to steady her pounding heart, she nodded. "Hank told me to wear it always. I think it has a tracking device in it."

"Smart man." He lifted the pendant and touched his lips to it. "You're beautiful."

She started to raise her arms to cover her bare breasts.

"Don't." Chuck captured her wrists and held them for a moment.

Kate raised her eyebrows, a shiver rippling across her skin. "I seem to be the only naked one here."

He winked. "But you do it so well." Then he pulled off his shirt and flung it to join her nightgown. "I'd go further, but it might be harder to explain my being naked to a three-year-old."

"True."

"And I don't need to be naked to do this." He bent to press his lips to the base of her throat. "Or this," he whispered against her beating pulse. His mouth slipped over her collarbone and down to capture a nipple between his teeth.

For the next few moments, he nibbled, nipped and flicked that nipple.

Kate moaned softly and clutched the back of his head, her fingers digging into his scalp.

"Like that?" he asked.

"Yesss…" She leaned her head back and let him have his way with that nipple and then the other.

By the time he abandoned them, she was squirming

on the back of the couch, ready for him to take it downward.

And he did.

Chuck dropped to his knees and dragged his lips over her ribs, one at a time. He dipped his tongue into her belly button and continued downward to the fluff of hair at the juncture of her thighs.

Kate widened her legs automatically, her breathing ragged, her pulse racing.

Parting her folds with his fingers, Chuck leaned in and blew a warm stream of air over that heated strip of flesh.

Kate gasped and applied pressure to the back of his head, urging him to do more.

With his tongue, he flicked her clit, sending a jolt of electricity racing across her body.

"Oh my," she whispered.

He tapped that spot with the tip of his tongue, teasing her to the point she wanted to scream.

"Please," she begged.

Chuckling, he ran his tongue across her sweet spot again and again until she dropped her hands to her knees, pulled back her legs and gave in to the orgasm that rocked her to her very soul.

Chuck curled one hand behind her to keep her from toppling over the back of the couch while the other spread her folds for the magic of his mouth.

For what felt like a lifetime and yet was so short it could only have been a length of a breath, Kate flew to the heavens and back, her body spasming, her hips rocking to the rhythm of Chuck's tongue.

When she floated back to earth, she couldn't have remembered her name, where she was from or the color of summer grass.

Chuck rose from his knees, stood her on her feet, then left her to gather their clothes from where they'd landed on the floor.

With care and kisses, he dressed her in her nightgown, guiding the fabric over her head, across her shoulders and down her torso, his hands touching her skin all the way.

Kate sighed and leaned into him, her legs like jelly, her body completely relaxed against his. "Wow."

A warm chuckle reverberated between them. "I've never known a woman to come that completely undone."

"I've never come so close to dying." She lay her head against his chest, listening to the rapid beat of his heart. "I believe you've ruined me."

"How so?"

"I don't think anything can top that."

"No?" He tipped back her head and brushed a strand of her hair back behind her ear.

"Not even ice cream," she said, her brain fuzzy, her body still humming from her incredible experience.

Chuck laughed out loud, and then slapped his hand over his mouth. "I'll take that as a compliment. Better than ice cream?"

"Mmm-hmmm." She lifted up on her toes and pressed her lips to his. They tasted of her. It made her tingle down there again. And if she didn't step away soon, she'd beg him to do it all again.

A soft sound came from the bedroom down the hallway, pulling her out of the spell he'd cast on her.

Kate sighed. "I'll check on Lyla."

"I'll make another round of the house," Chuck said. "And then we need to get some sleep. We don't know what tomorrow will bring."

Kate smiled. "You mean today." She nodded toward a clock on the wall.

"Right." He winced. "And children have a habit of getting up at the crack of dawn."

Though she knew she needed to check on Lyla, Kate found it difficult to let go of Chuck. She had the feeling that once she did, everything would change. Things would go back to the way they were before. Him being the bodyguard, her being the client. Purely professional.

Oh, but they'd crossed that bridge and there was no going back. Not for Kate.

Chuck checked the windows and doors once again, even though he'd done it only minutes before. It gave him an excuse to step away from Kate. If he stood too close to her, he'd be too tempted to keep her in his arms and make love to her all over again.

They had been very lucky that Lyla hadn't walked in on them while they were in the heat of passion. Witnessing people who aren't her parents getting it on would be hard to comprehend at her age. And Chuck was certain Kate's sister wouldn't appreciate them exposing themselves to the little girl.

He ran a hand down his face. This lack of control

wasn't like him. Being focused was what he did, how he'd stayed alive on all the missions he'd conducted with the Navy SEALs and on special assignment with the DEA. He'd done whatever had to be done to accomplish his mission. Emotions and relationships couldn't get in the way. People died when one lost focus.

Kate emerged from Lyla's room and stood in the hallway. Her nightgown hung down to mid-thigh.

Chuck knew she wasn't wearing underwear and vaguely wondered where she'd ditched them. But it didn't matter. She wasn't wearing any, and it made him hard all over again.

"Go to bed," he said, his tone a lot sterner than he intended.

Kate nodded, as if she understood his struggle. She turned and walked barefooted to the master bedroom, her shoulders back, her head high.

God, she was beautiful.

With every ounce of self-control he could muster, Chuck resisted following Kate and making love to her for the rest of what was left of the night.

They didn't need Lyla waking up to find them naked in bed together. They could do without that kind of trauma. The kid had enough stacked against her as it was.

He settled in the lounge chair and kicked up the footrest. Day One on the new job had seen him set up house with a beautiful woman and child, go to dinner with the old people of the town and make love to his client. It wasn't a SEAL mission or busting a drug dealer, but it might be the most important mission of his life. He'd better get his shit together before someone got hurt.

He suspected it might be him. Already, his heart was on the line. *After only one day.*

Closing his eyes, he willed himself to catch some shuteye. He'd learned the skill of falling asleep quickly as a young Navy SEAL. He drew on that skill now to keep his body refreshed and ready to go should the need arise.

HE MUST HAVE SLEPT, because when he opened his eyes again, sun shone around the curtains hanging in the windows and tiny footsteps sounded in the hallway.

Lyla stood in the middle of the hallway, her stuffed sloth clutched to her chest, her eyes wide, scared.

"Hey, Lyla," Chuck called out softly. "It's okay. You can come sit with me until…Mama wakes up."

She stared at him for a long time.

Chuck sat up, folding the leg rest under him.

Lyla remained standing in the hallway, her bottom lip quivering.

His heart squeezed hard in his chest. "Oh, baby. It's okay," he tried to reassure her. "Did you have a bad dream?"

She nodded.

Chuck held out his arms. "Come here. Nothing can hurt you while you're with me."

Lyla took in a shaky breath, and then ran toward him.

He rose from his chair in time to catch her as she flung herself into his arms.

"Oh, sweetheart, you're going to be just fine." Chuck held her close, rocking back and forth from one foot to the other. "You're in a new house, in a new place, and everything takes a little getting used to."

She wrapped her arms around his neck and buried her face against him, Sid Sloth crushed between them. Her body was stiff in his arms, as if she was tight with fear.

After a while, Lyla relaxed and loosened her grip around his neck.

Chuck crossed to the window to let in the sunshine. Everything seemed to get better when the sun was shining. The sun would scare away the shadows where bad things hid.

Lyla sat up and stared out the window, her sloth clutched under her chin.

"Feeling better?" Chuck asked.

She nodded.

"Hungry?"

Again, she nodded.

Still carrying Lyla, he entered the kitchen, then found a bowl and the cereal they'd purchased at the grocery store. He carried Lyla to the table. When he tried to place her in one of the seats, she refused to let go of him.

"Okay then." He chuckled. "We'll just make a few more trips. No worries." Chuck ferried milk, a cup, a bowl and a spoon to the table. Once he had everything set out, he took his seat and settled Lyla in his lap. "Want to move to your own chair?"

She shook her head.

Chuck poured cereal into a bowl and sloshed milk over it.

Lyla picked up the spoon and scooped cereal into her mouth. With liquid dripping down her chin, she turned and gave him a milky smile.

"Whatever makes you happy." He sat while she finished her cereal, with Sid Sloth in the chair beside them.

"You two seem to be getting along rather well this morning."

Kate entered the kitchen, wearing jeans and a soft, baby-blue sweater. She was barefooted, and her hair was pulled back into a loose ponytail.

Chuck sucked air into his empty lungs. The woman took his breath away without even trying.

"I make a mean omelet," she said and bent to pull out of the cabinet the frying pan they'd purchased at the grocery store. When she straightened, her gaze met his. Her pupils flared, and her cheeks reddened.

She had to be remembering what they'd done in the living room the night before.

Chuck sure as hell was remembering.

Lyla set her spoon on the table, having finished her cereal. She raised her arms to Kate.

Kate set the pan on the stove and crossed the kitchen to lift Lyla into her arms.

Chuck cleared his throat. "Why don't you get in some morning cuddles while I fix breakfast."

Kate smiled down at Lyla. "You're on. Since I live on my own, I don't do a lot of cooking. No use cooking for one."

"I used to cook for my buddies on my SEAL team when we got together. Most of it involved a grill and huge amounts of steaks and ribs. But I've been known to make a decent breakfast when I have to."

She waved her hand. "I'm not arguing. By all means." Kate hugged Lyla close. "Where's Sid?"

"He's finishing his breakfast," Lyla said, pointing to the chair where Sid sat as if he were waiting for someone to serve him cereal and milk.

Chuckling softly, Chuck manned the stove, pulled out the carton of eggs, shredded cheese, green onions, bell peppers and tomatoes. He started bacon in the skillet, cooking it while he chopped the ingredients for the omelets.

By the time everything was ready, Lyla had moved into the living room by herself and was playing with Sid and the doll Sadie had sent.

"Need any help, or did I time that right?"

He smiled. "Sit. I'll serve."

"Yes, sir." She popped a sharp salute and took a seat at the little table.

Chuck set a plate full of a fluffy, yellow omelet and three slices of bacon in front of her.

"This looks amazing," she said and sniffed. "Smells even better. But I can't eat all of this. I'd be in a food coma before noon."

"You need to keep up your strength. We never know what to expect or when."

With her fork poised over the omelet, she stared up at him. "Do you think they'll find us here?"

"I don't know, but even if they don't, it doesn't hurt to be ready." He sat opposite her with a plate filled just like hers. "Eat up."

They ate breakfast together like a young married couple, talking and finding out more about each other.

"What does your boss think about you taking off for such a long period of time? Will you have a job to return to when Lyla and your sister are all settled?"

Kate smiled. "I should. I own the company."

Chuck leaned back. "I'm impressed."

She shrugged modestly. "I started out as a company of one employee. I now have twenty, and one of them is my general manager. She'll have everything under control. I've been handing the reins to her over the past year, ready to move on to another challenge."

"Like?"

Kate shrugged again. "I'm not sure. I haven't found anything that inspires me yet."

"The timing for relinquishing authority couldn't have been better, what with Lyla showing up on your doorstep."

"I know." She shook her head. "Some things can't be explained. You could say it was fate."

Chuck stared down at the food on his plate. "Fate can be benevolent at times, and sometimes she can be a bitch." He stabbed his fork into the omelet and raised a bite to his lips.

"Like when your family died in the car crash?" she asked softly.

He nodded. "And like finding Hank and the Brotherhood Protectors. I count myself lucky that I can use my training as a SEAL, taking care of others who might not be able to take care of themselves."

Kate nodded. "I'm just glad I could be here for Lyla. She's a beautiful little girl with a wonderful personality. I hope we can reunite her with her mother soon. I'm sure Rachel is beside herself worrying about her."

"Hank's working on finding her."

Kate set her fork down beside her plate. "I'm glad she knew to call on Hank and the brotherhood. I wouldn't have known which way to turn."

"Fate," Chuck concluded.

They finished their breakfast and laid out a plan to keep busy for the next few days. It included sprucing up the house with fresh paint on the interior walls.

After another trip to the hardware store for the supplies they needed, they spread plastic sheeting on the floors and furniture, opened the windows and went to work painting one room at a time.

For the next three days, Chuck kept his hands to himself, though it was a challenge.

The more time he spent with Kate and Lyla, the more he wanted to spend with them.

In the evenings, they sat around the living room. He or Kate read to Lyla, or Lyla played with Sid and the doll Sadie had given her.

Chuck insisted on cooking meals to keep from having to go out each night when Lyla was tired and cranky. Kate always pitched in, helping chop vegetables or setting the table. Lyla helped too, drying dishes and folding napkins.

An outsider looking in would think they were one happy family.

Even Chuck was beginning to feel that way. But he knew it couldn't last.

He touched base every day with Hank to keep abreast of anything Kujo found out about the cult in Idaho. So far, Kujo hadn't seen Rachel or made it past the cult's security. He'd reported that in order to get inside the camp, he'd have to join the cult. And the cult members weren't very open to outsiders at the time.

After the third day, they'd finished the painting inside by completing the touchup on the baseboards.

Three days inside was enough. Chuck cleaned the paintbrushes and washed his hands. "Who wants to go to the park?"

Lyla clapped her hands. "I do. I do."

Kate stood behind Lyla, her eyebrows pulling together. "You think it will be all right?"

Chuck nodded. "All three of us will go as a family."

Kate nodded and smiled. "Great! These walls were closing in, and the paint fumes are getting to me."

"We'll leave the windows open to air out the house. Ten minutes enough to wash the paint off the tip of your nose and change into clean clothes?"

Lyla ran for the bathroom.

Kate followed, touching the tip of her nose and looking down, cross-eyed, to see where the paint might be.

Chuck laughed, his heart light for the first time in

what felt like years. He liked being with Kate and Lyla. If, at the end of this assignment, they parted ways, he would have at least learned something.

Life continued after losing a loved one. And he needed to live it.

With that in mind, he decided to enjoy the day while keeping a close watch on the two ladies in his care.

CHAPTER 9

Kate scrubbed the paint off her nose, hands and arms and helped Lyla do the same. After she helped her niece into clean clothing, she ran to her own room and dressed in freshly laundered jeans and a white, cotton blouse. She brushed her hair out and left it hanging long around her shoulders.

Chuck seemed to like it when she left her hair loose. His eyes darkened and his nostrils flared when she came into a room with her hair down around her shoulders.

For the past three days, she'd done her best to keep from begging him to make love to her again. And it was just as well she hadn't. Lyla had made a habit of waking up in the middle of the night calling out for her mama.

If she'd done that the first night in the house, the situation would have been embarrassing for all three of them and might have generated a barrage of questions Kate didn't want to have to provide the answers for. Rachel should have that honor, several years down the road.

When Kate emerged from the bedroom, Chuck was attempting to teach Lyla how to play the Miss Mary Mack hand-clapping game in the living room.

Kate laughed when she saw them. "Where did you learn how to do that?"

A grin tipped up the corners of his mouth. "I have an older sister. She made me play this game until she had it down." He returned his attention to Lyla and tried again to get her to clap in the correct sequence. They both laughed.

Kate smiled at the silly game, but her smile faded as she remembered how she and Rachel had played that game and others when they were little girls, not much older than Lyla.

She wished Hank would find Rachel soon. She missed her sister and hoped she could help her out of whatever mess she'd landed in.

Chuck straightened, his gaze going to Kate. "Hank's people are on it. They'll find her," he said, as if reading her mind. "For now, we're going on a picnic to the park."

He lifted a backpack off the kitchen counter.

She blinked. "You made lunch that fast?"

"You ladies took more than ten minutes. I had plenty of time to make sandwiches and pack some chips, bottled water and a blanket."

"You're an amazing man." She cupped his cheek with her hand and leaned up to plant a kiss on his lips. She did it all as if it was the most natural thing to do. When she realized what she'd done, she shrugged. What the hell? Why not?

Without an apology, she swung her hair back over her shoulder and headed for the door. "Last one to the truck is a rotten egg."

She flung open the door and would have run out, but Chuck's hands caught her arm and Lyla's before either one could race outside.

That's when Kate noticed a man on the road outside the house, walking a dog.

He slowed as he passed the yellow cottage, his gaze swinging toward them, his eyes narrowing.

"I'm going to be a rotten egg," Lyla cried and wiggled free of Chuck's hand. She ran outside, straight for the truck.

Kate's heart stuttered, and then her pulse kicked into high speed. She ran after her, but Chuck reached her first, swinging her up into his arms. He carried her the last few steps to the truck and let her lean forward to touch the truck first.

"I win!" she called out.

"Yes, darlin', you win," Chuck said, his gaze on the man and dog. "Hop in so I can buckle your seat belt." Chuck opened the door and deposited Lyla on the seat, buckling her in and then closing the door firmly.

Kate stood beside him, trying not to be too obvious about watching the man walking his dog. She could see him in her peripheral vision. He'd walked to the end of the road, turned around and was on his way back.

"Hop in, sweetheart." Chuck held the passenger door for Kate. "He doesn't appear to be armed unless the dog is his weapon of choice. In which case, you need to get in."

Kate jumped up into the seat, and Chuck closed the door.

Her heart continued to race as Chuck rounded the truck and climbed into the driver's seat.

"Do you think he—" Kate broke off her sentence and nodded toward the stranger.

"I don't know, but apparently he's the one Mrs. Turner was talking about the other night."

"Should we stay at the house?"

"No. We're going on a picnic on the other side of town. Hopefully, he won't follow us there."

"And if he does?"

Chuck opened his jacket, displaying a shoulder holster with a handgun tucked inside.

Kate's eyes rounded briefly, but then she settled back in her seat, reassured he was prepared to protect them. As a SEAL, he had to be a good shot. She prayed he wouldn't have to use the gun, but she was glad he was packing.

The drive across town took less than five minutes, and only that long because they had to stop to let an old woman using a walker cross Main Street.

The sun was shining, the day was warm without being too hot and Kate was ready to breathe fresh air.

Yet she couldn't get over the feeling they were being watched. Perhaps it was seeing the man walking his dog that had set her on edge, but she had a hard time shaking the feeling.

At the park, they found a grassy spot beneath the spreading branches of an oak tree and laid out their blanket.

They were only a few yards away from the playground equipment.

"I need to call Hank," Chuck said.

Lyla grabbed Kate's hand and dragged her toward the swing. "Push me. Please."

Kate looked over her head at Chuck. "It's not far. You can keep an eye on us while you talk to Hank." She nodded toward a woman who'd just arrived with her daughter. "Isn't that the woman from the grocery store?"

Chuck stared across the field at the woman as she and her daughter walked toward the swings. "I think so."

"We'll be fine. I'll stay close to Lyla. Join us when you're finished with your call."

"Okay, but don't go any farther."

"We won't."

"And Kate…" Chuck said.

"Yes?"

"Don't share information with anyone, no matter how inconsequential. Words have a way of finding the wrong ears."

"I'll be careful." Kate let Lyla lead her to the swings, while Chuck anchored the blanket with the backpack and pulled out his cellphone.

The woman she'd met in the grocery store was already at the swing set, gently pushing her daughter.

"Hello," Kate called out as she neared. "Becca and Mary, right?"

"That's right." The woman smiled. "And you're Kate and Lyla."

Kate nodded toward the woman and helped Lyla up into the swing. "Seems we keep running into each other."

"Hard not to, since it is such a small town."

"How are you settling in?" Kate asked, glad for a little variation in her adult conversation. Coming from a thriving marketing company in LA to being sequestered in a house with one man and one small child, she found she craved a little more social interaction.

"Actually, we're staying in a camper just outside of town while we look for just the right piece of property to buy." Becca pushed Mary in the swing in a steady rhythm. "We'd like to have a garden to grow our own vegetables."

"Wow. A camper?" Kate glanced around the park. "No wonder you're at the park. I'm sure the camper walls were closing in around you."

Becca nodded. "Yes, they were. It's nice to be outside in the fresh air. We needed the exercise."

Lyla looked back at Kate. "I want to climb on the slide."

"Okay, but be careful on the ladder." Kate stopped the swing.

Lyla jumped off and ran for the slide.

Becca stopped Mary and tipped her head toward the slide. "Why don't you go with Lyla and show her how it's done."

"Yes, ma'am," Mary said and hurried off to join Lyla.

Kate walked more sedately behind Lyla and found a bench within easy reach of Lyla and the slide. She sat on one end and was glad to see Becca settled onto the other end.

"Is Mary your only child?" Kate asked.

"No, I have two sons I left with my mother back where we're from. They're in school, and I didn't want to uproot them before we found a place to live."

"That's understandable." Kate glanced at Becca before turning back to watch Lyla. "It must be hard to be away from your children."

"It is, but they're used to being with my mother. She takes very good care of them."

Still, Kate couldn't imagine leaving even one of her children behind.

Her lips curled upward. Here she was thinking she wouldn't leave her children behind when she hadn't had any and probably never would. She was getting to that age when women had trouble getting pregnant. At the ripe old age of thirty-five, she'd resigned herself to being alone.

Until Lyla came into her life, and then Chuck.

The two of them had opened a door she thought completely closed. Now that she knew what she was missing...

Sweet heaven.

She wanted a family.

Her gaze went from Lyla to Chuck and back.

She'd always thought her life was perfect. She was a successful career woman with a nice apartment in an upscale area of LA. She had employees who looked up to her and clients who trusted her work and tastes. What more could she ask for?

A husband to come home to and a child to love.

Kate swallowed hard on the lump forming in her throat. She loved being with Lyla. Sure, she was a lot more work that she'd ever thought a three-year-old could be, but her niece gave the warmest, sweetest hugs. How could she not love that little girl? And Chuck... there was so much about the man that Kate could love. Her chest swelled, and her pulse quickened. God, she hoped their first night of passion wouldn't be their last.

He'd been her most amazing lover. But he was more than that. He'd more than proven his daddy skills, and he was fun to be with, smart and strong. He cared about the people around him and would do anything to protect them from harm.

After less than a week with Chuck, Kate could already tell she was falling for him. Hard.

"Are you and your husband settling in nicely?" Becca asked.

Kate frowned. "Did I say we were new in town?"

Becca shot a glance her way, and her cheeks reddened. "I don't remember. I just assumed you were new because you said you hadn't seen many children in town when we were back at the grocery store."

Kate remembered what Chuck had told her about sharing too much information with anybody. "Oh, we've been around for a while. I just meant that so many of our young couples leave town because there just aren't that many jobs in the area. Thus, fewer children Lyla's age."

Not that she considered Becca a threat, but what Becca shared with another stranger, might be that little

MONTANA SEAL UNDERCOVER DADDY

bit of information an attacker could use to abscond with Lyla.

Kate wasn't taking any chances, but she wasn't going to be rude to the woman who only seemed to want a friend to talk with.

Mary and Lyla climbed the ladder and slid down the slide a number of times before they grew bored and climbed the monkey bars a few more steps away from where Kate sat.

Kate leaned forward, her gaze scanning the park for threats. So far, the park was empty, except for a man on the far side wearing a baseball cap and playing with a puppy.

He was far enough away, he wouldn't be a threat. Kate could reach Lyla before he could make it there.

She settled back and enjoyed the sunshine, her gaze again swinging from Lyla to Chuck and back. This was what life with the Navy SEAL could be like. If he was interested.

She cautioned herself not to raise her hopes too much. Just because he'd made love to her once, didn't mean he wanted to do it again. Hell, he hadn't made a move on her since.

Her lips twisted. Had making love to her been that bad?

CHUCK HELD the cellphone to his ear, trying to make out what Hank was talking about. The reception was spotty. He'd done his best to give his boss an update, but he'd had to redial a couple of times already because of dropped calls.

He was most interested in learning more about Kujo's investigation of the cult community in Idaho.

"Kujo…into the camp…tight security," Hank was saying.

Chuck hated that he was only getting part of the conversation, and he had to ask for repeated clarification. "He got into the camp?"

"No. He couldn…"

"Has he seen Rachel?" Chuck asked.

"Not yet…and children seem to…guarded and…out of sight."

"Pretended to wander…the camp and… stopped before he…within a hundred yards."

Chuck snorted. "Why would they be that closed and have that good of security unless they were hiding something?"

"Or someone," Hank said.

"Exactly."

The phone went silent.

"Hank?" Chuck listened. Nothing. He looked down at his display only to find *Call Ended* written across the screen.

Muttering a curse, he dialed Hank's number again.

"The reception where you…is poor. Call me…cottage."

"Will do," Chuck said and ended the call. He'd spent more time than he cared to away from Lyla and Kate. And they had yet to partake of their picnic lunch.

He glanced toward Lyla who was playing on the

monkey bars with Mary, the little girl they'd met at the grocery store.

His gaze went to Kate seated on a bench, not far from where Lyla was playing. She seemed content to chat with Becca while she watched Lyla play.

Anyone watching would think nothing of Kate watching her child play. She kept a close eye on Lyla, her glance rarely moving away from her niece. Then she leaned forward, her brow furrowing.

Chuck looked back toward Lyla, and he frowned.

Where she'd been a moment before, she was no longer. Then he saw both little girls running across the open field toward a man with a puppy.

Chuck was off like a rocket, running as fast as he could, pumping his arms and legs.

Lyla had a pretty good head start.

Kate was off the bench and well ahead of him, running for Lyla. She'd make it to her first.

The thing that had him scared was that Lyla could make it to the man and his puppy before Kate or Chuck could reach her.

His heart pounding and lungs burning, he ran fast, but not fast enough.

Lyla's little legs carried her across the grass and right up to the puppy.

The man stepped forward and leaned over the child, his hands outstretched.

"No!" Kate yelled. "Don't take her!"

Chuck caught up with Kate, passed her and dove for Lyla just as the man's hand came in contact with the little girl.

With the grace of a hawk swooping in to claim his prey, Chuck snatched Lyla out of the clutches of the man and crushed her to his chest.

Kate came to a skidding stop in front of them, breathing hard, her hair in wild disarray around her face. "Is she all right?" she demanded between deep breaths of air.

"She's okay," Chuck said, his gaze on the man.

He'd scooped up the puppy and held it away from the small children, a frown creasing his forehead. "What the hell was that all about?" he asked.

"You were about to take my n—daughter," Kate said, a glare drawing her eyebrows into a V.

The man laughed. "No, your daughter was about to touch my puppy." He glanced down at the animal in his arms. "Duchess isn't used to small children. She might have bit your little girl. I was reaching down to rescue her."

Kate's frown deepened. "But I thought…and you were reaching…and I couldn't get…" She bent double and placed her hands on her knees, dragging in deep, ragged breaths. She waved toward Chuck. "Tell him."

"We thought you were trying to steal our little girl. Our mistake. Now, if you'll excuse us, we'll leave you alone."

Carrying Lyla in his arms, Chuck walked back toward the playground equipment.

Kate grabbed Mary's hand and led her back, following behind Chuck.

Becca met them halfway across the field. "What was that all about?"

"Nothing," Chuck said. "Just a misunderstanding."

"Mary, did you get to pet the puppy?" Becca asked.

"No, ma'am," she said and stood quietly next to her mother.

"Are you going to be here much longer?" Becca asked.

Chuck answered, "No. We have to be leaving. Remember that appointment we had?"

Kate glanced up at Chuck, her gaze questioning. But she nodded and played along. "Oh, yes. I almost forgot." She turned to Becca. "I enjoyed spending time with you and Mary. Perhaps we can do it again, soon."

"I'd like that, too. Will you be out tomorrow?" Becca asked, giving her a tentative smile.

"I'm not sure." Kate shot a glance toward Chuck.

His lips tightened. He hoped Kate picked up on his desire not to make plans. Set up times to be places could be used against them. An attacker could arrange to be there ahead of time and surprise them, make a grab for Lyla and be gone before they knew what had happened.

"I'll see you around," Kate finally said and hurried over to grab the blanket off the ground and swing the backpack over her shoulder.

They walked back to the truck in silence. Even Lyla was quiet.

Chuck buckled her in and held Kate's door for her while she climbed inside.

His heartbeat had barely settled back into a normal rhythm by the time he climbed into the driver's seat.

If the man with the puppy had decided to grab Lyla and make a run for it, he could have done it.

Kate and Chuck might not have gotten to her in time.

The whole situation made Chuck realize just how lax he'd gotten in his duty. He vowed to tighten up and take better care not to let his guard down for even a moment. Kate and Lyla were depending on him.

CHAPTER 10

Kate waited in the truck with Lyla while Chuck entered the house, checked it over thoroughly, and then returned with the all-clear sign of a thumbs-up.

She'd almost struck up a conversation a couple times on the short drive back to the cottage, but every time she glanced his way, his jaw was tight and his lips were pressed into a thin line.

Chuck appeared completely unapproachable and downright scary.

Instead, Kate clamped her lips together and waited for Chuck to loosen up. Apparently, Lyla running off to pet a puppy had rattled the SEAL. So much so, he had gone into professional bodyguard mode and was taking everything to the extreme.

Supper was the sandwiches Chuck had made.

Lyla pouted when they sat down at the dinner table. She was disappointed they hadn't had time to have a picnic in the park.

To make up for it, Kate spread the picnic blanket on

the floor of the living room, and they ate their sandwiches, as if they were on a picnic.

Chuck even pretended an ant got on his sandwich, sending Lyla into a fit of the giggles.

By the time Kate's niece had her bath and dressed in her pajamas, she was already yawning.

Kate tucked her in, sat on the edge of her little bed and stroked her hair while reading from her favorite book.

Not three pages into the story, Lyla's eyes drifted closed.

Making her voice quieter and softer, Kate kept reading. When she was certain Lyla was fast asleep, she rose from the bed. She tucked Sid Sloth under the child's arm and dropped a kiss on her forehead. "Sleep tight, sweetheart. I love you."

Kate stared down at Lyla, wishing with all her heart her sister was okay and would be back soon to claim her daughter. When Rachel did come back, Kate would miss being Lyla's temporary mother. She'd miss reading stories to her and having picnics in the living room. She'd miss painting walls and eating hotdogs at the kitchen table. She'd miss being a family with Lyla and Chuck.

Her eyes blurring with unshed tears, Kate turned toward the door and stumbled into a hard wall of muscle.

Strong hands came up to cup her elbows. "What's wrong?"

Chuck's deep voice sounded so close to her ear, she leaned toward it, blinking back the tears so that he wouldn't see them. "Nothing. I'm fine. Lyla's fine. We're all so freakin' fine."

Kate attempted to push past him, but he refused to release her arms.

"Seriously, what's got you all wound up?"

"Is it wrong for me to want my sister to come back but want her to stay away at the same time?" She swallowed back a sob and looked over her shoulder at Lyla. "I never thought I wanted children."

"Until you spent time with Lyla?" he said softly.

She nodded and a tear slipped from the corner of her eye. "Rachel had to be desperate to leave her. What could have gone so wrong that she would abandon that sweet little girl?" More tears spilled from her eyes. Tears she was helpless to contain.

Chuck tipped her chin up and pressed a kiss to her damp eyelids. "Rachel is going to be okay."

"I hope you're right." Kate sniffed. "And when she comes back for Lyla…" Her lips twisted, and the tears fell faster. "I'll miss her."

"Yeah. Me, too." Chuck pulled her into his arms and held her. "She has a way of fitting right into your heart, doesn't she?"

"Yes." Kate rested her cheek against Chuck's chest, listening to the reassuringly steady beat of his heart. She'd miss Chuck, too. How could two people have become so much a part of her life in such a short time?

Kate curled her fingers into the fabric of Chuck's shirt. She didn't want to let him go. Not now, not ever.

What was she thinking? She couldn't be in love with the guy. Kate Phillips, marketing executive and career woman, couldn't possibly be in love with a man whom she'd only recently met. She'd never believed in love at first sight, or even insta-love. Relationships took time to build and grow. Didn't they?

"I don't know what I'm going to do," she whispered. "I don't want to let go."

Chuck brushed a strand of her hair back behind her ear. "You're a mess, you know that? For a woman who knew exactly what she wanted out of life, you're going all wishy-washy on me."

She laughed, the sound catching on a sob. "I know. It's not like me to lose it." Now, her tears were falling in earnest down her cheeks.

Chuck brushed away some of them with his thumbs, but there were too many to catch. "Darlin', you've got to shut off these waterworks, or you'll have me bawling before you know it."

Kate smiled at the thought and scrubbed at the tears on her cheeks. "I didn't think SEALs could cry."

"Oh, they can, all right. Just don't tell anyone. They'd never believe you anyway." He bent and scooped her up in his arms.

"Are you taking me to bed to make mad, passionate love to me?" She cupped his cheek in her hand. "Because, if you are, could you please hurry?"

He hesitated in the hallway, his glance going to the open door of her bedroom. Then he must have thought better of it because he turned the opposite direction. "Let's take this conversation to the living room. I can't think when you're naked."

She looped her arm around his neck as he carried

her to the couch. "Do you mean that in a good way or a bad way?"

"Both." He sat on the couch and settled her across his lap.

"Are we going to talk? Or neck like teenagers?" She pressed her lips to his cheek. "You know where I want to go with it."

He cupped her cheeks between his palms and held her still. "Kate, what are we doing here?"

Her heart stilled for a second, and then thundered against the walls of her chest. "I thought it was pretty clear. Why else would you carry me here and sit with me in your lap." She frowned. "Am I getting mixed signals?" Kate wiggled on his lap, certain of a growing erection beneath her bottom.

"You're right. I had every intention of kissing you, but it's more than that. What are we doing? Where are we going?"

Her heart slid slowly into her gut, a bad feeling creeping through her soul. "I thought what we were feeling was mutual." She swallowed hard. "Is it not?"

Chuck nodded. "I can't deny that I have feelings for you. But I'm not sure where they're going."

"No?" Kate's voice choked into a whisper.

"I was married once. I had it all. A wife, a little girl much like Lyla, and a home to go to."

"And you lost it," Kate concluded softly. "I'm sorry you had to experience that. But that was years ago. You can't live forever in the past."

"No, but it's tainted my expectations for the future."

"I don't understand."

"What if I fall in love again?"

An icy blade stabbed Kate's heart. He'd said *if*.

Kate moved off his lap and sat on the couch beside him. "Go on," she encouraged, though she wasn't sure she wanted to hear what came next.

"What we've had this past week has been amazing. I feel like I'm a part of a family again. And frankly, it scares the hell out of me."

She frowned. "But you're a Navy SEAL. You've been in battles that would leave me quaking in fear. How can a family come close to that kind of trauma?"

He closed his eyes for a moment, before opening them again and giving her a bleak look. "I don't know if I could handle losing my family again. If I give my heart to someone and she dies, I don't think I could go on living."

Kate pushed up off the couch, and walked to the picture window and stared at the curtains drawn for the night. "So, what you're really saying is you don't want to commit to anyone, for fear of losing them."

"Yeah."

"I see." She turned to face him, pasting a smile on her face, though her heart was cracking into a million pieces. "And what happened the other night?"

"It was amazing. You're amazing." He stood and walked toward her, his arms outstretched as if to embrace her. "But it should never have happened."

Kate held up a hand and shook her head. "Stop."

"Kate, I don't want to hurt you."

"Who said you hurt me?" She lifted her chin and widened her smile. "All of this week has been a big act for the sake of protecting Lyla. I don't expect anything else from you. The other night was just a bonus fling. Nothing more." She ducked around him and headed for the bedroom, her eyes stinging.

"Kate..." Chuck called out after her.

"I'm tired. I'm going to bed." At that point, she gave up trying to make a graceful exit and ran the rest of the way to the bedroom.

When she closed the door behind her, she leaned against it and slid to the floor, tears flowing silently down her cheeks.

What had she expected? A confirmed bachelor like Chuck wouldn't just fall for a career-minded, almost middle-aged woman. Not when he could have any woman on the planet with just the crook of his finger.

When he'd made love to her the other night, it had been sex. Not love. To think otherwise was setting herself up for a heaping helping of heartache.

Kate pressed a hand to her chest, the pain radiating throughout her body.

"Damn. Damn. Damn." She'd committed the ultimate folly and fallen in love with a man who couldn't love her in return. They wrote songs about it. Unrequited love. That would be the story of her life.

When Rachel returned to claim Lyla, Kate would go back to her life as a corporate executive. Back to her tastefully decorated apartment in LA and a life she thought she loved and had...until now.

She'd been a fool to start believing that the past few days they'd been acting as a family were real. They weren't. Everything had been an act to fool potential attackers. Only it had backfired.

Kate had begun to believe that fairytales really could come true.

She stared at the bed through her watery eyes, but couldn't drag herself up off the floor to get there. Instead, she lay down on the hardwood flooring and closed her eyes.

Maybe if she went to sleep, everything would be better in the morning. Chuck could have had second thoughts about never marrying or having children. They'd go on being a happy family— and pigs could learn to fly.

CHUCK PACED the living room floor, crossing the length in a few short strides then conducting an about-face and crossing again. Two, then three times, he caught himself short of marching down the hallway and pounding on Kate's door.

She had to understand where he was coming from. He couldn't open his heart again. It hurt way too much to lose someone you loved. The pain was worse than being shot and lasted so much longer.

He couldn't fall in love and risk losing everything all over again. But Kate made it easy to fall in love. Strong, capable and confident in herself, she was so very different from Anne. They weren't anything alike.

So, why couldn't he leave her alone? Why did he want to hold her, kiss her and make love to again and again? He knew he couldn't commit to a relationship.

Kate deserved a man who wasn't afraid of loving. A man who could give her the babies she now knew she wanted.

Chuck wasn't the man for her.

But the thought of any other man being with her, holding her in his arms, kissing and touching her intimately nearly brought Chuck to his knees.

How could he let her go into another man's life when he wanted her?

Holy hell. Was he falling in love with Kate?

He stared toward the door at the end of the hallway. Was that what had him running scared?

His head tried to tell him no, but his heart screamed yes!

The truth stared him straight in the eye. He'd fallen for Kate. Totally, completely and irreversibly. No amount of denying it could change that fact now.

Pushing her away had been a stupid defense mechanism he'd used on other women who'd tried to get close to him. The problem was that when he'd pushed her away, his heart went with her.

As if of their own accord, his feet carried him down the hallway to the master bedroom door. He lifted his hand to knock.

Before he could touch the wood-paneled door, pounding sounded on the front door in the living room.

He hesitated, knowing he had to undo the damage he'd just done or risk Kate walking away without giving him a second chance.

More pounding that had a desperation to it sounded. Chuck couldn't ignore it.

He gave one last glance at the door to the bedroom and ran for the front entrance.

"Chuck! Help!" cried a shaky female voice on the other side.

Chuck yanked open the door.

The elderly Mrs. Turner fell inside and into his arms. "Oh, please, help me."

"Mrs. Turner, what's wrong."

"My house—" She coughed and drew in a ragged breath. "My house is on fire and Geraldine is still inside!"

Even as she said the words, Chuck could smell the smoke.

"Kate!" he yelled. "Kate!"

Kate jerked open the door to the master bedroom, her hair in disarray, her eyes red-rimmed and puffy. When she saw Mrs. Turner, she hurried toward them. "What's happening?"

"My house is on fire, and Geraldine is still inside," Mrs. Turner wailed.

Chuck held onto Mrs. Turner's arms. "Who is Geraldine? A friend or relative?"

"No. She's my cat. Geraldine has been with me since my husband died. I can't lose her." The older woman pulled free of Chuck's hands. "I have to find her." She ran back out into the night.

Chuck shot a glance at Kate. "I have to help her."

"Go," she said. "I'll call 911 and stay here with Lyla."

"Lock the doors behind me and don't open for anyone but me." He reached for her and pulled her into his arms. "When I get back, we have to talk."

"No, we don't." Kate pulled back out of his grip. "You've said enough. I'm not dumb. I get it when I've been brushed off."

"No, Kate. I was wrong. Very wrong. But I can't do my apology justice until I make sure Mrs. Turner doesn't run into a burning house to save a cat."

"We'll be all right. Just go." Kate held open the door.

Chuck didn't want to leave her, but Mrs. Turner would go back into a burning building to save her cat if he didn't go after her and stop her.

"Wait." Kate ran to the kitchen, grabbed a dish towel and soaked it under the faucet. Quickly ringing it out, she handed it to him. "She can't run all that fast. You can catch her before she goes in."

"Thanks." He bent and brushed a quick kiss across her lips. "I was wrong, and you're amazing. We'll talk."

Then he ran out the door and across the yard to Mrs. Turner's house. Smoke leached out of the open windows and flames shone through the glass of one of the bedrooms.

The old woman was just reaching for the front doorknob.

"Mrs. Turner, wait!" he called out.

Mrs. Turner glanced back over her shoulder. "Geraldine."

"Don't go in," he shouted. "I will."

Mrs. Turner stood back as Chuck ran up the stairs.

He touched the doorknob with the tip of his finger. It wasn't hot, so he knew there wasn't much of a blaze yet in the living room. If the smoke and fire was only in the bedroom, he might have a chance to find the cat and get out before the whole house went up in flames.

"She's probably hiding under the couch or in the closet in my bedroom, the first door on your left down the hall," Mrs. Turner said. "She hides when she's scared."

Chuck opened the door and was immediately assailed with smoke.

He ducked low. "Promise me you'll stay out of the house, Mrs. Turner."

She nodded. "I promise."

"I'll do my best to find Geraldine." Chuck held the damp towel over his nose and entered the house, hunkering as low as he could to remain below the rising smoke.

Inside the house, the lights in the living room were still working. Apparently, the fire hadn't reached the breaker box or the lines connecting the house to the power pole.

He dropped to his knees and checked beneath the couch, feeling his way with his hands. Though he didn't encounter a furball, he felt dust bunnies and cat toys.

His eyes stung, but the towel helped to filter the smoke to keep him from breathing it into his lungs.

Chuck checked the kitchen as he passed and entered the hallway. Smoke poured out from beneath one of the bedroom doors. He touched the door handle to find it extremely hot. The sooner he got out of the house, the better. Old houses were tinderboxes that fed a fire. When the fire spread into the walls and attic, it would be all over.

Fortunately, the cat couldn't have gone into the bedroom with the closed door or it would likely have already died of smoke inhalation.

The first door on the left was open. Chuck pushed it wider and stepped inside. At first glance, he didn't see any sign of the cat. But then he didn't expect to. If the cat was in the bedroom, it would be under the bed or in the closet as Mrs. Turner had suggested.

The closet door was open as well with a clothes basket on the floor inside.

Though there were clothes in the basket, no cat was tangled amongst them.

Chuck pulled the basket out and searched the back of the closet and up on the shelf above.

No cat.

The smoke grew thicker, making his eyes burn and water. Even the damp cloth over his mouth and nose wasn't quite keeping him from breathing the thickening, tainted air.

Chuck dropped to his knees and crawled to the bed. The lights flickered and extinguished, leaving him feeling around in the dark.

He first encountered what felt like a plastic storage container. Dragging that out from beneath the bed, he touched on what felt like a suitcase.

The smoke was getting worse. He didn't have much time left before he had to get out. The roar and heat of the fire intensified. Over his head, flames penetrated the ceiling and large flakes of burning embers and ash fell down around his legs.

He scooted farther under the bed until he finally felt

something furry. Grabbing onto a leg, he dragged Geraldine toward him and was scratched for his efforts.

Refusing to release the leg he had, he pulled her closer, latched onto the scruff of her neck and inched backward until he cleared the bed.

Fire raged around him, smoke making it impossible to breathe. He covered his mouth with the damp cloth, inhaled as deeply as he could and wrapped the cloth around the cat's head and body and then dove for the door.

Just as he neared the threshold, the hallway ceiling crashed down, blocking his escape. He slammed shut the door and ran for the window.

When he tried to open it one-handed he couldn't get the window to budge and he couldn't put down the cat or it would go right back under the bed.

With time running out, he snatched a pillow off the bed, removed the pillow out of the case and shoved the cat into the pillowcase.

Quickly tying the opening in a knot, he set the cat on the floor, grabbed a vanity stool from near the dresser and bashed it against the window.

The old glass shattered.

Using the stool legs, he knocked the shards loose, tossed the cat in the pillowcase out on the grass and dove out just in time to breathe.

Behind him, the ceiling of the room he'd been in, crashed in, flames and sparks shooting out in a spray of fireworks.

Chuck sucked in air and coughed. Locating the pillowcase with the cat, he decided the cat was better off contained in the case. He lifted the cat, bag and all and rounded the front of the house.

Sirens screamed in the distance, and soon, the Eagle Rock Fire Department arrived in force.

Chuck located Mrs. Turner and handed her the cat in the bag. "Leave her in the bag for now or she might run away and get lost."

Mrs. Turner cried ugly tears as she clutched the smoke and soot-covered bag to her chest.

Inside, the cat yowled.

Chuck didn't care. He'd saved the woman's cat. Now, he had to get back to the little, yellow house and make sure the sparks from the Turner house didn't catch his home on fire.

CHAPTER 11

Kate stared out the side window facing Mrs. Turner's house, her heart beating fast, worry making it impossible to settle down. She'd dressed in jeans and a sweatshirt and pulled on her shoes.

She had to be ready in case the fire spread from one house to the other. It hadn't rained the entire time she'd been in Eagle Rock, which meant the vegetation was dry and could catch fire from one of the many flying embers kicked up by the wind.

"Mama?" Lyla's voice sounded behind her.

Kate turned away from the devastation and held open her arms. "Hey, sweetie. Come here."

Lyla padded across the floor and into Kate's arms. "I couldn't sleep."

"Did you have another bad dream?" she asked and combed her fingers through her niece's hair. "I could read another book to you, if you like."

Lyla shook her head and looked over Kate's shoulder to the window. "Is that a fire?"

Kate took her hand and held it in hers. "Yes, it is."

"Will the fire come here?"

"No, sweetie," Kate said, though she wasn't so sure herself. She'd be ready if it did. Getting Lyla to safety was her number one goal.

Pounding sounded on the door. "Police, open up! You need to evacuate, now."

Lyla squealed and buried her face in Kate's neck. "I'm scared."

"It's okay, honey. They just want us to get out in case the fire does spread. We're okay."

Lyla dared to lift her head. "Where's Daddy? I want Daddy Chuck."

Kate did, too.

More pounding sounded on the door. "Open up. You have to evacuate now," the voice called out.

Again, Lyla shrank against Kate.

Kate grabbed her purse from the counter and Lyla's blanket from the bedroom, and she ran for the door, carrying Lyla.

For a second, she hesitated. Chuck had warned her not to open the door for anyone but him. Surely he didn't expect her to ignore the police.

She unlocked the deadbolt and the lock on the knob. When she twisted the knob to open the door, it slammed inward, knocking her backward.

A man rushed in followed by a woman.

Kate didn't have time to think, nor the ability to defend herself with her hands full of Lyla. A cloth was shoved into her face, and she inhaled a sickly-sweet scent.

"Get the girl," the man said, his voice rough, urgent.

Kate's legs weakened, and she couldn't hold onto Lyla as someone yanked her from her arms.

"No, you can't take her," she mumbled, her vocal cords no longer hers to control as she slipped into the darkness and fell into the man's arms.

Her last coherent thought was of Chuck.

Please, help us.

The Eagle Rock Fire Chief waylaid Chuck as he crossed Mrs. Turner's yard, taking precious seconds of his time. He told the chief he'd be back to answer all his questions once he checked on his wife and daughter.

Chuck ran back to the little, yellow house and took the porch steps two at time, arriving at the front door.

His heart sank to the pit of his belly when he found the front door ajar. Without going inside, he knew.

Kate and Lyla were gone.

Inside, Kate's purse lay spilled across the floor, and Lyla's blanket lay beside it.

He raced through the little house, praying he was wrong but knowing the truth. When he returned to the front door, he had his cellphone out, dialing Hank.

Hank answered halfway through the first ring. "I was just about to jump in the truck. I heard on the police scanner that Old Lady Turner's house was on fire. Are you guys all right?"

His hand tightened on the phone. "I'm all right, but Kate and Lyla are gone."

"How?"

In a few abrupt sentences, Chuck explained about Mrs. Turner's cat and finding the door open, Kate's purse and Lyla's blanket.

"Any sign of forced entry?" Hank asked.

"No."

"Based on the purse and blanket, she opened the door, thinking she had to get out," Hank surmised.

Knowing he'd failed them, Chuck couldn't give up. He had to find them. "Where would they have taken them?"

"If Kate's still wearing the necklace I gave her, we can track her. Let me get Swede on it right now. And I'll be there in fifteen minutes—ten, if I own the road." Hank ended the call as abruptly as he'd answered.

Chuck left the house and returned to find Mrs. Turner sobbing in the arms of the fire chief.

When Chuck walked up, the chief took the opportunity to untangle himself from the older woman. "I have to check on a few things."

Mrs. Turner faced her house, tears slipping down her wrinkled cheeks. The fire had been extinguished, but the firefighters were still unloading gallons of water on the smoldering embers.

"Everything I own is gone. Everything. Including my husband's ashes."

"Mrs. Turner, you have Geraldine," Chuck reminded her.

She sniffed and hugged the cat still confined to the pillowcase. "Poor thing is beside herself."

As if on cue, the cat yowled a long, pained sound.

"If you need a place to stay, you can stay at our place," Chuck offered.

"I wouldn't dream of putting you out," Mrs. Turner said. "I can stay with Hugh and Greta or Wanda."

Chuck's jaw tightened. "You won't be putting us out. In fact, you'll have the place to yourself. Kate and Lyla had to leave. Family emergency."

Mrs. Turner touched his arm. "Oh, dear. I hope it isn't major."

"Me, too. We'll know more with time. For now, though, I have to leave as well. Work called. I have to go."

"You sure you won't mind if I stay in the house?"

"Not at all."

"Thank you. I'd rather be close by in case someone needs to ask me anything. And when they let me back into the wreckage, I hope to be able to salvage something. Anything." She sniffed and more tears slid down her tired face.

"I'm sure Kate wouldn't mind if you borrow some of her clothing. Help yourself to anything. I'll be back as soon as I can."

Hugh and Greta arrived a moment later, giving Chuck the chance to make his escape. He started toward Main Street and found a man walking his dog talking to a policeman.

"Excuse me," the man called out.

Chuck slowed, his eyes narrowing.

"Do you live in the yellow house?" the man asked.

"I do," Chuck replied.

"I've been trying to tell this officer that I saw something that worried me."

Chuck sucked in a breath and let it out slowly. "What did you see?"

"I'm new in town, but I like to walk my dog out here, because I can let Brutus off his leash to run and no one cares. I was at the end of the road when the shit hit the fan with the old lady's house." He waved toward the darkened end of the road. "Damned dog got a wild hair up his ass and chased off after a rabbit in the dark."

Chuck glanced over the man's shoulder toward Main Street, watching for Hank's truck. He wished the man would get to point.

"Anyway," the stranger continued. "I was back in the woods, trying to get Brutus back on his leash, when I heard the woman yelling. I got back to the road in time to see a man carrying a large sack over his shoulder, getting into a van. Then a woman carrying a crying child got into the van, and they drove away." He pointed toward the yellow cottage. "They came from that direction. I was afraid they were ransacking the house, but I wasn't there in time to stop them."

"Thank you for letting me know," Chuck stuck out his hand. "What's your name?"

The man shook his hand with a firm grip. "Lance Rankin." He nodded toward the police officer who had walked away. "I guess he's not interested in finding out if the house was looted."

"It wasn't, but the sack he was carrying was probably

my wife and the crying child was my daughter." Chuck spied Hank's truck. "Gotta go find them."

"Well, good luck, man. If you need anything, look me up. I'd be happy to help."

"Thanks."

"Semper Fi," Lance said.

Chuck did a double take. "Marine?"

Lance nodded. "Fresh out of the military. I'm here to look up a guy named Hank Patterson. I hear he might have some work for me. Want me to help get your wife back?"

"I'll let you know." Chuck didn't want to spend time with introductions to Hank. He'd get around to that after he found Kate and Lyla. He ran toward Main Street as Hank turned down the side street and eased to a stop behind all the emergency vehicles.

Chuck reached the truck before Hank could climb out and come looking for him.

"Good. I wasn't sure how to find you in that cluster." Hank backed out onto Main Street and headed out of town.

"Just talked to a marine who saw the people who took Kate and Lyla. They were in a van."

"Even better," Hank handed him a device with a green dot blinking on a screen. "Swede was able to get Kate's tracker to come up. We're following them."

Hank leaned forward in his seat. "Where are they going?"

"Looks like they're headed for Bozeman."

"Shouldn't we call the state police and have them head them off?"

Hank tightened his hands on the steering wheel. "I didn't have an idea of what kind of vehicle they might be in. Go ahead and call it in. Tell them to look for a van."

Chuck checked his cellphone and cursed. "No service."

"Want me to head back to town so that you can make that call?"

"How far ahead are they?"

Hank stared down at the device in Chuck's hand. "I'd say they have a fifteen-minute lead."

"You got any of your guys south of town or even in Bozeman?"

"Sorry. I have a call out to all of them, but they were assigned to outlying ranches providing security. Duke Morris is in Great Falls. His client owns a plane and offered to fly him into Bozeman in case we need him. Tate Parker is coming in from his ranch. I told him we were headed south and to get on the road toward Bozeman. He might catch up to us by the time we hit the city limits."

"That's four of us. You think whoever took Kate and Lyla will put up a fight?"

Hank's lips pressed into a tight line. "If they're from the same cult Kujo's been following, they might. He said the perimeter guards are armed with machine guns."

Chuck's gut tightened. "Let's hope we reach them before they get to Idaho."

Hank cast a sideways glance at Chuck. "We should be able to catch up to them well before that."

Thirty miles out of Bozeman, they'd made up at least

eight of the fifteen-minute lead Kate's captors had on them.

Hank shot a glance at the screen. "Uh-oh." He pulled up a GPS screen of Montana and enlarged the area.

Chuck tensed. "What?"

"Looks like they're headed for the airport in Three Forks."

"There's an airport at Three Forks?" Chuck asked, his heart thudding in his chest.

"A small one used mostly by general aviation flights."

"We're six minutes out." Hank laid his foot hard on the accelerator, pushing his truck past one hundred miles per hour. "Hold on."

Chuck clutched the armrest and prayed an elk or antelope didn't step out in front of the vehicle.

Rather than look at the road ahead, he studied the green blip on the screen. It had ceased moving. "They stopped." Hope rose in his chest. He stared at the dark road in front of the truck. Just a few more miles.

Hang in there, Kate and Lyla, he prayed.

Hank took the Three Forks exit and blew through town. The airport was southwest of the little burg. When it came in sight, Chuck could see the blinking light of a plane taking off into the sky.

"Please don't be them," he muttered beneath his breath. His gaze shifted back to the tracking device, and he let out a sigh of relief. The green blip hadn't moved.

They pulled up to the small airport.

Chuck pointed to a gray van parked near the gate. "There," he said. "The location device says she's in there."

MONTANA SEAL UNDERCOVER DADDY

Hank skidded to a stop behind the vehicle and both men jumped out.

Chuck pulled his handgun from the holster beneath his jacket and aimed it at the vehicle. "Cover me. I'm going in."

"Got your six," Hank reassured.

Chuck eased toward the van and around the side. The sliding door was open all the way, and the interior was empty.

Chuck cursed. "That plane that just left…I think they were on it." He leaned into the van and shined his cellphone flashlight at the interior. Something glinted beneath the beam.

Chuck pulled out the necklace with the tracking chip and clutched it in his palm. "They're on their own. We can't track them." He stared up into the sky, but the plane that had taken off was long gone, swallowed up by the indigo night sky.

Hank pulled out his cellphone. "I'm calling Kujo to give him the heads-up. Hopefully, that's where their abductors plan to go. If not, we have no way of locating them on the US continent."

Chuck pocketed the necklace and straightened, his heart in the vicinity of his knees, all hope fading. "What next, boss?"

"I'm going to reroute the plane Duke is in and have them land at this airport. We can fly out to just about anywhere. I'll get Swede on tracking the plane that left here. It must have a transponder code—unless they didn't file a flight plan and are flying without using instruments to guide them."

"And if Swede can't track them?"

"I'm putting a call into Kujo to stake out the closest airstrip to the cult community. If that's their destination, they might fly there."

"And where will we fly?" Chuck asked.

"Aiming for Idaho." Hank pulled out his cellphone and dialed. "My gut tells me that's where we'll find them." His attention turned to his cellphone. "Kujo, we have a problem I hope you can help us with."

Hank coordinated with Kujo and the other Brotherhood Protectors originally en route to Bozeman. Kujo would stake out the airport. Duke and Bear would meet them at the Three Forks Airport for pickup when the plane from Helena arrived.

Meanwhile, Chuck paced, wondering what was happening with Kate, praying they weren't on a wild goose chase to the wrong location. Kate and Lyla could be flying to Canada or Mexico, for all they knew. If they didn't locate them in the first forty-eight hours, they might never find them. Hell, they hadn't found Rachel and it had been almost a week since she'd disappeared.

Chuck walked faster, his steps taking him to the end of the taxiway. He turned and walked back in time to see Bear arrive.

Hank briefed them on the situation and had them meet at his truck. He opened the tool box to display an entire array of AR15s, similar to the M4A1 with SOPMOD upgrades used by members of DEVGRU. His stock also included handguns, Ka-Bar knives and ammunition.

Each man selected dark clothing, black armored

vests, helmets, night vision goggles and communications equipment, testing the radios as they waited for the plane to arrive. They packed the equipment in the go-bags Hank provided.

By the time they were ready, a plane touched down on the runway and taxied over to where they were waiting.

Steps were lowered and John Wayne "Duke" Morris stepped down and crossed the tarmac. "Thought we were landing in a cow pasture." He extended his hand to Hank. The two shook. "The pilot has instructions to take us anywhere we want to go, courtesy of Lena Love."

"The actress?" Bear asked. "You still covering her six?"

"Between Angel and I, we've got her covered."

"I thought she was a raging lunatic," Bear said.

"She is, but she trusts us to keep her from jumping off the deep end or someone shooting her because she's so hard to get along with." Duke chuckled. "We don't put up with her crap. I think she respects that."

"You sure you're still good for working with her?" Hank asked. "We don't need the business so much you have to put up with her orneriness."

"Don't worry." Duke waved a hand. "We have it covered. Besides the job has its perks. We're supposed to fly to St. Maarten Island in the Caribbean soon for a movie location shoot. That should be interesting."

The whole time they were talking, Hank was handing Duke the same equipment he'd outfitted Bear and Chuck with.

Duke weighed the AR15 in his hands. When he looked up, his eyebrows were high. "Are we expecting an all-out war?"

"We don't know what exactly to expect, but if we learn Kate and Lyla have been taken to the cult's location in Idaho, we have some intel. Kujo's been there on reconnaissance." Hank handed him a helmet and night vision goggles. "They've set up the perimeter with machine guns and loads of ammunition."

"Sounds like a friendly bunch. All on American soil. Go figure." He shook his head and helped himself to magazines full of ammunition for the rifle and handgun he selected.

Once Duke had all he needed, they loaded into the plane and the pilot set a course for the airstrip closest to where Kujo had been hanging out in the mountains of Idaho.

Normally, Chuck's gut was a reliable gauge of what was happening. But this time, all he could feel was cold dread. Perhaps he was too heavily invested in the outcome. Worst case scenario, the plane Kate and Lyla were on would crash. Much like the story of his wife and child. Or the team would get there too late to save Kate and Lyla from whatever horrific fate the cult had in store for them. Or they'd get there to discover Kate and Lyla weren't there at all and never were. They'd have to start their search all over. At least in the last scenario, they might have the chance of finding them alive.

Chuck forced himself to think positive. Kate and

Lyla were at the cult's camp. They'd swoop in and rescue them and Rachel.

He'd tell Kate he loved her. She'd tell him the same, and they'd live happily ever after.

A man had to have his dreams. Otherwise, life wasn't worth living.

CHAPTER 12

Kate came to with a splitting headache, her face lying against a cold, hard floor and darkness. She blinked her eyes several times just to make sure she was actually awake and not in some terrible nightmare.

Pain throbbed in her hip where it lay against the solid floor. She shifted and moaned.

Soft sobbing echoed against the walls, forcing Kate to go that extra little bit to full consciousness. "Hello," she called out.

The sobbing grew louder.

"Hey, who's there?" she called out, the hairs on the back of her neck standing at attention. The sobs sounded soft and feminine, but not childlike.

Child. Lyla!

Kate pushed to a sitting position. "Lyla?"

"She's not here," a voice said from a different direction. "I don't know where they took her."

Kate knew that voice. It sounded so much like hers. "Rachel?" Oh, dear, sweet Lord. "Rachel? It's you."

More sobs sounded from the other side of the room. Were there two women?

Kate ignored the sobs and felt her way across the floor until she bumped into another person. "Rachel?" Tears welled in her eyes and spilled down her face.

Rachel's cold arms wrapped around her. "Oh, Kate. They have Lyla." She shook with the force of her silent sobs. The woman in the other corner had the market on noisy crying.

"I tried to keep her safe," Kate said. "They tricked us by setting the house next door on fire."

"You did the best you could. I should have known I couldn't keep her safe. Once you're in their fold, they don't give up. They don't let go." Rachel hugged Kate, laying her head on Kate's shoulder. "I tried to make a run for it, but they found me. And now they have Lyla."

"We'll get her out of here. You'll see." Kate forced confidence into her voice. Though she wasn't sure how she'd make it happen, she would get Rachel and Lyla out of this hell.

"I tried to protect her. When they said she had to marry at eight years old, I knew we couldn't stay. They do horrible things to the women and young girls. I didn't see it at first. When I did, I begged Myles to leave. But he wouldn't listen. They brainwashed him. He became just like James."

"Who's James?" Kate asked.

"James Royce, the leader of the People of Ascension. He says he's the voice of God." She cried into Kate's shirt. "What man of God preys on little girls?"

"None, sweetie." Kate smoothed a hand over Rachel's hair. "He's a monster."

"And that's why I had to leave."

Kate held her sister close, thankful they were finally together. If only the circumstances could have been different. "Why didn't you leave sooner?"

"I didn't know. They keep their secrets until you're assimilated into the cult. I just happened to take longer than the others. Myles and I lived on the outskirts in a log cabin. We grew our own food, taught Lyla to respect nature and I thought we had a good life. Until Myles was inducted into the inner circle. He changed. From the kind, gentle man and father of our child to an evil, horrible being willing to give over his own daughter to the leader as one of his wives."

Kate's heart lodged in her throat. "That's what they wanted? To make Lyla one of the leader's wives? She's only three years old."

"I know. At first, I thought it was just a way to protect her. James's wives and children are treated the best. They get the best food, the best lodging and clothing. The community shares the bounty of each family's harvest. But I never saw James's family contribute to the rest. When I asked why, I was beaten with a broomstick."

"Oh, Rachel. Why didn't you tell me what was going on?"

Rachel shrugged against her. "We barely talked anymore. Myles and I had already given up so many worldly things like television and telephones. When I could get to town and call you, I thought you wouldn't believe me if I told you what was going on. And I tried to convince Myles to leave and take our family somewhere far away from the madness."

"And what did he say?" Kate clenched her fists, already knowing it hadn't been good.

"He told James what I'd said. James gave him a leather strap and told him the only way to bring me in line was to beat the resistance out of me. I had to be taught what was expected." Rachel cried harder. "And he did. He beat me. Myles wasn't the sweet, kind man I married anymore. I couldn't stay. But I had no money, and I couldn't take much with me. All I could do was walk with Lyla out of the woods, all the way to a highway, where I hitched a ride with a kind, old trucker who took me all the way to California."

Kate's heart ached for her sister. All the while Rachel had been suffering, Kate had been living the life of a high-powered executive, with more money than she could ever spend. Shame made her heart heavy. "I'm so sorry, Rachel. I should have known. I should have been there for you."

Rachel shook her head. "You couldn't have known. I didn't tell you. I was afraid and ashamed of what I'd let happen. Running away seemed the only option. I don't know what would have happened if the truck driver hadn't been going my way. He even went as far as to give me enough money to take a taxi to your apartment, and he bought a stuffed animal for Lyla. I owe that man my life."

Kate smiled though her heart ached. So that's where Lyla had gotten Sid Sloth, perhaps her first and only stuffed animal. When they got out of the mess they were in, Auntie Kate was going to give that child all the stuffed animals she could ever want and to hell with James Royce.

The sobs grew louder from the woman in the corner.

"Who is she?" Kate asked.

"Margaret, one of the sister wives James grew tired of. When he no longer has a use for them, he kicks them out of his house, claiming they've sinned." Rachel snorted. "The only sin they've committed is being trapped in this hell."

"How long have you been here?" Kate asked.

"They caught me the day after I left Lyla with you. I've been here in this cell ever since."

"Oh, Rachel. I'm so sorry." Kate hugged her sister. "We're going to get out of here. I swear on my life. And we're going to get Lyla out as well. I love that little girl. She's amazing."

Rachel laughed, the sound breaking on a sob. "I've missed her so much. I tried hard to give her a normal life, despite James and his insanity. She deserves a chance to be a child. She deserves happiness."

"Yes, she does. And we're going to give it to her." Kate pushed to her feet. "Do they feed you and let you relieve yourself?"

Rachel let Kate pull her to her feet. "Twice a day they bring a meal. Once in the morning and again in the evening. We use a bucket in the other corner to relieve ourselves. Someone comes in once a day to empty it."

"Is it always dark in here?" Kate couldn't get over how pitch-black it was in the cell.

"When the sun comes up, we get a little light from beneath the doorway. Other than that, yes." Rachel sighed. "I've felt my way around the entire room. It's made of concrete blocks. I've even used the handle on the waste can to try and chink away at the grout, thinking I might dig my way out eventually. It's no use. This cell is escape-proof."

Kate's jaw hardened. "Nothing is escape-proof when people are involved." She reached for her sister again and hugged her close. "We have each other. You know we're stronger when we work together."

Rachel wrapped her arms around her sister and held on tight. "I'm sorry you got dragged into this mess, but I'm so glad you found me."

"Me, too." She set her sister to arm's length. "Rachel, they brought me in unconscious. Where exactly are we?"

"We're in the mountains of Idaho."

Hope swelled in Kate's chest, and she dropped her voice to a whisper. "I think we might get out of here sooner than you think."

"Really? How?"

"Do you remember telling me to go to Montana and find Hank Patterson?" The mere thought of the Brotherhood Protectors gave her courage. They would come. Chuck would be beside himself until he found them. Yes, he'd told her he didn't want a relationship. But the man was committed to his mission. He wouldn't stop until he found and freed them. Of that, Kate was absolutely certain.

Rachel squeezed her sister around her waist. "The truck driver told me that if I ever needed help from someone I could trust with my life, I should look up Hank Patterson in Montana. He said his son worked for him. He employs former military men and women. Did you find Hank?"

Kate laughed. "I did. And if I'm not mistaken, he and his guys will find us."

"Thank God." Rachel hugged her sister again. "I don't know if it's fate or divine intervention, but I think someone or something has a plan. We just have to learn what it is."

"Though Hank's guys will be coming, we can't wait for them to get here. We have to help ourselves and Lyla out of this situation." A plan formed in Kate's mind, and with that plan, confidence and a fierce determination returned. "For now, we should rest until daylight. We need to be ready when they bring in the morning food."

BY THE TIME they landed outside the small town of Angel's Rest, Idaho, the eastern sky had lightened with the gray of predawn.

The pilot offered to stay around for twenty-four hours to take them back to Eagle Rock when they were done with their business.

Hank thanked the man and led the way out of the plane onto the tarmac.

Kujo and his retired military working dog, Six,

crossed from the fixed base operator's building where the general aviation planes were serviced. "You guys are a sight for sore eyes," Kujo said. He reached out and shook Hank's hand and then greeted the others as they descended from the plane, carrying their go-bags.

"What's the scoop?" Hank asked.

Kujo's brows drew together. "A plane landed here a couple of hours ago. A van, with several heavily armed men, met them on the tarmac. They offloaded their cargo and drove away. I followed them up into the hills. They were headed for the cult compound."

"Did you see what their cargo was?" Chuck held his breath, waiting for Kujo's response.

"No. I didn't want to get too close in case they saw me. But whatever it was took two people to load one of the bundles, and I think a woman loaded the other. I'm guessing it was the woman and child you thought it might be. The sizes looked about right. They must have given the woman something to knock her out. She wasn't struggling at all."

Chuck let go of the breath he'd been holding and pushed forward, his heart squeezing so hard it hurt. "Take us to the camp."

"It'll be daylight by the time we get there," Kujo warned. "We'll need to move in slowly. They have a pretty tight perimeter, and they mean business. They're fortified with manned machine guns and men armed with semi-automatic rifles."

"Think they know how to use them?" Hank asked.

Kujo nodded. "I know they do. I found where they

practice. It looked like something mocked-up for military training in urban terrain. These guys are badass."

Hank frowned. "Then we have to tread lightly. We're not in a war zone. We're on American soil. If they own the land, they might have the right to defend it." He glanced around at the men. "Number one…don't kill anyone, unless it's your last choice. Number two…be careful, there might be collateral damage if anyone starts shooting."

"And there would be." Kujo's mouth set in a grim line. "Inside the perimeter is an entire community with women and children."

"Which means, we can't go in shooting everything that moves," Hank said. "Killing women and children isn't what we do."

"And it's bad for business," Kujo agreed.

"What *do* we have going for us?" Duke asked.

"Someone inside that compound kidnapped two women and a child," Chuck said.

Hank nodded. "Those people are on the wrong side of the law. We're only going in to rescue our clients."

They followed Kujo to the large SUV he'd rented for his stay in Angel's Rest, and loaded their gear in the rear and then climbed inside, filling all the seats.

Six lay on the floor between the captain's chairs and rested his head on his paws.

The ride up into the mountains would have been nice if Chuck wasn't worried about Kate, Lyla and Rachel. The road wound through national forests, across rivers and past stark bluffs. The soft morning sun shone through the canopy of leaves, giving a false sense of peace in a place sure to test their abilities.

Eventually, they turned off the paved highway and bumped along a dirt road for another couple of miles.

"I found this road while out hiking the area. It parallels the one leading into the cult compound," Kujo said. "It's not as well maintained, but it serves the purpose of getting us closer without having to walk several more miles unnecessarily."

He tipped his head toward a cooler on the back seat. "There are sandwiches and drinks in the cooler. You might want to fuel up before we start our hike. The hills are steep and rocky. It'll take some time getting in. If we play our cards right, we can get close enough that I can show you where the perimeter guards are located before dark. Then when night falls, we can sneak past them or take them out. Either way, we'll get in."

Chuck wasn't hungry, but he ate anyway. He understood the necessity of providing his body with fuel. If he wasn't in top physical condition, he put his teammates at risk. So, he ate a sandwich, wondering if Kate and Lyla's captors were feeding them so that they could keep up their strength.

He hated that Kate had been kidnapped and hated even worse that Lyla had been subjected to this nightmare yet again. At this rate, the poor kid would have bad dreams for the rest of her life.

He vowed to find the three of them and get them out unscathed. Failure wasn't an option.

Kujo parked the SUV beneath the spreading branches of an oak tree.

The men climbed out, donned their gear and performed a comm check with their radios. When everyone was ready, they moved swiftly through the woods while they could. Kujo explained that once they crossed over a certain ridge, they'd have to slow down and move carefully to avoid detection.

Chuck had to resist the urge to charge through the woods and right into the camp. He would be of no help to the women if the perimeter guards shot him and left him for dead.

The men spread out, using the skills they'd attained while training with special operations teams. Noise discipline was fully enforced. Along the way, they gathered additional leaves and foliage to camouflage their helmets and clothing.

Kujo led the way, pausing at the top of a ridge to point out where they were heading and the location of the cult's camp. "From here on, move slowly, deliberately and keep low. They're using real bullets in those machine guns and rifles."

Hank waved his hand indicating they should move out.

One by one, they slipped over the top of the ridge and descended into a broad valley.

In the distance, Chuck could make out a few buildings and a farm field. As they dropped lower, climbing over rocks and boulders, he lost sight of the village, but he knew about how far it was and hope built in his chest. He had a hard time slowing down when he wanted to race ahead, find his girls and get them out of harm's way.

But he followed Kujo's lead. The man had spent time spying on the closed community. He would know what they had to do in order to stay safe, get past the perimeter guards and rescue the women.

By the time Kujo brought them to a halt, it was past noon.

Though the air in the mountains was still a bit chilly, Chuck had worked up a sweat, climbing over hills and easing past some rugged obstacles.

"We stop here," Kujo said into Chuck's headset. "The guard manning the machine gun is at our ten-o'clock position. Look closely. He's using camouflage netting to blend into his surroundings, only the camouflage is lighter than the surrounding green of the trees. Do you see it?"

A moment of silence passed.

"I see him," Duke acknowledged.

"Me, too," Hank said.

Chuck raised his mini binoculars and studied the terrain until he too spotted the camouflage netting. "I see him."

"Got 'em," Bear chimed in.

"Now," Kujo said. "Look toward the two-o'clock position. There's a man sleeping at his post. He's armed with a semi-automatic rifle."

Once again, the men chimed in when they spotted the second guard.

"There are three more positions in the woods and a pair of guards on the road leading into the community." Kujo had done well with his recon mission.

"We can't see anything of the community from here?" Hank said.

"No, you have to get past the perimeter guards to get close enough to see what's going on in the village," Kujo admitted. "I was able to sneak past the two guards on the northern end of the perimeter a couple of times. But other than the training they're conducting, I didn't see much else. They have gardens they tend and fields of wheat and corn. They farm using mules and primitive plows."

"Kate, Lyla and Rachel have to be in there somewhere," Chuck said.

"Most of the buildings are made of logs cut from the surrounding forest. But there is one larger structure made of concrete blocks, located in the center of the community," Kujo said. "I didn't see a whole lot of movement around it, but that would be my bet if they're being held captive."

"That's our objective," Hank said. "We'll wait until nightfall to enter the camp. By then, the women and children will be inside, eating their evening meal or in bed and sleeping. For now, rest in place. We move as soon as it gets dark."

Chuck stared at the woods ahead, every muscle in his body tense, ready to rush into the village and free the woman he'd fallen head over heels for. Love? Yes, he loved her. Was it too soon to know? Hell, no.

Why else would he feel so horrible? If he didn't care about her, he might not be so anxious to get this extraction operation under way.

He lay on the ground, his weapon pointed toward

the machine gun nest. Drawing on his experience as a SEAL, he focused on controlling his respiration and heart rate. If he didn't relax and let his body rest, he'd be worn out before he took one step toward the camp. At the ripe old age of forty-seven, he worked out, ran and lifted weights. But he knew enough to recognize that he had to pace himself.

Chuck lay still, his pulse slowing, his breathing becoming more regular. He had a mission to accomplish, and he needed every bit of strength and stamina to do it right.

When the sun dipped over the edge of the western ridgeline, the lengthening shadows blended into the dark gray of dusk.

They'd be moving soon. It wouldn't be long before he would be reunited with Kate and Lyla. He could barely wait another minute to see them, but he practiced patience, praying they were all right and everything would turn out okay. He sure as hell couldn't lose them now. Not when his heart was fully committed to the love he felt.

"Time to move out," Hank said into Chuck's headset.

He gave his full focus to the mission ahead, and set out to do it to the best of his abilities. Lives depended on him. Lyla's, Rachel's and Kate's lives.

CHAPTER 13

Kate waited through the day for someone to open the door to their cell. But no one came. Her stomach rumbled and by the fading light beneath the door, she guessed the sun was setting. And still, no one came to give them food or water.

"This is the first time they've skipped feeding us breakfast," Rachel said.

In the limited light, Kate studied her sister. Her skin was pale, except where shadows made dark crescents beneath her eyes. She'd lost weight since Kate had last seen her, appearing almost gaunt.

When they got out of there, Kate was going to feed her sister good food and take care of her. She'd never have to be afraid again.

First, they had to get out of their prison.

Darkness claimed the cell again. Night settled in. Hunger knifed through her belly, but Kate refused to let it bring her down. She hadn't been there as long as Rachel. One day without food wouldn't slow her.

Footsteps sounded outside the metal door of their prison, and keys rattled and scraped against the lock.

The door opened, and a woman entered carrying a tray of food.

A man stood behind her, holding a lantern.

Kate recognized the woman as Becca, the lady who, with her daughter Mary, had befriended her in the park in Eagle Rock. "Becca?"

Becca cast her eyes downward. "You should eat," she said softly.

"You were part of bringing me and Lyla here?" Kate shook her head. "Why?"

"It's not for me to explain. I only do as my husband commands," she said and slid her eyes sideways as if motioning toward the man with the lantern. Her husband, Daniel.

Anger burned in Kate's gut. "You lied to me and took my child."

"She was not yours to take," the man said from the doorway. "The child belongs to the collective."

"She doesn't belong to the collective." Kate's hands balled into fists. "She should be with her mother."

"Please," Becca begged. "Take the tray. You need to eat to keep up your strength."

Clearly, the woman was cowed by the man behind her. This made Kate even angrier. But she held her temper in check, channeling it into a plan.

She took the tray from Becca and then tipped it. The food slipped onto the floor.

"Oh, now look what you've done." Becca ducked to

pick up what she could, leaving a clear line from Kate to the man in the doorway.

Curling her arm, Kate flung the tray like a frisbee, aiming it at Daniel's throat. Her aim was true. The tray slammed into the man's Adam's apple. He dropped the lantern. The lantern oil spilled onto his jeans, and the flame caught his pant leg on fire.

Daniel clutched at his throat, gasping for breath while the flames climbed up his leg.

Kate grabbed Rachel's hand and ran for the door.

Blocking her path, Daniel hopped up and down in an attempt to put out the fire.

Once again, Kate put her kickboxing class to use and planted her heel in Daniel's gut, knocking him backward. His head hit the concrete wall with a loud thud, and he slid to the ground.

"Run!" Holding Rachel's hand, Kate dashed past Daniel and ran for a set of stairs.

"Wait," a voice called out behind them. "Take me with you."

Kate paused with her foot on the bottom step and glanced back at Becca, her hands outstretched.

As Becca passed her husband, Daniel reached out and snagged her ankle. She fell hard, landing on her stomach.

Daniel raised his fist to punch her.

Kate ran back and kicked his arm before he could land the punch.

He roared, rolled to the side and lurched to his feet, towering over Kate. "I should have killed you instead of bringing you here."

Kate crouched in a fighting position, her eyes narrowing. "You're not going to do either."

The big man's face glowed a ruddy red in his anger. He seemed to have forgotten the fire climbing up his leg, burning his skin.

Kate cocked her leg and hit him in the kneecap.

Daniel clenched his fist and swung hard.

Kate ducked but not fast enough.

His fist clipped the top of her head, sending her staggering backward.

"Kate!" Rachel cried.

Before Kate's vision could clear, Daniel swung again.

Only this time, his fist didn't make it to her face.

Becca had swung the lantern, catching Daniel's arm, blocking the blow meant for Kate. Oil spilled out of the crushed lantern onto Daniel's arm, and his shirt burst into flames.

The man screamed and staggered backward.

Becca grabbed Margaret's arm and dragged her out of the cell.

The four women raced up the steps and out into the open, night air.

"Where are your children?" Kate demanded.

"In James's house," Becca said. "But you won't get inside. He has guards."

"We're getting inside," Kate vowed. "I'm not leaving Lyla with that lunatic. Show me the way."

Becca backed up several steps. "I c-can't."

"You can, and you will." Kate snagged the woman's arm. "Show me. I'll do the rest."

Margaret stepped forward. "I'll show you the back

way into the house. I lived there for seven years. I know how to get in and out without being seen." She darted a glance left then right. "Follow me." Then she slipped into the shadows cast by the stars lighting up the sky.

"Stay and risk being caught, or come with us," Kate said to Becca. "We're going after Lyla and Mary."

Becca bit her lip, her eyes wide with fear. "You don't know what he's like."

"We're going." Kate left Becca standing in the doorway of the camp prison. A moment later, she heard the sound of footsteps behind her. Becca hurried to catch up.

Margaret had the lead, slipping from shadow to shadow alongside the buildings lining the road through the village. At the northern end of the village stood a much larger building made of stone and cedar, not the rustic log cabins so many had built with their bare hands and lived in with nothing more than wood-burning heat.

Margaret skirted the front of the building and scurried around to the back.

Kate paused between buildings and gripped her sister's arms. "Stay here. There's no need for both of us to go in. I'll get Lyla out. If anything happens to me, get out of the camp and find help."

"Kate, I can't let you go in there alone," Rachel said. "You don't understand. James is…" she shook her head. "He's evil. He's charismatic, charming when he wants to be, and he makes you believe what he wants you to believe."

"I won't fall for his nonsense," Kate promised.

"I didn't think I would either, but I watched so many others caught in his spell, and I was too."

"I'm not one of them, Rachel. And you aren't either, not anymore. You got out once. You'll get out again. Now, wait here and be ready to go for help if I don't come out with Lyla in the next five minutes. Got it?"

Rachel hugged Kate hard and let her go. "I love you, sister."

"I love you, too." Kate left Rachel hiding in the shadows.

CHUCK TOOK point on neutralizing the machine gun. He slipped through the night, placing each foot carefully to avoid making a sound.

Circling wide, he came from the rear of the machine gun nest, dropped into the fox hole and grabbed the man from behind in a choke hold.

Fortunately, the gunner hadn't had his finger on the trigger. He struggled but was no match for Chuck's superior strength. When the man went limp in Chuck's arms, he lowered him to the ground, checked quickly for a pulse and then secured him with zip ties. He slapped duct tape over the man's mouth and left him lying in the foxhole.

"Machine gun neutralized," he informed the others.

"Got my rifleman," Duke reported.

"Should we take out the others?" Bear asked.

"No time. We need to keep moving," Hank said. "If

they check in with the perimeter guards and find the ones we tied up, they'll set off an alarm. Things will get sticky."

The men moved through the night, easing into the little village.

Kujo led the way to the cinder-block building.

Chuck followed as close as he could, covering his teammate's six.

Although it had been years since he'd been on a mission working with a team, his training came back to him. Once they were in the village proper, Chuck covered while Kujo moved forward. Then Kujo covered him while Chuck moved forward.

They didn't know what to expect in the way of resistance inside the camp. The occupants might consider themselves sufficiently protected with the perimeter guards and the two on the road leading in. Then again, they might have snipers perched on the rooftops of the log cabins.

Chuck doubted that, but then he wasn't willing to put it to the test. He covered Kujo as if snipers were waiting to pick them off, one by one.

Hank, Duke and Bear followed Chuck, leap-frogging their way from building to building.

Chuck made it to the concrete-block building first. The entrance door stood open with a set of stairs leading downward.

He paused long enough to shift his night vision goggles into place. A giant green blob of a human staggered out of the darkness, cursing. "That damned woman. I'll kill her."

Shifting the goggles back up on his helmet, Chuck stepped through the door, closed it behind him and switched on the flashlight clipped to his vest, shining it right into the eyes of the man threating to murder a woman.

That's when he recognized him. This was the same man he and Kate had run into in the grocery store in Eagle Rock. "Where's Kate?" Chuck asked in a low and dangerous voice. He dropped down a step. "I'll give you two seconds to answer, which is more than you gave her before kidnapping her."

"I don't know where the bitch went." His lip curled up in a snarl. "She won't get out of camp. No one does."

"That's where you're wrong." Chuck descended another step. "Time's up." As he rushed down the rest of the stairs, Daniel roared and ran up.

They met like clashing Titans.

Though Daniel was younger, he didn't have the same set of battle skills as Chuck. With minimal effort, Chuck twisted the man's arm up behind his back and pinned him face-first against the wall. "Where's Kate?" He shoved the man's arm higher up the middle of his back.

Daniel cried out. "I don't know. She kicked me in the gut and ran out of here with three other women."

The door at the top of the stairs opened. "Everything all right?" Kujo whispered into Chuck's headset.

"They were in here," Chuck said. "If you'll give me a hand…"

Kujo hurried down the stairs.

Chuck made quick work of binding the man's wrists with a zip tie and then his ankles.

Kujo covered his mouth with duct tape.

Leaving Daniel at the bottom of the stairs, Chuck and Kujo stepped out of the building.

"Where to now?" Chuck asked.

"Chuck, Kujo, head north. We found two women hiding in the shadows. One says she's Kate's sister, Rachel."

Chuck resisted the urge to race up the road. Instead, he and Kujo covered each other as they slipped from shadow to shadow until they joined the other three Brotherhood Protectors.

A woman who looked a lot like Kate shivered in the shadows with the woman Chuck recognized as Becca, Daniel's wife.

Chuck's fists clenched. "What have you done with Kate?" he demanded in a hushed tone.

Becca held up her hands. "I helped her escape," she said.

"The hell you did." Chuck fought to keep from wrapping his hands around the woman's neck. "You and your husband helped kidnap her and Lyla."

"I had to," she said. Her chin dipped to her chest. "My husband made me. If I didn't help, he would have beat me and my daughter."

Chuck didn't want to believe her, but after meeting Daniel…He tightened his lips. "Where's Kate?"

"She went after Lyla." Rachel stepped forward and pointed. "She's in that building."

The men studied the rock and cedar structure.

"It belongs to the cult leader, James Royce." Rachel's voice shook. Her teeth chattered in the cool night air.

"He has Lyla and Mary. Kate made me promise to find help if she wasn't out in five minutes." She stared into Chuck's gaze. "She's been in there longer than five minutes." A sob choked her last words. "Please, help her."

CHAPTER 14

Kate and Margaret slipped through a gate in the walled garden at the rear of James Royce's house.

"They lock the back door every night, but I can pick the lock," Margaret said.

Following the woman, Kate weaved her way through a garden of vegetables and flowers to a door half-hidden by a rose trellis.

The scent of roses filling the air was incongruous with the terror constricting Kate's lungs.

She pushed past the fear, knowing she might be Lyla's only hope of escape. Yes, the men of Hank's brotherhood would be there soon. She had no doubt of that. But she couldn't risk James taking Lyla hostage or making a run for it, taking the child along as his insurance policy.

Kate had to get to the little girl before James realized the women had escaped, and before the former special operations guys converged on the complex.

Margaret reached the door first and felt about the

doorframe with her hand. She retrieved a narrow metal file and stuck it into the lock on the doorknob.

With a few quick jiggles, she unlocked the door and pushed it open. Pressing a finger to her lips, she led the way into the house and down a long corridor.

The doors on either side opened outward and had padlocks on the outside.

A chill raced across Kate's skin. What kind of monster locked the people of his household inside their rooms? What if there was a fire? They'd all perish before anyone could get them out.

Even more determined to find Lyla, Kate pushed forward with Margaret leading the way.

The hallway ended in a large, starkly-furnished living area. The floor was made of stone tiles with no soft rugs for bare feet to walk on.

There wasn't a speck of dust or dirt anywhere to be seen. The area barely appeared to be lived in.

Margaret turned and walked along the wall to another hallway much like the first. She stopped halfway down that hall and used her file to pick the padlock hanging on the hasp.

The lock clicked, echoing loudly in the quiet corridor.

"What are you doing here?" a woman's voice called out from behind Kate and Margaret.

Margaret pulled off the lock and turned to face the woman. She pushed Kate behind her and whispered. "Find your girl." Louder she said, "I came back for my son."

"He is no longer your son," the woman said. "You

were cast out of this household. Your children belong to James."

"No," Margaret said. "I will not abandon my children. They belong with me."

Kate fumbled with the door handle and pulled hard. The door didn't open. Glancing upward, she noted a latch. She reached up and flipped the latch over then jerked open the door. "Lyla?" she called out. "Mary."

"Mama?" a little voice responded. The five-year-old Kate had met at the park rose from a pallet of blankets on the floor.

"Mary, come with me, now." She rushed in, grabbed Mary's hand and led her toward the door.

Half a dozen little heads lifted from their pallets. All eyes looked toward Kate. They were all little children, probably no more than five years old. Kate's heart pinched hard in her chest. And none of them were her niece. She turned to Mary. "Where's Lyla?"

"He took her." Mary's face scrunched, and tears welled in her eyes. "I want my mama."

"Who took her?" Kate asked. In her gut, she already knew.

"Our father," Mary said, tears rolling down her cheeks. "Please. I want my mama."

The other children in the room heard Mary crying, and started crying too.

Kate hated leaving them, but she had to find Lyla before James did something stupid.

She backed out of the room to find Margaret pressed against the wall by a woman twice her size and a man standing nearby, holding Lyla in his arms.

Kate straightened with Mary's hand in hers. "Let Lyla go, James. She's done nothing to hurt you."

"Mama," Lyla called out and leaned toward her with arms outstretched.

James tightened his hold on the little girl. "Quiet!" he thundered, his eyes narrowing. "I value each of my children. They are the future. I will not allow them to be poisoned by the heathens existing outside our paradise."

Kate snorted. "Paradise? What kind of paradise forces its residents to stay when they want to leave? What kind of paradise locks its people in at night?"

"They are locked in for their protection."

"Against whom?" Kate demanded. "The only person I see who poses a threat is you."

He raised a finger and pointed. "You are a pariah. You know not of what you speak."

"Oh, cut the preacher crap. You don't impress me. A man who threatens women and children isn't a man at all. He's a coward who can only control those who are weaker." Kate let go of Mary's hand and eased past the woman holding Margaret hostage.

One rescue at a time. Lyla needed her.

"Let go of the child," Kate reiterated, her voice dropping to a low, menacing warning.

"Or what?" James cocked an eyebrow. "It appears I'm the only one with anything to bargain with." He tipped his head toward Lyla, who was crying softly in his arms. "If I like, I could snap her neck before you reach me. Is that what you want?" He asked like he was inquiring what flavor of ice cream she preferred. Then his tone grew deeper and his lips pulled back in a feral snarl. "Because if you come one step closer, that's what I'll do."

Kate stopped five feet short of where James stood with Lyla. The man was insane. She wouldn't put it past him to hurt Lyla.

"Just put Lyla down. Take me in her place. She's just a little girl."

"Mama," Lyla cried. She wiggled and slipped free of his grip. Sliding down the man's body.

James grabbed at air, unable to catch her.

Lyla landed on her feet and darted toward Kate.

James dove after her, grabbing her by the hair.

Rage ripped through Kate, and she lunged for James, plowing into him headfirst.

When Kate hit him in the gut, he released Lyla's hair as he flew backward and slammed against the wall.

Kate yelled, "Run, Lyla!"

James grabbed Kate around the waist, rolled her over and straddled her back. "You have been nothing but trouble since you and Myles came. I should have done away with you when I did away with Myles." He gripped a handful of her hair and pulled back her head. "If you aren't a believer, you're done."

Kate was pinned to the ground with no way to fight back. She closed her eyes, prepared for the man to slam her head against the hard stone floor. Her head would crack open like a melon. "James, don't," she said, her voice raspy, her throat stretched with the force of him pulling her backward.

"What you don't understand is that I do as I please. I'm the messenger of God."

"Not anymore, you're not," a deep voice rumbled off the walls. The weight on Kate's back lifted, but the hand in her hair dragged her up with it.

Kate's heart filled with joy. Chuck had found them.

"Let go of her," Chuck commanded.

"No." Royce's voice was nothing more than a gasp.

"Do it, or I'll snap your neck like you threated to snap Lyla's."

Kate couldn't see behind her, but she could tell Chuck had a hold of Royce and was hurting him.

Eventually, the man released his hold on Kate's hair.

She dropped to her knees and crawled forward. Once she was well out of his reach, she leaped to her feet.

Chuck had Royce in a chokehold, his face set in grim lines. "Nobody threatens my family," he said, his voice a low growl. "Do you understand?"

Kate's heart thudded dully. She'd never seen that look on Chuck's face.

Royce could only nod, his face turning red and then blue from lack of oxygen.

"He's not worth it, Chuck." Hank entered the hallway behind Chuck. "I have the state police on their way. This man is going to jail for the rest of his life. He deserves to die there."

Still, Chuck refused to release the man.

Kate touched his arm. "Chuck. Let him go. He can't hurt us anymore."

Chuck stared down into Kate's eyes. "He would have killed you."

"But he didn't." She smiled, although her scalp still hurt from how hard Royce had pulled her hair.

Lyla ran to her and wrapped her little arms around her legs.

Kate lifted her up and hugged her tight. "We're okay. Let him go."

Finally, Chuck relinquished his hold to Kujo who bound the man's wrists with zip ties and led him out of the building into the night.

Margaret stood beside Hank. The woman who'd held her captive sat on the ground, her face buried in her hands. Her wrists were bound in front of her.

"Give Margaret the keys," Kate commanded of the woman.

The woman unhooked a huge ring of keys from a belt around her waist, and handed them to Margaret.

Margaret went from room to room, unlocking the padlocks. Duke and Bear helped. Soon, all the women and children were freed, many of them crying, not knowing what was happening or what would happen to them now that they weren't under James Royce's control.

Chuck took Lyla in his arms and wrapped his arm around Kate's waist.

Kate held onto Mary's hand, and they walked out of Royce's house into a clear, star-studded Idaho night.

Becca ran to Mary and pulled the little girl into her arms. "Thank you, oh, thank you," she cried and hugged her daughter to her.

Rachel reached out for Lyla, who went to her mother and clung to her, crying.

By the time the police arrived, the Brotherhood Protectors had the men lined up and cooperating. With their leader subdued and sequestered in the same cell he'd locked Kate and Rachel in, the others didn't protest. They laid down their weapons and waited for the sheriff to arrive.

Along with the local sheriff's department came the state police and a contingent from the ATF.

Hank had his men ground their weapons before the authorities arrived to make certain no one got trigger-happy and started firing at the Brotherhood Protectors, thinking they were the bad guys.

For the next few hours, Hank fielded most of the questions, while buses were brought in to take the women and children to shelters.

"It'll take the authorities a long time to sort through everything Royce has done," Chuck said.

Kate nodded. "And longer still for those touched by his madness to recover." Her heart ached.

Her sister sat on the ground with her daughter. Someone had brought out a blanket and wrapped them in it. Rachel rocked back and forth as she held Lyla who'd fallen asleep in her arms.

"She'll need time," Kate said. "Despite how badly Myles had treated her, she was still shocked that Royce had killed him."

"Time and the love of her family will get her through." Chuck pulled Kate into the curve of his arm. "I'd like to be there with you to help."

Kate leaned into him, glad for his support. "I think we have room in our hearts. But are you sure? Sticking with us might come with a commitment clause." She arched an eyebrow.

Chuck laughed. "I'm one hundred percent committed. I knew it as soon as I opened my big, fat mouth and said I couldn't. Like I said, I made a mistake." He turned her to face him. "Please, forgive me and let me make it up to you."

"Don't promise anything you aren't comfortable with."

"If there's even a slim chance you could fall in love with me, I'm all in."

Kate's heart soared. "Slim chance?"

He wrapped his arms around her waist and stared down into her eyes, his reflecting the stars above. "I never thought it possible to love again, but you've proven me wrong. I never believed in love at first sight, but then I met you. I want you in my life. Forever. If it takes me the rest of my life to convince you, I will. Just say you'll give me a chance to earn your love."

Kate leaned up on her toes and pressed her lips to his. "Will you shut up?"

He frowned though his lips quirked upward at the corners. "Not exactly what I was hoping to hear."

"Because you won't let me get a word in edgewise." Kate laughed. "There is no slim chance of me loving you."

Chuck's smile faded. "Well, dang, I guess I have my work cut out for me. Just so you know, this SEAL doesn't give up easily."

Kate cupped his cheeks between her palms. "Chuck, there's no slim chance," she kissed him, "because there's a *big* chance I already love you." Then she claimed his lips, sealing her declaration with a kiss.

Duke bumped into Chuck's shoulder.

Chuck broke the kiss and looked up, frowning. "Hey, watch it."

"You two need a room?" Duke grinned.

Kujo stood beside Duke with Six sitting by his feet. "Didn't Hank give you the talk?"

Chuck frowned. "What talk?"

Hank clapped a hand on Chuck's shoulder. "The one about not falling for the client?"

Chuck pulled Kate close. "Nope. Didn't get that talk."

"Well," Hank said. "It wouldn't have done you any good." He shook his head. "You two would have found each other anyway. Can't argue with fate. Not when it comes to love."

"Nope," Kate said. "Fate has a wicked sense of humor."

"And she knows what the hell she's doing," Chuck brushed a soft kiss across Kate's lips.

"Is everyone ready to go home?"

"Yes," Kate said, already thinking of Eagle Rock as home.

"Yes," Chuck said. "Though I loaned the cottage to Mrs. Turner. We might have company."

Kate smiled. "We'll have a full house with my sister and Lyla moving in until they can get settled in a new life."

"That's all right by me," Chuck said. "Looks like we need to find a bigger place."

"Yes, we do. And I'm looking forward to spending more time with my family." Kate opened her arms.

Rachel rose from the ground with Lyla and walked into Kate's hug. "I love you, sis."

Kate hugged her sister tightly. "I love you, too. And by the way, have you met the man in my life? This is Chuck."

Rachel smiled up at Chuck. "No, we haven't officially met. But I like him already. Any man who can make my sister smile like that is more than okay in my book." Instead of shaking his hand, she hugged his neck. "And thank you for saving her and Lyla."

Kate couldn't stop grinning. She had her sister and her niece back in her life, and the man of her dreams loved her. Life couldn't get better.

But it did. Chuck kissed her again.

Yeah. Life did get better.

EPILOGUE

Two months later...

Chuck adjusted the heat on the grill as he stood on the back porch of the house he and Kate had purchased within a week of returning to Eagle Rock. It was a rustic cedar and river stone, two-story structure with huge picture windows overlooking the foothills of the Crazy Mountains.

As soon as he and Kate had seen it, they fell in love with it and made an offer. A month later, they were all moved in and starting a life together.

Rachel and Lyla had moved in with them until Rachel could find work and save enough money to get a place of her own. Which meant Kate and Chuck got to spend more time with Rachel and Lyla.

And Lyla was thriving. She loved having an uncle who gave her piggyback rides and the equivalent of two mothers to spoil her.

"I take it you and Kate are happy together," Hank said. He sat back in an Adirondack chair, a beer in his hand.

Sadie was helping Rachel and Kate prepare the steaks inside.

"Couldn't be happier," Chuck said.

"Are you two going to get married?" Hank held up his hands. "Sadie told me to ask you. She's all for planning another wedding. She enjoyed helping Viper and Dallas with theirs and wants to take a crack at the next one."

With a snort, Chuck lifted his beer and drank a long swallow before answering. "I asked her. She said yes, but we haven't decided on a date."

Hank pushed to his feet. "That's great news. Congratulations." He hugged Chuck, clapping him hard on the back. "Sadie will be beside herself. I couldn't be more pleased. You seem so much happier."

"I am. I didn't know how miserable I was," Chuck said, laughing, "until I wasn't."

"So, I take it you'll be staying with the Brotherhood Protectors."

Chuck nodded. "As long as you'll have me."

"Good, because I'll be taking some time off later this year, and I might need you to wrangle some of the new guys."

"I'm game."

"Most of the guys manage on their own, but I might need you to assign cases as they come up." Hank grinned.

Chuck frowned. "Okay, what's up that you're not telling me?"

Hank's grin spread from ear to ear. "Sadie's pregnant."

It was Chuck's turn to hug and pat Hank's back. "That's great! Emma's going to have a little brother to pick on."

Hank nodded. "Or sister. We don't know what it's going to be yet. And really, I don't care. As long as Sadie and the baby are healthy, I'm happy." He shook his head. "I can't believe I'm going to be a daddy again."

Amid his happiness for Hank, Chuck couldn't help a flash of envy.

He and Kate had talked about having kids, but he was already forty-seven and Kate was thirty-six. Was it fair to bring a child into the world when they were getting older? Assuming they could even have children. His swimmers might already be dried up along with Kate's eggs.

He'd told Kate he'd be fine if they didn't have children. They would continue to be Lyla's favorite aunt and uncle. He'd told her that would be enough for him.

But hearing Hank and Sadie were expecting made Chuck wish things could have been different. He'd loved being a daddy to Sarah. And he was at a point in his life that he was willing to risk loving another child of his own. Alas, fate had her hand on the outcomes. If they were meant to have a baby, they would. If not, Chuck would be happy as long as he had Kate's love.

Sadie stepped out on the deck, carrying a tray of

seasoned steaks, hotdogs and chicken breasts. She was followed by Rachel, Emma and Lyla.

"Where's Kate?" Hank asked.

"She had a little tummy upset. She'll be out in a minute," Sadie said, a small smile playing at the corners of her lips.

"Yeah, she'll be out in a minute," Rachel echoed, her lips also tipping upward. "You might want to get that food on the grill. These girls are hungry."

Emma and Lyla jumped up and down, clapping their hands.

Chuck laughed, took the tray from Sadie and went to work laying out the meat on the grill.

"By the way," he said, "I hear congratulations are in order for the Patterson family."

"Oh, Hank told you?" Sadie laid a hand across her flat belly and sat in Hank's lap. "I'm excited and can't wait to find out what we're having."

"I could wait. I like surprises," Hank said.

"I hear having two children is entirely different than having one child," Sadie said. "I look forward to the challenge."

Rachel sighed. "I always wanted two children. I didn't want Lyla to grow up an only child."

The door opened, and Kate stepped out, her face pale.

Chuck set down the spatula and hurried toward her. "Kate? Are you feeling all right?"

"No, I feel like hell." She looked at something in her hand and then looked at him, a smile spreading across her face. "But I couldn't be better."

Chuck cupped her elbow and helped her to a chair. "I don't understand. You feel awful, but you couldn't be better?"

Sadie laughed out loud. "Don't you get it? Look at what she has in her hand. She's got morning sickness."

Chuck was so worried about Kate, he wasn't sure of what Sadie was saying. "Do I need to call a doctor? Maybe an ambulance?"

Rachel and Hank joined in Sadie's laughter.

Kate lifted the stick she had in her hand and held it in front of his face. "I'm going to be fine in nine months."

The stick, the blue line, nine months and the smile on Kate's face all added up to hit Chuck in the gut like a sucker punch.

He staggered backward, all the blood in his head draining at once.

"Catch him, he's going down!" Rachel cried.

Hank dove for Chuck and looped one of his arms over his shoulder. "You might want to save the passing out for when you're in the delivery room. It's better to have trained doctors and nurses around when you crack your skull on the floor." Hank chuckled. "I guess congratulations are in order all around."

"You're pregnant?" Chuck shook loose of Hank's hold and knelt beside Kate's chair. "Are you sure you're all right?"

"I'm sure. Just a little queasy." Her eyebrows dipped. "Are you going to be okay? We talked about having kids, but now, are you happy? You're going to be a daddy."

Chuck pulled her into his arms and hugged her

tight. "I've never been happier. I have you in my life, and now…a baby." He shook his head. Then a thought occurred to him. "Guess we'll be setting a wedding date."

Kate nodded. "Uh-huh."

"And we have a wedding planner, if she should choose to accept the mission." He shot a glance toward Sadie.

Sadie waggled her eyebrows. "I'm in as long as you have it before I give birth," Sadie said.

"You're on." Kate and Chuck said simultaneously.

"And here I thought life couldn't get better." His heart soaring, Chuck kissed Kate.

ABOUT THE AUTHOR

ELLE JAMES also writing as MYLA JACKSON is a *New York Times* and *USA Today* Bestselling author of books including cowboys, intrigues and paranormal adventures that keep her readers on the edges of their seats. When she's not at her computer, she's traveling, snow skiing, boating, or riding her ATV, dreaming up new stories. Learn more about Elle James at www.ellejames.com

Website | Facebook | Twitter | GoodReads | Newsletter | BookBub | Amazon

Or visit her alter ego Myla Jackson at mylajackson.com
Website | Facebook | Twitter | Newsletter

Follow Me!
www.ellejames.com
ellejamesauthor@gmail.com

ALSO BY ELLE JAMES

Shadow Assassin

Delta Force Strong

Ivy's Delta (Delta Force 3 Crossover)

Breaking Silence (#1)

Breaking Rules (#2)

Breaking Away (#3)

Breaking Free (#4)

Breaking Hearts (#5)

Breaking Ties (#6)

Breaking Point (#7)

Breaking Dawn (#8)

Breaking Promises (#9)

Brotherhood Protectors Yellowstone

Saving Kyla (#1)

Saving Chelsea (#2)

Saving Amanda (#3)

Saving Liliana (#4)

Saving Breely (#5)

Saving Savvie (#6)

Brotherhood Protectors Colorado

SEAL Salvation (#1)

Rocky Mountain Rescue (#2)

Ranger Redemption (#3)

Tactical Takeover (#4)

Colorado Conspiracy (#5)

Rocky Mountain Madness (#6)

Free Fall (#7)

Colorado Cold Case (#8)

Fool's Folly (#9)

Brotherhood Protectors

Montana SEAL (#1)

Bride Protector SEAL (#2)

Montana D-Force (#3)

Cowboy D-Force (#4)

Montana Ranger (#5)

Montana Dog Soldier (#6)

Montana SEAL Daddy (#7)

Montana Ranger's Wedding Vow (#8)

Montana SEAL Undercover Daddy (#9)

Cape Cod SEAL Rescue (#10)

Montana SEAL Friendly Fire (#11)

Montana SEAL's Mail-Order Bride (#12)

SEAL Justice (#13)

Ranger Creed (#14)

Delta Force Rescue (#15)

Dog Days of Christmas (#16)

Montana Rescue (#17)

Montana Ranger Returns (#18)

Hot SEAL Salty Dog (SEALs in Paradise)

Hot SEAL, Hawaiian Nights (SEALs in Paradise)

Hot SEAL Bachelor Party (SEALs in Paradise)

Hot SEAL, Independence Day (SEALs in Paradise)

Brotherhood Protectors Vol 1

Iron Horse Legacy

Soldier's Duty (#1)

Ranger's Baby (#2)

Marine's Promise (#3)

SEAL's Vow (#4)

Warrior's Resolve (#5)

Drake (#6)

Grimm (#7)

Murdock (#8)

Utah (#9)

Judge (#10)

The Outriders

Homicide at Whiskey Gulch (#1)

Hideout at Whiskey Gulch (#2)

Held Hostage at Whiskey Gulch (#3)

Setup at Whiskey Gulch (#4)

Missing Witness at Whiskey Gulch (#5)

Cowboy Justice at Whiskey Gulch (#6)

Hellfire Series

Hellfire, Texas (#1)

Justice Burning (#2)

Smoldering Desire (#3)

Hellfire in High Heels (#4)

Playing With Fire (#5)

Up in Flames (#6)

Total Meltdown (#7)

Declan's Defenders

Marine Force Recon (#1)

Show of Force (#2)

Full Force (#3)

Driving Force (#4)

Tactical Force (#5)

Disruptive Force (#6)

Mission: Six

One Intrepid SEAL

Two Dauntless Hearts

Three Courageous Words

Four Relentless Days

Five Ways to Surrender

Six Minutes to Midnight

Hearts & Heroes Series

Wyatt's War (#1)

Mack's Witness (#2)

Ronin's Return (#3)

Sam's Surrender (#4)

Take No Prisoners Series

SEAL's Honor (#1)

SEAL'S Desire (#2)

SEAL's Embrace (#3)

SEAL's Obsession (#4)

SEAL's Proposal (#5)

SEAL's Seduction (#6)

SEAL'S Defiance (#7)

SEAL's Deception (#8)

SEAL's Deliverance (#9)

SEAL's Ultimate Challenge (#10)

Texas Billionaire Club

Tarzan & Janine (#1)

Something To Talk About (#2)

Who's Your Daddy (#3)

Love & War (#4)

Billionaire Online Dating Service

The Billionaire Husband Test (#1)

The Billionaire Cinderella Test (#2)

The Billionaire Bride Test (#3)

The Billionaire Daddy Test (#4)

The Billionaire Matchmaker Test (#5)

The Billionaire Glitch Date (#6)

The Billionaire Perfect Date (#7) coming soon
The Billionaire Replacement Date (#8) coming soon
The Billionaire Wedding Date (#9) coming soon

Ballistic Cowboy

Hot Combat (#1)

Hot Target (#2)

Hot Zone (#3)

Hot Velocity (#4)

Cajun Magic Mystery Series

Voodoo on the Bayou (#1)

Voodoo for Two (#2)

Deja Voodoo (#3)

Cajun Magic Mysteries Books 1-3

SEAL Of My Own

Navy SEAL Survival

Navy SEAL Captive

Navy SEAL To Die For

Navy SEAL Six Pack

Devil's Shroud Series

Deadly Reckoning (#1)

Deadly Engagement (#2)

Deadly Liaisons (#3)

Deadly Allure (#4)

Deadly Obsession (#5)

Deadly Fall (#6)

Covert Cowboys Inc Series
Triggered (#1)
Taking Aim (#2)
Bodyguard Under Fire (#3)
Cowboy Resurrected (#4)
Navy SEAL Justice (#5)
Navy SEAL Newlywed (#6)
High Country Hideout (#7)
Clandestine Christmas (#8)

Thunder Horse Series
Hostage to Thunder Horse (#1)
Thunder Horse Heritage (#2)
Thunder Horse Redemption (#3)
Christmas at Thunder Horse Ranch (#4)

Demon Series
Hot Demon Nights (#1)
Demon's Embrace (#2)
Tempting the Demon (#3)

Lords of the Underworld
Witch's Initiation (#1)
Witch's Seduction (#2)
The Witch's Desire (#3)
Possessing the Witch (#4)

Stealth Operations Specialists (SOS)

Nick of Time

Alaskan Fantasy

Boys Behaving Badly Anthologies

Rogues (#1)

Blue Collar (#2)

Pirates (#3)

Stranded (#4)

First Responder (#5)

Blown Away

Warrior's Conquest

Enslaved by the Viking Short Story

Conquests

Smokin' Hot Firemen

Protecting the Colton Bride

Protecting the Colton Bride & Colton's Cowboy Code

Heir to Murder

Secret Service Rescue

High Octane Heroes

Haunted

Engaged with the Boss

Cowboy Brigade

Time Raiders: The Whisper

Bundle of Trouble

Killer Body

Operation XOXO

An Unexpected Clue

Baby Bling

Under Suspicion, With Child

Texas-Size Secrets

Cowboy Sanctuary

Lakota Baby

Dakota Meltdown

Beneath the Texas Moon

Printed in Great Britain
by Amazon